Laura Place

The Watson Novels

ANN MYCHAL

Dedicated to the memory of
Margaret Cadman

Will it not be wiser to accept the society of those good ladies in Laura Place, and enjoy all the advantages of the connexion as far as possible?

Persuasion Jane Austen

CHAPTER ONE

On reading in the *Chronicle* the news of Lady Allersham's arrival at Laura Place, Lady Russell was almost persuaded to delay her departure from Bath until the end of the season. The news was not without intrigue, for Lord Allersham's name was curiously absent from the piece. Lady Russell's displeasure at having received no prior notice of the announcement was acute, for the opportunity to be the bearer of such news among her acquaintance of rank, an undertaking that was rightfully hers through the claims of family, had been denied her. She felt slighted by His Lordship, for although her connexion with the family was as his father's distant cousin, she considered Henry Fitzroy, the young Lord Allersham, a *nephew*; consequently, she had maintained a greater and more enduring interest in the family than was required of most distant relations. Yet, despite having a plentiful supply of first cousins with offspring enough to populate Somerset, none among them had the good fortune to be in possession of an earldom; therefore, they were little thought of or cared about.

There was but one person who had equal claim on Lady Russell's attention. A woman over whom she had exercised her counsel in former years and provided direction almost in place of a mother. The daughter of Sir Walter Elliot, Mrs Anne Wentworth, to whom Lady Russell was now engaged for the summer, would not have acted so. Anne would have known what was due to her as a friend and confidante. Anne would not have spared the cost of an express.

No excuse would suffice to explain Lord Allersham's oversight, and nothing could save him from censure in her estimation, for the satisfaction of being the first to impart news of such interest was the principal purpose of her daily exercise and conversation.

Would that I had received word from Allersham Park directly! Would that my nephew had accorded his aunt the courtesy of informing her himself! Would that she had not read of it in the *Chronicle*!

Her vexation with Lord Allersham would not be easily assuaged. Lady Russell put aside her newspaper and glanced impatiently at the clock. A letter – an express – might yet suffice!

She waited until shortly after four when the post came in, but at the hour of its arrival, the mail, served up on a silver dish, yielded little to speak of: an invitation to a card party in Pulteney Street, a lengthy missive from Uppercross, a bill from the haberdasher and a brief communication from the apothecary in Queen Square concerning a tonic for the relief of heartburn. But not a line from Allersham! After a cursory glance at each item, she tossed the letters aside, being in no humour to read them, and took up the *Chronicle* once again.

Consolation was to be found on the pages of the newspaper, and for the rest of the hour Lady Russell turned to those columns that regularly claimed her attention, for it was there that her mind found occupation and was most favourably engaged. A thorough perusal of the page, however, returned little to speak of and, with a sigh of disappointment, she was obliged to conclude that no person of consequence had been named in the obituaries of the day.

Her attention returned to the announcement of Lady Allersham's arrival in Bath, and after further consideration, she was inclined towards the view that it may be no bad thing. I might, perhaps, be of service to my nephew's young wife, thought she. And, were I inclined to overlook *his* shortcomings, I might assist *her* in some small way, for she appears to be quite unconnected in these parts.

The newcomer to Bath was to be accompanied by her aunt, Mrs Beresford, the widow of the late Colonel Beresford of Whitcombe; and, whether known to the newcomers or not, they were to be blessed with the very best of neighbours. Lady Allersham and Mrs Beresford were to reside near another family of rank with whom Lady Russell claimed more than a passing acquaintance through her association with the Elliot family: the Dowager Viscountess Dalrymple was Sir Walter's cousin. Lady Russell had, three seasons ago or thereabouts, been introduced to Lady Dalrymple when, together with her daughter, the Honourable Miss Carteret, they had taken possession of a house in Laura Place.

An idea took hold in Lady Russell's mind; and the more she gave thought to it, the greater her desire became to bring about its execution. Laura Place! To find two families of rank so closely situated! There could be no more fitting residence in the whole of Bath for two such families, and nowhere more conducive to comfort than the proximity of equals, thought she. And as Lady Russell could justly claim a

3

connexion and interest in both parties, she saw that the service of performing the necessary introductions must fall to her. Circumstances, however, prevented her from making any serious alteration to her own plans, and so Lady Russell contented herself with the prospect of accomplishing the gratifying office before quitting Bath for the country.

The act of introducing one noble family to another was achieved with the greatest of ease and convenience the following morning. The meeting could not have been more propitious had the Almighty himself ordained it. On approaching the Pump Room at a fashionable hour, Lady Russell was pleased to find one party at its entrance, wholly unaware of the other party stationed not ten yards within its walls.

With an almost imperceptible nod of the head, the Dowager Viscountess uttered the least that was required on such occasions, while eyeing the young Lady Allersham with languid indifference.

'When might Bath expect to welcome Lord Allersham?' said she. 'A young woman moving about the country without the protection of her husband is singular.'

'And yet I do not move alone, as you see.' Lady Allersham exchanged a playful grin with Mrs Beresford.

'Allow me to present Lady Allersham's aunt, Mrs Beresford,' said Lady Russell to Lady Dalrymple and Miss Carteret. 'Mrs Beresford is Lord Osborne's sister, and Lady Allersham his daughter.'

'Yes, yes,' said the Dowager. 'The Surrey family. My husband had some dealings with Osborne Castle at one time. I forget why. I expect Osborne Castle is as grim in winter as most ancient houses. Allersham must appear the height of comfort and convenience by comparison.'

Mortified by her mother's ill humour, Miss Carteret, being of similar age to the young Lady Allersham, was eager to please; and to prevent further embarrassment, she promptly extended a cordial invitation to the newcomers to take tea with them the following day.

'What could be more convenient? No need of a chair, or an umbrella, for the best society in Bath is to be found next door,' said Lady Russell. 'And now, sadly, I must take my leave of you all for circumstances require my presence elsewhere. I am to visit my godson.'

'A godson, you say?' said the Dowager.

'Master Frederick,' replied Lady Russell. 'Did you not hear the news? Anne Wentworth is delivered of a fine baby boy. The infant, I am reliably informed, is so gentle in nature and countenance — the very image of his mama! Indeed, he could have no better mother in all the world. As to the father, I perceive no resemblance of any kind from the description so far afforded me in dear Anne's letter. But I have always been of a sanguine disposition and have every hope that the child will turn out well, despite any deficiency of character present in the father.'

'I am astonished that no news of the infant's arrival has yet reached Laura Place, though why it should astonish me I do not know. Sir Walter never attends to such things,' said the Dowager. 'As to Captain Wentworth, I perceive no particular imperfection of the kind other than that which commonly afflicts the male temperament. But let us at least hope that the boy is blessed with more wit and sense than his grandfather.'

'Mama!' Her daughter spoke in a low but firm voice of disapproval.

'Sir Walter Elliot?' said Lady Allersham, who marvelled at the intriguing exchange between mother and daughter. 'At least,' said she, in a whisper to Mrs Beresford, 'Osborne Castle is not solely singled out for ignominy and disgrace.'

'Are you acquainted with the Kellynch family?' said Miss Carteret, unsteadily.

'I have not had the pleasure, though I have heard stories of Sir Walter. His reputation goes before him,' replied Lady Allersham. 'I should like to make his acquaintance.'

Miss Carteret replied, 'Then I am sorry to disappoint you. The Elliots are gone to Bristol — Sir Walter and Miss Elliot, that is. And I cannot provide you with more information than that. It is quite a mystery, I assure you.'

'Sir Walter delights in assuming an air of mystery,' said Lady Dalrymple. 'He is apt to think it gives him greater consequence. It does not, of course. Last season, I was obliged to remove a very fine French gilt looking-glass from the drawing room for he was never done with admiring himself in it. I have a mind to return it to its proper place now that Sir Walter has quitted Bath.'

Lady Allersham and Mrs Beresford exchanged glances of amusement that appeared to heighten Miss Carteret's discomfort.

'Well then, let us not stand on ceremony,' said Lady Dalrymple. 'Come Jane, give me your arm.' The

Dowager took Miss Carteret's arm, impatient to be on her way. 'Until tomorrow then,' said she.

The curious encounter had delighted Lady Allersham for reasons Lady Russell had not intended; and Mrs Beresford was no less intrigued by the meeting. The former, once out of earshot of their new acquaintance, observed, 'Do you not, Aunt, have a great desire to make the most of our new neighbours? I own, I could not help but think of Papa. How dare she speak of Osborne Castle that way? Have you ever heard anything quite so impertinent? But would not Papa have been diverted by Lady Dalrymple's declaration of those imperfections *of the kind that commonly affect the male temperament*? Poor Miss Carteret! What pains she must take to keep her mama in check!'

'Emma,' replied Mrs Beresford to Lady Allersham, 'I wish neither to dampen your spirits nor curb your enthusiasm, but for my part I have no desire to foster connexions with Lady Dalrymple beyond those of a commonplace acquaintance.'

'Nor I, Aunt, I assure you,' said Lady Allersham. 'But I doubt that will be possible. And Miss Carteret is surely in need of a friend. I am determined that when you are engaged about the business which brought us to Bath, I shall make it my business to further my acquaintance with Miss Carteret. We might start with an expedition to Sydney Gardens. I have a great desire to see the gardens and an even greater one to learn more of the Dalrymples and the Elliots.'

'Oh, my dear,' said Mrs Beresford, 'Miss Carteret does not look like the kind of person to invite gossip. And at the risk of judging on first impressions, I suspect Miss Carteret is not possessed of an open temperament.'

'I expect you are right, Aunt,' replied Lady Allersham. 'She looked rather ill at ease when first we were introduced. I wonder why?'

'Why does Miss Carteret interest you so?' said Mrs Beresford.

'Unless I am mistaken and there is more than one *J Carteret*, my dear husband has in his possession a copy of *Paradise Lost* belonging to our new neighbour. I came across it a few weeks ago when I was looking for *Mansfield Park*.'

'Milton?' said Mrs Beresford.

'You seem surprised,' replied Lady Allersham. 'Milton is a great favourite with Henry. But there, as clear as day, inside the volume, in a woman's hand — elegant — without flourish — was written *J Carteret*. It is unquestionably the hand of our very own *Miss* Carteret. Did you not hear Lady Dalrymple call her *Jane*?'

Mrs Beresford replied, 'There is sure to be a simple explanation. Did you ever seek one from Lord Allersham?'

'Of course I did. Henry insisted he had never before set eyes on the volume.'

'And you have no cause to doubt him?'

'No,' she replied. 'I have no reason to think him inconstant. He is, I suppose, inclined to speak with candour when invention might better serve his purpose. It is his way. Only last month he declared that I have a tendency to mistake fiction for fact. Quite untrue, of course. I cannot imagine what caused him to form such an impression. Plain speaking is generally to my liking for I do not care for falsehood of any kind, but neither do I believe that a little indulgence from my husband, a little generosity with the truth from time to time, goes amiss.'

'I see.'

'And yet, my dear Henry's reprimands are accomplished so agreeably and with the greatest good humour that I cannot be vexed with him for more than a day.' She sighed at the thought of him. 'Still, I find no satisfactory explanation in this instance. How did that volume find its way into the library at Allersham?' said she. 'I should like to know.'

'And shall you ask Miss Carteret to account for its presence there?' said Mrs Beresford.

Lady Allersham smiled, amused by a mischievous impulse. 'Perhaps, on our walk I might compare one paradise to another. My dear Miss Carteret, I may observe, Sydney Gardens puts me in mind of that other garden so often depicted by artists and poets. Does it not bear comparison to Eden itself? Would it not be diverting to witness Miss Carteret's response?'

'My dear Emma,' said Mrs Beresford, 'I counsel against it. Contrivance is rarely deployed to good purpose. Miss Carteret may likely comprehend your meaning. The mortification that must follow exposure is hardly ever forgotten. We, none of us, like to be found out.'

'There may be a simple explanation, I suppose,' said Lady Allersham. 'Jane Carteret may have a brother called John, or James, or Josiah. Still, it would not, I suppose, account for the volume's presence in the library at Allersham.'

Mrs Beresford replied, with a smile, 'What good purpose can come of seeking to expose something that might not be what you first imagined it to be.'

'It might turn out to be entirely innocent. But I should still like to know the facts. For the present, however, I shall satisfy myself with good intentions. I shall perform a service to *very* good purpose and find Miss Carteret a husband of her own,' replied Lady Allersham.

The following day, Lady Allersham, stationed for the greater part of the morning at the window, observed the comings and goings in Laura Place until the appointed hour for tea. 'Lady Dalrymple is scarcely encumbered by callers. There, you see! The rotund gentleman with a stick and his female companion stayed but a quarter of an hour.'

'Of the society of some callers, a quarter of an hour is quite sufficient,' said Mrs Beresford, with a smile.

'Lady Dalrymple has received *only* two callers this past hour, and one of them quite infirm! Poor Miss Carteret. The gentleman is practically lame.'

'The gentleman of whom you speak might be the greatest wit in Bath,' said Mrs Beresford.

'Or the greatest complainer,' she replied. 'I suppose he takes the waters. I expect they all do. Laura Place, it seems to me, thrives on infirmity. I have observed all the comings and goings this past hour and I can confirm, but for you and I, and Miss Carteret, who have no ailments to complain of, I have seen not a soul without a stick or a limp. It puts me in mind of Brinshore where there is no more interesting topic of conversation than the extent and severity of one's ailments, each complainer seeking to outdo another. Indeed, Bath lacks only sand, sea and stillness, or one might easily mistake one place for the other. Henry says that there is not a silent moment to be had anywhere in Bath.'

'Have you heard from His Lordship? When does he arrive?' said Mrs Beresford.

'In a week, or thereabouts,' sighed Lady Allersham. 'And I shall not sleep until he is once again safely returned to us. I do not know why he must visit Brinshore at this time of year. It was the same last year. I wish he would wait until the autumn to make his annual survey. But it is of no matter what I think. It seems it must all be accomplished at the start of the season.'

It was another half an hour before Lady Allersham and Mrs Beresford were issued into their neighbours' drawing room for tea. Mrs Beresford at once admired the sapphire silk drapes at the windows while her niece complimented Lady Dalrymple on a most excellent fireplace.

'I expect it is not so very dissimilar from the fireplace in your own set of apartments,' said she.

'Yours, ma'am, is of finer quality, I believe. Do you not agree, Aunt?' said Lady Allersham, her eyes willing Mrs Beresford to concur with her own view.

Mrs Beresford could perceive no material difference between the two but smiled and nodded accordingly. Lady Dalrymple, gratified by the compliments paid by both guests, ordered tea and continued to describe to Mrs Beresford the many fireplaces she had encountered, for good or ill, during the course of her existence. 'Mrs Beresford, I am sure you would agree, that a fireplace is both to be admired and to be *used*.'

'A fireplace without a fire is like a chest without tea leaves.'

'Or a ship without a sail,' added Mrs Beresford.

'Or a key without a box,' said Miss Carteret.

'Do not you mean a box without a key, Miss Carteret?' said Lady Allersham.

Miss Carteret replied in a whisper out of earshot of her mother. 'No indeed. A key without a box is of no use at all, whereas a box without a key can be forced open to reveal its secrets.'

Lady Allersham, fascinated by Miss Carteret's curious observation, pondered its likely meaning. To be in possession of a key and not the box to which it belongs is rare, thought she, for it is easier to lose a small item than a large one.

'Are you accustomed to misplacing precious items, Miss Carteret? Keys, boxes, books? That kind of thing,' continued Lady Allersham.

Miss Carteret looked anxiously at her mother and replied, 'I speak only in a general sense. I had in mind no particular box, and no particular key.'

Lady Allersham noticed that Miss Carteret was wearing a gold chain half hidden beneath the fold of her collar. 'Had I the key to a precious object, I should wear it about my neck, on a chain long enough to conceal its existence and secure enough to ensure that I do not lose it. A chain such as the one *you* are wearing, Miss Carteret.'

She blushed and replied in a soft voice, 'Oh dear! You have found me out. Am I to be so easily understood?'

Lady Allersham returned her smile but said nothing in reply. Yes, thought she, you most certainly are. My supposition was correct. Miss Carteret is full of intrigue.

'I came upon the key some time ago. I imagined it lost to me forever. But I beg you, do not press me further. It is impossible to speak — I cannot speak of it to anyone.'

'Then no mention of it shall pass my lips,' said Lady Allersham, curious to know why, if it were so great a secret, Miss Carteret had alluded to the key in the first place.

'How do you like Bath? Shall you stay for the season?' said Miss Carteret, in an anxious bid to alter the course of the conversation.

'I am not yet acquainted with Bath, at least not as well as I should like to be. Our plans are not wholly settled but I believe we shall stay for several weeks. I had no wish to stay at Allersham alone. Henry, that is Lord Allersham, is from home. He is gone to Brinshore. You have probably never heard of it. It is a small town situated on the coast and lies between Brighton and Eastbourne.'

'I believe I know of another town thereabouts on the coast that also lies between Brighton and Eastbourne,' said Miss Carteret, with some hesitation. 'A place by the name of Sanditon, though I have never had the pleasure of —'

'Sanditon?' said Lady Allersham, with surprise. 'It is but three miles from Brinshore! How came you to hear of Sanditon?'

Miss Carteret blushed again. 'My memory fails me. The gossip that circulates in Bath has no bounds! One hears so much chatter and nonsense, and none of it to any purpose. I have likely heard Sanditon spoken of at the Pump Room or the church.'

'Sanditon of all places spoken of in Bath! I must write and tell my Aunt Fowle. And then again, perhaps I shall not. My aunt would want to know why Brinshore it not spoken of in equal measure. But I can well believe what you say about gossip. I can tell you that my own grandmamma and great aunt years ago adored the old rooms at Bath for that very reason,' said Lady Allersham. 'Gossip was, and remains, their mainstay. It will not surprise you to learn that I have heard stories of the old rooms that would make your hair stand on end.'

'Then we must seem very dull indeed,' said Miss Carteret. 'We might just as well reside in the country for we see little society in Laura Place — an occasional musical evening, a card party, a dinner. I accompany Mama to the Pump Room three days out of seven for she likes to take the waters. But as Mama prefers to maintain the distinction of rank —'

'Your circle is much reduced,' said Lady Allersham, grasping her companion's train of thought.

'Persons of rank are fewer in number these days. But please do not suppose my remarks tend towards despondency. I am not downcast. Not very downcast.'

'My dear Miss Carteret, your countenance tells me otherwise. *I* am convinced you have need of society even if *you* are not,' said Lady Allersham. 'And as your mama insists on preserving the distinction of rank, she will not object if I were to request the pleasure of your company from time to time. Indeed, I should like to visit Sydney Gardens very soon, and I should like you to accompany me if you will.'

'I am sure Mama would raise no objection to that,' said Miss Carteret, brightening at the prospect.

'Tomorrow then. It is as good a day as any,' replied Lady Allersham.

'And Mrs Beresford?'

'Mrs Beresford has business of her own at present and will be engaged upon it tomorrow morning.'

'I see,' said Miss Carteret. 'I hope the business is as agreeable as a walk to Sydney Gardens.'

Lady Allersham drew closer to Miss Carteret and whispered, 'My aunt's spirits have been low since the death of poor Colonel Beresford. Bath, I feel certain, will raise them. It is, in part, why I insisted on spending some of the season here. But more than that, my aunt is in receipt of a letter from my late uncle's cousin, a Mr James Beresford, who has taken up residence in Bath until some personal matters are settled to his satisfaction. We know nothing of the nature of these matters. We know only that Mr Beresford is lately returned from the East Indies and wishes to pay his respects in person to Mrs Beresford, having been absent from the country at the time of Colonel Beresford's death. My aunt believes herself duty bound to receive him and would prefer to do so in Bath rather than summon him to Whitcombe.'

'And you do not consider your aunt duty bound in any way?' said Miss Carteret.

'No, indeed! I question the gentleman's motives,' replied Lady Allersham. 'To take such pains now — Miss Carteret, what must his purpose be if not to invent some claim to an inheritance?'

'Might he desire simply to express his condolences?'

'It is sufficient to express one's condolences in a letter. And Mr James Beresford has already undertaken to do so at great length. His sentiments

15

appear sincere enough, I suppose. But Colonel Beresford hardly spoke of his cousin while he drew breath.'

'I see what you mean. One must certainly question the gentleman's intentions in such a case. Is the Beresford estate entailed?'

'Whitcombe? No, it is not, thank heaven,' said Lady Allersham.

'Might the gentleman in question have a genuine claim to some part of it?' replied Miss Carteret.

'Certainly not!' said Lady Allersham. 'Colonel Beresford took great care to provide for his widow. If only you had known him. He was a man of principle and honour. Colonel and Mrs Beresford loved each other so very dearly right to the end.'

'I can believe it. The truest love does not die,' said Miss Carteret, in a wistful tone. 'Does Mr James Beresford stay in Bath long?'

'I am not acquainted with his plans.'

'Then I too fear this gentleman's purpose. Mrs Beresford must be on her guard,' said Miss Carteret. 'I hesitate to say so, but something of the kind happened to a widow, some ten years younger than Mama two seasons ago. She was left in severely reduced circumstances. I do not know what became of her. If this be Mr Beresford's purpose — were he to play upon your aunt's goodness and generosity, I fear — poor Mrs Beresford.'

'My aunt shall be on her guard. I shall make sure of it.'

'I suppose your aunt has consulted an attorney?'

'No. If such a course of action were required, my Uncle Watson is as formidable an attorney as one might find in the whole of England. He will stop at nothing if the cause justifies the action.'

'Excellent!' replied Miss Carteret.

CHAPTER TWO

The following day Lady Allersham and Miss Carteret set out from Laura Place and proceeded along Pulteney Street to Sydney Gardens at an unhurried pace, impervious to the chill in the air or the gathering clouds. Miss Carteret was pleased to draw attention to certain points of interest on the way, most notably those houses belonging both to families of distinction *and* notoriety, the latter being greater in number and of greater curiosity to the newcomer.

When Sydney Place came into view, Lady Allersham seemed surprised by its proximity to Laura Place.

'We have hardly set foot out of the door, and here we are! How very convenient!' said she. 'A tour of Allersham Park would take a great deal longer and become more arduous underfoot.'

'Yes —' Miss Carteret broke off, recollecting herself. 'I am sure you are right.'

'Every amusement in Bath seems so conveniently placed,' said Lady Allersham.

'Laura Place is perfectly situated for a morning's walk, as you see. And there is no better place in the world for distraction than Sydney Gardens,' said Miss Carteret. 'At times, it has afforded a very pleasant refuge from the world.'

'And you visit the Gardens alone?'

'Oh no! Yes! I have not —'

'I suspect it is a venue like no other, for all sorts of schemes and assignations,' said Lady Allersham, with a smile.

Overcome by confusion, Miss Carteret made no reply. The pair entered Sydney Gardens through the Tavern. Within its walls, Lady Allersham saw only industry. Breakfast was the preoccupation of many, with waiters dashing about with tea trays piled high with bread buns and cakes, and all in plentiful supply. On emerging at the other end of the building, Lady Allersham saw before her a charming tree-lined walk that beckoned them onwards towards the heart of the gardens.

'How delightful!' said she.

'Yes, indeed!' said Miss Carteret. 'Let us take this path. This path will suit us very well. There is so much to see along this path.'

Lady Allersham perceived that her companion had recognised a small party advancing towards them and meant to avoid them.

Once the danger had passed, Miss Carteret glanced anxiously at her companion. 'Forgive me, Your Ladyship. I believe I should explain myself.'

'Not on my account, I assure you,' replied Lady Allersham. 'You acted swiftly to avoid an awkward encounter. I cannot count the times I have done so myself.'

'I do hope the attentions of the Misses Ibbotson were engaged elsewhere. I should not wish them to feel slighted. But I would have been obliged to enquire after old Mr Ibbotson. His gout worsens by the day, and one is only spared the details of it by making no enquiry at all. I cannot tell you how many hours have been given over to the progress of Mr

Ibbotson's foot. Only last week a recital at the Upper Rooms was blighted for that very reason. We might all have been enraptured by a most glorious Italian tenor had it not been for Mr Ibbotson's foot. Lady Allersham, if only you had heard him sing! It was heavenly. But the performance was ruined. Quite ruined! For Mr Ibbotson would not be silenced. He spoke without drawing breath for twenty minutes complete. He was even to be heard amid the exquisite tones of Bononcini's *Per la Gloria d'adorarvi* giving as full an account as was in his power, and as far as his voice would carry, of the removal of his blackened and festering toenail. Had you heard it, you would have despaired as I did,' said Miss Carteret.

'What about his gout?' said Lady Allersham, with amusement.

'It constantly defies improvement,' Miss Carteret replied. 'Were we seen?'

'I believe we were,' said Lady Allersham. 'But have no fear. Should we come upon the party further on, leave me to account for our detour.'

'Thank you. You are very good,' said Miss Carteret. 'I am sure Your Ladyship encounters none of the foibles and eccentricities at Allersham that we are exposed to in Bath.'

'Nonsense! I encounter them all the time wherever I go,' said Lady Allersham. 'And had circumstances been different, I should have been a parson's wife! Then my exposure to all manner of human frailties and eccentricities should have increased tenfold.'

'How fortunate you are to be so well situated now.'

'Yes,' said she, 'yes, indeed.'

'How do you like Allersham Park?' said Miss Carteret.

'It has a most pleasing aspect. And yet, I do not like it at all when Lord Allersham is from home. What is the point of living in such a vast abode when one can only occupy one room at a time? I know my husband feels the way I do about it.'

'And yet, it must be the greatest good fortune to be mistress of Allersham,' said Miss Carteret.

Lady Allersham paused to survey the vista before her. 'My husband was not meant to inherit. And though I appear to deride the life for which he was intended, I believe it would have suited him much better. It was his greatest desire to take holy orders. And I do not see why he should not do so even now, except that there are not sufficient hours in the day to devote to any endeavour but Allersham — and Brinshore. I believe we should have been just as content with the living at Stanton.'

'Stanton?' said Miss Carteret.

'Stanton is not far from the home where I was born, Osborne Park, although there was a time when I should not have imagined — well, that is the past and we cannot return to it.'

'No. We cannot,' replied Miss Carteret.

'My grandfather, you see, once had the living at Stanton, and when it became vacant, Papa purchased it, for it was where he proposed to Mama, and where she accepted him, in the rain, as they took shelter under the church porch.'

'How very romantic,' sighed Miss Carteret.

Lady Allersham caught a distant look in her companion's eye.

'How slim the line between the greatest good fortune and the gravest misfortune!' said Miss Carteret.

'I do not follow your meaning,' Lady Allersham replied.

Miss Carteret sighed. 'Is not happiness a matter of accident? One can neither earn it nor expect it.'

'Some strive for it.'

'Perhaps,' she replied. 'One may strive for the whole of one's life and never attain it.'

Lady Allersham's attention was suddenly drawn to the spectacle before her. 'Look!' said she. 'How charming! How novel!'

'Yes,' replied Miss Carteret. The scene before them was familiar to her. 'At certain times, the figures move, and water appears to cascade. It looks almost real.'

Lady Allersham drew closer, enchanted by the novelty of a rural scene. 'I do not think I have ever seen its equal! It is quite delightful! Come, let us sit here and watch for a while.'

Miss Carteret lingered a few steps behind until her will to continue ceased completely. She could venture no further; it was as though the place held her in its grasp and she was enfeebled by its power over her.

'It is no good,' said she. 'I can go no further. Forgive me.'

'What is it?' replied Lady Allersham. 'Are you unwell? Shall I seek help?'

CHAPTER THREE

Mrs Beresford had given Lady Allersham every assurance that she felt no uneasiness at the prospect of receiving Mr James Beresford alone.

'Equanimity shall be my maxim, Emma.'

'It would not be mine. Would that yours were tenacity, or severity,' her niece replied. 'Promise me, Aunt, that you will be on your guard at all times. Should Mr James Beresford make you uneasy in any way, throw him out forthwith! Do not give him the time of day!'

Mrs Beresford smiled. 'Thank you for your advice, my dear. You are quite right, but I doubt I shall have need to follow it.'

'I am serious, Aunt. If you sense any misgiving as to his character or intent, I shall write to Uncle Watson directly. I am quite prepared to postpone my walk with Miss Carteret if you harbour any doubt about meeting with this man alone.'

'There is no need,' said Mrs Beresford. 'I am quite equal to the encounter, I assure you. In fact, I might even go so far as to say that I look forward to meeting Mr James Beresford.'

When Lady Allersham returned from her walk with Miss Carteret, Mrs Beresford was nowhere to be found. On enquiring of the footman the whereabouts of her aunt, she was perplexed to find that Mrs Beresford had received a message half an hour earlier and had left Laura Place immediately on hearing it. Mrs Beresford had left instructions that Lady Allersham was not to be alarmed, that all was well, and that her aunt would return within the hour.

Her Ladyship reproached herself for abandoning her aunt and placing her in the power of a scoundrel. Without a moment's thought, she prepared to set out to find her. In that instant, however, Miss Carteret was admitted in a great hurry to the drawing room.

'Miss Carteret!' said Lady Allersham. 'Do you bring news of my aunt? She is missing, and I do not know where she is gone.'

'A carriage has overturned in Henrietta Street,' said she. 'I have just heard it from Mrs Bacon, Mama's dressmaker. Mrs Beresford was seen hastening from the house some five and thirty minutes ago.'

'I must go,' Lady Allersham replied. 'May I trespass on your kindness? You would do me a great service if you would remain here while I am gone. Should my aunt return in my absence and require assistance, I —'

'Of course,' she replied. 'Have no anxiety. I shall not move from here. You may depend on it. I shall await your return.'

Lady Allersham set off in the direction of Henrietta Street quickening her pace with each step, while conceiving every misfortune imaginable visited on her aunt. I daresay, said she, under her breath, were Mr Beresford the victim, we should not care so very much.

Miss Carteret surrendered her coat and bonnet and stationed herself at the window that gave the fullest view of Laura Place. She surveyed the room to ascertain whether any slight adjustment might be required to aid Mrs Beresford, or any other person, unlucky enough to sustain injury to mind or body. The sight of mutilation would be certain to cause distress to any person of weak mind unused to witnessing such horrors. Miss Carteret prepared herself for any eventuality.

The placement of a footstool by the chair, and an additional cushion upon it, seemed all that was needed to complete the already comfortable arrangements. But were the wounded to be admitted, what would be called for then? thought she. Bandages, wine, poultices, compresses, a surgeon! Should I be required to tend some poor unfortunate creature, crushed beneath the weight of a carriage, stoical to the last, despite the agony, I hope I should know how to act!

Suddenly, the door opened to admit a gentleman whose buoyant gait was as much a stranger to pain as his conduct to propriety. An apologetic footman followed soon afterwards, unable to prevent the encounter.

'My dear cousin! Emma!' said the stranger, dismissing the footman. 'You do not recognise me, I see! Nor I you! Your hair has grown very dark indeed. How long is it since I pulled your locks and pinched your slice of gooseberry tart in Grandpapa's dusty old parlour at Stanton? Don't be so standoffish! It is I. Your cousin. Robert. You may be a countess, but I'll wager you are still a flouter of convention. Send for tea and tell me how you managed to persuade Lord Allersham into matrimony. You look surprised. Are you not delighted to see me?' said he.

'You, Sir, are a stranger to me. I am not Lady Allersham. Therefore, it is neither my business to feel delight nor dismay at your arrival. I am merely curious to know why you should mistake me for Lady

Allersham,' said Miss Carteret, turning fully towards him. 'I am not, as you see, your cousin.'

'Ah,' said he. 'My apologies.' The gentleman surveyed the young woman, and then the room, and waited for an invitation to be seated. The invitation did not come, and an awkward pause ensued.

At length, the stranger broke the silence. 'Captain Harding at your service. May I enquire to whom I have the pleasure of speaking?'

'Miss Carteret,' said she, with a curt nod of the head.

'I take it my cousin is from home at present.'

'Lady Allersham is expected shortly. There has been an accident,' said she.

'Oh that. Yes,' said Captain Harding. 'A sorry business. I heard of it on my way here. The carriage will likely require the attention of a wheelwright. But it is not beyond repair in the right hands.'

'But what of its occupants? What of the horses?' said Miss Carteret.

'I daresay there will be nothing amiss there. I have twice overturned on the road and escaped with nothing more than a bruise or two on both occasions. Potholes, Miss Carteret. In almost every case, potholes are the culprits.'

Perplexed by Captain Harding's continued presence despite the impropriety of their meeting, and his insistence on prolonging the encounter, Miss Carteret said nothing in reply. She turned away and took up her position by the window once again, and the room fell silent.

Captain Harding looked about him before making himself comfortable by the fire, and with a casual, almost careless demeanour, proceeded to hum a

Scottish air while conducting an imaginary orchestra with his forefinger.

'Sir,' said Miss Carteret, exasperated by his continued presence, 'I am commissioned by Lady Allersham to assist her should any unforeseen event arising from the incident in Henrietta Street occur. And although you are perfectly entitled to await Her Ladyship's return, your presence in this room, and mine, must be seen in a very poor light. I do not need to tell you that it is highly irregular and will require explanation.'

'You wish me to leave then?' replied Captain Harding, affecting surprise.

'That would be the natural impulse of a gentleman,' said she.

At that moment the door opened to admit Lady Allersham and Mrs Beresford, none the worse for their exertions in Henrietta Street.

'Cousin Robert!' said Lady Allersham, astonished to find her cousin in Laura Place. 'Is it really you? What brings you to Bath? When did you set foot on dry land? Oh! Miss Carteret. What must you think of me? I had no knowledge of anything of the kind or I should never have — Allow me to introduce my cousin, Captain Harding.'

'Miss Carteret and I are already acquainted. Had you delayed another five minutes, I feel sure we should have been almost betrothed.'

'I must apologise for my cousin,' said Lady Allersham. 'He is the greatest mischief-maker in the world. Do not believe a word he says. When he is in such a humour, there is nothing to be done except ignore him or scold him severely.'

'Then I am already undone for I received my marching orders from Miss Carteret,' said Captain Harding. 'I see I shall be obliged to make amends for the greater part of five minutes.'

'I have never known you to be prevailed upon to make any alteration of the kind,' added Mrs Beresford, with good humour.

'Mrs Beresford,' said Captain Harding, 'how good it is to see you once again. And you see I am hardly altered at all. I have no more acquired a serious air than a fondness for decorum. I am as ever I was. Miss Carteret, though, seems fonder than I of decorum.'

'Certainly, I am,' said she.

'Miss Carteret is not used to your ways, Robert. In my cousin's defence, Miss Carteret, Captain Harding is not wholly without manners. It is just that he chooses now and again to refrain from employing them,' said Lady Allersham.

Another ten minutes went by in cheerful raillery at Captain Harding's expense, delighting Lady Allersham and Mrs Beresford. At length, Miss Carteret returned to the subject of the overturned carriage. But before the matter was spoken of in full, Lady Allersham and Mrs Beresford apprised Captain Harding of the business that had led to it, the business surrounding the visit of Mr James Beresford.

'And so, Mr James Beresford is your late husband's nephew,' said Captain Harding to Mrs Beresford.

'His *cousin*,' said Mrs Beresford, correcting their visitor. 'I should have made the same error myself, for Mr James Beresford is a young man, not unlike my dear late husband in manner and appearance twenty years ago. At times I perceived a look, a gesture — I

27

was reminded of him — it was quite disconcerting. My husband's father had two brothers. There existed a difference of one and twenty years between the eldest, Admiral Beresford, and the youngest. Mr James Beresford is the only child of the youngest brother, if you comprehend my meaning. The Admiral had no children. My husband was an only child. And so, Mr James Beresford alone is left.'

'I never served with Admiral Beresford, but I understand he was a good man,' said Captain Harding.

'I met him but twice in my life,' said Mrs Beresford. 'He was said to treat the families of those fallen in battle with great compassion.'

'Indeed,' said the Captain.

'And was Mr Beresford's carriage damaged beyond repair?' said Miss Carteret, curiously keen to establish the facts.

'The carriage belonged to a gentleman from Kent,' Mrs Beresford replied. 'Mr Beresford witnessed the scene and took charge until his assistance was no longer required. He sent word to Laura Place that he would be delayed. But the messenger did not convey the message accurately, and so I assumed that Mr Beresford was the injured party. He is now gone back to his lodgings.'

'Mr Beresford was not fit to be seen by the end of it. His jacket was thick with mud and dust,' added Lady Allersham. 'He promises to call at Laura Place in the morning.'

'One hopes, in a clean jacket,' said Captain Harding.

'And this is the gentleman lately returned from the East Indies?' said Miss Carteret.

'I am indeed,' said Captain Harding, misunderstanding to whom she was referring.

'I meant Mr Beresford,' said she.

Lady Allersham explained to Miss Carteret that her cousin had also been in the East Indies. The extraordinary coincidence, that both her cousin and James Beresford were lately returned from the East Indies, prompted her to solicit Captain Harding's help. She turned to him and said, 'Cousin, perhaps you know or have heard Mr James Beresford spoken of in the East Indies.'

Captain Harding laughed. 'The East Indies is a very vast continent. I expect I should have remembered the name Beresford had the gentleman crossed my path, but I feel sure he did not.'

'And yet your knowledge of the East Indies may yet serve us well,' continued Lady Allersham. 'Might you enquire about his travels there, find something that —'

'You mean, ascertain whether the gentleman is who he says he is?' said Captain Harding. 'Imposters are a great favourite with our family, Miss Carteret. What was the name, Emma, of the rascal who persuaded old Aunt Turner into matrimony, spent her fortune and left her without a penny?'

'Never mind that,' she replied. 'Just make sure you call here in the morning. I have need of you. Where are your lodgings?'

'Sydney Place,' said Captain Harding. 'It is quite the place to be. I'm told that when our good and noble Queen resided there, she brought with her a large regiment of attendants from the Palace.'

'Sydney Place is very well situated. In fact, Miss Carteret and I had a most pleasant walk in Sydney Gardens this morning,' said Lady Allersham.

'Then perhaps you might allow me to accompany you when you plan another adventure there,' said Captain Harding.

CHAPTER FOUR

'I do so enjoy conundrums,' said Lady Allersham to her aunt, when they were alone. 'Jane Carteret puzzles me greatly.'

Mrs Beresford had seen nothing in Miss Carteret's disposition to raise her curiosity. 'She is, perhaps, a little sombre, but I should suppose that to be Lady Dalrymple's doing. She seems to keep a keen eye on her daughter.'

'There is more, I think. In her air and expression at times there appears something akin to despondency. Lady Dalrymple, of course, may be the culprit. Or perhaps she has been crossed in love,' said Lady Allersham. 'I know the signs and have felt the pain.'

'Emma, my dear,' said Mrs Beresford, 'we have all had our hearts broken. I am sure Miss Carteret is no exception. But I do not think she would seek or welcome our interference, however kindly intended.'

'A heart once broken is soonest mended when affection is channelled in another direction, and bestowed on a worthier object —'

'A heart once broken is soonest mended when others refrain from conduct that is meddlesome and misapplied,' said Mrs Beresford.

Lady Allersham was not to be deterred. To be occupied about the business of mending Jane Carteret's heart, if indeed it had been broken, was as estimable a scheme as one could hope for in Bath. Where else in the whole of England might so plentiful a cohort of suitors be found?

Alas, thought she, of her acquaintance in Bath, only two candidates were known to her and neither one would do: Cousin Robert had neither fortune nor manners; and nothing good was known of Mr James Beresford.

'This is a sorry state of affairs,' said Lady Allersham. 'I know of no eligible young men at all.'

The remainder of the day was spent in pleasant occupation: writing letters, reading notices in the *Chronicle*, and making plans for visits to the theatre and assembly rooms.

'There is to be a recital on Wednesday evening at the Upper Rooms. Lady Dalrymple was most insistent that we attend. What do you say, Emma?' said Mrs Beresford.

'Was not the invitation accompanied by the suggestion that only *one* carriage would be required. And as Lady Dalrymple did not place her coach at our disposal, I assume her intention being that we should offer ours instead,' Lady Allersham replied.

'I believe you are right. Yet, it is a reasonable proposition.'

'There is wisdom in it for Lady Dalrymple. She gives herself no trouble over the hire of the horses, saves herself a shilling or two in the process, and is assured of every comfort and attention, and at no expense to herself. I do hope, Aunt, that Lady

Dalrymple does not see fit to impose on us every time it pleases her to do so.'

At that moment, Lady Allersham was distracted by the sound of footsteps on the stairs. No one was expected at that hour, and so it was with surprise and delight that the door opened to admit Lord Allersham.

'Henry!' said Lady Allersham, jumping up to meet him. 'We did not expect you.'

'Have I surprised you? I confess, it was my aim. The business in Brinshore took less than half the time. I had planned to break my journey and call at Osborne Castle, but as your parents are to visit Allersham in the autumn —'

'The autumn?'

Lord Allersham nodded, amused by his wife's surprise. 'Yes. And so, I decided to forgo the pleasure for the present and continue on my way. I was eager to see what you have made of Bath, my dear, or perhaps what Bath has made of you.'

'Very little, I'm afraid,' said Lady Allersham, 'but we have had the good fortune to become acquainted with our neighbours in Laura Place through the kind solicitations of your self-appointed aunt. Lady Russell was generosity itself, and she made every effort to conceal her vexation with you. Henry, my love, Lady Russell was obliged to read of our arrival in the *Chronicle*.'

'Ah,' said His Lordship, as he sank into a chair.

'But never mind that. We have made the acquaintance of Lady Dalrymple and Miss Carteret through your aunt's good offices. I must say, it gave Lady Russell great pleasure to perform the introductions, and I believe she left Bath fully content with *her* efforts, even if she seemed less than satisfied with *yours*, my dear,' said Lady Allersham.

'Ah.'

'Have you nothing more to say in reply?' said she.

About Lady Dalrymple and her daughter, he declared he had nothing further to say except that he hoped not to be drawn into their society every hour of the day. Lady Russell would require more careful handling. A letter was the least that would suffice.

'We might invite her to Allersham in the autumn,' said he.

'An enchanting prospect,' replied Lady Allersham, without a hint of delight in her voice.

He smiled and turned to Mrs Beresford and enquired whether she had news concerning Mr James Beresford.

'I have indeed,' said she.

The incident that occurred in Henrietta Street was related in detail to Lord Allersham. He listened intently and sought clarity over certain aspects of the report before declaring the actions of the gentleman in question to be benevolent and honourable, sufficient in his eyes to wholly recommend Mr James Beresford. Lady Allersham was less inclined to give way.

'His intention may well have been to impress, to secure our approval and, by so doing, gain our good opinion. I expect he saw his chance and made the most of it,' said Lady Allersham. 'Is it not prudent to be on one's guard until we know more about Mr James Beresford?'

'Be on your guard as your conscience dictates, but keep an open mind,' said Lord Allersham. 'Not every individual is governed by wickedness and deceit.'

'Henry,' said Lady Allersham, 'you are too generous by half. You refuse to see wickedness in others. You insist on seeing good even where there is no goodness to be found.'

'Is it not better to think well of someone until we can be certain that the reverse is true?'

'There can be no other explanation for Mr James Beresford's appearance now,' said Lady Allersham, 'If only we were not so often at odds. But I believe I shall be proved right in the end.'

'We all have our imperfections,' said Lord Allersham.

Lady Allersham sighed heavily.

'Come, my dear,' said Lord Allersham, with a teasing smile, 'I find your imperfections perfectly charming. Please do not imagine any alteration is needed on my account.'

'And I find your affability extremely vexing,' replied Lady Allersham. 'Tell me how you found Captain and Mrs Blake.'

'The picture of wedded bliss,' said he.

Mrs Beresford made her excuses and retired earlier than was her custom. News of Captain and Mrs Blake, though eagerly awaited, would bear postponement until the morning. On climbing the stairs to her bedchamber, Mrs Beresford recalled, as a boy, Charles Blake striding up and down the staircase at Osborne Castle, the home where she was born. He had once been a frequent visitor there. As a child, he had loved to dance; in his eyes there was nothing in the world to compare to a ball, except for hunting foxes and other creatures. Mrs Beresford sat on the edge of the bed and removed a gold chain worn many years ago at one such ball, some weeks before Colonel Beresford had summoned the courage to propose. The night of the Delham Ball was permanently inscribed on her memory. She recalled how displeased her brother had been when she had broken her promise to stand up with Master Charles and had danced that night with Colonel Beresford instead. In the event, the boy's disappointment had been short-lived; another young woman had taken pity on him and soon afterwards offered to dance with him, restoring his enjoyment in an instant. That young woman was Emma Watson, the beautiful but penniless daughter of a local clergyman. Within a twelvemonth Miss Watson's engagement to Mrs Beresford's brother, Lord Osborne, would astonish the world, and despite the many objections and expressions of surprise when first it was announced, it had been a good and enduring match. And it had been in no small part due to Mrs Beresford's intervention, for when she saw her brother's regard for Miss Watson, she knew that he would settle for no one but her; consequently, she had done all in her power to promote the match.

Lady Allersham, the daughter of Lord and Lady Osborne, was not entirely satisfied with the account that her husband had carried of Captain and Mrs Blake. Yes, they were in good health. Yes, their Sanditon home was much altered and improved through the pains the young Mrs Blake had taken with it, all of which had added to its comfort and utility. Yes, they extended their good wishes to Her Ladyship and promised to spend Christmas at Allersham Park should circumstances allow.

'And what news of Captain Blake's mother? When is she expected to visit Sanditon? Is she in good health?'

'I have no reason to doubt it,' Lord Allersham replied.

'No? I have not received a letter from her for six weeks.'

'If Mrs Blake had been in poor health, the matter would have been mentioned and it was not,' said he.

Lady Allersham continued, 'And the weather? Was Sanditon all sunshine and Brinshore rain?'

'It rained three days out of five. The air was mild,' he replied. 'But Emma, my dear, are you not curious to know how fares your Aunt and Uncle Fowle?'

'I cannot say that I am,' she replied.

Lord Allersham wondered at his wife's indifference. 'Are you unwell? Ordinarily, you delight in every absurd detail.'

Lady Allersham laughed at her husband's concern. 'Aunt Fowle has a cold and blames Mr Fowle for it, and Mr Fowle complains that Mr Granby is stealing his patients.'

'How on earth did you hear about Granby? I was told not to breathe a word of it.'

'Cousin Robert is in Bath,' said she. 'He surprised us all with a visit this morning. We received a very full report of the goings on between the Fowles.'

'Harding?' replied Lord Allersham. 'How can that be? I was given to understand he was in Portsmouth.'

'You may see for yourself, my love. He promises to call on us tomorrow. And I do believe he may prove himself useful. Mr James Beresford also threatens to call on us.'

'I suppose you have asked your cousin to quiz Mr Beresford about his business interests in the East Indies,' said Lord Allersham.

'His *business* interests? I had not thought to include his business interests. Thank you, my love.'

'Emma!' said Lord Allersham. 'From every report I have received concerning Captain Harding, including, I might add, yours, I should no more rely on his opinion of Mr James Beresford than his view of the sea worthiness of a tea strainer.'

Lady Allersham raised half a smile. 'Henry, my love, promise me you will not be persuaded to go away again, at least not without me. I have missed you more than you can know.'

'You have my word,' said he. 'I shall not be prevailed upon to leave you ever again.'

'Thank you,' she replied.

'Unless,' he added, 'it is absolutely necessary.'

CHAPTER FIVE

Captain Harding's mother, Mrs Fowle, had married for a second time following the death of Dr Harding. A young man of four and twenty years, Captain Harding had spent twelve of them at sea. As a child, he was wild and wilful, a matter of constant anxiety to his parents, which led them to suppose that the best hope of correction was to be found among the ranks of the Navy. As a young naval recruit, Harding encountered the discipline he had lacked in earlier years. His heroic exploits had seen him rise quickly through the ranks, and though he had made a success of his time at sea, he had returned with a somewhat modest sum in prize money.

His occasional presence on dry land had brought Captain Harding into the way of a Miss Shaw of Chichester, an unworthy object of affection in his mother's estimation. He had proposed and was accepted. The engagement did not last long, and came to an end when the young woman, wearied by Harding's long absences and indifferent fortune, sought and succeeded in making a more advantageous alliance with a gentleman of means, to the relief and delight of Captain Harding's mother.

Old Dr Harding had provided his son with a legacy that would have tempted some, but one which gave no inducement to the kind of young woman who, through choice rather than necessity, aspired to marry as well as fortune would allow. Captain Harding's mother, having been handsomely provided for through Dr Harding's estate, was not long in quitting Chichester after her husband's demise, and setting up in a little-known town on the south coast by the name of Brinshore. There, her interests in promoting the town coincided with the exertions of a local physician, Mr Fowle, who extolled the town's beneficial and medicinal qualities. Matrimony soon followed, though Mrs Harding's love of Brinshore and its possibilities was greater than her love for Mr Fowle and his. For his part, Mr Fowle, whose passion for Mrs Harding at first knew no bounds, found to his dismay that unfettered devotion had its limits. He was disposed to overlook certain defects of character and temperament in the woman to whom he was joined forever, and yet he would have raised no objection to any man who six months later had had at his disposal the means to put their union asunder.

Mrs Fowle's disappointment in her husband was felt with less force, for her expectations of matrimonial bliss had been far lower from the outset. Shrewd and practical, Mrs Fowle found that she was able to tolerate her situation in life with greater forbearance than he. Complaints and grievances were what now gave purpose to her existence, and when at times her tolerance had reached its limits, she found release through occasional visits to Osborne Castle. There, due to the sisterly affection and patient ministrations of Lady Osborne, Mrs Fowle was free to give voice to the displeasure occasioned by her husband's petulance and felt the better for it. The matrimonial discord that pervaded the Fowle household was thus contained; and Brinshore society was saved the knowledge of it, for among her circle Mrs Fowle was at pains, as was her husband, to preserve the appearance of marital harmony at all costs.

Captain Harding's business in Portsmouth had been completed to his great surprise and amusement. The matter concerned the will of his late father's friend, Mr Brooks, a man whose frugality in later life had led to the belief that his means had been greatly reduced through poor business transactions. Captain Harding, who had been summoned by Mr Brooks' attorney, found to his astonishment that the deceased, who had lived a modest existence, had acquired land and property, the rents from which had accumulated into a handsome fortune. Having no immediate heir and being able to do with his wealth as he pleased, he had chosen to bestow the entirety of it upon the son of his good friend. The legacy had not been made on a whim, however, for Captain Harding, believing Mr

Brooks to be impoverished, had made provision for him to be cared for, and in the final weeks of his life had visited him as often as circumstances would allow on his return from the East Indies.

The attorney charged with oversight of the late Mr Brooks' affairs had insisted on conveying the news of the beneficiary's good fortune in person according to the deceased's express instructions. Six, possibly seven, thousand a year, land and property besides, represented a marked change in providence for one without expectations of the kind. Captain Harding quitted the offices of the Portsmouth attorney with one thought in mind: for as long as he was able, he would not speak of the matter to anyone at all except his man of business.

When Captain Harding reached Laura Place, he found Lord and Lady Allersham and Mrs Beresford, the Dalrymples and Mr James Beresford in animated conversation. Introductions were made on his admittance to the drawing room and the usual salutations were given and received. Lady Dalrymple had already established Captain Robert Harding's minor connexion with the Osborne family, and showed little interest in advancing the acquaintance further. An occasional invitation to a card party, should it be necessary to make up the numbers would suffice, and only if Captain Harding proved to be a reasonable card player.

Mr James Beresford appeared to be of greater interest, not only to Mrs Beresford and Lady Allersham, but to Lady Dalrymple's daughter also. Before the hour had passed, Miss Carteret had established that Mr Beresford's taste in music, art and poetry was identical to her own. Lady Allersham, a keen observer of what passed between them, was struck by the possibility that happiness might not be quite so out of reach as Miss Carteret had supposed.

'Do you read, Cousin? Poetry, perhaps?' said Lady Allersham, turning to Captain Harding. 'I remember how well you liked to make up silly rhymes.'

'The Navy List is a favourite volume of mine,' Captain Harding replied. 'Within it one might find some nonsense or other. I once commanded a vessel described therein as a frigate of the sixth-rate. How it had acquired so dazzling a description, I do not know.'

'Mr Beresford, we have heard nothing of your travels in the East Indies,' said Lady Allersham. 'Captain Harding has spent much time in that part of the world, have you not, Cousin?'

'Most of it at sea,' he replied.

'My knowledge is limited to a small island off the southern tip of India. Ceylon. I expect you have heard of it. A most beautiful and exotic land,' said Mr Beresford. 'And of Ceylon, my knowledge, I must confess, is limited too. I had hoped there might be business possibilities there.'

'And the nature of the business being tea?' asked Miss Carteret helpfully.

'Coffee, tea, coconut oil perhaps, and more besides,' replied Mr Beresford.

'And have you plans to return to Ceylon in due course?' said Mrs Beresford.

'I cannot say categorically that I have,' said Mr Beresford. 'But forgive me. I have trespassed on your kindness long enough. Mrs Beresford, may I wait on you this day week or another day hence? At your convenience, of course. Name the day if you will. I have no further engagements that claim my attention.'

'Of course,' replied Mrs Beresford. 'I shall send word to Paragon Buildings as soon as I am able.'

Mr Beresford took his leave and departed Laura Place; he proceeded along Argyle Street to Bridge Street, but rather than taking the direct route to The Paragon, continued towards Milsom Street and soon arrived at his destination in Queen Square.

The drawing room at Laura Place saw no further decline in numbers for almost an hour after Mr Beresford had quitted it. Lady Dalrymple was disinclined to move, having secured a comfortable chair by the fire.

'Well,' said she of Mr Beresford, 'a man of mystery. Has he connexions in Bath?'

'Mr Beresford and my late husband were cousins,' said Mrs Beresford.

'Mr Beresford wishes to make amends for his absence at the time of Colonel Beresford's death,' said Lady Allersham.

'Does he? Has he a view to benefitting from the Colonel's demise in some way?' continued Lady Dalrymple, with unabashed candour.

'Of his motives we are uncertain, Lady Dalrymple.' Turning to Captain Harding, Lady Allersham enquired, 'Well, Cousin? In your opinion, has Mr Beresford ventured further east than Margate? Has he spent time in the East Indies as he claims?'

'I have no reason to suppose that he has not,' said Captain Harding.

'So, you do not think him a storyteller of sorts?' said Lady Allersham.

'Mr Beresford? Impossible!' said Miss Carteret. 'No one could be less so.'

'There, Miss Carteret,' said Captain Harding, 'I cannot agree. Scoundrels never look like scoundrels. And before you yield to the temptation of saying that which is on the tip of your tongue —'

Lady Allersham could not suppress her amusement. 'My thoughts precisely, Miss Carteret. Cousin, if anyone has the appearance of a scoundrel it must be you.'

'You may think of me as you will, Emma,' said he. 'I should never deny you diversion at my expense. Nor you, Miss Carteret. Indeed, I am certain that my own mother would agree with you wholeheartedly.'

'There is but one name that fits such a description,' said Lady Dalrymple. 'A person, the very height of absurdity and recklessness! But I shall not speak of him.' The Dowager lent towards Captain Harding and whispered loud enough for the whole gathering to hear, 'Sir Walter Elliot.'

'Tell me, Madam,' said he, 'am I as fine-looking as he? I know of him only by reputation, but I believe he is reckoned handsome for his age.'

Lady Dalrymple broke into laughter. 'My dear Captain Harding!' said she, 'No one is as handsome as he! At least that is *his* belief. He has quite worn out my looking glass establishing it to be so! I have never known a man so full of vanity.'

'Mama!' said Miss Carteret.

Lady Dalrymple's mirth would not be curbed. 'Captain Harding,' said she, 'Are you a vain man?'

'Vanity, Madam, is my forte,' said he. 'I am determined to perfect it in all its aspects.'

'Shocking, Sir!' said Miss Carteret. 'Quite shocking! Have you no shame?'

'At this moment, Miss Carteret, I have not the greater need of it,' said Captain Harding, in a whisper. 'Your mama is quite beside herself. Does she often laugh so heartily?'

Lord and Lady Allersham and Mrs Beresford looked on in bemused silence as Lady Dalrymple endeavoured to recover her countenance. Lord Allersham whispered to his wife, 'Your cousin is rare indeed. He succeeds in recommending himself by purposely seeking to discredit his very character in every way possible.'

'Lady Dalrymple does seem pleased with him. If only he had more than wit to recommend him, she might even think of him for Miss Carteret, not least to satisfy her own need for amusement,' whispered Lady Allersham.

'My love,' whispered Lord Allersham, 'If only you would desist from ordering the happiness of others.'

'How can I when I have ordered my own and have nothing else to do. I am as well placed as anyone to offer encouragement. And I shall do so where I can,' said she.

'It was not so long ago that you had me in your sights for another,' said Lord Allersham.

'I know,' said Lady Allersham. 'How foolish of me! I need no reminder. And to prove that I am not so lacking in judgement as you suppose, Cousin Robert would never do. He and Miss Carteret are so dissimilar. And, I fear Miss Carteret finds Mr James Beresford more agreeable. If only we were sure of *his* character. Despite his engaging manners, I cannot quite make him out.'

Lady Dalrymple was disinclined to quit the company of Captain Harding despite her daughter's entreaties.

'Mama,' said Miss Carteret, irked by Captain Harding's total abandonment of decorum, 'are not we to call upon Mr Ibbotson and the Misses Ibbotson. Did we not give our word?'

'The Ibbotsons will not take offence. They are pleased to be noticed at all. You may call on them tomorrow if you will,' said Lady Dalrymple.

From the severe look cast by Miss Carteret in his direction, Captain Harding saw that she held him entirely responsible for her mother's uncommon geniality. He supposed that his success with Lady Dalrymple had impaired any progress he might hope to make with Miss Carteret, and though he had no object in mind beyond that of an amiable acquaintance, the challenge of cultivating the daughter's good opinion, as well as the mother's, was not without its appeal, for Captain Harding enjoyed a challenge. He made his excuses and took leave of the residents of Laura Place, having secured unlimited further invitations from one party, and an invitation to a card party from the other; all had been achieved without giving trouble to himself, without exertion or affectation, and all within a week of arriving in Bath.

Lady Dalrymple and Miss Carteret soon afterwards took their leave; the former, who had at first found her seat by the fire the perfect degree of warmth, now found the heat overpowering and wished to be gone.

As the usual farewells on parting were given and received, Lady Allersham observed an uneasiness in Miss Carteret's manner towards Lord Allersham. In contrast, he appeared to exhibit a general air of unstudied ease and good humour. Nevertheless, Lady Allersham felt a slight pang of doubt. Lord Allersham and Miss Carteret had spoken only briefly during the morning, and nothing had passed between them but several commonplace remarks. Moreover, Lady Allersham had detected nothing in the demeanour of either to raise alarm, except the curious, almost nervous, adieu of her new friend.

She was reminded of the presence of *Paradise Lost* in the library at Allersham and Miss Carteret's name inscribed within it; its existence there had still not been properly explained, and until the matter had been clarified, doubts would remain and cause her uneasiness of mind.

The afternoon passed quietly and uneventfully. Lady Allersham sat by the window with the intention of hemming a handkerchief but found the activity in the street outside of greater interest. Mrs Beresford set about letter-writing and Lord Allersham took the opportunity to walk into town to settle some business with an attorney acting on behalf of the estate adjoining Allersham Park.

From the window above, Lady Allersham watched her husband depart Laura Place. Five minutes passed before something quite troubling caught her attention. She observed Miss Carteret setting out alone and hastening towards Bridge Street in much the same direction as her husband.

CHAPTER SIX

The concert at the Upper Rooms was spoken of with great excitement and anticipation in Laura Place, the exception being Lord Allersham, who had shown little inclination for the occasion despite the many assurances that it was to be an excellent evening and was not to be missed.

'It promises to be an evening like no other, according to Lady Dalrymple,' said Lady Allersham. 'My dear, how shall I account for your absence? I should not mind it so very much had we the carriage to ourselves, for explanation would then have been unnecessary. But what shall I say when Lady Dalrymple asks where you are, as she most certainly will?'

'As there will be no room in the carriage for me, I see no problem in telling her so,' said he. 'Does she not possess a carriage of her own?'

'She did not want the trouble of ordering it,' said Lady Allersham.

'Do not mistake me, my dear,' said he. 'I am perfectly content with the arrangement. I can advance no better argument of my own to defend my absence. Enjoy your evening. I shall enjoy mine.'

Lady Dalrymple, having availed herself of a seat in her neighbours' carriage prior to the event, was determined not to give it up, and despite the unexpected arrival of Lord Allersham, saw no need to make any alteration to her own plans.

'Even so, my dear, I should like your company,' said Lady Allersham to her husband.

'Lady Dalrymple will require an entire seat to herself,' said he. 'You will all be obliged to squeeze onto the seat opposite. And were I to join you, I should only add to your discomfort.'

'The Upper Rooms are not far. It is not beyond a walk. And you like walking,' said Lady Allersham, frustrated by her husband's reluctance to join the party. 'I daresay Cousin Robert would accompany you should he be disposed to attend. I shall send a note immediately to Sydney Place and ask him.'

'My dear,' said Lord Allersham, 'it will serve me extremely well to stay where I am and read a book. Invite Harding if you will but leave me out of it. I am perfectly content to remain where I am.'

'If only I had not been persuaded to promise Lady Dalrymple a seat in our carriage.'

'Too late now, my love,' said he. 'She is a woman who brooks no refusal. And I am sure you will do very well without me and find much at the Upper Rooms to take pleasure in; and as society in general is disposed to ascribing the greatest importance to rank and consequence, you are certain to command all the best seats between you.'

Following his elder brother's demise and his accession to the Allersham estate and title, regard for Henry Fitzroy increased in equal measure to his consequence. The esteem in which he was held as the young Lord Allersham, however, gave him no pleasure. He regarded it with some consternation for he had always scorned that aspect of society that tended towards obsequiousness, and never more so than the present, having become the object of it. As the third son of a nobleman whose aim in life had been to enter the Church, his lesser standing in the eyes of the world at one time had provided a refuge from the condescension that displeased him most. In every other aspect he was disposed to acknowledge his good fortune; for, as Lord Allersham, he knew that any man lucky enough to accede to such an inheritance had no business complaining about it, for if condescension was an evil to be fought against, poverty and degradation was the greatest evil of all. Oddly, Allersham, despite all it stood for, offered the comfort that Bath could not supply. For the present, he was obliged to tolerate the foibles and excesses of the town — it was unavoidable — but for one evening he was content to sit by the fire with a book and savour the silence.

Mrs Beresford, having spent the morning shopping in Milsom Street, on her return to Laura Place examined her purchases, and was pleased to find that she had chosen well. She was content to spend the rest of the afternoon in preparation for the much-anticipated evening concert.

The procurement of several yards of grey silk for a new gown was a prudent purchase, and a pair of gloves a bargain, and though one did not fit quite as well as the other, it required no more than a little stretching to make it perfectly acceptable. Her greatest regret of the morning, however, was having had no time to visit Molland's.

The enjoyment of shopping had eased her melancholy; and she was surprised to discover that two hours had passed without a single thought given to Colonel Beresford. But as she sat alone in her room, the remembrance of him brought with it guilt; that she had taken pleasure in a morning's purchases without once lamenting his loss caused her to suffer the pain of remorse for her inconstancy and neglect.

Mrs Beresford was reminded of the wise words of Charles Blake's mother, a woman whose widowhood had endured for more than twice the duration of her marriage: *mourning cannot be rushed or brushed away like a speck of dust on a coat sleeve. Society must wait, and patience must be applied until grief is brought under good regulation with time.* Like many before her, Mrs Beresford continued to entertain the self-reproach that sometimes afflicts those left behind when the deceased are gone but remain in the conscience and thoughts of the living. A necklace lay on the dressing table, a modest piece, elegant in its simplicity, a bittersweet reminder of her late husband. It was the last, and one of the most cherished gifts she had received from him.

An unhurried hour was spent in her preparations for the evening. When the assistance of her maid was no longer required, and she was satisfied that everything was as it should be, she placed the necklace around her neck and for some moments studied her appearance in the looking glass.

Mrs Beresford was ready to enter society again.

Word came that Lady Dalrymple was impatient to set off. There was one disappointment: Miss Carteret was not to be one of the party. A sore throat was the cause of her indisposition, and being more severely affected than she had at first supposed, she had found that the apothecary's remedy she had sought the previous afternoon had done little to improve it, hence, complete rest was advised.

'Scarcely is relief to be found in the application of apothecaries' tonics and potions. But Jane would make a point of purchasing some such concoction against my advice. I advised her to take to her bed, but she would go out. She would not be told. Apothecaries will say anything to sell a cure-all. That is my view,' said Lady Dalrymple, as the carriage pulled out of Laura Place. 'White soup and a little rum are the very best restoratives of all.'

'Might I suggest a little lemon juice mixed with honey and oil of sweet almonds?' said Mrs Beresford. 'I have used such a mixture myself for twenty years and have found it efficacious in every instance.'

The curative properties of each remedy were compared and debated for the duration of the journey. Lady Allersham felt some relief when the Upper Rooms came into view and an end to the discussion was in sight. Her thoughts, however, were much preoccupied by the absence of Miss Carteret, and her own husband's disinclination to attend the concert. She dismissed any notion of intrigue, but doubts arose from time to time to cause her just enough discomfort to distract her attention from the evening's event. The pleasure of the recital had been diminished because of it, and when asked for her view of the performance at the close of the first act, to the surprise of her aunt, she had remarked that it had seemed ten minutes too long.

Lady Allersham was anxious to return to Laura Place. Even the promise of a dish of tea was of little comfort to her. The temptation to feign a headache, or even the first signs of a cold, was great indeed; but to see her aunt's pleasure at being in society once again was enough to dismiss the thought from her mind completely.

Mrs Beresford would have wanted nothing more than the presence of her late husband to make her joy complete; but she was now a little more readily disposed to accept less than the impossible and endeavour to enjoy those aspects of society that raised her spirits and enabled her, from time to time, to allow him to slip unobtrusively from her thoughts.

'Poor Miss Carteret,' said Mrs Beresford to her neighbour, as they made their way to the tea room. 'Your daughter has missed a most delightful evening.'

Lady Dalrymple agreed, but observed that it was a lesson to her daughter to take more care in her choice of attire.

'Jane insists on wearing silk stockings in cold weather,' said she.

'One does not wish to wear wool in May,' said Mrs Beresford.

'When the weather is cold, the month is of little matter. I have told her on more occasions than I care to recount that wool stockings are far superior to silk and guard against all manner of ailments whatever the season. And I see that I am proved right.'

The conversation continued in the same vein as Lady Allersham left her two companions to their tea to take some air. As she approached the door, she was addressed by a familiar voice whispering in her ear.

'Emma, what do you make of the fiddle player?' said Captain Harding.

'Robert?' said she.

'Is it such a surprise to you to find me here?'

'Yes, it is. You made no mention of it two days ago.'

'I was not disposed to attend a musical evening two days ago,' said he. 'And then I thought, why not? I'll put on my best jacket and surprise you all. But I don't see the redoubtable Miss Carteret among your party this evening.'

'Or my husband,' added Lady Allersham. 'He insists on spending the evening in peace and quiet, with a book.'

'He prefers a book to a screeching soprano? Singular,' Captain Harding replied. 'And how did Miss Carteret excuse herself? Her enjoyment of music surpasses all other pleasures, or so we are led to believe. Do not you recall, Emma, your friend's fervent plea that we all attend a musical evening in Bath. This very one, in fact. I expect she cried off claiming she had a violent headache when she found that the paragon of all virtue in the form of Mr B had no plans to attend.'

'Miss Carteret has a cold,' said Lady Allersham, observing, with a smile, the interesting change in her cousin's countenance. 'Do I detect a hint of disappointment?'

'Disappointment?' said he with incredulity.

'Arising from the absence this evening of Lady Dalrymple's daughter?' continued Lady Allersham.

Captain Harding dismissed the idea out of hand and declared it a reprehensible proposition. 'Nonsensical woman!' said he.

She was amused by Captain Harding's protest. And despite her teasing, Lady Allersham perceived that her cousin, amid his declarations of astonishment at the idea, had uttered no firm denial.

She persuaded him to join their party, an invitation that was met with universal surprise and delight. An additional seat was called for immediately, and Lady Dalrymple insisted that the seat be placed beside hers.

'Well, Captain Harding,' said Lady Dalrymple, as the second act was about to begin, 'this is an unexpected pleasure. What think you of our charming soprano? Who can deny her brilliancy?'

'Not I,' he replied. 'Though I'll wager that had a thirty-six pounder been half as deafening, we'd have seen off the French in half the time. If we are lucky enough to see another war, she'd be the Navy's greatest asset.'

'Dear me, Captain Harding!' said Lady Dalrymple, unable to conceal her amusement. 'For shame!'

'I am an insolent wretch,' said he.

'You are indeed,' replied Lady Allersham.

'I shall be obliged to mend my ways, for I see a look of disapproval in my cousin's eye,' said he to Lady Dalrymple.

'Too late, Cousin,' said Lady Allersham. 'You are utterly beyond amendment!'

He turned to Lady Dalrymple and whispered, 'I see I shall be the talk of Bath for all the wrong reasons.'

Lady Dalrymple smiled. 'Should you like to be the talk of Bath, Captain Harding?'

'Had I a vast fortune, I expect I should have no choice in the matter. As it is, I am, thankfully, quite safe.'

The second act brought Lady Allersham greater pleasure than the first as certain familiar songs and airs were sung in brighter tones; and by the end of the evening, she was quite sure that the music had brought a change in her mood and an easing of the misgivings that had earlier disturbed her mind. The evening concluded with an encore, and to great applause the gathering of Bath's leading music lovers began to disperse.

CHAPTER SEVEN

An account of the previous evening was half listened to the following morning in Laura Place; with an ear to his wife and an eye on the *Chronicle*, Lord Allersham was selective in the news that competed for his attention. The knowledge that Captain Harding had attended the concert and had once again succeeded in entertaining Lady Dalrymple from the opening of the second act to its conclusion, caused Lord Allersham to observe that there could be no argument more persuasive for having stayed indoors by the fire with a book. Of Captain Harding's purpose in wishing to recommend himself to Lady Dalrymple, Lord Allersham was doubtful.

'An hour or two spent in the company of Miss Carteret, and you think Harding half in love?' said he.

Lady Allersham replied, 'I do. But, my love, you must help me keep Cousin Robert out of Miss Carteret's way if you possibly can. I am serious.'

'I do not doubt it for a moment,' said he. 'But if Miss Carteret does not object, what possible good would come of keeping them apart? If Harding has her in his sights, and I sincerely doubt that he has, let them decide it between them.'

'Miss Carteret does not have my cousin in her sights. Of that I am certain. I think only of Robert. I should like him to avoid the inconvenience of another broken heart. You do not know how he suffered over Miss Shaw.'

'Thankfully not. And I have no wish to know,' said he.

'It will all come to nothing with Miss Carteret too. He has no fortune to speak of. Nothing to warrant serious consideration on her part.'

'Lady Dalrymple seems to approve of Harding,' replied Lord Allersham. 'That element alone makes the way infinitely less arduous.'

'Indeed, it does not! Cousin Robert may be as droll as he likes, but Lady Dalrymple will not let her daughter marry a jester. We must think of someone else for him,' said Lady Allersham. 'I am at a loss to know who would have him.'

'As am I,' agreed Lord Allersham. 'So, let the matter rest. He does not require your assistance in matters of the heart. And as to describing Harding as a jester, that may be one aspect of his character. Indeed, it is the only aspect of his character I have been obliged to witness; but a young man does not distinguish himself or attain the rank of captain in the Navy at two or three and twenty on the merits of being a clown. Invite him to dinner if you will. If he is as poor as you claim, a good dinner will suffice. He will be happy enough with that.'

It was a fine morning and one not to be missed. Mrs Beresford came down to find Lady Allersham at her writing desk. The latter, needing no persuasion to postpone her task, put down her pen, favouring instead a walk to Milsom Street to sample the sweet delicacies at Molland's.

'There we might enjoy a dish of hot tea and a slice of cake, or marzipan, or whatever appears the most appealing. It is certainly worth the exercise,' said Mrs Beresford.

'What is letter-writing compared to a slice of Molland's fruit cake? I have heard so much about it,' said Lady Allersham. 'And while we are there, I shall buy some liquorice for Miss Carteret. There is nothing better than liquorice for a cough, which always follows a sore throat and a cold in the head. Henry's favourite is marzipan, and I may buy him some too, for he will be quite put out that he did not join us. He is gone to meet Mr Dauber who is in town on parish business or something of the sort. I expect he will stay a day or two if he brings Miss Dauber with him. She likes to spend money. I hear she is acquainted with all the shops in Bath.'

'Then she is likely accompanying her father to purchase wedding clothes,' replied Mrs Beresford, 'for Mrs Dauber has hardly set foot outside the Rectory this past year and Miss Dauber can wait no longer for her mother's assistance in the matter.'

'Of course. It slipped my mind. Miss Dauber is to be married,' said Lady Allersham. 'But Mr Dauber is so seldom parted with his money that I do not think the purchase of wedding clothes will take long.'

Lord Allersham had been obliged to meet with the clergyman in town. He was, as Lady Allersham had predicted, accompanied by his eldest daughter. Miss Dauber had indeed come to buy wedding clothes, but it was also her object to take advantage of the opportunity to call on a school friend in Gay Street.

During the three years she had spent at Mrs Price's establishment in Gay Street, Miss Dauber had formed a friendship with another boarder there, a Miss Fox. The two young women had not met for almost a year, and in that period Miss Dauber had become engaged to a local farmer and was thought to have done exceedingly well for herself.

The same could not be said of Miss Fox. Circumstances over which she had no control had left the young woman without family or means. Miss Fox, a parlour boarder whose unknown benefactor had ceased providing regular payments to Mrs Price some time ago, with the result that substantial arrears had accrued, had been obliged to continue less as a boarder than as a servant. Mrs Price had seen fit to provide Miss Fox with a roof over her head in return for the performance of a variety of daily tasks. Attending to the needs of the younger boarders, reading aloud, darning, caring for the sick and carrying out errands as and when required, were among Miss Fox's duties, and she executed them kindly and meticulously, without remonstrance or self-pity. The generosity of Mrs Price was celebrated by all among her acquaintance, and Miss Fox was daily reminded of her immense good fortune, in case she should forget it.

When Lady Allersham and Mrs Beresford entered Molland's, Miss Dauber and Miss Fox were already seated. As many seats were taken, Miss Dauber was insistent that their own seats should be placed at the disposal of Lady Allersham and Mrs Beresford. It was no trouble in the least — they were shortly to leave Molland's — Her Ladyship would find no place more private, no seat more comfortable or conveniently situated away from the draught. Lady Allersham, though preferring another part of the shop, graciously accepted their offer and asked to be introduced to Miss Dauber's friend, Miss Fox. Surprised by the request from so great a personage as Lady Allersham,

Miss Dauber made the introduction but seemed almost ashamed of her friend.

After the two young women had left Molland's, Lady Allersham observed that Miss Fox was a pretty girl, modest and unaffected. 'I am a little surprised that she and Miss Dauber are such particular friends. Miss Fox clearly sees the constant need to display the kind of gratitude that is often present in a friendship where the terms of it are less than equal.'

Mrs Beresford was preoccupied by thoughts of her own and made no reply. After the tea things had been set down, however, and the cake sampled and approved of, she said, 'I know of no family by the name of Fox, but there is something about Miss Fox's countenance that is strangely familiar. Perhaps I have seen her in Whitcombe or thereabouts. I cannot quite recall where or why.'

'Possibly you glimpsed her visiting Miss Dauber,' said Lady Allersham.

'Perhaps so,' replied Mrs Beresford.

Lady Allersham would have liked to discover more about Miss Fox of whom nothing was known other than that she was the friend of Miss Dauber. Indeed, only the smallest leap of imagination was required to form the notion that someone like Miss Fox would be just the type of young woman to distract her cousin from his interest in Miss Carteret.

The cake was declared the best in Bath, even though it was the first they had sampled outside Laura Place, and the tea infinitely superior to that which had been served the evening before at the Upper Rooms.

The visit to Molland's was a subject of great interest later in the day when Lady Allersham called to see how Miss Carteret fared. Lady Dalrymple had taken to her bed for the afternoon, and Miss Carteret, having had a good night despite feeling feverish, was alone and thankful for the company.

'Liquorice is a favourite with me. It is so very good of you to think of it. I confess, I feel a great deal better already,' said she. 'I was exceedingly sorry to miss the concert. I trust you enjoyed it.'

'It was a very pleasant evening,' replied Lady Allersham.

'Mama was much amused by Captain Harding,' said Miss Carteret. 'It surprises me greatly, for she is never normally amused by anything.'

'My cousin's conduct leaves much to be desired. I am sorry if it vexes you.'

'Captain Harding's behaviour is singular, but I am not vexed by it. I do not think of it from one day's end to the other,' replied Miss Carteret, and changing the direction of the conversation she enquired, 'And how did you like Molland's?'

'I liked it very much indeed,' said Lady Allersham. 'Molland's is everything I had hoped for.'

Miss Carteret's smile was one of resignation. 'Everyone visits Molland's. I go but rarely, for it is the place where one is sure to meet everyone in the world one most seeks to avoid. I confess, I take little pleasure in conversation there for when once one enquires about another person's health, which is a major preoccupation wherever one goes, the question bestows consent on all and sundry to unleash the topic one least wishes to hear or speak about. The entire history of a person's ailments and infections, almost always of a putrid nature, are broadcast in every minute detail so that the world might hear. And it must always occur at the very moment one sits down to enjoy a splendid piece of Molland's cake. I should not mind so very much if half the world were really ill. It is those with the mildest ailments that make the loudest noise.'

'Well,' said Lady Allersham, 'I heard nothing of the sort this morning. But we did happen upon the Rector's daughter from Whitcombe, whom we know, and her friend. Miss Dauber is to be married shortly and is come to buy wedding clothes. She introduced us to a Miss Fox. They did not stay long and insisted on giving up their seats so that we might have them. I should have preferred a seat by the window for there is so much in the street outside to see and wonder at. So much goes on in Milsom Street.'

'Did you say Miss Fox?' replied Miss Carteret.

'Yes.'

'A Miss Fox used to sit with Mr Ibbotson's wife every Tuesday afternoon.'

'Used to? Why does she not sit with her now?'

'Mrs Ibbotson died some months ago.'

'How very unfortunate for Mr Ibbotson.'

'His preoccupation with his own health shields him from anything approaching despondency. He is never more animated than when he is granted the opportunity to speak of it.'

'Is Miss Fox connected with the family?' said Lady Allersham.

'That I do not know. But I recall Mr Ibbotson once saying that his wife could not do without her. I have heard him speak of a Miss Fox on one or two occasions.'

CHAPTER EIGHT

Three days passed before Lady Allersham saw Miss Carteret again. Restored to health, and eager to impart some information of interest she had obtained that morning, Miss Carteret called on Lady Allersham the same afternoon. As Lord Allersham had accompanied Mrs Beresford to call upon Mr James Beresford at Paragon Buildings, she was pleased to receive her neighbour alone.

'Wherever there is an accident, James Beresford is to be found,' said Lady Allersham. 'This time he is the patient. I do not know the details, but I understand his physician has ordered two days' rest. Mrs Beresford would insist on visiting Paragon Buildings to call on him, though I believe she is also curious to see how everything looks inside.'

'I hope his recovery is swift,' said Miss Carteret.

'It ought to be. For his physician is a dear one. He is said to be the best in Bath,' said Lady Allersham, 'which surprises me greatly.' At that moment, the thought occurred to her that Mr James Beresford might have employed an expensive physician on the expectation that Mrs Beresford would pay his bill. To distract herself from another troubling thought, Lady Allersham rang for tea.

Eager to impart her own news, and with an animated look in her eyes, Miss Carteret began. 'Mr Ibbotson and the Misses Ibbotson called at Laura Place this morning. While Mama was busy giving Miss Ibbotson advice, I took the opportunity to speak to Mr Ibbotson. To enquire about Miss Fox. I thought you might like to know what I discovered.'

'Yes, I should like to know very much,' said Lady Allersham.

'Miss Fox is not connected to the Ibbotson family, but there is a connexion of another kind. Miss Fox is a parlour boarder at Mrs Price's establishment in Gay Street. Mrs Price had been acquainted with Mrs Ibbotson for some time. During her final illness, Mrs Ibbotson, God rest her soul, required the assistance of a nurse and companion for certain duties the Misses Ibbotson were disinclined to perform. Hence, Mrs Price provided Mrs Ibbotson with the services of Miss Fox.'

'How interesting,' said Lady Allersham. 'But how did Miss Fox come to be a parlour boarder at Mrs Price's establishment?'

'She was placed there by *someone*. Mr Ibbotson believes it was a clergyman, but could provide no more information than that, and even then, he was not so very sure that the clergyman had any connexion to the young woman. Miss Fox, you see, was not necessarily placed there by her benefactor,' said Miss Carteret. 'A third party is often employed in such matters as these. I believe Your Ladyship mentioned that the father of Miss Fox's friend was a clergyman?'

'He is Rector of Whitcombe,' said Lady Allersham.

Miss Carteret glanced knowingly at Lady Allersham. 'There is more,' she went on. 'Provision, it seems, was made for Miss Fox by an unknown benefactor for several years, but latterly the payments have ceased. Thus, Miss Fox finds herself in a position of dependency. Little better than a beggar, I understand. Some say Mrs Price dealt kindly with Miss Fox for she did not throw her on to the streets as others might have done. She kept her on and gave her employment.'

'And I suppose one of her tasks was to sit with Mrs Ibbotson?' said Lady Allersham.

'Yes,' replied Miss Carteret.

'Poor Miss Fox,' said Lady Allersham. 'She is virtually a slave.'

'Mrs Price is praised to the hilt for her generous nature,' Miss Carteret replied.

'And yet all the advantages of the arrangement seem to be on Mrs Price's side.'

'Though Miss Ibbotson was not explicit, she implied that Miss Fox's duties are not inconsiderable. It is my belief that Miss Fox is imposed upon.'

'Of course she is,' said Lady Allersham. 'I despise the *appearance* of goodness. It is a masquerade of the worst kind.'

Their conversation lasted for much of the afternoon, and when the injustices that afflict women at the mercy of the Mrs Prices of this world had been debated and condemned, Miss Carteret took her leave.

When Lord Allersham and Mrs Beresford returned to Laura Place, Lady Allersham was obliged to withhold the details of her intelligence concerning Miss Fox and give way to her aunt who was anxious to relate the particulars of their visit to Paragon Buildings. Mr James Beresford had been a most charming host despite being incommoded by his present ailment; he had made light of his discomfort and would speak only of Colonel Beresford and the high esteem he had always had for his cousin. Colonel Beresford was declared the best of men. Every recollection was listened to with unwavering attentiveness, every detail of the Colonel's character and disposition was extolled, and facts about the Colonel's last days and hours on this earth were eagerly sought and remarked upon in a most compassionate and kindly manner. Lord Allersham had been pleased to sit quietly by and watch the proceedings as Mrs Beresford spent two hours happily engaged in cheerful recollections that had been brought to mind through the gentle prompting of a patient listener. Mr James Beresford had praised his cousin for leaving his widow in comfort and security and insisted that should she have need of anything at all, in the Colonel's memory, he would be honoured to provide it.

'James Beresford is no inheritance hunter,' said Mrs Beresford. 'There is nothing to suspect him of, Emma. I was most impressed by his civility and understanding.'

Lord Allersham agreed and added that he found neither calculation nor deceitfulness in his manner. 'He has an open temper and was at pains to account for his movements abroad and the years of his absence. There was but one matter that he passed over more quickly than the rest, which perhaps merited some explanation. Mr Beresford seemed disinclined, or unable, to account for his presence in Bath.'

'I believe he seeks to establish himself once again in the county of his birth. He has been so long in foreign lands that he now finds himself friendless, removed from society. James Beresford is alone in the world,' said Mrs Beresford. 'Surely it is reason enough to renew the connexions of family that have long been denied him.'

'And you are certain, Aunt, that his motives are pure?' said Lady Allersham. 'You believe he has no other purpose in mind?'

Mrs Beresford could not have been clearer. 'I can see no better argument for taking up residence in Bath than its proximity to Whitcombe. After all, I am the only family he has.'

The account of the visit to Mr James Beresford continued over dinner and beyond, supplanting the interesting news of Miss Fox that Lady Allersham had been eager to report. When Lady Allersham's reservations regarding Mr James Beresford had been answered to her satisfaction, she was willing to concede that she had judged him more harshly than he deserved. He had proved himself worthy, and when eventually Lord Allersham entered the drawing room, the conversation between the two women had proceeded to the proposal of a dinner to be held in James Beresford's honour as soon as preparations could be made. It was not to be a grand affair, but such a dinner would serve as a declaration of Mr James Beresford's connexions with the Allersham family and, consequently, secure his entrance to the highest circles in Bath. Lady Allersham was of the view that no better service could be bestowed on him than this.

'I did not form the impression that Beresford cared about such matters. He does not appear to be the type of man who courts society, nor does he seem to care about his own consequence or the good opinion of others,' said Lord Allersham.

'That is because you, my dear, are of the same view,' said Lady Allersham. 'You dislike having to yield to the vagaries of society. But it is important that you are seen to do so, even though I cannot provide you this instance with a good reason why it should be so.'

Lord Allersham smiled at his wife's disarming admission. 'My dear Emma, I should happily endure a dinner given in Beresford's honour for your sake alone.'

'There,' said Lady Allersham to Mrs Beresford. 'That is settled then.'

Mrs Beresford expressed her gratitude to them both and, with a sigh of relief, said, 'You are both very dear to me, and I thank you not for myself alone for I know that this act of kindness would surely —' Overcome by the emotion of the moment, Mrs Beresford was unable to continue.

'Yes. I, too, believe it would be Colonel Beresford's express wish,' said Lady Allersham. 'We shall honour *his* memory also.'

Mrs Beresford, speechless with gratitude, took hold of her niece's hand and held it in both of hers. After some moments she composed herself sufficiently to say, 'I am reminded of him at every turn. James Beresford has a certain look that is unmistakable — and his disposition is so very akin to the Colonel's. The similarity is quite astounding.'

'Then let us set about our task,' said Lady Allersham. 'Dinner guests. I propose we invite Miss Carteret.'

'In which case you will be obliged to invite her mother,' said Lord Allersham.

'And if Lady Dalrymple is to attend, should we not include Captain Harding, as he is such a favourite with her,' said Mrs Beresford.

'Yes, indeed. Cousin Robert will keep Lady Dalrymple entertained. And I shall place Miss Carteret next to James Beresford.'

'I thought you wished to keep Harding away from Miss Carteret?' said Lord Allersham.

'A dinner does not need to be an intimate affair. Indeed, if you recall, my dear, it was your suggestion a day or two ago that we invite Cousin Robert for dinner. I shall place him next to Lady Dalrymple and they shall sit by you.'

Taking up a book, Lord Allersham gave a sigh of exasperation and began to read silently.

'A table of seven will never do,' said Mrs Beresford. 'We must have an even number.'

'Oh, yes. That is true,' agreed Lady Allersham. Turning to her husband, she said, 'My dear, does Mr Dauber and his daughter stay long in Bath?'

'Mr Dauber?' said Lord Allersham, with surprise.

'Mr Dauber? What an excellent thought!' replied Mrs Beresford.

'And Miss Dauber,' said Lady Allersham.

'The addition of Miss Dauber would not be desirable,' replied Lord Allersham.

Lady Allersham and Mrs Beresford were puzzled by his remark.

'I merely allude to the problem of arithmetic,' said he. Lord Allersham found his place on the page once again and recommenced reading.

His wife saw that any further attempt to engage her husband on the subject was futile. 'It is easily settled,' said she to Mrs Beresford. 'We shall invite

Miss Dauber's friend. You remember, Aunt. The young woman to whom we were introduced at Molland's.'

'Miss Fox?' whispered Mrs Beresford.

'Yes,' whispered Lady Allersham in reply. 'As a matter of fact, I have today received some interesting information concerning Miss Fox. Miss Carteret was the bearer.'

Mrs Beresford listened with increasing curiosity to the history of Miss Fox.

'I should not be surprised if Mr Dauber is party to the secret,' said Lady Allersham.

'The secret?' enquired Mrs Beresford.

'Concerning Miss Fox's benefactor who now appears to have abandoned her. Is it not likely that Mr Dauber is the clergyman who first placed Miss Fox with Mrs Price in Gay Street?' said she. 'After all, he is sworn to the secrecy of the confessional. And, Miss Fox, being the particular friend of Miss Dauber enables Mr Dauber to keep an eye on her.'

'You do not suspect her benefactor to be Mr Dauber?'

'What do you say to one of Whitcombe's parishioners, perhaps?' said Lady Allersham. 'You said yourself that Miss Fox seemed familiar to you. You might well have seen her in Whitcombe.'

CHAPTER NINE

The following morning, Lady Allersham proposed a walk to the Pump Room, insistent that they should not forego the opportunity to benefit from exercise and fresh air on so fine a day. Lord Osborne had no other pressing claim on his attention, hence he could make no objection beyond the unpleasantness of the spa water itself. Lady Allersham dismissed her husband's view that it was too hot to drink and tasted of boiled eggs and declared that something so foul-tasting was sure to have curative qualities in abundance.

'In proposing the exertion, my dear, I thought only of you,' said Lady Allersham. 'Are you not pleased to spend a morning in the company of your wife? While we are there, we might invite Lady Dalrymple and Miss Carteret to our dinner. Even James Beresford, it seems, is known to visit the Pump Room from time to time.'

'The Dalrymples are sure to be present, for Miss Carteret said that her mother is rarely dissuaded from her routine,' said Mrs Beresford.

Lord Allersham took his wife's hand and kissed it. 'And I suppose she will have no objection to a dinner that does not oblige her to order her carriage or place it at the disposal of others,' said he.

Mrs Beresford was to accompany them as far as the Pump Room for she had made up her mind to visit a shop in Bath Street that had been highly recommended for its excellent silk thread at very reasonable prices; moreover, the Daubers' lodgings being but a stone's throw from Bath Street would provide a welcome place to sit for a quarter of an hour on her return. And she would be happy to take with her Lady Allersham's invitation to dine at Laura Place.

'So, you see, the arrangement will serve me very well,' said Mrs Beresford. 'The White Hart is not out of the way, and I am anxious to hear news of Whitcombe from Mr Dauber. I have lately received reports from more than one source of a very dear neighbour's rapid decline to an alarmingly poor state of health. I should like to enquire whether Mr Dauber has received any further communication from Whitcombe this morning.'

The arrangement proved satisfactory and the party set out in bright sunlight a little before eleven o'clock. On approaching the Pump Room, Lord and Lady Allersham parted company with Mrs Beresford and paused at the entrance momentarily to watch as she walked towards Bath Street.

'I am sure I should not find my way back to Laura Place from there,' said Lady Allersham. 'Perhaps we should go with her.'

'Your aunt was quite clear that it was her express wish to go alone,' Lord Allersham replied. 'I offered to secure a chair for her, but she would not hear of it. Mrs Beresford is not a stranger to Bath.'

'And what if she is set upon by robbers?'

'I expect Mrs Beresford will spend a pleasant morning purchasing thread at cheap prices and drinking tea with the Daubers' at the White Hart.'

Lady Allersham sighed. 'I do hope she remembers to ask Miss Dauber to bring her friend Miss Fox to dine.'

'Who?' said he.

'Miss Fox, Miss Dauber's particular friend,' said Lady Allersham. 'I made her acquaintance in Molland's. We spoke of it last night. Have you forgotten already? Miss Fox will make up our table.' Lady Allersham observed a curious change in her husband's countenance. 'My dear, it was at your prompting. Was it not you who brought the problem of arithmetic to my attention?'

Her husband made no reply. They proceeded inside to join the promenading throng and were soon spotted by Lady Dalrymple and her daughter.

Lord Allersham offered his arm to Lady Dalrymple who gratefully accepted it and the two went on ahead while Lady Allersham and Miss Carteret lagged behind to observe the unusual style of hat worn by a fashionable bystander.

'It must be the new style,' said Miss Carteret. 'I expect it is in the French mode for it is so elegant.'

'And heavy,' replied Lady Allersham. 'I prefer comfortable attire that is lightweight and easy to clean. I am the least stylish creature of anyone I know.'

'Oh no!' said Miss Carteret. 'I have never seen a better style than yours. A simple style must always be the most elegant.'

'I do hope so,' she replied, in jest. 'Perhaps I shall start a new fashion, or more likely expose myself to all the quizzing glasses in Bath!'

'I have never owned a quizzing glass and never will,' said Miss Carteret. 'To be the object of another's gaze is the height of discomfort.'

Lady Allersham was in full accord with Miss Carteret's sentiments, but was reminded of a time when she had suffered as a consequence of similar behaviour of her own.

'I once had use of a spy glass. It was a most welcome object at the time and afforded some measure of amusement. I was staying with my aunt, Captain Harding's mother, in Brinshore. Captain Harding was at sea at the time, but I don't recall where precisely. I was obliged to stay indoors for several days with a sprained ankle on the orders of Mr

Fowle, Brinshore's celebrated physician, who later proposed to my aunt, I might add, and was accepted. The prospect from the drawing room window offered full sight of the bay, and having use of the spy glass, I was afforded a clearer view of the shore, boats, bathing machines and dippers, all sorts of people and their movements.'

'And did you witness something disagreeable, something that caused you pain?' said Miss Carteret.

'Something disagreeable to me alone,' Lady Allersham replied. 'It is done with now, and the pain was thankfully of short duration, but a spy glass reminds me of what I felt then, of thoughts and actions that were not what I should have wished them to be.'

Miss Carteret fell silent. The impulse to speak, to make known that which oppressed her mind was great indeed. Lady Allersham's candid admission, the nature of which was usually confined to the intimacy of friendship, had opened the way; and demanded a similarly frank confession in return, but Miss Carteret was unable to provide one, for her willingness to reciprocate gave way to hesitancy. She looked up. Her eyes settled on Lord Allersham; the strangeness of her expression was not easily read, but neither was it lost on Lady Allersham. Her husband seemed unaware that he was the object of attention as he stood, ear lent towards Lady Dalrymple, deep in conversation. At such a distance it was impossible to ascertain the subject that appeared to be so animating to both parties, and Miss Carteret was obliged to content herself with conjecture only, for there was nothing to be done until their return to Laura Place, where she would then be at liberty to discover the nature of the discourse that had held Lord Allersham and her mother enthralled.

Lady Allersham had been quick to observe how at ease her husband had seemed in the Pump Room despite his protests against the artifice of those social practices he claimed were so distasteful to him.

'I know how it pains you to feign pleasure in pursuits that hold no interest for you,' said she, as they left the Pump Room behind and walked towards Cheap Street. 'I know how those affectations in others that appear empty and false to you are at times almost beyond endurance. And I know how you dislike parading about like a peacock.'

Lord Allersham smiled but made no reply.

'But I thank you for your efforts with Lady Dalrymple. Miss Carteret assured me that her mother had enjoyed a most pleasant morning, and it was all your doing.'

'I'm pleased to hear it, but it was not my doing,' said he. 'I expect you want to know what was said between us.'

'Only if you wish to reveal it, my love,' said Lady Allersham.

Lord Allersham smiled once again and maintained his silence until they reached the bridge.

'If you wish to tell me, my dear, I am happy to hear it,' said she presently, repeating the offer.

'It is of no great import. Lady Dalrymple received a letter in the post this morning with news that has surprised her,' he replied.

'Oh?' said Lady Allersham.

'Sir Walter Elliot wishes to return to Kellynch Hall, but his tenant, a retired admiral of the Navy cannot find a suitable alternative arrangement. Apparently, the Admiral's wife is related to Sir Walter's son-in-law. And so, it is not quite as straightforward as it seems. To insist on them quitting Kellynch would not be viewed in a good light.'

'And I suppose Lady Russell was the informant,' said she.

Lord Allersham nodded.

'And does you aunt support Sir Walter in his aim?'

'Lady Russell is wholly opposed to the idea and seeks to rein him in.'

'And Lady Dalrymple?'

'Dismisses it out of hand. It seems he is just as wasteful as he ever was. Dislikes Bristol and has had enough of Bath.'

'And so that was the extent of your conversation?' enquired Lady Allersham.

'That was the gist of it, yes,' said he. Lord Allersham could see that his wife was less than satisfied with his reply.

'What is it, my dear?' said he.

'Why should news of Sir Walter Elliot, which is hardly news at all, be so disconcerting to Miss Carteret? I saw how nervously she glanced in your direction. I believe she was anxious to know what passed between you and her mother.'

Lord Allersham expressed surprise that anything he should say would be of interest to Miss Carteret.

'But I assure you, my dear, something most certainly was of interest. Is Miss Carteret connected in some way with Allersham? Had she or Lady Dalrymple some association with Allersham Park in former years?'

'No, indeed,' said he. 'At least not to my knowledge.'

'Then how is it Miss Carteret's copy of *Paradise Lost* found its way into your library?'

'I cannot tell you,' said he.

'You cannot tell me, or you will not tell me?'

Lord Allersham came to a halt and turned to his wife. He looked directly into her eyes and said, 'I cannot tell you, my love, because I do not know. And surely other matters are infinitely more worthy of your concern.'

'And if you were sworn to secrecy?' said she.

'Like you, I am bound by my word,' he replied. 'If an assurance is given, such a confidence must be honoured. I should have no business therefore exposing a secret to the world. But in this matter, I give you my word. I know of no reason why Miss Carteret's volume should have been placed in my library. And I might add, there are more Carterets in the world than your new friend. It might belong to any one of them. When we return to Allersham you are at liberty to restore the offending object to Miss Carteret forthwith if it pleases you, and with my blessing.'

'Thank you,' said Lady Allersham, 'I shall.'

'Indeed, I wonder why you have not spoken of it to Miss Carteret if it matters to you so very much.'

'I have not spoken of it in case she might think I suspect her,' replied Lady Allersham.

'Oh what?' said he.

'I don't know.'

They walked on in silence for some minutes attending only to their private thoughts.

Lady Allersham was the first to break the silence. 'If you truly have no knowledge of how that volume found its way into your collection, I believe the best explanation must be that Lady Russell borrowed it, brought it with her and misplaced it when she visited Allersham on some past occasion. It is a perfectly reasonable assumption, I think.'

'Perfectly reasonable,' said Lord Allersham, with a mischievous smile. 'And it is a rather fine volume. I'd like to own a copy myself. The exceptional quality of the binding and the clarity of the print cannot be bettered.'

'And your being an admirer of Milton, you must surely see how it is bound to be misconstrued.'

'I am in no doubt that when Miss Carteret is reunited with her lost volume, she will be as happy as I in the knowledge that paradise is once again universally restored,' said Lord Allersham.

It was a little after three when they returned to Laura Place, and though the hour was not late, the absence of Mrs Beresford created some uneasiness in the mind of her niece. Lady Allersham was unable to sit down for more than five minutes together before moving backwards and forwards to the window to look out on to Laura Place for any sign of her aunt. Almost an hour passed before she observed her aunt alight from a smart carriage, her countenance cheerful and bright, and without the slightest trace of anxiety. A few minutes more and Mrs Beresford was once again among them and eager to report the news of the day.

'I came upon Captain Harding outside the White Hart. He insisted on sending me home in his carriage. And I must confess, I was thankful for it. My feet are sore, and my ankles swollen. I wish only to sit down and rest them properly,' said Mrs Beresford.

'Cousin Robert owns a carriage?' said Lady Allersham.

'I am as surprised as you. A fine chaise and four,' said Mrs Beresford.

'That cannot be,' she replied. 'I expect he has hired it.'

'No,' said Mrs Beresford. 'I formed the impression that it belonged to Captain Harding. It looks almost new and is excessively well sprung.'

Lord Allersham said that he knew nothing of Captain Harding having purchased a carriage.

Mrs Beresford conceded that she might have mistaken the matter and was sure that Captain Harding would correct any information given in error. She turned to a different topic. 'I was pleased with Bath Street and found exactly what I was looking for at half the price of the thread in Milsom Street. The owner was most attentive and would insist on showing me everything on the shelves. I left with a large parcel of items and spent only four shillings and eleven pence. The parcel is to be delivered, for I did not wish to carry it with me. But had I known that Captain Harding was to place his carriage at my disposal, I should, of course, have declined delivery of my purchases,' said Mrs Beresford.

'And did you call on Mr Dauber and his daughter at the White Hart?' Lady Allersham enquired.

'I did,' Mrs Beresford replied. 'It was providential, for Miss Fox was also present. She was but ten minutes ahead of me and could not stay long for she was on her way to read to one of Mrs Price's invalids. Miss Fox is obliged to work very hard and on rather poor terms. Miss Dauber confirmed it, though not in Miss Fox's hearing. She was most discreet and waited until Miss Fox had departed. I mentioned the dinner to Mr Dauber, who was eager to attend, but to do so must extend his stay another day. And Mrs Dauber has urgent need of him, according to a letter he received this morning from Whitcombe. She has a nervous complaint that worsens by the day. He will send a note tomorrow to make his plans known. His attendance at the dinner is not certain, but he hopes to be present. Miss Fox cannot be spared, though I daresay if Mrs Price were to be applied to directly we might receive a more favourable outcome. I did not press the matter. I thought it advisable to wait for Mr Dauber's reply, for Miss Fox will not be disposed to attend if Miss Dauber does not. And Miss Dauber will not remain in Bath if her father does not.'

'Quite right,' said Lord Allersham. 'Had I known earlier, I should have advised against it from the start. Mr Dauber I have no objection to, or his daughter. But we know nothing of Miss Fox.'

Lady Allersham was astounded by her husband's remark. 'I am shocked that such a remark should come from *your* lips. In fact, we know a great deal about Miss Fox from Miss Carteret. I like Miss Fox and I feel very sorry for her. Hers is a most cruel situation and she has been left without hope or expectation through no fault of her own.'

'Nevertheless, I think it best that Dauber keeps to his plan to return to Whitcombe without the inconvenience of so unnecessary a delay, and Miss Fox stays where she is. Invite Dauber and his whole family to Allersham if you will on our return. A dinner will be easily managed there and enjoyed by all.

Here we shall be obliged to sit for too long in a room cramped and hot and airless. We do not need to invite the whole of Bath to Laura Place,' said he.

'My dear, if it had not been for your interference in the first place, I should not have given a single thought to the Daubers or Miss Fox,' Lady Allersham replied. 'I desire only to make up an even table according to your own recommendation.'

Mrs Beresford was disinclined to interpose or meddle in any way and slipped out of the room unseen to allow Lord Allersham and her niece the liberty of continuing their debate in private. Closing the door behind her as quietly as possible, she went down to ascertain whether her parcel from Bath Street had arrived.

Dismayed by her husband's obstinacy, Lady Allersham suspected that the cause of their lively exchange must be the inferiority of Miss Fox and her situation. Such a startling disagreement was a new thing: she thought she knew her husband well, but in this instance his opinion was wholly incomprehensible to her. Their conversation was neither severe enough to be called an argument, nor mild enough to be considered entirely amicable; but she had seen him in a new light and struggled to quell her disappointment.

The matter was settled without further disquiet the following morning when a note arrived from Mr Dauber politely declining the invitation to dine on the grounds that his wife's condition had deteriorated further. Mr and Miss Dauber were to leave Bath the same morning.

'My dear,' said Lady Allersham, passing the note to her husband, 'here is news that will please you.'

Lord Allersham observed his wife with apprehension as she passed the note to him. His eyes skimmed the page and he said presently, 'Perhaps it is for the best.' Passing the note back to his wife, he added, 'I see it does not please you.'

'It is you that I am displeased with, not Mr Dauber's note,' she replied.

'Then I am sorry indeed,' said he, 'for I should never intentionally seek to provoke your displeasure.'

After a brief glance to ascertain the expression in his wife's eyes, Lord Allersham resumed his perusal of the correspondence before him. She was disappointed in him and continued to be so.

The post brought yet another communication that caused further dissatisfaction on her part. It was from her husband's steward concerning a matter that needed immediate attention. After reading it twice, he glanced at his wife and said, 'Emma, I must go to Allersham. I shall stay but two nights. It is important that I go.'

'Can it not wait?'

'No, my dear. My presence is needed. There are decisions to be made that cannot be made without me.'

'I hope the laying of a path to the lake according to my design is among them.'

'There are more pressing matters to be considered,' said he.

Lady Allersham sighed with disappointment. 'Will you return before —'

'I shall be present to receive our guests. You may depend upon it.'

CHAPTER TEN

Lord Allersham's departure from Bath was swift and disappointed his wife greatly. Was it business alone that drove him away from her? She could not endure the thought that he had left by design, that he wished to be parted from her, that it was a relief to him to leave her behind in Bath.

Distraction was essential, and soon came unexpectedly in the form of an invitation from Captain Harding to breakfast in Sydney Gardens. The invitation could not have been more welcome or more opportune. The message was short and the reply even shorter: Lady Allersham and Mrs Beresford would be delighted to accept.

'I took the liberty of reserving a table inside for the sky does not look too promising,' said Captain Harding, as they approached the building. 'But should there be a break in the clouds later, I propose a walk in the labyrinth.'

'I should like that very much indeed,' said Lady Allersham, brightening at the idea.

Mrs Beresford was similarly pleased with the plan, but as to the labyrinth, she warned that she was wholly dependent on their sense of direction. 'I cannot count the years since I have entered a labyrinth of any description,' said she. 'It is not the path to the centre, but the way out. I can never seem to recall how I got there in the first place.'

'No better metaphor for life,' said Captain Harding. 'I once had a similar experience in the middle of the Indian Ocean. A slight miscalculation can add days to a journey. Fortunately, the prevailing winds were in our favour.'

'If only the same were true of all our journeys,' said Mrs Beresford.

'What is life for but the weathering of tempests?' said Captain Harding, with a sigh.

'Shall you stay in Bath long?' said Lady Allersham. 'I thought Brinshore might have held greater appeal, being on the coast, by the sea.'

'Brinshore? I did not travel half way round the world, fight battles, avoid shipwrecks, disease, and mutiny, all for the sake of ending my days in Brinshore. Bath suits me well enough for the present. It is as convenient a place as any,' Captain Harding replied.

Lady Allersham was not entirely satisfied with her cousin's answer. 'My aunt tells me the chaise and four you placed at her disposal yesterday belongs to you.'

'I am happy to be mistaken,' said Mrs Beresford.

Captain Harding sighed. 'I suppose the truth will out. It was a bequest.'

'And a very handsome one,' said Lady Allersham.

'Yes,' he replied.

'How pleasant to receive such a gift,' said she. 'And how gratifying that the deceased, whomever he or she may be, left it to you.'

'And surprising, I hear you say,' said Captain Harding.

Lady Allersham was eager to establish the name of Captain Harding's generous benefactor and glanced at him in the hopeful expectation that he might provide it; but it was not forthcoming.

To circumvent any delay in being seated, Captain Harding went on ahead to inform the waiter of their arrival. Once out of earshot, Lady Allersham remarked, 'A chaise and four is a fine thing, but it is also expensive. How will Robert afford the upkeep? That is what I would like to know.'

'Perhaps he is less impoverished than he would like us to believe,' said Mrs Beresford.

'Who among our connexions would make such a bequest? No. I believe Mr Fowle is his mystery benefactor and pays to keep him at a safe distance from Brinshore,' said Lady Allersham, teasingly.

Mrs Beresford smiled and said, 'From what I hear, there's more likelihood of him receiving payment to stay in Brinshore than to avoid it altogether.'

'You are right,' said Lady Allersham. 'Aunt Fowle is quite put out about it. She cannot understand why her son remains in Bath when he might enjoy the many delights of Brinshore.'

They were soon seated, and the table spread with a plentiful selection of buns and rolls, tea and coffee. Both Lady Allersham and Mrs Beresford selected Bath buns to take with their tea.

'I have long wished to sample the famous Bath bun, but you must promise me, Cousin, to say nothing of it to your mother,' said she.

Captain Harding laughed and picked out a Bath bun for himself. 'I shall write to her directly and extol the virtues of the Bath bun, its health properties, its appetising appearance and its delicious taste. And I shall say that I am not alone in doing so.'

'I shall never speak to you again if you do,' said Lady Allersham, with a smile.

Mrs Beresford added, 'I have heard that nothing surpasses a Brinshore bun, but I have not had the good fortune to try one.'

'Then you are fortunate indeed,' said Captain Harding. 'The Brinshore bun, Mrs Beresford, is much like a hot cross bun. It neither bears a cross, nor is it hot. But, oddly, the characteristics most often exhibited in the household where the Brinshore bun was first conceived are those absent from the bun itself: hot and cross.'

'Captain Harding,' said Mrs Beresford, 'when you are married, you will discover that those characteristics are not confined to the Fowle household. I was very lucky myself, for Colonel Beresford was the mildest and kindest of men. Ours was a rare and peaceful alliance.'

'I cannot argue with you,' he replied. 'How much greater your loss must be.'

'Yes,' said she. 'And yet I was blessed with the greatest good fortune. I have much for which to be thankful. In marriage, where true devotion and constancy prevail, little irks or tends towards provocation.'

Lady Allersham was silent. Hers was a marriage born of the deepest affection, and yet there were occasions when her opinions and those of her husband seemed to be at odds. His return to Allersham, even for two days, felt akin to abandonment, and when once she had begun with one cheerless thought, her mind soon gave way to another, and another, until she was left with the notion that her husband may not love her at all.

'Thank you, Cousin,' said she, 'for I do not think I should have stirred from Laura Place today, and I am pleased that I did. And it is all your doing.'

Captain Harding placed a hand on hers. He was not without understanding despite sometimes making a pretence of having no feelings of his own, to conceal those sensations he would rather disown. He had read his cousin's mood completely. 'Emma,' said he, 'I should like to take the credit for this, but I must confess, I played little part in it. It was Lord Allersham who arranged it all.'

'Then he did so because of guilt for his neglect,' she replied. 'I suppose that is some consolation.'

'An estate as vast as Allersham does not run itself,' said Captain Harding. 'I'll wager he suffers guilt for his neglect and would choose differently for himself. But that is not always possible. And so, if you can bear it, I am at your disposal until Lord Allersham's return.'

The conversation took a lighter turn as each offered various suggestions of places to visit and people to call on over the following two days. There was unanimous agreement that they should attend a ball at the Upper Rooms, but they were equally decided that they would await Lord Allersham's return to accord him the pleasure of accompanying them.

As breakfast came to an end, so did the fine weather. A chilly breeze in the air and grey clouds overhead soon gave way to rain. Consequently, their walk to the labyrinth had to be postponed.

At the entrance to the building a large group of people had assembled, some with umbrellas, others railing against the rain, but all with one mind: how soon they might leave Sydney Gardens to reach their respective homes, and be once again warm and dry, and seated comfortably by the fire.

There was nothing to be done until the worst of the downpour had eased. Captain Harding and Mrs Beresford lingered to look at a painting while Lady Allersham's attention was drawn elsewhere, to a young woman who appeared to have in her charge an even younger woman seated in a wheeling chair. Her interest increased when she made the discovery that the young woman in attendance was very like Miss Fox. A few moments more and a few steps closer established that it *was* Miss Fox.

Lady Allersham observed that the invalid in her care appeared anxious to leave at once despite the rain. Miss Fox's efforts to pacify her charge appeared as fruitless as her attempts to secure the hire of a sedan, for it seemed that the chairmen were each disinclined to perform the service she required. Lady Allersham saw with increasing dismay that no one standing nearby stepped forward to act.

Shocked by the indifference of those who had it within their power to intervene, Lady Allersham ventured forward and took charge, immediately drawing even more attention to Miss Fox's predicament, and adding to her confusion. At first Miss Fox declined assistance, ashamed of the fuss she had caused. A profusion of apologies for the commotion and inconvenience to Her Ladyship followed, though each protest was instantly swept aside. Having obtained a clearer understanding of the problem, Lady Allersham summoned the chairmen and censured them for the despicable way they had conducted themselves. She insisted they apologise to Miss Fox and her charge forthwith. Without a single voice raised in protest, they relented and their manner towards the young women underwent a sudden and complete transformation until nothing was too much trouble. Bystanders who had observed the scene from the beginning now joined in, voicing disgust at the chairmen's treatment of the young women, but Lady

Allersham, holding them equally responsible, spurned the insincerity of their theatrical indignation.

The point at issue was soon understood and quickly rectified. Miss Fox had been prevented from hiring a chair for her charge, having only five pence ha'penny in her possession. The fare, being sixpence, left her a ha'penny short of the full amount.

Lady Allersham ordered the chairmen to assist the invalid out of the wheeling chair and into the sedan and summoned a further chair for Miss Fox's use. All protestations from Miss Fox were instantly dismissed: she would not be permitted to walk in heavy rain without an umbrella while her charge was conveyed in comfort and in the dry.

At length, the scene caught the attention of Captain Harding and Mrs Beresford. They saw that Lady Allersham was at the centre of the commotion, and quickly made their way through the throng to offer their support.

'What has happened, my dear? Are you hurt?' said Mrs Beresford.

'Emma?' said Captain Harding.

Lady Allersham explained the reason for the commotion and swiftly put their minds at ease by confirming that the matter had been resolved. The approval and admiration of both aunt and cousin for her quick action was fulsome; but, vexed by the behaviour of those who had done nothing to aid Miss Fox, Lady Allersham was in no humour to accept praise.

'Poor Miss Fox. She was a ha'penny short and had no other means at her disposal to pay the fee. The young woman in her charge was in quite a temper and wilfully knocked the coins out of poor Miss Fox's hand, and she was only able to retrieve five pence ha'penny.'

'Who was she, the young woman in the wheeling chair?' said Mrs Beresford.

'Another means for Mrs Price to make money out of Miss Fox, I expect,' said Lady Allersham.

Captain Harding explained that he had seen a young woman in a wheeling chair once before in Sydney Gardens, and had been given to understand that the family to whom she belonged resided in Pulteney Street, but he could say with no certainty that Miss Fox had attended her on that occasion.

Captain Harding returned Lady Allersham and Mrs Beresford to Laura Place but declined an invitation to join them for the rest of the day. Lady Allersham had little to occupy her until dinner, and with listless indifference took up a piece of embroidery that she had long neglected. The house was quieter than usual for Mrs Beresford had taken to her bedchamber with a headache, and Lord Allersham was not expected until the following day.

After accomplishing a few stitches, she put the embroidery aside. Her thoughts turned to her parents. There had been no word from Osborne Castle in almost a fortnight, and so, after a further half hour of fruitless endeavour borne of procrastination, she began a letter to her mother. Barely had she written a sentence when a note was brought to her accompanied by sixpence ha'penny. Lady Allersham immediately directed the footman to send the bearer up to her, and if she had already set out, to go in search of her and insist on her returning to Laura Place.

Almost a quarter of an hour went by before Miss Fox was shown into Lady Allersham's drawing room. But, fearful of Mrs Price's displeasure, she explained her need to return to Gay Street without delay.

'I have need of Captain Harding and his conveyance. Ask him to come at once,' said Lady Allersham, instructing a footman to treat the message as a matter of urgency. Turning to Miss Fox, she said, 'Do not worry about Mrs Price. I shall accompany you and provide an acceptable explanation for your delay. You will see, all will be well.'

Miss Fox expressed her gratitude but added that she had not spoken to Mrs Price regarding the incident at Sydney House and was certain it would be seen in a poor light.

'I am told there are many gossips in Bath,' said Lady Allersham. 'Mrs Price is likely to hear a report of it before long. Better the account comes from my lips than the lips of a tell-tale.'

The assurance given by Lady Allersham appeared to lessen Miss Fox's anxiety, and when invited to sit down, she was almost happy to comply.

'Is Mrs Price as formidable as she sounds?' said Lady Allersham.

'Mrs Price has been very good to me, Your Ladyship. I do not know what would have become of me without her kindness,' Miss Fox replied.

'Have you been at Gay Street long?'

'It seems a very long time.'

'And before that?'

'It is so long ago that I can hardly remember,' said Miss Fox. 'I believe I lived with a farmer's family some distance from Bath when I was very young.'

'And your parents?'

'I know nothing of my mother or my father.'

'And so, you are all alone in the world,' replied Lady Allersham.

'Oh no. Not alone. For I have occupation. Nor am I completely friendless. Miss Dauber is very kind to me. In fact, I am invited to her wedding, and if Mrs Price can spare me, I have every hope of attending.'

'And you have the means to travel to Whitcombe?'

Miss Fox looked down, hesitant to reply.

'Forgive me. I do not mean to pry,' said Lady Allersham.

Miss Fox composed her thoughts, and said at length, 'From time to time I take in a little extra mending for which I receive thrupence of my own.'

'Thrupence? I see. And Mrs Price is aware of this arrangement?'

Miss Fox replied, 'No.' Her eyes expressed shameful acknowledgement of the fact.

'You have nothing to fear from me. You have every right to receive payment in exchange for work done. I am only surprised that it is thrupence and not half a crown,' said Lady Allersham.

Miss Fox looked tired, as though the weight of her situation was almost too heavy to bear. 'I shall decline further requests of the kind and direct them to Mrs Price instead. It is the only way to peace of mind. I am not proud of my deception.'

'You have done nothing wrong, Miss Fox. You are not to blame for your situation. Why should you not receive payment?'

Lady Allersham ordered tea and insisted on Miss Fox taking some refreshment.

'We shall take tea and then you shall return to Gay Street. I am sure my cousin will not be long in coming,' said she.

A weakness seemed to come over Miss Fox as her strength ebbed away. Lady Allersham rang for immediate assistance and reached for some smelling salts to revive her guest. The sound of commotion in the hall caused Mrs Beresford to come out on to the landing, anxious to discover what had happened.

'We need a physician, Aunt,' said Lady Allersham. 'Miss Fox is here and looks very ill indeed. Will you stay with her? Try her with a glass of wine. I have sent for Captain Harding and I expect him shortly. He will know where to find a physician.'

Lady Allersham penned a rushed note to Mrs Price and instructed a messenger to deliver it to Gay Street directly.

'James Beresford speaks highly of a Mr Wood in Queen Square,' said Mrs Beresford. 'I know of no other physician by name. There is a new apothecary in Milsom Street which is a little nearer at hand.'

The sound of a carriage drew Lady Allersham to the window. She found, as she had hoped, that the carriage was Captain Harding's. 'He is come,' she said, with a sigh of relief.

There was no time to be lost. She hurried down to meet him, and when the situation was explained to him he proceeded without a moment's delay to Queen Square.

Miss Fox rallied a little, but lacked strength in her limbs and, drifting in and out of consciousness, occasionally uttered words incomprehensible to the hearer. Mrs Beresford brought extra cushions to make her comfortable. Without the strength to swallow a sip of wine when pressed to her lips, her head slumped to one side, and the liquid trickled from the edge of her mouth. Lady Allersham rubbed her hands and spoke without pause, striving to keep Miss Fox conscious.

Half an hour after Captain Harding had set out, the sound of a carriage outside signalled his return. This time Mrs Beresford went to the window to look out.

'Mr Wood is with Captain Harding,' she said.

'That is a relief,' said Lady Allersham, 'for I fear I have run out of things to say.'

Moments later Mr Wood was shown into the drawing room. Little improvement had been observed in Miss Fox's condition since the illness had taken hold, and after obtaining all the information required to assess the patient's condition, he conducted his examination.

A message was brought up to Lady Allersham to inform her of the arrival of Mrs Price and of her wish to see Miss Fox.

'I shall speak to Mrs Price,' said Mrs Beresford. 'You are needed here.'

'Thank you,' said Lady Allersham. 'Please inform her that Miss Fox is too ill to receive visitors. Explain that she is receiving the best of attention, and that a message will be sent to Gay Street in the morning. She will receive news of Miss Fox's condition and how she fared overnight. Extend my thanks to Mrs Price for her concern but make it clear there is nothing to keep her here. And Aunt, would you see that the guest room is prepared? Ask Pike to stoke up a good fire and warm some sheets.'

On completing his examination of Miss Fox, Mr Wood took Lady Allersham aside and explained that the young patient was suffering from exhaustion and lack of proper nourishment. 'Fluid, a little and often should be given — clear soup, or a little warm milk and honey — by the spoon. Bed rest and some wholesome food when the patient rallies will have the desired beneficial effect. I shall call in the morning to see how the patient goes on. Should there be any change overnight, you know where to find me.'

Captain Harding instructed his coachman to take Mr Wood to Queen Square and afterwards to return to Laura Place.

'You did not go?' said Lady Allersham to her cousin.

'Miss Fox is very weak. How do you intend to move her into the guest room?' said he.

'It had not crossed my mind.'

'Precisely,' said he. 'Don't worry, Emma. I have carried heavier loads aboard ship amid cannon fire and against the swell — wounded men, blinded and bleeding. Miss Fox will present a lesser challenge.'

'Thank you, Cousin,' said she.

Miss Fox hardly stirred as Captain Harding lifted her into his arms. Mrs Beresford collected her shawl, bonnet and reticule while Lady Allersham stood and watched, struck by the scene before her. What a charming couple, thought she. Cousin Robert might not be the most eligible of men, but there could be no better prospect for Miss Fox.

The invalid was deposited on the bed and made comfortable with pillows and blankets. Pike was instructed to stay by her bedside and raise the alarm should any change in her condition occur.

'Small spoonfuls and often,' said Lady Allersham, making sure that the fluids recommended were present and in good supply.

Captain Harding took his leave with the promise of calling the following morning to see how the patient had fared overnight.

CHAPTER ELEVEN

Signs of an improvement in Miss Fox's condition were evident the following morning as she partook of five spoonfuls of gruel and a little conversation. When Lady Allersham observed the progress of the patient a little after eleven o'clock, she was pleased to find Miss Fox sitting up in bed.

'I am so very sorry for the inconvenience I have caused,' said Miss Fox. 'I shall return to Gay Street as soon as my feet will carry me.'

'Nonsense,' said Lady Allersham. 'I am instructed by Mr Wood that you are not to be moved. You are his patient now, and you must listen to *his* advice.'

'A physician attended me?' said Miss Fox. 'Oh dear.'

'If you are anxious about his fee, do not be,' said Lady Allersham. 'You are not to concern yourself with such matters. Mrs Price will be kept informed of your progress, but I have impressed upon her that for the present you are not well enough to receive visitors. You are to stay here and that is the end of it.'

Miss Fox raised a shy smile. 'I do not know what to say. Such kindness I have rarely encountered.'

'Say nothing,' she replied. 'For now, you are to have complete rest, and once you regain your strength, we shall see what is to be done.'

'May I ask what ails me?'

'You are worn out, and lack nourishment. Nothing that cannot be put right through proper rest and wholesome food. Now, I expect you to drink a full dish of tea before luncheon.' Lady Allersham placed the dish into Miss Fox's hands.

As she left the room, Lady Allersham reflected, and said, 'Should anyone enquire after you, would you like to see them? A friend or confidante, perhaps?'

Miss Fox shook her head. 'Miss Dauber is gone to Whitcombe. There is no one I should care to see,' said she, hesitantly.

'I see.' Lady Allersham needed no further explanation. Mrs Price would not be welcome in Laura Place. 'Well, perhaps it is for the best. Rest and quiet is what are needed.'

Lady Allersham found Mrs Beresford in the drawing room accompanied by Captain Harding who had just appeared, and Miss Carteret who had arrived but five minutes earlier.

'I thought something must be amiss,' said Miss Carteret, 'when I looked out of the window and saw Mr Wood. How strange that the patient should be Miss Fox. We were only speaking of her the other day.'

'Did you not hear about the incident at Sydney House?' said Captain Harding.

'No,' Miss Carteret replied, turning to Lady Allersham, anxious to know more.

'That was the start of it,' she said, and explained the clash with the chairmen and the missing ha'penny. 'No one, not a soul, came to poor Miss Fox's aid.'

'I can well believe it,' said Miss Carteret. 'There are few that would take the trouble to step forward as you did, Your Ladyship. And so, Miss Fox came to Laura Place to return a ha'penny?'

'Sixpence ha'penny to be precise,' said Lady Allersham.

'Emma insisted that Miss Fox should have a chair too and paid the chairman from her own pocket,' said Captain Harding.

'It was nothing,' Lady Allersham replied. 'But sixpence ha'penny is a great deal of money to Miss Fox, and hard earned besides. I accepted it, of course, for to do otherwise would have injured her pride. Miss Fox has an independent spirit.'

Mrs Beresford whispered to Miss Carteret, 'I don't know where we would have been without Captain Harding. He carried Miss Fox up the stairs as though she were as light as a feather.'

Miss Carteret looked across at Captain Harding who was standing at the window deep in thought. His pensive mood puzzled her, and as she observed his fine figure by the curtain, she was perplexed to discover that her earlier estimation of his character and manners had perhaps not done him justice. It occurred to her that Captain Harding might not be as careless or as profligate as she had first supposed. Indeed, as she continued to observe him, she was surprised to find that he began to appear almost handsome.

He turned suddenly and caught her eye, and having surprised her in return, was equally puzzled by her gaze. She quickly looked away and for the rest of the morning afforded him nothing more than an occasional cautious glance.

'Will Miss Fox remain with you long?' said Miss Carteret.

'For several days, I think,' replied Lady Allersham.

Mrs Beresford's practicality came to the fore, and she suggested that Miss Fox would need a change of clothes. 'I shall call on Mrs Price to arrange for some to be sent to Laura Place,' said she. 'It would be no trouble at all. To afford Mrs Price a visit in person would demonstrate the concern felt in Laura Place for the seriousness of Miss Fox's condition. And I might call on James Beresford on my return. I promised to lend him my copy of Cowper and have been remiss in doing so,' said she.

Captain Harding, having business in Milsom Street, was pleased to offer Mrs Beresford a seat in his carriage and would be happy to take her as far as Gay Street. Mrs Beresford could think of no better plan, and was pleased to accept his offer, requiring only five minutes to make herself ready.

'Have you any errand that takes you to town, Miss Carteret? Allow me the honour of conveying you as far as Milsom Street or beyond.'

'Thank you, no,' said she, glancing awkwardly in his direction.

Sensible of her confusion and a little amused by it, he smiled and turned to his cousin. 'When is Lord Allersham expected?'

'This evening or tomorrow, I believe,' she replied. 'I shall expect you all for dinner, of course, tomorrow evening. Please remind Mr Beresford of his invitation, Aunt.'

'Perhaps Miss Fox will be strong enough to join us,' said Miss Carteret, glancing at Captain Harding who was preparing to take his leave.

'Yes, indeed,' said Lady Allersham, who had formed the notion, despite her husband's objections, that the presence of Miss Fox among them would make up the table admirably.

'Would it not be a formidable prospect for one so little accustomed to society, and depleted of strength, to suffer the company of strangers, however amiable and solicitous they might consider themselves to be. Should we not have compassion on Miss Fox?' said Captain Harding. 'And yet, I suppose a little company may prove beneficial to the patient. Where a dinner table might overwhelm and proving taxing, might half an hour in the drawing room suffice?'

Surprised by Captain Harding's remark, all eyes were turned upon him with looks of wonder and curiosity. That he should take so great an interest in the patient and her welfare and display unusual consideration for the delicacy of her situation was singular for a man who frequently and purposely took pleasure in feigning a want of understanding.

'You are quite right, Captain Harding,' said Mrs Beresford.

'What has brought this about? This is not at all like you, Cousin,' said Lady Allersham, with an artful smile.

'I am not completely devoid of feeling,' said he, light-heartedly.

'And yet you are fond of the appearance of it,' said Lady Allersham.

'Now and then, perhaps,' said Captain Harding. 'It doesn't suit everyone, I suppose. Miss Carteret does not like to be teased.'

'I hope I am not completely devoid of wit,' Miss Carteret replied. 'In your case, Captain Harding, I cannot determine whether you act from design or compulsion.'

'There I cannot help you,' said he. 'But to be thought about at all is an improvement on the alternative, Miss Carteret.'

When all had departed Laura Place, Lady Allersham went up to see how Miss Fox fared. The patient had, as directed, consumed one full dish of tea and was soon to partake of some white soup that had been freshly prepared and sent up from the kitchen.

'There is to be a dinner here tomorrow evening,' said Lady Allersham. 'If you are a little better by then, should you like to be one of the party? It will not be a large table, and you are acquainted with half the guests already.'

'Thank you,' said Miss Fox. 'Please do not think me ungrateful. But I should feel out of place. I have never —'

'I should not wish to add to your discomfort. But you have no need to be anxious. You will be among friends,' said Lady Allersham.

'I should not know what was expected of me,' replied Miss Fox. 'I do not know how to act among —'

'I hope we are not so formidable as to frighten you away,' said Lady Allersham. 'There are people of rank among my acquaintance who have no regard for their own behaviour and little understanding of what it should be. You have no need to worry on that score, I assure you. But I shall not press you. My cousin is of the belief that a mere half an hour in pleasant company is a great restorative.'

'Captain Harding?' said Miss Fox.

'Yes,' Lady Allersham replied.

'Half an hour?'

'Yes, or longer if you so wish.'

'Would half an hour suffice, Your Ladyship?' said Miss Fox.

'It would,' said Lady Allersham, gently. 'It is neither a demand nor an expectation. You are free to do as you please.'

'Even half an hour seems so great an imposition —'

'You do not impose upon me or anyone else. We think only of your welfare.' Continuing, Lady Allersham observed, 'And, as you see, there are helpers enough at hand to guard against neglect of any kind. You will be better looked after here than in Gay Street for nothing is expected of you in Laura Place except a full recovery.'

The early return of Lord Allersham to Laura Place was met with delight. Lady Allersham had not expected his arrival for another four hours. News of Allersham Park was the foremost subject of conversation, the primary matters of concern being repairs to parts of the roof and improvements to some portion of the land that had flooded.

'Emma,' said he, 'I am not persuaded that it is a good thing to remain in Bath until the end of the season.'

'What of Aunt Beresford? Her spirits are not so low as when we first arrived. And James Beresford? You have seen for yourself my aunt's pleasure in his company. She is reminded of the Colonel in the most beneficial of ways,' said Lady Allersham.

'And I have no doubt that their acquaintance will continue whether she remains in Bath or returns to Whitcombe. It is not so very great a distance after all.'

'But I should like to remain in Bath a few weeks longer, my love, for I have seen so little of it.'

Lord Allersham hesitated before offering a solution. 'And if I were to return to Allersham without you, what would you say?' said he.

'I should not like it at all,' Lady Allersham replied.

'Nor I,' he replied.

Some minutes went by before he spoke again.

'Emma, you know that my need for society is not equal to yours. Bath is pleasant enough in small measure, but I cannot pretend to take pleasure in it as you do. There is so much work to be accomplished, improvements to be made and projects to supervise at Allersham, and all, hopefully for the good, and to universal benefit.'

'And to remain in Bath a few weeks longer will make a difference to such schemes?' asked Lady Allersham.

Lord Allersham placed her hand in his. 'If you wish to remain in Bath until the end of the season then that is what we shall do.'

'As much as I wish never to be parted from you, I should not desire you to remain here against your will. If you have no objection, I should like to stay for another month complete, but I release you from any obligation of the kind. You may come and go as it pleases you. Indeed, I find that when you are absent there is nothing sweeter than the anticipation of your return. And anyway, at present I am much preoccupied with matters of my own here in Laura Place.'

'Oh?' said he.

'There has been an addition to the household,' said she.

'A dog, I suppose,' said he. 'Where did you acquire the creature? Had you consulted me first, I should —'

Lady Allersham laughed and replied, 'Not a dog. A fox of sorts. Miss Fox in fact. Do you recall how —'

'Miss *Fox*?' said he. The sudden change in her husband's countenance vexed Lady Allersham.

'When I have related the details in full, my dear, you will agree with me that it was for the best.'

Lord Allersham sat in silence while his wife recounted the events of the previous day.

'And when all is said and done,' Lady Allersham observed, 'I am certain that another situation must be found for Miss Fox when she is fully recovered.'

'Emma,' said he, 'I do not doubt that you acted with the best of intentions and that Miss Fox receives the greatest of care, but I do advise you strongly to return Miss Fox to the protection of Mrs Price the minute her health improves.'

'But why?' said she, astonished by her husband's lack of feeling. 'What is it? What do you have against Miss Fox? I cannot make you out. My love, if there is something I should know, please tell me.'

Lord Allersham sighed and strode over to the window to compose himself. 'Dauber came to see me at Allersham on parish matters. For your sake, I took the opportunity to ask what he knew of the business concerning Miss Fox.'

'What did he say?' said Lady Allersham.

'Dauber, as a man of the cloth, is not at liberty to betray the secrets of the confessional as you well know and consequently would not be drawn on particulars. Indeed, I was surprised that he spoke as openly as he did. But I must warn you, Emma, that you have stumbled upon a most delicate business in Miss Fox.'

'My love,' said Lady Allersham, 'that is simply not good enough. I must know what you mean. What delicate business?'

'I shall say this, and no more, and then I beg you, let the matter rest,' said he. 'Dauber intimated to me that Miss Fox is not wholly unconnected —'

'Unconnected to whom? To what?' said she.

'No name was given, but I believe he implied Allersham.'

'*Allersham*? But how? Did Mr Dauber infer that the reputation of Allersham was at stake? Did he suggest a scandal of some kind?'

'As I said, he would not be drawn on the details of the matter. Now let that be an end to it, Emma,' said he.

'Impossible!' she replied. 'Surely you must see that I cannot let go so easily. If Allersham is implicated in Miss Fox's plight, you, my dear, and I, must bear some responsibility for it, whatever might or might not have transpired in the past. It is incumbent upon us both to make amends for any wrong committed against her. At the very least she must be released from the abominable conditions to which she has been subjected through no fault of her own. Who paid for her to board with that dreadful woman, Mrs Price? And who withdrew her allowance? That is what I should like to know. I should not have allowed Mr Dauber to intimate so much and explain so little.'

Before Lord Allersham had chance to reply, Mrs Beresford, who had returned from her afternoon expedition and was anxious to provide an account of it, entered the room. She was surprised to find Lord

Allersham present and was eager to hear if the road from Bath to Whitcombe had been mended. Having ascertained that it had and that the journey had been accomplished without incident of any kind, Mrs Beresford asked what news there was from Allersham.

'Of rooftops, floods and drains news is in bountiful supply,' said he.

'Then I should prefer not to hear it,' said Mrs Beresford, with a smile.

'Quite right,' he replied. 'Excuse me.' Lord Allersham withdrew and was not seen again until dinner.

Mrs Beresford had enjoyed a mixed afternoon, having first called on Mrs Price in Gay Street with a report of Miss Fox's progress. The sense of disorder within the household was palpable, as Mrs Price's exertions to constrain the turmoil appeared to be in vain. The absence of Miss Fox was in no small part the reason for the disarray. That Mrs Price reigned supreme was not in dispute but, without the efforts of Miss Fox, the ever-pressing demands of the establishment could not be met by the proprietor alone. Indeed, the request for some of Miss Fox's clothes was met with alarm by Mrs Price who refused to part with them until firm assurances had been given concerning Miss Fox's early return. Miss Fox was to be returned to Gay Street the moment she was fit to resume her duties.

'Well, we shall see about that,' said Lady Allersham. 'Mrs Price may request whatever she wishes but that does not mean her wishes will be granted.'

105

'I was obliged to give my word, Emma,' said Mrs Beresford.

'Evidently Mrs Price cannot do without Miss Fox. And I have no doubt from your description of the state of things there, that her duties will have increased tenfold by the time of her return.'

Mrs Beresford had not stayed long in Gay Street and, on leaving Mrs Price's establishment, had found Captain Harding's carriage once again at her disposal.

'I could not have been more relieved to find him there,' said she.

'I am glad he did not abandon you. He must have known how it would be,' said Lady Allersham.

The afternoon, according to Mrs Beresford, had improved from that point onwards, as Captain Harding accepted the invitation to accompany Mrs Beresford to Paragon Buildings to visit James Beresford. All three had spent a convivial hour in conversation, much of which involved stories of the East Indies and adventures on the high seas.

'And I returned to Laura Place in Captain Harding's carriage once again. He was most insistent,' said Mrs Beresford.

'I am glad to hear it,' replied Lady Allersham.

'And now he is gone to back to Sydney Place to spend the evening alone.'

'He should have dined here,' said Lady Allersham.

'That is what I said, but he would not hear of it. Captain Harding bid me tell you that he looks forward to dining at Laura Place *tomorrow* evening,' Mrs Beresford replied. 'Now, I shall go up to look in on Miss Fox. Mrs Price would have me say to Miss Fox that she must not embellish her symptoms or stay a moment longer than is necessary. But I shall say only that Mrs Price wishes Miss Fox a speedy recovery. Captain Harding would have me wish her the same, though I wonder whether a slower one would be of greater benefit in the long run.'

'Aunt,' said Lady Allersham, 'you once mentioned that Miss Fox seemed familiar to you in some way, that you had perhaps caught sight of her in Whitcombe.'

'Yes,' said she, 'there is something in her look that is familiar. I cannot be certain, of course. Where or when I might have seen her, I cannot say.'

'Mr Dauber has been Rector of Whitcombe for some time, I suppose,' said Lady Allersham.

'Oh yes,' she replied, 'for many years. It is perfectly possible therefore that Miss Fox should have visited Miss Dauber in Whitcombe. Yes, indeed. That must surely account for it.'

'Did you ever hear of a scandal connected with Allersham in former years?' said she.

'I knew little of Allersham at all before your marriage to Henry. Colonel Beresford and I lived quiet lives. We moved in different circles.'

'The reputation of Henry's elder brother was common knowledge, was it not?' said Lady Allersham.

'I suppose it was,' Mrs Beresford replied. 'My dear Emma, am I to understand that Miss Fox is connected in some way to Allersham Park?'

Lady Allersham sat down beside her aunt and sighed. 'Henry asked Mr Dauber what he knew of Miss Fox's history. He seemed to imply some past connexion with Allersham but would not be drawn further on the matter. I have just learned of it.'

'I see,' said Mrs Beresford. 'And does that explain his reluctance to have Miss Fox under your roof?'

'Perhaps. Perhaps not. I do not know what to think. Whatever ensues, surely, we must do what we can for Miss Fox whether Allersham is found to be the cause of her troubles or not. Had her benefactor been Henry's elder brother!' She paused, uncertain of the grounds of her suspicion. 'He had a shocking reputation. Miss Fox's allowance ceased some time ago, did it not? Henry's brother may or may not have made provision for her after his death, until the money ran out. That would explain a great deal,' said Lady Allersham.

'I see what you mean,' said Mrs Beresford, choosing her words carefully. 'Then, you may need to tread carefully, my dear. Should information subsequently come to light, the name of Allersham might be sullied were you to continue your association with Miss Fox.'

'And so, Miss Fox must return to Gay Street?' said Lady Allersham. 'I cannot believe that Henry would place the reputation of Allersham above the plight of a young woman who has been injured by his own family. I begin to think I do not know my husband at all.'

CHAPTER TWELVE

The next day brought good news concerning Miss Fox's condition. Mr Wood attended his patient early and declared that her recovery was proceeding well; another two days would see the patient fully restored. Lady Allersham broke the news to the patient herself to ascertain Miss Fox's wishes and determine whether a better situation might be sought for her with lighter duties and proper recompense. To her surprise, she found, on speaking to the invalid, that she was perfectly complaisant with the notion of returning to Gay Street as soon as her health allowed and spoke of it in a tone of cheerful acceptance.

'I do not know how I shall ever repay your kindness,' said she, 'It will be a comfort to me to know that I trespass no longer on your goodness and generosity. Mrs Price expects my return without delay. Of that I have no doubt. And it will ease my mind to know that I might lessen her burden also.'

'Well,' Lady Allersham replied, 'it does not ease mine. Are you certain that you desire it? I should not wish those same duties that caused your illness in the beginning to do so again. Allow me to search for another situation for you.'

'I have given my word to Mrs Price,' said she.

'Are you bound to keep it?' asked Lady Allersham.

'I am, Your Ladyship,' Miss Fox replied.

'Nevertheless, I should like to help you,' said Lady Allersham. 'But I need some information to assist me. Tell me, Miss Fox, have you any recollection, any item or document in your possession that might proffer evidence pertaining to your history, your birth, your parentage? Believe me, it is not my purpose to pry. You see, were it in my power to do so, I should like to pursue reparation on your behalf, but only if you have no objection to such intrusion. Please understand, I desire nothing more than your welfare in this matter. If an oversight or injustice has occurred, I should wish for it to be put right.'

Confused by Lady Allersham's interest in her circumstances, Miss Fox received the request with some measure of apprehension. Having no wish to displease Her Ladyship, however, or deny her appeal, Miss Fox answered with cautious diplomacy.

'Please do not concern yourself on my account. I am perfectly reconciled to my situation. I do not measure my life by what it might be, or might have been, or what it might become. I am content that I am not completely friendless; nor am I without food or shelter. There is misfortune far worse than mine in the world. As to my history, there is but one item I possess, a silver vinaigrette, that provides no clue to the giver or their connexion to me. I cherish and fear it in equal measure in case it should become to me like the vessel that Pandora held in her possession.'

'May I examine it?' said Lady Allersham.

'It is in there,' said Miss Fox, pointing to a threadbare reticule on the table by the window.

Lady Allersham passed the reticule to Miss Fox.

'It is the sweetest thing,' said she. 'I carry it with me always.'

Miss Fox felt inside her reticule for the small silver box and retrieved it. She placed it into Lady Allersham's hand; Her Ladyship examined it with care, intrigued by the initials engraved on the lid.

'It bears the letters M and F,' said Miss Fox. 'I am Maria. Maria Fox, you see.'

Lady Allersham was less certain that the letters were those that Miss Fox imagined them to be. The engraving was so worn in places that there remained only the hint of an F. And the M was barely distinguishable from an N or even a W. The vinaigrette was, nevertheless, an elegant piece, and almost certainly the work of a silversmith of some repute. But while the initials could not be determined with any certainty, the possibility that the second initial was indeed an F, caused Lady Allersham to consider another explanation. F, thought she, might indeed denote *Fox*. It seemed the most logical conclusion; but other surnames also began with the letter F, and *Fitzroy* was one of them.

'Shall you join us this evening? For half an hour?' said Lady Allersham.

'I shall,' said Miss Fox, 'if you wish it.'

'I do,' Lady Allersham replied, and placed the vinaigrette into Miss Fox's hand. 'Take care of your most precious possession. It may yet aid us in our search.'

Dinner at Laura Place was not the lavish or immoderate occasion to which some of Bath's distinguished residents were accustomed, for the party was small and the guests, but for Lady Dalrymple, were simply attired. Despite the modest display and absence of grandeur, and appeals to sit a further ten minutes, Miss Fox was not persuaded to stay beyond the agreed half hour.

Lady Dalrymple's opinions held sway over all others, and for much of the half hour the conversation was given over to those remedies for ailments to which young women were especially prone.

The conversation alone was enough to send Miss Fox back to her room as soon as the promised half hour had been spent, for no one seemed able to silence Lady Dalrymple on the subject. The retreat of Miss Fox occasioned several remarks from members of the party, although Lord Allersham discouraged it, and was disinclined to be drawn into any speculation regarding their guest.

On Miss Fox's part, the opportunity to thank Captain Harding and Mrs Beresford for their kindness had been accomplished; the patient had spoken warmly, both of her gratitude and her conviction that she would forever be in their debt.

'What a strange creature she is,' said Lady Dalrymple, when Miss Fox was safely back in her room.

'She is indeed,' said Lady Allersham. 'Miss Fox possesses an irrepressible spirit, makes no complaint, feels no self-pity and has nothing but praise for everything and everyone, and yet she has more reason to complain than any one I know.'

Miss Carteret was inclined to agree.

'That may be so,' replied Lady Dalrymple, 'but Miss Fox's circumstances are not singular. Her care of Mrs Ibbotson was described as excellent, but all this talk of Miss Fox, all this attention given over to a young woman who is nothing to us, elevates her beyond her station. It may tend to her undoing. Indeed, it may turn her head and give her airs unbefitting to her situation in life.'

Lady Allersham could not agree and spoke of the apprehension she felt on having agreed to return Miss Fox to Gay Street. Mrs Beresford, though of the same mind as her niece, saw no possibility of a reversal.

James Beresford remained silent. He looked on in quiet contemplation as Miss Fox's situation was discussed and decried among them, nodding only occasionally when comments drifted in his direction. Miss Carteret observed that he had remained so for the entire half hour, and sought to draw him out.

'What is your opinion of our Miss Fox? Should she return forthwith to Gay Street? Or should she be found another situation?' said she.

'It is not a subject about which I am qualified to speak. I suspect Miss Fox will make up her own mind,' he replied.

'But if she has not the power of choice,' said Miss Carteret, 'what then? Are we to abandon her to her fate?'

'No,' interposed Lady Allersham. 'Abandonment is unthinkable. Something must be done.'

The subject of Miss Fox continued until dinner was announced and everyone had had their say on her plight and its solution.

Seated beside Lord Allersham in the dining room were Captain Harding and Lady Dalrymple; the latter, however, soon tired of the subject of Miss Fox and appealed for a new topic of conversation.

Captain Harding obliged with an account of a card party he had recently attended in Camden Place. The most interesting aspect of it in Lady Dalrymple's eyes was the mention of Sir Walter Elliot.

'And was Sir Walter spoken of with affection there?' said Lady Dalrymple, expecting the opposite to be the case.

'There can be no more desolate place in Bath than Camden Place without Sir Walter Elliot,' said Captain Harding, with a wry smile. 'Camden Place is filled with regret at his departure.'

'That I cannot and do not believe,' said she. 'Captain Harding, I believe nothing you say! You delight in teasing us all.'

Captain Harding replied, 'Nevertheless, I hope you will believe one piece of news that I gleaned from my host in Camden Place. Indeed, I believe it might be of great interest to you, Lady Dalrymple.'

'Oh?' said she.

'Miss Elliot is to be married. There was much made of it, I can tell you. I do not know the name of Miss Elliot's intended, but it seems the acquisition of a baronet's daughter is designed to add to the respectability of the bridegroom's family, or so I am told.'

'The family must be in trade,' said Lady Dalrymple. 'I'm surprised Sir Walter agreed to it. I expect it was Miss Elliot's only offer. She could not have expected better, for she cannot be a day under one and thirty. She is fortunate to find anyone who will take her.'

Lady Dalrymple was secretly put out to find that such interesting information had not been conveyed to her by Sir Walter in person, and more so because it afforded her cousin the opportunity to boast of finally finding someone to take Miss Elliot off his hands. Her dissatisfaction, however, had yet another foundation: that Miss Elliot should marry before her own daughter. This was, of all she had heard, the most disappointing news of all.

'I received a letter from Sir Walter last week. It is strange that he did not mention it,' said Lady Dalrymple.

'I understand that it was settled but two days ago,' Captain Harding replied.

'Even so, I have yet received no communication from *him*. I suppose his daughter's marriage, or the possibility of it, was in Sir Walter's mind when he mentioned returning to Kellynch. Now that Elizabeth Elliot is to marry, I expect he intends to seize his opportunity,' said Lady Dalrymple. 'But that would never do.'

'Perhaps Sir Walter himself will remarry,' said Captain Harding. 'Kellynch must be inducement enough for any prospective bride with ten thousand pounds. And as we all know, he is considered handsome for his age.'

Lady Dalrymple choked on her wine. 'There was some nonsense of the kind a year or two ago with a Mrs Clay. Unfortunate creature. Penniless. And quite unsuitable in every regard. Nothing became of it. She was found to be as thick as thieves with that rascal who is to inherit Kellynch.'

'William Elliot, I presume,' said Captain Harding. 'It is said he left considerable debts behind him when he quitted Bath, or so I am told by my informant in Camden Place.'

'If only Lady Elliot had not been so eager to meet her Maker. I expect the alternative was less appealing. The only sensible course is to leave Kellynch in Admiral Croft's hands. Sir Walter must be persuaded to extend Croft's tenancy. Lady Russell will see to it. She will put things to rights. It is the only sensible course of action guaranteed to preserve Kellynch.'

'I know Admiral Croft. He is an excellent man,' said Captain Harding. 'I served under his command when I first entered the Navy. Indeed, I have observed that a ship is much like a home. If Kellynch has Admiral Croft at its helm, it is in the best of hands. And more so when Mrs Croft is in command of her husband. I recall, it was a matter of dispute who was the better sailor.'

'Captain Harding,' said Lady Dalrymple, 'you never cease to amaze me.'

'I shall take that as a compliment,' said he.

'I understand you keep a carriage,' said she, changing the subject.

'A chaise and four,' he replied. 'It would not have been in my power alone to own so fine a carriage. I am the fortunate recipient of a bequest. The benefactor to whom I owe my good fortune acquired it for his own use but was shortly afterwards confined to his bed.'

Lady Dalrymple sighed. 'Oh, the cost of keeping a carriage rises constantly. I should be just as content to do without one myself, but that is simply not possible.'

'A carriage is my one luxury,' Captain Harding replied.

'That is because you have no thought at present of matrimony, Captain Harding,' said she.

'You must be right,' he replied. 'And now that I have become accustomed to owning a carriage, and have no thought of giving it up, I see I shall be obliged to marry a woman of good fortune to maintain it.'

Lady Dalrymple could not determine whether Captain Harding spoke candidly or in jest. The notion of a match between her daughter and Captain Harding had crossed her mind, but to acknowledge openly his need of a good income made no sense to her at all. Were he indeed a fortune hunter, he would surely not admit to it.

'Do not be uneasy, Lady Dalrymple,' said he. 'You are quite right. I have no thought of marriage at present. Be assured, heiresses are quite safe from me.'

Lord Allersham, whose conversation with Mrs Beresford about Whitcombe Woods had reached its conclusion, now turned to Captain Harding and Lady Dalrymple.

'Does one ever tire of Bath?' said Captain Harding.

'I do not,' said Lady Dalrymple. 'Consider the amusements Bath has to offer — health benefits in abundance — shops and tea rooms, gardens, concerts, balls, the theatre and so much more. I find I am quite content where I am. I do not need to frequent them all, of course. To know that I have the means to do so should I desire it is enough for me.'

'That is all very well,' said Lord Allersham, 'but one must have a purpose. And the sole purpose in Bath is pleasure. I must have something more than this.'

'That is because you are a man,' said Lady Dalrymple.

'Does it not also apply to a woman?' said Captain Harding.

'You surprise me, Captain Harding. Usually, it is assumed that a woman has no greater purpose than matrimony and children. But that is not a woman's *purpose*. That is a woman's fate. And when she has achieved what is expected of her, her usefulness is diminished,' replied Lady Dalrymple.

'Do you sincerely believe that to be the case?' said Captain Harding.

'I do,' she replied. 'Remember, I speak from experience. Think of me as you will, but I have no wish to see my own daughter subjected to the same fate if she does not choose it for herself. And yet her only alternative is to remain single and suffer the contempt and derision of others. So, matrimony it must be. I surprise you Lord Allersham, and you

Captain Harding. But it is a matter I have given much thought to.'

'No doubt Miss Carteret is acquainted with your views,' said Captain Harding.

She looked across at her daughter who was oblivious to her name being mentioned among them. 'We have not spoken on the subject,' said she. 'I do not know my daughter's mind.'

Lord Allersham's eyes were drawn to his wife who was unaware of his gaze upon her. She continued in cheerful ignorance, pleasantly engaged in an animated conversation with James Beresford and Miss Carteret. His thoughts turned to Allersham; he knew that she found little purpose there, while his obligations perpetually claimed his time and attention. Was her happiness the equal of his? Could it ever be, given the difference in the expectations placed upon them? Might his objections to his wife's interest in Miss Fox's plight be a symptom of his own lack of understanding? Had he been unreasonable in his expectations of her, urging her to abandon her efforts, to give up that which gave her life purpose beyond the inanity and shallowness so often at the heart of social intercourse?

The conversation between Lady Allersham, James Beresford and Miss Carteret had taken an interesting turn. Poetry was the subject of the moment, and the works of Cowper and Byron were disputed with passion among them. Lady Allersham asked whether James Beresford had ever come across any man on his travels who bore a likeness to Childe Harold, while Miss Carteret decried the claim by some that Byron was a poetic genius who surpassed the brilliance of Cowper and Herbert. James Beresford sought to establish morality as the heart of the matter, and wondered whether poetry, to be considered worthy, must have a moral foundation.

'Can man be perfected through experience and suffering?' said he.

'Every man should strive towards perfection if he possibly can,' said Miss Carteret.

'And every woman?' he replied.

'A man may strive as much as he pleases, but perfection is unobtainable,' said Captain Harding. 'Perfection is found only in novels and only then in the eyes of those blinded by desire.'

'Blinded by desire?' said Miss Carteret.

'*But love is blind, and lovers cannot see the pretty follies that themselves commit*,' James Beresford replied. 'One might argue, I suppose, that to be blind to certain faults in the beloved is a blessing. Where love is blind, all is forgiven, and all difficulties overcome.'

'A blessing or a curse? For when the scales are removed, and one sees the true character of the beloved, love disappears like melting snow,' said Lady Dalrymple.

'I am of the view that the faults we find with others are but a reflection of the faults we despise in ourselves,' said Miss Carteret. 'If love obscures them from view, therefore, that must be a good thing.'

'Pray, whose reflection looks back at you when you gaze into your looking glass?' whispered Captain Harding in reply, as the ladies prepared to leave the dining room.

Miss Carteret hesitated. Her eyes were momentarily drawn to Lord Allersham. 'An object of regret,' said she.

As the time to separate came around, the women sauntered into the drawing room and divided into pairs. Mrs Beresford took Lady Dalrymple aside to show her the various colours of silk thread she had purchased in Bath Street.

'A bargain indeed,' said Mrs Beresford. 'Now that I think of it, I should have purchased double the quantity, for silks are a great deal more expensive in Whitcombe and the range there is limited. I cannot recommend Bath Street too highly.'

Lady Allersham took Miss Carteret's arm. She noticed that her attention was drawn to a silhouette of a family gathering which hung on the wall beside the fireplace.

'The Fitzroys in all their splendour,' said Lady Allersham. 'The scene was captured in the year five, I believe. After the victory at Trafalgar. Henry's naval brother, depicted here, was a midshipman in the year five. There you see is old Lord Allersham, Henry's father, and seated at the pianoforte is his late mother. The tall fellow is Henry's elder brother. And there is Henry, the young boy standing by his mama. When I look at this happy scene, I am reminded that Henry is the only family member who lives. Of course, Henry was not expected to succeed his father.'

Miss Carteret grasped the ledge of the mantelpiece to steady herself. 'Forgive me,' said she. 'I am a little dizzy. That is all. It will pass.'

Lady Allersham led Miss Carteret by the arm to a nearby chair and examined her friend's countenance. 'Are you quite well? Is there anything I can do to assist you?'

'I am a little heady. I have taken too much wine,' said she.

'Wine has the same effect on me,' said Lady Allersham. 'Do not be uneasy. It is nothing that cannot be remedied.'

'Please excuse me. If I sit here a while in silence, I am sure the feeling will pass soon enough.'

'Be assured, if the feeling does not pass you shall stay here the rest of the night,' said Lady Allersham. 'We have another room to spare. Perhaps I should make adjustments upstairs in case anyone else should fall ill. The ballroom might well be put to better use as a sickroom. Let me fetch you a glass of water.'

'A little water. Yes. That is very kind. Thank you,' said she. 'Forgive me.'

Lady Allersham poured some water into a small glass and placed it in Miss Carteret's hand. 'Shall I summon your mother or would you rather I —'

'Please do not disturb her. I shall be myself again presently.'

CHAPTER THIRTEEN

Mrs Beresford took great pleasure in recounting the best parts of the previous evening's events. Her opinion of James Beresford had not changed; if anything, her esteem for him was even greater than before. He had proved himself a gentleman of manners, learning and understanding, altogether worthy of the surname he bore. She could find no fault with him, except that he ate less heartily than anyone at dinner. But what surprised her most was Lady Dalrymple. Circumstances had thrown them into each other's company for the latter part of the evening. She had not expected to find a topic of mutual interest and was resigned to obtaining nothing more from their conversation beyond the usual commonplace civilities. She was happy to be proved wrong.

'I was agreeably surprised by our conversation,' said Mrs Beresford. 'Lady Dalrymple spoke of her late husband with rare sensitivity. I am ashamed to say that I had not thought her capable of such feeling. As the evening went on, I found that we were at one on more subjects than I can recall. We found that we had an acquaintance in common: a Miss Carr. Neither she nor I have heard news of Miss Carr for some considerable time. There was a time when an alliance was expected between Miss Carr and your papa. The expectation was a universal one, but came to nothing. Mercifully, he made the better choice. The very best.'

Lady Allersham smiled. 'Was Miss Carr very disappointed?'

'Indeed she was,' said Mrs Beresford, wistfully. 'That was all a very long time ago. Now, to the point. Lady Dalrymple is anxious to visit Bath Street and I have promised to accompany her for I have in mind a few purchases of my own. Miss Carteret is unlikely to attend - '

'Poor Miss Carteret! I expect she is feeling the effects of the wine and a sore head. She was quite overcome with intoxication. And I do not think she was full sober when they departed, though she made an excellent impression of being so. Cousin Robert saw how it was and insisted she take his arm. I do hope he was careful not to tease her about it in Lady Dalrymple's hearing, for she is quite opposed to wine in excess. Did you see how she took only a sip here and a sip there for appearance sake? Most of the wine remained in her glass. Seeing Miss Carteret inebriated put me in mind of Aunt Fowle the night of the Brinshore ball. I remember how she had drunk rather too much negus and made quite a spectacle of herself. She was left with a terrible headache the following day.'

Lord Allersham had taken an early morning walk and returned to Laura Place much restored by it. 'It occurred to me, Emma, that you haven't yet attended one of Bath's famous balls,' said he. 'And considering all the stories you have heard of them I should have thought a ball a necessity. After all, what more interesting news is there to send to Osborne Park than an account of a ball at the Upper Rooms. Imagine the reaction of your grandmother and Mrs Turner at such news.'

'I suppose Cousin Robert mentioned it, for it was indeed our plan,' said Lady Allersham. 'Will you attend? Or shall you return to Allersham?'

'Harding did not mention it to me. And yes, I shall attend. Allersham can wait a week or two. I should like to accompany you if you will have me. I haven't seen you dance for some time,' said he.

Lady Allersham reached for her husband's hand and smiled. 'Yesterday you were determined to abandon Bath altogether.'

'And yesterday, I confess, I was wrong.'

'What changed your mind?' said she.

'It was something Lady Dalrymple said,' he replied.

She smiled. 'I must see to it that I invite Lady Dalrymple to dine more often.'

Not long afterwards, a note from the Dalrymple household arrived addressed to Mrs Beresford. The note was brief: Lady Dalrymple had no pressing engagements, and should Mrs Beresford be similarly unencumbered, she would be pleased to accompany her on a visit to Bath Street directly.

'I hope she orders her carriage and does not expect ours. Lady Dalrymple is not inclined to walk further than the bridge,' said Lady Allersham.

Mrs Beresford confirmed that on receipt of a positive reply Lady Dalrymple would have her carriage brought round.

'There, you see,' said Mrs Beresford.

'I am amazed,' replied Lady Allersham. 'The morning is full of surprises.'

Another surprise was yet to come. Mr Wood's daily visit brought news that had been anticipated. Miss Fox was now fully recovered and well enough to leave Laura Place.

'Surely another day or two of convalescence would do Miss Fox the world of good,' said Lady Allersham.

'I do not disagree, but Miss Fox is resolute in her desire to return to Mrs Price,' Mr Wood replied. 'I cannot prevent it.'

'I suspect it is a case of misplaced loyalty. Mrs Price imposes on Miss Fox greatly. It was for that reason alone that Miss Fox suffered as she did in the first place.'

'Then I am sorry indeed,' said he. 'I cannot deny that a day or two longer under Your Ladyship's care would fortify her constitution. But you must persuade her yourself, for I cannot.'

Miss Fox would not be persuaded; she would impose on Lady Allersham no longer, nor shun her duty towards Mrs Price. She *would* return to Gay Street. Every expression of gratitude that could be made was made, and every offer of further assistance was declined with grace and firmness.

One thing that Lady Allersham would not allow was for Miss Fox to return to Gay Street unaccompanied.

'I shall accompany you myself,' said she, 'and I shall brook no refusal. I have given way on everything else, but I *shall* have my way on this matter alone.'

Lady Allersham ordered the carriage and made sure that Miss Fox was laden with provisions for Mrs Price.

'There is nothing better for soothing resentment than a joint of ham, game pie and a visit from a countess,' said she, with light-hearted laughter.

Lady Allersham knew that Miss Fox's return would likely lead to recriminations from Mrs Price for the inconvenience caused by her absence. As the carriage turned into Gay Street, Lady Allersham observed Miss Fox's growing anxiety and sought to ease her mind.

'I shall deal with Mrs Price,' said she. 'She will not utter one word of reproach, I assure you.'

Mrs Price was astounded when Lady Allersham was announced and was led into the parlour; she had never received a countess before and felt the embarrassment that arose from the disarray that surrounded her. A profusion of apologies followed as Mrs Price urged Lady Allersham to overlook the chaos, declaring that had she received warning she should have been better prepared. As it was, she begged forgiveness for the disorderly state of affairs and swore that it had never happened before. The cause, said she, was wholly of Miss Fox's making, and that had she not succumbed to those neurotic tendencies fashionable among young women, both she and Her Ladyship would have been saved a great deal of trouble.

At length, when every item had been removed from the best chair in the parlour, save for a small feather cushion, Lady Allersham was invited to sit down. Mrs Price smoothed the creases from her own dress and primped her hair before taking a seat opposite her visitor. As she did so, she noticed Her Ladyship's carriage outside. The carriage, clearly bearing the Allersham livery for all her neighbours to wonder at and envy, was indeed a wondrous sight. And with the basket of provisions, a gift from Lady Allersham herself, it was almost enough to grant Miss Fox absolution for the sin of desertion. Mrs Price instructed Miss Fox to take the basket to the kitchen and straightaway return to her duties. Miss Fox seemed unperturbed, and thanked Lady Allersham once again for all she had done for her, before quitting the room.

Lady Allersham surveyed the parlour with an affected air of languid self-importance of the kind she had often encountered in the society of her equals.

'That is a curious object,' said she. Mrs Price followed the direction of her gaze. Her eyes rested on an old jug displayed on a shelf in a small alcove.

'It is too plain for the sole purpose of ornamentation, and too cumbersome for the dining table. It fills a shelf, I suppose,' said Lady Allersham.

'It was a gift from one of my boarders,' said Mrs Price. 'I shall remove it at once. I have always considered it very ugly indeed.'

'The painting above the fireplace is not unpleasant. It reminds me of Surrey. Have you visited Surrey, Mrs Price?'

'I have not been so fortunate. The scene is a very pleasant one. I have always admired it.'

'A gift from one of your parlour boarders?' said Lady Allersham.

'I believe so, Your Ladyship,' Mrs Price replied. 'Regretfully, I do not recall every —'

'Miss Fox came to you some years ago, I understand.'

Mrs Price suspected that Lady Allersham was in no hurry to leave until she had secured certain information pertaining to her boarder. The history of Miss Fox was a subject she would have preferred to avoid, indeed, at that moment she would have wished Lady Allersham elsewhere but for the enduring presence of the Allersham carriage at the entrance to her establishment. The patronage of a noble family would astonish the neighbourhood and do her reputation no harm at all, for the longer the carriage remained there the more likely it was that she might profit by association. Mrs Price saw her opportunity and ordered tea.

'Mrs Price, I should like to request Miss Fox's services. One afternoon a week should suffice. I shall pay Miss Fox's account and in return I expect you to reduce her duties accordingly. Is that understood?'

Mrs Price nodded in agreement.

'In addition, you will provide Miss Fox with an income commensurate with the work you require of her. I shall oversee the arrangement, but none of this is to pass your lips. Miss Fox will remain in ignorance of it. You may, if questioned, say that Miss Fox's benefactor has resumed payment of her allowance. I shall leave you to decide how to account for it.'

Mrs Price gave her word that she would comply with all of Lady Allersham's demands.

'Furthermore, you will release Miss Fox for two days complete for Miss Dauber's wedding, and I shall arrange her travel to Whitcombe.'

Mrs Price nodded vigorously.

'Finally, you will supply me with all the facts available to you pertaining to Miss Fox's history, including everything you know about her benefactor.'

With a semblance of dutiful diligence, Mrs Price went over to a chest of drawers and took out a volume containing a list of boarders' names and accounts. She found the page bearing the details relating to Miss Fox. The volume was placed into Lady Allersham's hands.

After scrutinising the page for some minutes, Lady Allersham said, 'Mr Dauber's signature appears.'

'Mr Dauber delivered Miss Fox, but the placement of his signature upon the page signifies nothing more than that. I have received many boarders in my time, Your Ladyship. They come and go. But on the whole, they are delivered through means of a third party. Like most, I understand Miss Fox to be the natural child of someone who does not wish his name to be known,' said Mrs Price. 'As you will see, Miss Fox's allowance was advanced through the office of an attorney. No payment has been forthcoming from Miss Fox's benefactor for some time. All enquiries have proven fruitless.'

'And you have no knowledge as to the identity of Miss Fox's benefactor?' said Lady Allersham.

'None,' Mrs Price replied. 'May I suggest that you apply to Mr Dauber? I know of no other person to whom you may apply for information.'

'You know as well as I that Mr Dauber is bound, as a clergyman, to maintain the secrecy of the confessional. But, thank you, Mrs Price. That is all I need to know for the present.'

A slight bow of the head was all the acknowledgement Mrs Price received. Having partaken of half a dish of tea, Lady Allersham was anxious to be on her way.

On leaving Gay Street, her sense of accomplishment gave her a decided air of satisfaction; Miss Fox may not see a complete change in her fortunes, but an easing of the demands placed upon her was certain to add solace and respite to her existence in some small way.

The knowledge that Mr Dauber and Whitcombe had played some part in Miss Fox's past was as intriguing to Lady Allersham as it was perplexing. She was in no doubt that something more must be done to reveal the facts in their entirety, but she was less certain about how to uncover them. Would her husband sanction her interference, or would he oppose it? His assistance, if offered, would be invaluable, but would he be disposed to do so if the reputation of Allersham were to be damaged by it? What might the consequences be should an unpleasant discovery see Allersham implicated? She would speak to him directly and hide nothing from him; she would appeal for his help, and if it were not forthcoming, his forbearance alone would suffice.

The details of her visit to Gay Street were received with greater tolerance than she had anticipated considering her husband's earlier misgivings. He replied with calm resignation, 'Be prepared for what might come to light, Emma. I hope you do not come to regret it.'

'I must do something,' said she.

Lord Allersham placed her hand in his. 'I see that it is futile to oppose you.'

'And in turn, I promise not to find husbands and wives for any one of our acquaintance.'

'That, I am certain, will be a great relief to them all,' said he. 'There is but one question that concerns me. How shall you maintain your side of the agreement when we return to Allersham? What will happen to Miss Fox then?'

Lady Allersham admitted that she had not considered that part of the arrangement. 'But I believe a suitable replacement will be found. Lady Dalrymple and Miss Carteret, or the Ibbotson household may find that they have need of Miss Fox one afternoon in seven.'

'Well, my love, I see you have no need of my help in this matter.'

'Still, I should like to know that I have your approval,' said she.

Lord Allersham took hold of his wife's hand and kissed it. 'You do not need it.'

CHAPTER FOURTEEN

Mrs Beresford had nothing but praise for Lady Allersham's handling of Mrs Price but advised caution in her quest concerning Miss Fox.

'Miss Fox's benefactor has gone to great lengths to guard against detection through careful concealment of the facts at every turn, and now finds that what seems to be a change in circumstances provides no other course of action than to abandon his charge. I suppose the shame of exposure might harm more than himself alone.'

'Whatever the circumstances, there is one person who knows the truth, and that is Mr Dauber. He alleges a connexion with Allersham but will not say what it is,' said Lady Allersham. 'His daughter befriends Miss Fox and he raises no objection, and even promotes their friendship by also placing her with Mrs Price and subsequently bringing Miss Dauber to Bath to visit Miss Fox. Why should he not speak plainly and reveal what he knows? It may be of benefit to more than Miss Fox, but most especially to Miss Fox.'

'It is not in his power to do so,' Mrs Beresford replied.

'I fail to see why clerical obligations should prevail over everything else.'

'Mr Dauber is a reasonable man. He would not withhold information that was within his power to make known, especially if it might be to the good.'

Lady Allersham sighed. 'I cannot rid myself of the notion that Henry's elder brother is the villain of the piece. And yet I do not know that he had any dealings with Mr Dauber directly even though all the facts point in his direction.'

'Do they?' replied Mrs Beresford.

'Of course,' said Lady Allersham, as an idea suddenly entered her head: the key to the solution was so simple that she was surprised she had not thought of it before. 'The answer is to be found at Allersham. There must be letters, documents. There must be accounts. There must be proof.'

'And you propose to —'

'Find it,' said she.

The speculation concerning Miss Fox came to an end when Lord Allersham entered the room and asked whether they should like to attend a ball at the Upper Rooms the following evening.

'Tomorrow evening?' said Lady Allersham. 'There is nothing I should like better.'

'I am sure I shall have no trouble persuading Lady Dalrymple to attend, and Miss Carteret, of course,' said Mrs Beresford. 'And I shall send a note to James Beresford. He will make a point of attending if we are certain to be there.'

'Cousin Robert is sure to come too,' said Lady Allersham. 'I cannot wait to see him steer Lady Dalrymple around the floor. And a ball will give Miss Carteret a chance to make up her mind.'

'Over what has Miss Carteret need to make up her mind?' said Lord Allersham.

'She cannot decide whether she admires James Beresford better than Cousin Robert,' said Lady Allersham.

'And you know this for a fact?' said Lord Allersham.

'Not a fact. A feeling,' Lady Allersham replied.

'Miss Carteret and Captain Harding?' replied Mrs Beresford. 'I thought she disapproved of him entirely.'

'I don't believe she disapproves of him half as much as she thinks she does,' said Lady Allersham.

'May I remind you, my love, of the conversation we had earlier,' said Lord Allersham. 'I seem to recall that you were determined to put such intrigue behind you. Furthermore, may I also remind you that it was not so long ago that you sought to enlist me in your scheme to keep your cousin and Miss Carteret apart. Has Captain Harding changed so completely that he should now have overcome those objections that once stood in his way, if indeed he had any serious thought of Miss Carteret in the first place? This is why I am ill-disposed to meddling in other people's affairs.'

Lady Allersham smiled at her husband and sighed, 'Henry, my love, I admit I may have been mistaken in my cousin. But you cannot deny that he knows how to curry favour with Lady Dalrymple. He succeeds with the mother, and I don't see why he cannot succeed with the daughter also.'

'We should go early to secure seats,' said Mrs Beresford, who had not attended carefully to the conversation concerning Miss Carteret's suitors.

'And watch the minuets? Yes, I should like that, though I should be surprised if either single gentleman of our party were to stand up. At one time my cousin could hardly manage a country dance,' said Lady Allersham. 'We shall go by chair of course, and you, my love, may go on foot with Cousin Robert. James Beresford will likely make his own arrangements for he has not far to walk. I suppose Lady Dalrymple will expect a carriage.'

'The Upper Rooms are best reached by a chair. Lady Dalrymple knows it to be so. *That* is the chief reason she is reluctant to offer her own carriage,' said Lord Allersham.

'I cannot deny it,' said Mrs Beresford. 'Lady Dalrymple has nothing good to say about chairs. She told me Mr Ibbotson was once dropped accidentally by careless chairmen. He sustained an injury to his hip and to this day it has not been put right.'

A note from Miss Carteret confirmed that she and Lady Dalrymple were certain to be in attendance. The note went on, 'It may please you to know that Miss Fox is quite well again and is to attend the ball. Miss Ibbotson is not expected to attend, and Mr Ibbotson has kindly offered a seat in his carriage to Miss Fox. Your visit to Gay Street is the talk of Bath and Miss Fox is become quite the romantic heroine. Miss Eliza Ibbotson is anxious to further their acquaintance and was most insistent that Miss Fox should go in place of her sister. She would not be gainsaid. Mr Ibbotson was obliged to plead with Mrs Price on his daughter's behalf, for Miss Fox was not inclined at first to accept, nor Mrs Price to give her consent. But it is now certain that she will attend. I must warn you that your patronage of Miss Fox has led to gossip of the worst kind. Allersham Park has been mentioned. I shall say no more about it. Yours JC. P.S. Has Miss Fox so much as a decent gown to wear?'

Poor Miss Fox! thought Lady Allersham. She has done nothing to deserve such odious attention as this; that I should be the author of it is wholly disagreeable!

She considered what should be done. The news preyed on her conscience and, seeing that Lord Allersham was engaged in writing to his steward, she left him in peace and went to seek Mrs Beresford's advice.

'What is to be done about such rumours?' said Lady Allersham.

'Retraction is impossible,' Mrs Beresford replied. 'Dissociation and concealment will only give rise to further speculation. I believe the best way to dispel the rumours is to acknowledge Miss Fox just as you would have done had you known nothing of the matter.'

'Surely that would serve only to confirm the rumours,' Lady Allersham replied.

'It will show that you care nothing for gossip and speculation. Remember, the world will think and say and behave as it will.'

'I do not wish to snub Miss Fox,' replied Lady Allersham. 'To submit her to such humiliation would be cruel indeed. I only wish to determine how best to act.'

'Stand firm, my dear, against critics and quizzers,' replied Mrs Beresford. 'It is the least ruinous path for all concerned. And if such speculation were proven correct, your conduct would, I believe, be judged more favourably. There are few examples in the world of generosity or liberality in such matters. You must show the way.'

'One thing troubles me,' said Lady Allersham. 'Who might be the originator of such rumours?'

'I would imagine it to be the only person who knows nearly as much about Miss Fox as Mr Dauber,' Mrs Beresford replied.

'Mrs Price,' said Lady Allersham.

Her Ladyship's conscience was almost eased, but she began to feel the weight of the unforeseen and unintended outcome of her actions, of which she had been warned repeatedly. She knew that Miss Fox would suffer disproportionately compared to any injury she and, by association, Allersham might sustain, and it was this knowledge that caused her to doubt the merit of her actions.

The impulse to conceal the matter from Lord Allersham was almost too great to resist, but she knew that concealment would never do. On entering the drawing room, she saw that her husband had completed one letter and was reading another, a letter that had arrived in the afternoon post. Before she had time to compose herself, Lord Allersham passed the letter to his wife and said with a grin, 'Here is news that will surprise and delight you, my love.'

The letter was from Captain Blake. 'The last paragraph will be of greater interest than the preceding one which describes the new alterations to Brinshore's spa,' said he.

Lady Allersham went straight to the final paragraph and read with a mixture of bemusement and surprise that Mr and Mrs Fowle were to visit Bath and were expected within the week.

The moment to speak of Miss Fox had passed, for Lady Allersham was called away to rectify a misunderstanding in the kitchen. Any further opportunity to speak appeared unlikely, for the hour to dress had arrived; there was much to be done and so little time in which to accomplish it. The rumours circulating in Bath concerning Miss Fox were put aside; she wished only that those pertaining to Allersham Park would not reach her husband's ears before she had had an opportunity to speak with him first.

CHAPTER FIFTEEN

The party arrived at the Upper Rooms a little before seven, and when all outer attire had been deposited in the cloakroom and cordial salutations exchanged with the Master of Ceremonies, they were escorted to the ballroom. On entry, before them stood expectant couples in minuet formation eager for the music to commence. The room was already full, and seats were scarce, but special provision was made for their party and they were pleased to sit down without fuss, obstacle or delay. Lady Allersham was assured that their seats provided a most advantageous position with the least possible disturbance from dancers and onlookers alike, and that country dancing was certain to follow at eight.

As the music began, Miss Carteret gazed at the floor where couples, with an ear to the tempo and eyes fixed on their feet or locked on each other, stepped forward in sink and rise motion, meeting and parting for the most part in harmonising movement. She had once danced as they now danced and hoped as they now hoped that those moments of pleasure would endure, that they would signify the imminence of a greater joy made perfect in a deeper, more permanent union. She lamented those whose hopes would be dashed, whose dreams would be crushed, whose hearts would be broken. Another assembly, in another time and place, was foremost in her thoughts; once such an assembly had been the site of her greatest triumph and forever after the place of her bitterest regret. 'It cannot endure,' she whispered under her breath. However strong her resolution might have been to put disappointment behind her, she remained fettered to the past, for there she was certain to find consolation in self-reproach.

James Beresford had engaged Miss Carteret for the first two country dances, and Captain Harding for the second. She admired the former in whom she found a gentleman of manners, with understanding and insight, comfortably situated and universally amiable. James Beresford was a man infinitely superior to Captain Harding in every way that mattered. Of the latter, she doubted her judgement, for her opinion of his character was constantly changing. Her inability to comprehend the true disposition of Captain Harding was something she found wholly disconcerting, for her estimation of him was not what it had been on first meeting, and against her better judgement her inclination to think well of him surprised no one more profoundly than herself. Perplexed and constrained by such conflicting sensations, she saw no prospect of a happy union with any man of her acquaintance; consequently, she began to embrace the notion that it was her fate, that such a union seemed wholly and forever improbable.

'Shall you dance, my love?' said Lord Allersham to his wife.

'I shall if you will take the trouble to ask me,' she replied.

Lady Allersham surveyed the ballroom for some sign of Mr Ibbotson's party. Her efforts were in vain for the benches and floor were full to overflowing, and late guests, being obliged to stand, obscured parts of the room from view. Almost half an hour had elapsed before the minuet reached its conclusion, and as couples prepared themselves for the next, Miss

Carteret drew Lady Allersham's attention to Miss Eliza Ibbotson and her dancing partner standing at one of the back benches at the far end of the room. It was then that Lady Allersham saw Miss Fox seated beside Mr Ibbotson. She appeared subdued, caught between Mr Ibbotson on one side and a woman of similar age to the gentleman on the other.

'Who is that woman sitting next to Miss Fox?' said Lady Allersham.

Miss Carteret replied that it was Mr Ibbotson's sister who often stayed with the family during the season. 'Mama does not like her, and she does not like Mama. Miss Ibbotson is acquainted with the Kellynch family. It seems she was once violently in love with Sir Walter, and to this day persists in defending him to the hilt. Mama thinks she would have him still if he were to offer.'

'She never married?' Lady Allersham enquired.

'No. She was not so fortunate. Mama says she waited too long for Sir Walter and when an offer did not come, she was past her first bloom of youth. Miss Ibbotson depends in part on her brother for an allowance and spends her time with whomever will invite her to stay, relations mainly, for it costs her less to avail of the hospitality of others than to keep rooms of her own.'

'Then I am sorry for her,' said Lady Allersham. 'Every person needs a home.' She watched as Mr Ibbotson got up and limped to the door, leaving Miss Fox in the care of his sister. And as she continued to observe them, she noticed that the place that had been occupied by Mr Ibbotson was now taken up by a woman who appeared to be acquainted with his sister. Miss Fox exchanged places, allowing the two women to sit together to enjoy a private conversation. Seemingly out of place and in the way, Miss Fox sat silent and alone, occasionally smiling as she caught the eye of Miss Eliza Ibbotson and her partner as the dance commenced and the couples stepped in time to the music.

'Mr Ibbotson is gone to play cards, I suppose,' said Miss Carteret.

'I hope someone has thought to secure a partner for Miss Fox once the minuets are done with,' Lady Allersham replied. Her impulse was to rescue Miss Fox and make room on their bench for her. There she might sit among friends and enjoy some conversation; there partners would be found for her and she would not feel overlooked or abandoned. She curbed the impulse to act, not for her own sake, for she cared little about the opinions of others, but for the sake of Miss Fox, whom she perceived would prefer to hide in the shadows than to find herself the focus of attention.

On the stroke of eight the much-awaited hour of country dancing began. James Beresford, with faultless good manners, fulfilled his promise to stand up with Miss Carteret; Captain Harding applied to Lady Dalrymple, but was turned down, for she never danced. On the rare occasion that Lady Dalrymple attended the Upper Rooms, she explained that it was her custom to watch the dancing until the interval and spend the rest of the evening in the Octagon Room at cards. There her mind might be better employed, and there she might learn the news of the day that was certain not to appear within the pages of the *Chronicle*.

Captain Harding made a similar application to Mrs Beresford who likewise declined his offer with the explanation that it was a little *too soon*. No further justification was needed, for the matter was comprehended immediately. 'Of course,' said he. 'Forgive me.'

Without a word, Lord Allersham sought the hand of his wife in complete expectation of it being given. To his surprise, she leaned forward to whisper something into Captain Harding's ear. An acknowledgement was given immediately, with an amenable expression and nod of the head from her cousin. She smiled with satisfaction and turned to towards her husband. Taking his hand, she said, 'That is a piece of work well done.'

Until they moved to the floor and took their places among the couples in the set, Lord Allersham had not comprehended the nature of the exchange that had passed between his wife and Captain Harding.

As it became clear to him, he said, 'Emma, I see what you have done.' Lady Allersham followed the direction of her husband's gaze: Captain Harding was leading Miss Fox towards the floor to complete another set, just as the signal to begin was given.

Smiles were exchanged between Lady Allersham and Captain Harding. Miss Fox appeared nervous but managed an obliging smile for her dancing partner and another for Lady Allersham. The pair appeared to be the subject of much attention, and as the music continued, Miss Eliza Ibbotson missed a step, for her concentration had been fixed solely on Miss Fox and Captain Harding to the consternation of her own partner.

Miss Carteret seemed perfectly content with *her* partner as comments and smiles were shared between

141

them, so much so that she appeared not to notice Captain Harding and Miss Fox at all.

'I could not watch as Miss Fox sat silent and ignored while everyone else seemed happy and engaged. My only fear is that my cousin is not much of a dancer,' said Lady Allersham to her husband.

Lady Allersham was prevented from watching Captain Harding's progress, except for an occasional glance behind her when the steps allowed, as her back was mostly turned away from him. Lord Allersham had a better view of Captain Harding's efforts as the dance proceeded and observed, 'You need not worry about your cousin. Harding must have become something of a proficient over the years.'

Lady Allersham gave a sigh of relief. 'That is good news indeed. And how does Miss Fox go on?'

Lord Allersham smiled. 'Admirably.'

'What is it?' said Lady Allersham. 'What amuses you?'

'Do you recall the first time we danced together?' said he.

'At the Brinshore Ball? I recall Aunt Harding, as she was then, and Mr Fowle! Who could not? How they danced! What a sight!' said she.

'You had sprained your ankle and was determined not to dance.'

'Not determined. Instructed,' said she. 'And you made me dance. Your insistence on inflicting pain on my poor foot is what I remember most of all.'

'It was for your own good. You spent far too long resting your ankle. Dancing that night did you greater good than harm, as you well know.'

'I was following Mr Fowle's advice,' said Lady Allersham. 'I had no desire to spend the summer in idleness. I suppose you thought I received far too much attention, that my aunt was oversolicitous of my health.'

'Yes, I did,' said he. 'After all, it was nothing more than a sprained ankle.'

'What did you think of me then?' she replied.

'Think of you?'

'Yes,' said she. 'Were you at least half in love by then?'

'No,' Lord Allersham replied.

'No?'

'Not half in love. I was never half in love.'

'But when did it begin?'

'I believe it was when you lectured me as you stood in a puddle of mud in Brinshore's famous town square.'

'You mean the moment you nearly ran me over,' said she, 'and spoilt my gown forever.'

'That moment precisely. Yes,' he replied. 'I take it the feeling was not mutual.'

'It certainly was not, as you well know,' said Lady Allersham. 'But I suppose like most men you expected me to come around in the end.'

'I had no expectations of the kind. I had hope,' said he. 'I still have hope.'

'That is an extraordinary thing to say. If ever you needed proof of my love, remember I accepted you in the full knowledge that you were determined to take holy orders, and I was not deterred by that,' said Lady Allersham.

'No, you were not. What greater assurance is there to be had?' said he, with a slight tone of irony in his voice. 'But I suppose Lady Allersham suits you better than Mrs Fitzroy.'

'My love,' said she, without a moment's hesitation, 'you are wrong. You will always be my Henry Fitzroy. The rest is of little consequence, I assure you. Nevertheless, if anything should bring shame on the good name of Allersham, I should be sorry for your sake, though it would have little effect on me.'

'Shame, my dear? Whatever do you mean?' said he.

The dance ended and prevented any further conversation until the interval. The matter uppermost in Lady Allersham's mind was how to bring to her husband's attention the rumours surrounding Miss Fox.

Lady Allersham was pleased to find that James Beresford, having relinquished his partner to Captain Harding, now applied to Miss Fox, and was accepted. What surprised her most was that both couples continued to dance two additional sets without a change of partner, and when at last the dancers broke up for tea, the rush for the tea room left Captain Harding and Miss Carteret adrift from their party, nowhere to be found. James Beresford returned Miss Fox to her station among the Ibbotson party and afforded her greater respect and courtesy than her own party had done or thought due to her. Having discharged his duty towards Miss Fox, he proceeded to find seats in the tea room for Mrs Beresford and Lady Dalrymple.

'Shall you join me after tea, Mrs Beresford? Are you a card player?' said Lady Dalrymple.

'Indeed, I am,' said she, 'though not a very good one. But I should be happy to join you nevertheless.'

'We are certain to find seats at Mr Ibbotson's table,' Lady Dalrymple replied, 'for his regular set begin to tire of bunions, blisters and bandages by nine o'clock. I hope you are not squeamish, Mrs Beresford.'

Lady Allersham at first saw no sign of Captain Harding and Miss Carteret in the tea room; when eventually she spotted them standing among the Ibbotson party, she was intrigued to see Miss Carteret appearing to perform the office of introducing Captain Harding to Mr Ibbotson and his sister.

Lord Allersham returned to their party, having been obliged to speak to one of Lady Russell's old friends he had spied earlier. Lady Allersham drew his attention to the Ibbotsons and said, 'Cousin Robert is surrounded by young women. Miss Carteret, Miss Fox and the younger Miss Ibbotson all appear to find him excessively entertaining. I wonder what he says to amuse them.'

'Whatever it is, it will probably not be of any great import,' said her husband. 'Emma, I have just been speaking with an old acquaintance of Lady Russell. What she says is concerning. I think you should hear it.'

'A friend of Lady Russell?' said Lady Allersham. 'What could she possibly have to say that concerns me? I shall wave and smile and have done with it. There, you see. She is perfectly content with a wave.'

'As you wish,' said he, in a serious tone. 'Then I shall tell you, for it cannot be left unspoken.'

Her eyes met his. 'What is it? What news? I hope nothing dreadful.'

'There are rumours circulating about Miss Fox.'

Lady Allersham sighed with relief.

'You knew?' he asked.

She smiled at him apologetically.

'And you did not think to tell me?'

'It was my intention, truly it was, but no opportunity presented itself, my love.'

'How long have you known?' said he.

'Miss Carteret sent me a note this afternoon and happened to mention it in a postscript. So, you see, it wasn't of the greatest significance.'

'I suppose Miss Carteret and presumably Lady Dalrymple are acquainted with the substance of the rumours. And your cousin?'

'Not to my knowledge. But I had to say something to Aunt Beresford, for I was at a loss to know how to act,' said she.

'You might have come to me,' he said.

'You were busy writing to your steward,' she replied. 'I did not wish to impede you for you said it was important.'

'This is important,' said he.

'Perhaps,' she replied. 'But I feel sure the rumours will be forgotten in time. They last a week or so and are always replaced in the end by other rumours more fascinating and shocking. But I *should* like to know if there is any truth in them.'

'And in the meantime, what of Miss Fox? Is she aware of the speculation concerning her?' Lord Allersham enquired.

'I do not know. When she comes to Laura Place I shall establish what I can then.'

As her husband was about to answer, Lady Allersham smiled and placed a finger against his lips, preventing him from speaking on the matter further. 'Let us forget the matter of Miss Fox for the present unless you wish to raise further speculation among the good people of Bath. I am sure you do not. Aunt Beresford advised me well. We shall carry on as normal and acknowledge Miss Fox just as we would have done had the rumours not come to light. I believe it is the best advice.'

Lord Allersham removed his wife's finger from his lips, looked at it, and kissed it. 'Well,' said he, 'I suppose there are two people I know of, each of whom I suspect would find the matter wholly entertaining.'

'Yes, indeed. I am only sorry that Grandmamma and Aunt Turner are not in Bath to hear it for themselves, for it would give them much to talk about in Delham. I should have invited them without a moment's hesitation. Alas, they are too infirm to travel.'

'You'd prefer an audience then?' said he.

'An audience?'

'To witness our undoing?'

'It is hardly our undoing, my love,' said she. 'Were it to be true, if Miss Fox were connected in some way to Allersham Park, it would not constitute *her* undoing either. I should make sure it would not. Why should any young woman suffer her entire life because of mistakes not of her own making. A young man would not find himself at the same disadvantage. It is women who suffer disproportionately. And it is unjust and wrong.'

For some moments, Lord Allersham studied his wife's countenance until, conscious of his gaze, she turned towards him and asked, 'What is it? What have I said to vex you?'

He smiled. 'Nothing at all. I was thinking of you. What a warrior you are.'

'Thank you,' said she. 'That is the finest compliment you have ever paid me.'

After tea, Miss Fox received two additional applications to dance; Mrs Beresford and Lady Dalrymple enjoyed a full hour at the card table; Lord and Lady Allersham danced two further dances; and James Beresford found himself cornered by Mr Ibbotson's sister who was anxious to seek advice on the availability of lodgings in Paragon Buildings.

As the assembly drew to a close, in the last half hour there seemed nothing to overturn the pleasure of the night. Captain Harding and Miss Carteret did not dance again. Instead, a contest was proposed by the former and accepted by the latter: Captain Harding challenged Miss Carteret to win at cards against him. Undaunted by the challenge, Miss Carteret agreed, and was keen to settle the matter.

As they entered the Octagon Room, Miss Carteret came upon a young woman with whom she had once enjoyed a brief but intimate friendship, and whom she had not seen or heard of for five years or thereabouts.

'Miss Buller!' said she, surprised to see the friend who was once her confidante.

'Mrs Baldwin,' she replied. 'I am married. Well and truly. Matrimony. There is nothing like it.' She dangled her ringed finger in front of Miss Carteret. 'I have been married these past two years. And you, my dear friend? What a surprise it is to see you after all this time. Let me guess.'

There was no time to reminisce, to explain the reason for the silence between them or to recollect shared memories. Mrs Baldwin turned to Captain Harding with a look of playful curiosity.

'Well, Jane, I think I know the name of this gentleman, and he is just as handsome as your description of him,' said Mrs Baldwin. 'Good evening, Captain Fitzroy.'

The mortification occasioned by the encounter could not have been more acutely felt: Miss Carteret was speechless. She blushed, her heart raced, she looked away; stunned by the unforgivable indiscretion of her once intimate friend, she fought to hold back tears of despair and humiliation. She had been found out in the worst manner possible. Her voice trembled as her reply dwindled to a weak and incomprehensible utterance.

Captain Harding was stunned by the revelation but quickly recovered his presence of mind and took charge of the situation. 'Your error, Madam, is unfortunate but not uncommon,' said he, addressing Mrs Baldwin. 'Regrettably, the gentleman to whom you refer is no longer among us, and I should, under different circumstances, request Miss Carteret to introduce us, but as you see, our friend is quite unwell and therefore I must beg you to release her.'

Mrs Baldwin gave way immediately, and in a state of confusion, with little more than an adieu, Miss Carteret quickly moved on. Captain Harding, confounded by the discovery of an astounding secret Miss Carteret had evidently gone to great pains to conceal, suggested a quiet place to sit down. 'Let me find you a seat,' said he.

'No. I thank you. That will not be necessary,' said she. 'I wish to leave.'

'Miss Carteret,' said he, 'allow me to say that you may rely on my complete discretion. I give you my word.'

Never had she seen in his look so complete an expression of serious intent or genuine concern. 'Thank you,' she replied.

In an instant she was gone. He did not — could not — prevent it; but he would go after her. Duty required it; courtesy, esteem, perhaps even love, demanded it.

At once he understood. That inexplicable coolness in Miss Carteret's dealings with the world was not to be found in a defect of character or temperament, but in the secret pain that must be endured in silence, that must be left unspoken. Only a full explanation of Miss Carteret's past dealings with the Allersham family would alleviate all manner of curiosity and speculation, and though he could not erase her extraordinary secret from his mind, he had given his word: he would speak of it to no one.

His search yielded nothing; Miss Carteret was nowhere to be found. In the end, he approached the table where Lady Dalrymple was about to declare a winning hand. Enquiring as to her daughter's whereabouts and receiving an indifferent reply, he said, 'Lady Dalrymple, I believe your daughter may be unwell.'

'Captain Harding, you are very good. Do not be uneasy. It is most probably the heat that affects her. She does not deal with heat well,' said Lady Dalrymple. 'You are certain to find her next to an open window or door. She will take too much air and, in a day or two, complain of a cold. But she will not be told. She will not listen to me.'

A further search of the Octagon Room and the tea room came to nothing. Some minutes later, Captain

Harding observed Lord Allersham returning from the cloakroom.

'Have you seen Miss Carteret?' said he.

'Emma has just taken her home, and I shall follow shortly,' Lord Allersham replied. 'Stay with Lady Dalrymple and Mrs Beresford, if you will, and see to it that they reach Laura Place safely.'

'Did Miss Carteret appear distressed?' said Captain Harding.

'An incident seems to have occasioned some unpleasantness,' he replied. 'Have you any understanding of the matter?'

Captain Harding chose his words with care. 'These things are often the result of disagreeable and unexpected encounters. I fear I was unable to protect Miss Carteret from such an encounter. But more than that I cannot say.'

'Point to the gentleman concerned or take the matter to the Master of Ceremonies at once,' Lord Allersham replied.

'That is impossible. The gentleman concerned is no longer,' said he, pausing to find the right word, 'present.'

CHAPTER SIXTEEN

Mr and Mrs Fowle were to stay in Bath for no more than a fortnight. When the day finally arrived, the couple reached Sydney Place under cover of darkness with boxes and trunks sufficient for a season. Fully laden, and with hardly a space to breathe, they alighted from the carriage on a night of bitter cold and driving rain, as their effects were lifted and stacked ready to be taken to their rooms. Mrs Fowle was careful to maintain a calm countenance despite the strong vexation she felt, for she preferred to travel with as little encumbrance as possible, including, and most especially, Mr Fowle. It was Mr Fowle who would not be persuaded to leave Brinshore without potions, powders, balms and remedies sufficient for every eventuality. His insistence on having his own way was so great that had his wife refused him, he had been prepared to abandon the journey entirely. Complaints and entreaties for moderation from the wife were dismissed as nonsense by the husband. Just as Mrs Fowle's forbearance had its limits, so had Mr Fowle's, though rarely did those limits find expression. On this occasion, Mrs Fowle found that she was obliged to give way, for the desire to see both her son and to visit Bath was greater than her need to triumph over her husband.

Captain Harding viewed the profusion of baggage and boxes with alarm in case his mother's intention was to spend, not simply a fortnight, but the rest of the season in Sydney Place.

The following day he saw very little of his mother as a large part of the morning was given over to rest and writing; she hardly stirred from her room. Letters and notes were despatched to inform interested parties of their safe arrival, and schemes were made to make the most of their stay in Bath. Mrs Fowle would have her rest, for she complained of a pain in her shoulder caused by the hours spent in a damp carriage in cramped conditions, having no adequate pillow on which to rest her head.

'Then you will be pleased to find that I have brought with me a balm to ease your discomfort,' said Mr Fowle. 'And I am sure you will agree that had I left this most excellent embrocation in Brinshore it would have been a misfortune indeed as you now appear to be in need it. I am pleased I had the foresight to include it in my box of necessities.'

'Had you left half of your necessities behind, room in the carriage would have been in ample supply. That being the case, I should have sat comfortably every inch of the way, and I would not now be nursing a soreness in my neck. Hence, I should not have required any embrocation of the kind to cure it.'

Mr Fowle placed the balm on the table beside her and marched out of the room. He disappeared, leaving Sydney Place in the full light of day, to Captain Harding's relief and satisfaction, and reappeared a short while before dinner, in a brighter mood, having spent some time at the Pump Room in contemplation of certain additional improvements to be made to Brinshore's own edifice of the kind. While his mind had been fixed on happier things, he saw that his stay in Bath might not be wholly unproductive and might even be put to very good use: the shrewd promotion of Brinshore and the brilliance of his reputation as a physician must be inducement enough to prompt an exodus from Bath mid-season for the promised land that was Brinshore, and the benefits and delights of the coast. Like Moses before him, Mr Fowle would endeavour to lead the way, for the vision was plain to see: Bath must move to Brinshore. It was a highly desirable prospect, and one from which he might profit well. Then, he might perhaps sustain fewer objections to the flagrant poaching of his patients by Mr Granby, for the infirm and disordered of Bath would fill Brinshore to overflowing and neither physician would ever again be in want of patrons to add to their lists.

Mrs Fowle, whose neck had undergone no improvement with the application of her husband's balm, was unmoved by the fervour of his ambition and cautioned that were the whole of Bath to move to Brinshore in July, or even August, Brinshore would not have room to accommodate them.

'And should the whole of Bath descend upon our esteemed shore at once, I hope they have better luck that me. They are sure to feel cheated, being promised a curative for every ailment, and then to find to their dismay, after paying out a great deal of money for the privilege, that the curative prescribed does nothing of the kind,' said Mrs Fowle. 'You might as well have left the balm at home for the pain in my neck has not eased in the slightest, and far from receiving any improvement through the application of it, I am certain that my condition has worsened considerably by its use. But my greatest objection is to its smell. Dripping. It smells of dripping; I have reeked of roast mutton all day long, and my spirits are much depressed by it.'

'I have a tonic for low spirits that has never failed,' Mr Fowle replied. 'But I see that it would be fruitless to prescribe any such restorative for you, my love, for you are determined to be ill, and when someone is determined to be ill there is nothing to be done. No remedy in the world will prove efficacious when a person in health makes up his mind to the contrary.'

'*Her* mind,' Mrs Fowle replied. 'I have never heard anything so duplicitous in my life. You raise no objections of the kind to those among your patients who fancy themselves ill, of which there are many.

Indeed, you are exceedingly happy to profit from anyone who will pay you handsomely enough to agree with the view that they are violently ill when they are not.'

'And how should you like to live on half the income you now enjoy?' said he.

The evening passed without resolution or compromise as Captain Harding sat for the most part in silence observation at the spectacle before him. Even though Mrs Fowle's pain had disappeared entirely during the evening, she had no intention of revealing the matter to Mr Fowle. Instead, she continued to give her finest performance of a woman in pain and despair until the day ended and sleep provided a welcome respite, each from the other and both from their host.

The visit of Lady Allersham, the following morning, was anticipated with pleasure by her aunt who bore no signs of the pain, real or imagined, with which she had plagued her husband the previous day. Lady Allersham's arrival was followed some minutes later by the return of Mrs Fowle's son. Captain Harding had taken an early morning walk in Sydney Gardens to escape the drama within. When all the pleasantries and enquiries about the journey had concluded, and news of Brinshore and Sanditon had been related in detail, Lady Allersham commented, 'Dear Aunt Fowle, what brings you to Bath and for so short a visit as this?'

'Mr Fowle insisted on it,' she replied. 'Did you not, my love? Mrs Fowle, said he, you deserve to go to Bath. Leave everything to me and I shall take you there. Is that not so, my love?'

'Yes, my love,' said he. 'Quite so.'

'Of course, I was anxious to see my son, for I have seen so little of him since he returned from the Indies. Evidently Bath has greater appeal than Brinshore. I was anxious to discover what it was. There are but two reasons that come to mind. The first is that my son is afflicted by an ailment for which no cure is to be found in Brinshore. An unlikely supposition. The second is that my son seeks to avoid his mother,' Mrs Fowle went on, reproachfully.

'Unless, my love, he has a more joyous purpose in mind. Perhaps he is contemplating matrimony and wishes to avoid interference,' said Mr Fowle.

Captain Harding replied, 'I am sorry you have had the inconvenience of coming all this way at great expense. But it is to no purpose. I suffer neither a disorder of the mind or body, nor, I might add, of the heart.'

'Your mother suffers greatly from neglect,' said Mr Fowle. 'Is that not true, my love?'

Mrs Fowle cast an accusatory glance at her husband, and replied sweetly, 'Quite true, my love.'

The room fell silent as tension filled the air. Lady Allersham was at a loss for something to say to ease the strain. At length, the silence was broken by the entrance of a servant with a tray of tea.

'Excuse me,' said Mr Fowle. 'I must attend to business that cannot be put off.'

'Shall we see you in Laura Place tomorrow evening?' said Lady Allersham. 'You are invited to dine with us. Please do not let us down. We dine at eight.'

The invitation to dine with the Allersham set was too great a distinction to be resisted, despite the drawback: Mr Fowle would be obliged to accompany his wife. An evening at Laura Place, however, would be viewed in Brinshore with great interest and provide his patients with a highly desirable alternative to the commonplace accounts of Mr Granby's visits to his uncle, an ordinary parson with a modest living in Delham.

The invitation was accepted with as much grace as it was given. 'Mrs Fowle and I should be delighted to attend, should we not, my love?' said he.

'Indeed, we should,' said Mrs Fowle. 'There is nothing Mr Fowle and I like better than to spend an evening among family.'

'Except to spend it apart,' whispered Captain Harding to Lady Allersham.

'What is that you say?' said Mrs Fowle, half hearing her son's quip.

'He said, spoken from the heart,' replied Lady Allersham, quickly.

Mrs Fowle appeared at greater ease after her husband had quitted the room, and immediately turned to the real purpose of her visit. 'Emma, my dear, I suspect my son has not been entirely honest with you. He must have his reasons, I suppose. He has certainly not been honest with his own mother, and I should like to know why.' She directed a glare of disapproval at her son. 'Well?' said she.

'I cannot imagine what you mean, Mother,' said Captain Harding.

'Can you not?' Mrs Fowle replied.

'Cousin?' said Lady Allersham, looking to him for an answer.

Captain Harding strode over to the fireplace and leaned against it but said nothing.

'I had a visit from one of your late father's close associates who was astonished, quite astonished, to find that poor old Mr Brooks had left behind so little in death, considering the vast amount of land and property he had acquired in life. Mr Brooks a wealthy man? said I. Impossible! I doubt he had two farthings to rub together. Said he, you are mistaken Mrs Fowle. Mr Brooks was a gentleman of considerable means. He was, however, not inclined to disclose the extent of it. The acquisition of property and land was his lifetime's work. Imagine that! I am shocked, said I. Quite shocked. I wonder how he meant to dispose of it? Ah, Mrs Fowle, said he. I see you have not heard the news.' Mrs Fowle turned to her son and said, 'What do you say to that?'

Captain Harding shrugged his shoulders and replied, 'I am equally astonished to hear it.'

'Are you?' his mother replied. 'Shall I go on?'

'There is no need.' He sighed with resignation. 'Emma, my mother has discovered something I have, without success, endeavoured to conceal. I suppose it must come out eventually.'

'What is it?' said Lady Allersham.

'Say it,' Mrs Fowle instructed her son.

'Mr Brooks made me his sole beneficiary.'

'Yes, I know,' said Lady Allersham. 'You said so. He left you a chaise and four.'

'And a great deal of land and property into the bargain,' Mrs Fowle added.

Lady Allersham looked at her cousin with astonishment. 'How wonderful! Robert? Is it true? Why did you not say?'

'Why?' said he. 'I had a rather foolish notion that were I to contemplate matrimony, I had no wish to allow the possession of a good fortune to determine my partner in life.'

'I knew it! This is all to do with Miss Shaw,' said Mrs Fowle, sighing in exasperation. 'I see how it is.'

Lady Allersham looked to her cousin for a response.

'A man is no less capable of having his heart broken at least once in his life. It is not the sole province of woman.'

'My son was completely taken in by Miss Shaw, as I knew he would be,' said Mrs Fowle. 'But it was a great relief to me when she cried off. She received a better offer. But she will be very sorry indeed when she hears what she has lost. And I shall make sure she hears every word of it.'

'No. No,' said he, with uncommon firmness. 'None of this is to be spoken of to anyone. I insist that it goes no further,' said he. 'I am serious. Do not oppose me in this. I will not have it spoken of.'

'My dear Cousin,' said Lady Allersham, shocked by the determination in his voice. 'Of course. I shall say nothing. Even Henry will not hear of it.'

Captain Harding quickly finished the remainder of his tea. 'You will get on better without me. I have some business in town. Stay as long as you wish, Emma. Luncheon will be provided if you desire it.'

'Thank you, Cousin,' Lady Allersham replied.

'Please excuse me,' said he, and without another word he took his leave.

When the door was shut firmly behind him, Lady Allersham sought a fuller explanation from her aunt.

Mrs Fowle explained that the business dealings of old Mr Brooks, Dr Harding's great friend, had been something of a mystery, and though it was thought

159

that he had lived the latter part of his life in reduced circumstances, a chance remark in Chichester had led to further enquiries. The remark had come from the attorney of a former client whose land had been acquired by Mr Brooks some years earlier.

'I do not know the extent of my son's fortune,' said Mrs Fowle, 'but I understand it to be considerable.'

Lady Allersham went over in her mind certain past remarks made by her cousin. 'I cannot understand why he went out of his way to give the impression that he had no fortune. I suppose his explanation must indeed be true. I never thought my cousin a true romantic, but he must desire to marry for love after all.'

'That is because you saw nothing first hand of the nonsense with Miss Shaw,' said Mrs Fowle.

'Does Mr Fowle know?' enquired Lady Allersham.

'He does not, and I have no mind to tell *him*.' Mrs Fowle fought to keep her feelings about her husband in check. 'Mr Fowle is not himself at present. I hesitate to speak so, I really do, but I cannot conceal matters for much longer. Mr Fowle is plagued by despondency brought on by Mr Granby's popularity in Brinshore. Had Mr Granby confined himself to Sanditon, according to the understanding reached when first he left Delham, Mr Fowle might have borne it better. But there it is. And I shall not, at present, trouble Mr Fowle with the business of old Mr Brook's will. I blame Aunt Turner for this and your grandmother. Between them, they contrived to send Mr Granby to Sanditon. And now the consequences are plain to see.'

'If not Mr Granby, some other young man would likely have acted in just such a fashion,' said Lady Allersham. 'But what concerns me more is Cousin Robert. I shall endeavour to keep my cousin's secret, however great the temptation to reveal it might be. In one quarter at least, such knowledge would, I suspect, be received with great interest.'

Lady Allersham would say no more for fear of disclosing something she suspected to be the case but of which she had no proof. Nevertheless, thought she, when the time comes, if it should come, Lady Dalrymple might be pleased to find that Captain Harding's portrayal of himself as a pauper is as far from the truth as Aunt Fowle's portrayal of married bliss.

CHAPTER SEVENTEEN

Lady Allersham returned to Laura Place to news that the Dalrymples had gone to Bristol. The decision was as sudden as it was astonishing. They had waited for half an hour for Lady Allersham's return but could delay their journey no longer as they were expected in Bristol by six o'clock. The reason for their departure, Mrs Beresford explained, was Miss Carteret's resolve to attend Miss Elliot's wedding.

'I commend Miss Carteret,' said she, who had received their neighbours in Lady Allersham's absence. 'She was anxious not to snub the Elliots. I thought that very noble of her. Lady Dalrymple was not possessed of the same scruples but did not wish to stand in her daughter's way, I suppose. It seems an invitation to the wedding was received from Sir Walter who was most anxious that they attend, although a letter announcing Miss Elliot's engagement had never come. Sir Walter, it appears, was very apologetic. You may recall, Lady Dalrymple first heard of it from Captain Harding of all people and she was not well pleased. But a profusion of apologies, accompanied by a similar surfeit of excuses for the unforgivable oversight, has done the trick. In the end, Miss Carteret was eager to go to Bristol and Lady Dalrymple raised no objection. I had not expected to change my view, but I now believe Laura Place will be the poorer for their absence.'

'How long do they intend to remain in Bristol?' said Lady Allersham.

'Lady Dalrymple could not say,' Mrs Beresford replied. 'The wedding is to take place there. Kellynch was offered at first but Sir Walter turned it down. I suspect, as landlord rather than master, it was a matter of pride: he did not wish to see his daughter married from there if he were but a guest in his own home. Nonetheless, I thought it a most generous offer from Admiral Croft, for it seems Mrs Croft enjoys indifferent health at present and might just as easily have had good reason not to issue an invitation at all. Captain and Mrs Wentworth are pleased with Bristol due to its proximity to their home, as they are also expected to attend. And Lady Russell is certain to be one of the party.'

The wedding of Miss Elliot had not been expected so soon, but the announcement suited Miss Carteret perfectly, for she was eager to leave Bath as soon as a compelling excuse was found. The invitation to attend Miss Elliot's nuptials, which might otherwise have been received with wry indifference, was now seized upon with resounding eagerness. Miss Carteret saw a way out of her predicament: the wedding of Sir Walter's daughter was the best possible explanation for the suddenness with which they had quit Bath. She found little to ponder or regret once her mind was made up, except the loss of their neighbours' society; and even then, any continuation of the intimacy both she and her mother had enjoyed with the Allersham set would further increase the chance of discovery. Hence, it had to be ended. The incident at the ball had served to emphasise the increasing risk of exposure if Mrs Baldwin remained in Bath. Captain Harding had given his word, and Miss Carteret had believed his pledge of silence; but the presence of her former friend gave her no peace, for *her* discretion could not be relied on. The regret felt by Miss Carteret was great; had she resisted concealment, had she spoken to Lady Allersham when the opportunity had first arisen, she should not have felt the depth of self-reproach that now consumed her.

'And they gave no indication when they might return to Laura Place?' Lady Allersham enquired.

'No,' replied Mrs Beresford.

'How strange. I had not thought the society of Sir Walter held so much appeal.'

'The Dalrymples attended Miss Anne Elliot's wedding. I expect they did not wish to snub Miss Elliot.'

'Yes, of course,' replied Lady Allersham. 'Miss Carteret is fastidious in such matters, though I expect Lady Dalrymple took some persuading.'

The dinner, given in honour of Mr and Mrs Fowle, was anticipated with a certain degree of apprehension.

There were six in all who sat down at eight o'clock. A reluctant Captain Harding was the only other guest in attendance and would have wished himself elsewhere but for the fact that he had no desire to disoblige his cousin. James Beresford sent apologies, having found that another commitment established some time ago could not be given up.

The conversation progressed without pause and continued well into late evening, driven along for the most part by Mrs Fowle.

'Emma, my dear,' said she, 'you would not believe your eyes were you to see the changes that have occurred in Sanditon. It has become very shabby. Very shabby indeed. I was astonished when we had occasion to pass through the town on our way here. Had there been a better road we should have taken it, but there is no more direct route than through Sanditon and so we were obliged to make the best of it.'

'Sanditon is the bane of our lives,' said Mr Fowle. 'Is it not, my love?'

'We were shocked by what we saw,' Mrs Fowle replied, 'and stopped there but ten minutes to visit the Blakes. I do not know what they find to be so cheerful about when they are obliged to live in such a place. Captain Blake's mother was there. She is to stay in Sanditon for one month complete. She promised to visit Brinshore on our return before setting out for Delham, for she is anxious to hear news of *dear Emma*. I expect she looks for any excuse to leave Sanditon when she can. Mr Fowle and I offered to break our return journey and bring the news ourselves, but Mrs Blake would not hear of it. There, you see, one will make almost any excuse to run away from Sanditon. Is that not so, Mr Fowle?'

'Yes, my love,' said he.

'Cousin,' said Lady Allersham, with a mischevious grin, 'do you plan to visit Brinshore? Or shall you quit Bath for Brighton before the season ends?'

'Neither,' said Captain Harding. 'I have no plans to vacate my present situation.'

'I expect you have heard that Lady Dalrymple and her daughter have quit Bath,' said Lady Allersham. 'We do not know when to look for their return, but I hope they will not stay away long.'

Captain Harding received the news with surprise. 'A rather sudden decision, is it not?'

'They are gone to Bristol,' said Mrs Beresford. 'Miss Elliot is to be married from there.'

'How did Miss Carteret seem?' said he.

'A little tired, I thought,' said Mrs Beresford.

'Why do you ask?' Lady Allersham enquired.

'I called on Miss Carteret the morning after the ball,' said he.

'You came to Laura Place?' replied Lady Allersham.

'Miss Carteret was taken ill at the ball, I believe,' said he.

'Yes. She seemed well, even animated, at first, and suddenly she was not. How did you find her?'

'I did not find her at all. She was indisposed. I sat for ten minutes with Lady Dalrymple and left,' said he.

'Perhaps she has a weak constitution, for she is often. ill. Poor Miss Carteret. Mr Fowle, can you recommend a tonic for a weak constitution?' said Lady Allersham.

'Certainly, I can. A most effective one,' said he.

Mrs Fowle ignored her husband, for her attention was fixed on her son and the interesting change she observed in his expression when Miss Carteret's name was mentioned. She was desirous of knowing more about the family.

Lord Allersham obliged with a short account of the Dalrymples, their rank, connexions and situation.

'So, she is an *honourable*. The Honourable Miss Carteret, daughter of the Dowager Viscountess Dalrymple,' said Mrs Fowle. Her countenance brightened. 'She must be three or four and twenty, I suppose. And not married. Is she plain and thin? Has she no fortune to speak of?'

'I expect she has,' said Lord Allersham, 'but she does not speak of it.'

'And we have no particular reason to speak of it either,' Lady Allersham added.

Mrs Fowle looked pointedly at her son.

'You may think what you will,' said Captain Harding to his mother, 'but leave me out of it. I am of no interest to Miss Carteret, I assure you.'

'But you might take the trouble to make yourself of interest, especially to the daughter of a viscount. I am sure your cousin would agree. Miss Carteret seems infinitely more —'

'Thank you,' said Captain Harding, quickly. 'That Miss Carteret is a viscount's daughter is of no interest to me. I shall manage my own affairs, and when I am disposed to contemplate matrimony, I shall inform you of it in my own time and in my own way.'

'See that you do,' said Mrs Fowle.

'My love,' Mr Fowle added, 'I do not wish to appear indelicate, but Miss Carteret is perhaps a little high, a little out of reach. Rank and fortune matter just as much to young people, as —'

'My dear Mr Fowle,' said Mrs Fowle, 'Miss Carteret could do worse. After all she is almost an old maid.'

'Have you news of Osborne Castle, Mrs Fowle? How does Master Frank go on? I expect he is much grown since last I saw him,' said Mrs Beresford, in an attempt to change the topic.

'He looks just like his father,' said Mrs Fowle, 'and is becoming quite the young man.' Turning to her husband, she added, 'And for all your talk of rank and fortune, might I remind you that my sister had no fortune to bring to her marriage and yet no one else would do for Lord Osborne.'

'Yes. I can vouch for my brother. Both my brother and I have been so very happy in our choice of partners,' said Mrs Beresford. 'I hear that Master Frank has a pony now and shows great promise.'

'My little brother has impressed them all at Osborne Castle with his riding,' said Lady Allersham.

'Do you still ride, Emma?' said Captain Harding. 'I remember you were a keen horsewoman once upon a time.'

'I am as keen a rider as ever I was and have often presented a challenge to Henry. We ride at Allersham.'

'Emma likes to race,' said Lord Allersham.

'He pretends to let me win. I win fair and square, of course,' said she. 'But I do not ride in Bath. Bath is for walkers.'

'Walkers are in great supply in Bath,' said Mr Fowle.

'But Brinshore has the edge over Bath, I believe,' replied Mrs Fowle. 'Streets, shore, lanes and terraces are so very accessible to walkers in Brinshore. Bath has its charms, of course, but the air here is vastly different and compares quite unfavourably with our fresh sea air.'

'My love, I could not have put it any better myself,' said Mr Fowle. 'Little persuasion is needed, I'm sure, to convince the residents of Bath that Brinshore is entirely worthy of their patronage. Our minds are at one in this endeavour. Are they not, my love?'

Mrs Fowle feigned a smile to mask the extent of her exasperation with Mr Fowle. 'I expect you find all this talk of Brinshore quite tiresome. It is not quite the paradise that it once was.'

Mrs Fowle knew that she had touched a nerve; her husband began to stiffen, darting a look of disapproval in her direction. It made no difference, for Mrs Fowle would not be silenced. 'Mr Granby has established something of reputation for himself in Sanditon and is now setting his sights on Brinshore. He is young, active, charming and amiable. The ladies like him a great deal. And he does not charge extortionate prices.'

Incensed by his wife's disclosure, Mr Fowle replied, 'My love, Granby is a fraud. He has little to speak of in the way of experience, has no learning in the field of science and gets by on his wits alone. I have seen how he operates.'

'As have I. Indeed, when I suffered from a rather unpleasant bilious attack brought on by something I do not care to mention,' said Mrs Fowle, with a glaring and resentful look directed at her husband, 'I seem to recall that you were quite dismissive. And so,

I sought Mr Granby's help. Do not look so shocked! What a delightful man! How charming! He quite won me over. Mr Granby recommended a special tonic of his own making. I was amazed. Quite amazed. One dose cured me in an instant. And he refused to take a penny for his trouble. Mrs Fowle, said he, I cannot begin to tell you what an honour it is to be of service to the enchanting wife of the famous and revered Mr Fowle. Those were his precise words. And I would send for him again if I had need of him.'

Silence fell as heads were bowed to suppress embarrassment and stifle amusement. But there was nowhere to hide from the looks of rage and indignation that passed between Mr and Mrs Fowle. At length, a disconcerted Lady Allersham broke the silence.

'Mr Wood is our man in Bath. He is widely recommended. We had need of him not long ago for poor Miss Fox.'

'Miss Fox?' said Mrs Fowle.

'I haven't mentioned Miss Fox, have I? She will come to Laura Place tomorrow afternoon and I daresay if the weather holds and you are tempted to make Laura Place your object too, you shall find her here.'

Mr Fowle continued in silence, reeling from the humiliation wrought by his wife's injurious words. Nothing could be done to cure the tension in the room that had arisen between them. To linger at the table would hardly have improved matters, and so Lady Allersham decided that the time had come to leave the gentlemen in peace. She stood up and led the way into the drawing room; and, with some relief,

Mrs Fowle and Mrs Beresford followed immediately afterwards.

'Perhaps I was a little unkind to Mr Fowle, but no more than he deserves.' Mrs Fowle sighed. 'I should not mind it, but he is possessed by such bitterness towards Mr Granby though the poor young man has done nothing to deserve it. Mr Fowle will not be told. I have tried and tried to impress upon him that speaking ill of Mr Granby to his patients does him no good at all. That is the reason half of them went over to Mr Granby in the first place. And I do not blame them. But let us speak of happier things, Emma. Tell me more about Miss Fox. Will she do for Robert if Miss Carteret will not?'

Lady Allersham and Mrs Beresford narrated in full their dealings with Miss Fox. Her story raised Mrs Fowle's interest, not least for the belief she expressed of having a superior talent for unravelling mysteries.

'My son is the biggest mystery of all,' said she. 'He can be so guarded at times and then at others candid to the point of imprudence. I cannot imagine who he takes after. It must be his father.'

'I thought Dr Harding mild mannered and yielding,' said Lady Allersham.

Mrs Beresford and Lady Allersham glanced at each other in silent bemusement.

'My son bears no likeness to his poor long-suffering mother,' Mrs Fowle continued, sighing deeply.

Having exhausted the subject of her son's failings, Mrs Fowle returned to a matter of greater interest: the question of an alliance. 'If he *should* marry Miss Carteret, I might visit from time to time. A month or two away from Mr Fowle would do me the world of good. It would suit me very well indeed to see my son settled at last. And what better place than Bath.'

'But, Aunt,' said Lady Allersham, 'would you not miss Brinshore?'

'I would, of course,' said Mrs Fowle. 'But that is all I should miss. Your mama understands. Osborne Castle has often been my refuge from Mr Fowle's melancholic tantrums.'

CHAPTER EIGHTEEN

Since her return to Gay Street, Miss Fox had been shown more leniency by Mrs Price than she had anticipated, and she concluded that the change in her mistress's demands must have been the work of Lady Allersham. The news that she was to visit Laura Place one afternoon in seven was both a pleasing prospect and a daunting one. Having received no notice in advance of the duties required of her by Lady Allersham, Miss Fox arrived at the appointed hour unprepared but eager to undertake whatever was expected of her, and to the best of her ability.

Laura Place was quiet, a pleasant relief from the constant noise and commotion of Gay Street. On being admitted to the building, Miss Fox was shown into the drawing room where she awaited further direction. It occurred to her that Lady Allersham might be from home, and that she might, therefore, receive her duties by means of the housekeeper or footman, and having previously received nothing but kindness from the highest to the lowliest in Laura Place, she was happy to have the opportunity to repay that kindness in any way she could. She sat cautiously on the edge of the chair, ready for the order to begin.

After several minutes the door opened and Lady Allersham entered.

'Forgive me, Miss Fox,' said she, 'I hope you have not been waiting long. Where *does* the time go?'

Miss Fox stood to greet Lady Allersham, curtsied, smiled at her patroness, and awaited instructions.

'The weather is not too promising,' Lady Allersham continued, 'so we shall stay by the fire until the hour for tea.'

'How might I assist Your Ladyship?' said Miss Fox. 'I understand that I am to undertake certain duties.'

'Yes. Indeed,' said Lady Allersham, turning over in her mind the possible tasks Miss Fox might usefully perform. 'Should you like a little needlework? Or are you tired of it? Are your fingertips sore?'

'I am told my stitching is neat and tidy, Your Ladyship,' said Miss Fox.

'Well then,' said Lady Allersham, 'I should like you to make some alterations to a rather pretty gown, if you will.'

'I should be very happy to do so. I am used to such work,' said Miss Fox, relieved to find that she had been given a task she was equal to undertake.

Lady Allersham went in search of an item of clothing from her own wardrobe and returned several minutes later with a fine muslin gown of pale yellow. She draped it over the sofa and smoothed out the creases.

'There,' said Lady Allersham. 'Will that do?'

'It is the prettiest gown I have ever seen,' said Miss Fox.

'The sleeves are a little tight, I find,' Her Ladyship replied.

Miss Fox examined the gown to see if the sleeves might be let out.

'What is your opinion?' enquired Lady Allersham.

'There is just room enough to let out the sleeve by almost half an inch,' said Miss Fox.

'Oh dear,' said Lady Allersham, 'I am afraid to say that half an inch will not do. It would need to be an inch at least.'

Miss Fox pondered how she might undertake the task without ruining the overall appearance of the gown. 'Perhaps I could take a small piece of muslin from the inside hem and place it into the sleeve under the arm where it will not show,' said Miss Fox, hopefully.

'I see,' Lady Allersham replied.

'I should of course take the greatest of care with it. You have my assurance — the gown would not be spoilt,' said Miss Fox.

'Let me see,' said Lady Allersham, holding the gown next to her skin. She looked at herself in the mirror and said, 'I do not think pale yellow becomes me at all well,' said Lady Allersham.

'Oh, indeed it does, Your Ladyship,' said Miss Fox. 'It is such a pretty shade that it complements Your Ladyship in every way.'

'Place the gown against you,' said Lady Allersham. 'Let me see how it looks. You will need to stand up straight and come over to the window to catch the light.'

Confused by the request, Miss Fox hesitated to do as instructed.

'Come,' said Lady Allersham.

Miss Fox complied with Her Ladyship's request and timidly stood holding the gown up to her chin.

Lady Allersham stepped back to examine the gown for colour and size.

'Pale yellow becomes *you* very well,' said Lady Allersham. 'The gown is a little too long at present, but the sleeves and the bodice will require very little adjustment if at all. The hem will need taking up by two inches. Can you do that?'

Miss Fox protested the idea and declared that she could not possibly accept such a commission.

'Nevertheless,' said Lady Allersham, 'it is what I should like you to do. It is a gown I have worn only once, and it has not seen the light of day in Bath.'

Surprised by Lady Allersham's remark, Miss Fox looked up.

'I realise one of the Ibbotson sisters lent you a gown, the one you wore for the ball at the Upper Rooms. It was, perhaps, well-meaning in its own way, but it was not so very kind of the younger Miss Ibbotson to declare it to all and sundry. Now, Miss Fox, this will be your task for the duration of your visit. And when it is accomplished I shall see that the gown is pressed and fresh and delivered to Gay Street.'

'I cannot —'

'I know that you did not expect to undertake such a task,' said Lady Allersham, 'but be at ease. We shall not speak of it again. And when Miss Ibbotson invites you to the Upper Rooms, you shall not be in her debt for you shall have your own gown.'

Miss Fox smiled shyly and began with hesitation to unpick the hem of the gown according to Lady Allersham's instructions; at the same time, Lady Allersham sorted through a basket of darning belonging to Mrs Beresford. She had never darned anything neatly in her life before but, willing to be industrious on this occasion, she set about the task with greater optimism than skill.

'Tell me,' said she, 'how did you enjoy the ball?'

'It was very grand. The ladies were very elegant,' replied Miss Fox.

'Some of them, perhaps,' said she. 'I know you did not dance every dance, but were you pleased with your partners?'

'Yes. I could not have had better partners. Captain Harding and Mr Beresford are excellent dancers. I forgot the steps and trod on Mr Beresford's toe, but he did not seem to mind it,' said Miss Fox. 'I happened upon Mr Beresford on my way to Laura Place.'

'Oh?' said Lady Allersham.

'He did not see me. I believe he was much occupied with his own thoughts.'

The sound of commotion in the hall outside reminded Lady Allersham that Mrs Fowle had promised to call if the weather permitted. She quickly directed Miss Fox to put down her needlework and take the dress through to the dining room so that it would not been seen.

Miss Fox did as she was instructed, returning to the drawing room moments before Mrs Fowle entered.

'I nearly did not set out at all for the clouds threaten rain,' said Mrs Fowle. 'Mr Fowle is gone out. I urged him to stay out for as long as he wished. I should not mind if it were the entire day nor, I believe, should my son. Mr Fowle, said I, I have no need of you today. But I know how it will be, for he never keeps his promise. It is all the same with men.

They are never there when they are needed and yet constantly in the way when they are not. And he often returns an hour, or even two, before he is expected. He cares not one whit that my peace is disturbed. Miss Fox, allow me to give you some advice. Do not marry if you can possibly avoid it, and if you cannot, make sure you marry a man whose pride is not injured over the smallest trifle.'

'Dear Aunt,' said Lady Allersham, 'I am sure Miss Fox will choose wisely.'

Miss Fox raised a timid smile. 'I do not think I shall ever marry.'

'You are wise beyond your years, Miss Fox. I do not know what possessed me to marry Mr Fowle.'

'Miss Fox's friend, Miss Dauber, is due to marry, and Miss Fox is to attend the wedding in Whitcombe,' said Lady Allersham.

'Whitcombe?' said Mrs Fowle. 'Is Mrs Beresford acquainted with the Daubers?'

'Miss Dauber is the Rector's daughter,' said Lady Allersham.

'Then her father must have buried Colonel Beresford,' Mrs Fowle replied.

'Yes, indeed,' said Lady Allersham.

'Mr Dauber once spoke of the Colonel,' said Miss Fox, 'but I cannot recall what he said.'

'How well do you remember Colonel Beresford, Aunt?' said Lady Allersham.

'I was acquainted with him briefly before your mama entered into matrimony. I recall the night of the famous Osborne Ball. It is clearly fixed in my memory, for it was the first time I had seen the inside of Osborne Castle. That was the night, Emma, your father amazed the entire neighbourhood.'

'Was that the first time he danced with Mama?'

'It was the first time he danced at all. But that was not the amazing part. I remember he had cut his hair. We did not recognise him. A crop was quite the new fashion then, of course. Your Uncle Musgrave had put him up to it. And we were all amazed, for he looked so very handsome as a crop. No one could imagine what had brought about the change in him. Your father never danced, you see, but that night it was as though Lord Osborne had become a different person altogether. In secret, your Uncle Musgrave had engaged the services of a dancing master who was held responsible for your father's transformation. And I am sure that it was all accomplished for the sake of love. You see, Miss Fox, as a consequence, Lady Allersham's father and my sister married, and she without a penny to her name.'

CHAPTER NINETEEN

The joyful event at Bristol, which was concluded to the satisfaction of one family and the forbearance of the other, took place without impediment, and to the relief of all. The Musgraves were neither present nor missed, except by the Wentworths, who were perplexed by their absence. Lady Dalrymple suspected the cause to be a simple one: a deficiency of rank and consequence in the Uppercross family would render the bride's family indistinguishable from the corresponding ranks of the groom's family, and therefore their presence at the ceremony was not wholly desirable.

Sir Walter dismissed the matter, claiming the reason for their absence was the great distance between Uppercross and Bristol. Anne Wentworth was deeply pained by her father's slight; nor could she forgive him for giving precedence to the pretentions of rank over the bonds of family. Lady Russell was less inclined to question Sir Walter's motives, and declared that an additional thirty miles travelled in indifferent weather was explanation enough and showed great understanding for the difficulty that the Uppercross family would likely encounter on the road. Captain Wentworth was unconvinced and reminded them that an alternative proposal had been made, pointing to Admiral Croft's offer of Kellynch, an offer which had been declined both by Sir Walter and Miss Elliot. Anne was certain that Mary would be exceedingly disappointed not to attend her sister's wedding. It had always been the case that Mary Musgrove had more enjoyment of such occasions than Anne and would not have allowed thirty miles of inclement weather to stand in her way of a wedding breakfast.

The church, which was more modest than Sir Walter would have desired, was almost half full, but the disproportionate division between the guests was striking; twice the number of guests made up the groom's side, while the bride boasted only five guests in all: Lady Dalrymple and Miss Carteret, Lady Russell and Captain and Mrs Wentworth. A cursory glance at the groom's family, however, gave Sir Walter the satisfaction he desired, for though fewer in number, the Elliot party outranked every guest in the opposing pews by a considerable degree.

Miss Elliot appeared pleased with herself despite the verdict of Lady Dalrymple on the difference in age and situation between the bride and groom. 'An improbable pair,' said she. 'The groom something of an oddity, the bride the picture of relief and resignation. I believe Miss Elliot thought only of her flight from spinsterhood.'

No longer would the word "spinster" be applied, no longer would Sir Walter's daughter be pitied and derided for her failure to secure a husband; nor would "poor Miss Elliot" again be obliged to give way to her married sisters or die an old maid; and if marrying into trade to achieve her object was the only path available to her, it was a necessary and prudent one.

Anne led the way and was first among the Elliot set to wish them joy with the warmth and sincerity of true sisterly affection. Miss Carteret followed and wished the happy couple a long and prosperous union. Lady Russell had expected Elizabeth Elliot to do better but was sanguine about her prospects — a bridegroom with three thousand pounds a year would surely prove compensation enough for any deficiency of breeding and refinement. What surprised Lady Dalrymple more than anything was Sir Walter's ability to overlook certain defects in his new son-in-law, a man who appeared to exhibit none of the qualities present in his father-in-law: vanity, excess or affectation.

'Sir Walter,' said Lady Dalrymple to Lady Russell, in a whisper, 'sees the means by which he might regain Kellynch. He believes his son-in-law's money will do the trick. And as far as Kellynch is concerned there is just enough veneration for rank and title on the groom's side to give Sir Walter some hope of succeeding.'

Lady Russell reluctantly could not disagree. 'The groom's mother is said to be the distant cousin of a baronet. I suppose that is some consolation.'

'And yet, too distant to invite their only connexion of rank to the wedding,' said Lady Dalrymple.

'Indeed,' she replied.

'It did not prevent every other relative and hanger-on descending on Bristol. What an assortment of curiosities! I applaud Sir Walter for his forbearance. I had not thought it possible. Let us see how far his tolerance extends. The Musgroves seem positively noble by comparison. I rather think his son-in-law will be disappointed in Sir Walter. Let me see them stroll side by side the length of Milsom Street and I shall take back every word.'

'Sir Walter will not return to Bath,' said Lady Russell.

'Oh? Is he to remain in Bristol? I had not thought it possible,' said Lady Dalrymple, with surprise.

'Sir Walter has made up his mind to visit the Wentworths after the wedding,' said Lady Russell. 'Poor Anne. I know well what his object is. Kellynch, of course. He will expect Anne to work on Captain Wentworth, and for Captain Wentworth to persuade the Crofts to find a tenancy elsewhere. Anne will do nothing of the kind, of course. But Wentworth may comply to keep the peace. That is why I intend to return with the Wentworths myself, for I am determined to oppose Sir Walter. The voice of moderation must and will be heard.'

'Then I wish you every success,' said Lady Dalrymple, doubtfully. 'I thank my blessings that I have no room in Laura Place to accommodate him, and even if I had, the thought would not enter my head. I wonder how far the Wentworths' patience will extend? How long will they tolerate his presence among them?'

Lady Russell looked across to where Miss Carteret was sitting. She had hardly uttered a sentence all day. 'Miss Carteret does not seem herself today,' said she.

Lady Dalrymple glanced at her daughter. 'Ever since we left Bath, she has been like this. I pay little attention to it. She gives way too easily to gloomy thoughts.'

'And yet,' said Lady Russell, 'she was most insistent on attending the wedding.'

'I suspect she glimpses her own future in Miss Elliot, or even worse, the prospect that she may not secure an alliance of her own. I have not pressed the matter. Perhaps I should have been more forthright. Jane has no need to marry. She is not poor, for we do not live to excess like Sir Walter,' said Lady Dalrymple.

'A husband can be a blessing and a curse,' said Lady Russell.

'My view entirely,' said Lady Dalrymple. 'The late Viscount was a blessing and a curse in equal measure. I could not ask for more than that. If only there were such a man as he.'

'Surely suitors are plentiful in Bath,' said Lady Russell.

'Jane never speaks to me about such matters. She hardly appears to show an interest in matrimony at all,' said Lady Dalrymple. 'I do not know what thoughts occupy her mind.' She sighed. 'Jane is not so plain as she appears at times, but she is rarely disposed to make an effort. If only she would make the most of herself.'

Miss Carteret, seeing that she was the object of attention, sat quietly at a distance caring little for the views and opinions that passed between her mother and Lady Russell. Her thoughts were elsewhere; chief among them was the alarming prospect of returning to Bath too soon, a matter she now pondered with trepidation. If it were in her power to delay the inevitable for a fortnight at least, then she might rest assured that their neighbours in Laura Place would almost certainly have quitted Bath for Allersham Park.

The name that was once so dear to her was never far from her thoughts. She had, in vain, endeavoured to put Captain Fitzroy out of her head forever. Never again would she hear his voice, but his words would fill her mind, words crafted in ink, faded over time, on paper worn out through constant unfolding. He would not age as she would, and yet the memory of his likeness, his look, his expression, had started to fade, like ink, with the passage of time; even the exercise of concentration would not bring his image back to her completely. She was losing Captain Fitzroy, not as before, suddenly and palpably, but slowly and surreptitiously.

Ever vigilant, ever on her guard against a chance utterance that might bear the name *Fitzroy*, Jane Carteret had cultivated a disposition of mind that had, for the most part, served her well in Laura Place, and even among her acquaintance in Bath, until the advent of Mrs Baldwin. On first reading of Lady Allersham's arrival in the *Chronicle*, she had prepared herself, half apprehensive, half riven with curious anticipation. The appearance of composure had prevailed; she had conquered her fear; she was safe. But soon came the test: for there before her in the form of Lord Allersham was a hint of his brother, and in Lady Allersham she saw the destiny that had been denied her, the prospect of what might have been, of what could now never be.

Had she mustered the courage to speak, had she confessed all to Lady Allersham, the feelings she had sought to disown might have found proper expression and relief. But her courage had failed her. Beset by self-reproach, Miss Carteret had become a feeble and faint shadow of the person she once was, the person to whom Captain Fitzroy had once given his heart. Had he lived, would he have loved her still?

She was stirred from her reverie by the voice of Anne Wentworth.

'I saw you sitting alone,' said she. 'If you do so by design, I shall leave you in peace.'

'No, not at all,' said Miss Carteret.

Mrs Wentworth sat down beside her. 'Thank you,' said she. 'I fear I may say something I should later regret were I to remain in the company of my father too long. My sister Mary will feel slighted, and justly so, when she hears that Elizabeth is married. It seems Mary was denied an invitation and yet her enjoyment of the event would have been far greater than mine.'

'I remember Mrs Musgrove. We met in Bath three or four seasons ago, I believe. Mr Musgrove's sister was there to purchase wedding clothes.'

'Yes, indeed,' replied Anne Wentworth. 'Henrietta is now blessed with two daughters and her sister Louisa has a son.'

'I understand Sir Walter and Lady Russell are to return with you when you leave Bristol.'

'They are indeed,' said Anne. 'I am fortunate to have a tolerant husband, a quality learnt, I believe, in the Navy.'

'How does Captain Wentworth like to be on dry land?' said Miss Carteret.

'Occasionally we visit our friends, the Harvilles, at Lyme. We stroll by the shore and he gazes at the sea with a distant expression in his eyes. I have sometimes noticed a look — of longing, perhaps, or fond remembrance. Mrs Harville tells me all men of the Navy have that look from time to time. I am thankful, for his sake, that the society of his fellow officers endures as it does.'

Miss Carteret looked into the distance and smiled weakly but made no reply.

'I recognise *that* look,' said Anne, searching her companion's face. 'Would you walk with me, Miss Carteret? There is a pretty path by the church. We will not be missed or disturbed.'

Relieved to exchange the dissonant voices of a crowded room for the tranquillity of a country lane, Miss Carteret agreed to Anne's proposal.

'It is a beautiful sight, is it not?' said Anne. 'It is the third time this week I have walked here.'

'Do you like to walk?' Miss Carteret replied.

'It is my habit to walk every day, even in the wet, and Frederick's too.'

'I do not walk as often as I should like, though I have lately enjoyed several walks in Bath in the company of Lady Allersham,' said Miss Carteret.

'I have heard Lady Russell speak of her nephew, Lord Allersham, but I have never met Lady Allersham,' said Mrs Wentworth.

They walked for some minutes before she continued, 'Forgive me if I speak plainly, Miss Carteret. On several occasions I could not help noticing that you seemed a little out of sorts. Please do not suppose me inquisitive for my own sake. Nothing could be further from my mind. I speak only out of regard and concern for *you*. Like many women before me, I know through bitter experience what it is to suffer alone and in silence. Whatever troubles you, if it be in your power to do so, I would urge you to confide in a trusted friend. Lady Allersham, perhaps?'

'I cannot,' said she. 'There is no one in whom I can confide.'

'When I was but eighteen, I fell in love. Lady Russell, whose intentions were good and honourable, counselled me to decline Captain Wentworth's offer of marriage. What followed was eight years of regret. I thought he was lost to me forever.'

They walked the length of the lane to the farthest extent of the churchyard wall before Miss Carteret broke her silence.

'May I tell you the story of a young woman who was also eighteen when she fell in love?' said Miss Carteret.

For half an hour more, they walked on until the story had been told. Desirous of avoiding detection, Miss Carteret left names and places unspoken, and obscured specific details that might have led her listener to a more complete understanding of the matter than she was inclined to supply.

Anne Wentworth listened rather than advised, and sought none of the particulars. Judgement was withheld, supposition spurned, and astonishment kept in check. The tragic circumstances of the case when compared to her own good fortune were ever present in her thoughts as she listened to Miss Carteret's narration. Anne Wentworth felt only sadness for the young woman who had loved at eighteen and whose dreams had been dashed by the cruellest of events. Every element of the account occasioned her sincerest sympathy, and Miss Carteret felt, as she had not had cause to do so before, the kindness of Anne Wentworth.

They had been acquainted for several years, the first season the Dalrymples came to Bath, the season Sir Walter quitted Kellynch for Camden Place. Neither Miss Carteret nor Anne Wentworth had cultivated the acquaintance. Anne had spent more time in Westgate Buildings with her friend Mrs Smith than in Laura Place with the Dalrymples. She had thought Miss Carteret aloof, superior and lacking in cordiality. But she now comprehended that she had judged harshly, for Miss Carteret was stricken with grief and of necessity had cloaked those emotions in a cold exterior. The sudden loss of the person who might have brought her the greatest joy and comfort so soon after her uncle's death had been almost too much to bear. Anne could see that the appearance of her cousins in the shape of the Elliot family at that moment had provided no comfort at all.

'I had no one to whom I could turn but for a friend whose discretion I relied on,' said Miss Carteret. 'I have not seen her these five years until we met by accident in the Upper Rooms. It was the work of a moment. My secret was exposed to the world when she mistook the gentlemen at my side for —'

Anne placed an arm around Miss Carteret's shoulder to comfort her. 'And now the secret you have harboured for so long is a secret no more.'

Miss Carteret nodded, unable to speak further as tears filled her eyes.

'Take this,' said Anne, placing a handkerchief in her hand. 'How widely is it known among your acquaintance in Bath?'

'I do not know,' replied Miss Carteret.

Anne Wentworth had comprehended considerably more than Miss Carteret's account had provided for she understood precisely why Miss Carteret had not chosen to confide in Lady Allersham. Officers of the Navy who die with distinction are not easily forgotten, and although she had never been acquainted with the deceased, she had heard Frederick speak of him: once during a dinner with the Crofts at Kellynch, and once with the Harvilles at Lyme. To be in possession of such knowledge presented Anne with a dilemma. Her aim was now to bring relief of some kind, to ease Miss Carteret's affliction; but each measure that came to mind risked the pledge of her silence.

Later that evening, when Captain and Mrs Wentworth were alone, and a review of the day's events had been recounted between them, and every detail exhausted, the subject of their son, Master Frederick, arose. He had been left to the capable care of his nanny who thought him too young to travel. Anne missed her son and was anxious not to delay their stay in Bristol longer than necessary. Captain Wentworth welcomed the idea and observed that he was of the same mind and saw no reason to extend their stay for three days more. They would leave the following day if the fine weather prevailed.

'And should Lady Russell wish to stay longer, she may accompany your father at their mutual convenience,' said Captain Wentworth.

Anne sat down beside him and placed his hand in hers. 'I was vexed with my father today,' said she.

'And you were not alone,' he replied. 'The Musgroves may not have travelled as far as Bristol, but the decision to decline an invitation on the sufficient grounds of weather and distance should have been placed within their power.'

'Poor Mary,' said she.

'Your sister will find some fragment of comfort in the business, I suppose. And more so because she will have something of substance about which to complain. She will doubtless receive more sympathy than she is used to,' said he.

Anne was lost in thoughts of her own and gave no reply. Wentworth was curious to know the subject of them.

'Weddings can be peculiar occasions, can they not?' said she.

'And none more so than the one we have just witnessed,' he replied.

'I wonder what my life would have been had we never had the good fortune to meet again,' said Anne, 'after I refused you all those years ago?'

'In a state I prefer not to contemplate,' he replied.

'Tell me, Frederick, in all the years we were apart, and you were at sea, was there anything — a word, a memory, a letter, a possession — that you turned to in moments of disquiet? Perhaps you were too preoccupied with more weighty matters.'

'Remember, I had no hope, no memory to cherish. But the object I most often wished I had within my possession was your likeness. Do you remember the day I was charged with the resetting of Captain Benwick's miniature for Louisa Musgrove?'

'The one he had commissioned at the Cape for poor Captain Harville's sister?'

'Yes,' said he.

Anne smiled at him and replied, 'How could I forget such a day?'

CHAPTER TWENTY

There had been no news from Bristol for almost a fortnight, except for a line in a letter from Lady Russell stating that the wedding had been exactly as expected, that she was to return to the Wentworths' in a day or two accompanied by Sir Walter and that she would remain there until her purpose had been accomplished. The letter was brief and gave no indication of the expected return of the Dalrymples to Laura Place but for the fact that Miss Carteret was 'pleased to have the occasion to explore Bristol's many attractions' and that a date had 'not yet been set' for their return to Bath.

Lady Allersham was disappointed in the letter for its complete lack of detail.

'What are we to understand from so unsatisfactory a description? What of the ceremony, the guests in attendance? How did the bride appear? And what of the family? I should have enjoyed reading an account of Sir Walter himself. Lady Dalrymple would have composed a more diverting missive. The wedding was *exactly as expected*. By whom, pray?'

Thankful for the lack of description, Lord Allersham declared that his aunt would likely provide a decidedly fuller account in person of those aspects of the event that she might not consider prudent to commit to pen and paper.

'Yes,' said Lady Allersham, 'Lady Russell is shrewd indeed. For if we are to hear anything of interest at all she will have to be invited to Allersham.'

'But only if curiosity outweighs all other considerations,' Lord Allersham replied. 'I should be far happier to know nothing at all about the wedding.'

'Then you will be outnumbered, my love, for I am sure I am not the only one curious to know more. Aunt, what is your opinion?'

Mrs Beresford smiled. 'I should imagine the disparity between the actual event and what we might perhaps surmise from the knowledge we already possess of the individuals concerned, is small indeed.'

'Bravo, Mrs Beresford,' said Lord Allersham, in jest. 'I might construct an account of the thing myself, and with equal accuracy, which would serve just as well.'

'If only the Dalrymples were to return to Laura Place before we are bound to quit it,' said Lady Allersham. 'I should like to see them once again, with or without an account of the wedding.'

As the time grew near for their return to Allersham Park, and the Fowles to Brinshore, Captain Harding proposed an expedition that had been put off for some time: a walk in the labyrinth. The party assembled for breakfast in Sydney Gardens, and as the morning looked promising, there was nothing to stand in the way of a good walk but idleness. Lord and Lady Allersham, Mrs Beresford and Captain Harding were to be accompanied by the Fowles and James Beresford.

'All we need to complete our party are the Dalrymples and Miss Fox,' said Lady Allersham. 'Unfortunately, the Dalrymples remain in Bristol, for I do not know how long, and Miss Fox cannot be spared. So, there we are.'

Mrs Fowle asked whether a suitable situation had been found for Miss Fox to replace her visits to Laura Place.

'The sister of Mr Ibbotson has taken lodgings in Paragon Buildings. Is that not so, Mr Beresford?' said Lady Allersham.

'It is indeed,' he replied.

'And I have heard word that Mr Ibbotson's sister has requested the services of Miss Fox. Her expectations appear moderate — some needlework and a little reading and writing from time to time, as Miss Ibbotson's eyesight is poor,' said Lady Allersham.

'What prompted Miss Ibbotson to leave her brother's establishment?' said Captain Harding.

'I believe I might have had a part in it,' said James Beresford. 'Miss Ibbotson was eager to know more about the Paragon and its neighbours. She had heard of rooms that had become available at a reasonable rent. I supplied what information I had to hand.'

Lady Allersham smiled. 'Miss Ibbotson kept you talking for some considerable time at the ball. I thought she would never release you.'

James Beresford suppressed a smile and the temptation to reply in kind. Instead, Lady Allersham was granted a slight nod of the head and was a little disappointed that it was the only response supplied.

'I hope Miss Ibbotson will not impose upon our Miss Fox,' said Lady Allersham. 'Cousin, you must keep an eye on Miss Ibbotson and make sure she does not treat Miss Fox as Mrs Price does. And you too, Mr Beresford. You shall be my spies.'

'Beresford will make a better spy than I,' said Captain Harding. 'He is perfectly situated for the endeavour.'

Once comfortably seated, and sheltered from the keen morning breeze, the party surveyed the gardens from their box. For want of something to say, all but Mrs Fowle believed the outlook was favourable for their walk.

'Why did you not advise me to wear my shawl?' said Mrs Fowle to her husband, accusingly.

'My dear, I should not be so bold as to advise you on your attire. I refuse to give advice that is certain to go unheeded,' said he. Mr Fowle looked about him and declared, 'I believe the pleasure of a public breakfast is greatly enhanced by the addition of music and, no doubt, liberal servings of Bath buns and hot buttered toast. As a physician, I consider the combination entirely wholesome and beneficial. Some arrangement of the kind would not go amiss in Brinshore. Strings, or even brass, would be a most agreeable innovation, especially by the shore. An orchestra by the sea! What a novel thought! Sydney Gardens is a very pleasant setting, a very pleasant setting indeed. But for the absence of sea and shore, Sydney Gardens has no equal.'

'Strings or brass would suit me very well and more appealing to the ear than those noises that sometimes pass for conversation. How did the parson have it last Sunday in his sermon? *If I have not charity, I am become as sounding brass or tinkling cymbal.* My love, if you would only place your chair a little further to one side, we might all admire the view a great deal better,' said Mrs Fowle.

Unmoved, and unwilling to move, Mr Fowle remarked, 'My love, might I suggest a less generous spreading of butter upon that most excellent and wholesome bun. Such a liberal portion is ill-suited to your constitution. Do not suppose me indelicate, but a surfeit of butter, or indeed sustenance of any description consumed to excess is best avoided, and more so because you, my dear, have less need of it than any one of us.'

Mrs Fowle gave no regard to his remarks. Taking up her knife, she cut into the butter and spread an extra helping on to the remaining portion of bun.

'I haven't enjoyed a morning such as this since my ship saw action in the Indian Ocean,' whispered Captain Harding. 'Am I to understand that your parents are to visit Allersham this year, Emma?'

'Their precise plans are at present uncertain while Grandmamma requires the daily ministrations of a physician,' said she.

'If all is well, we are to expect them at Michaelmas,' said Lord Allersham.

'Michaelmas has always been a favourite time of year at Osborne Castle,' said Mrs Beresford. 'I particularly love the daisies there that flower every year as summer reaches its end.'

'I have not seen Michaelmas daisies for many years,' said James Beresford.

'Then you must spend Michaelmas at Whitcombe. You will see such a splendid array there, almost the equal of those in Osborne Park,' said Mrs Beresford. 'I absolutely insist. And you, Captain Harding, if you have no other engagements, you must come too.'

'But only if you all promise to dine at Allersham every night,' said Lady Allersham. 'That is something I insist upon.'

After breakfast, they walked at a gentle pace towards the labyrinth. Mr Fowle strode briskly on ahead of the rest of the party in a bid to be the first to reach its centre. Mrs Fowle saw what her husband was about, slowed her pace correspondingly to a leisurely saunter, and sought the arm of her son.

'Mr Fowle is impossible,' said she. 'Did you hear how he spoke to me earlier?'

Captain Harding replied that the scene had been witnessed by every person present.

'What am I to do?' said Mrs Fowle.

'Spend as little time as possible in each other's company,' Captain Harding replied. 'You managed to arrange everything to your advantage when my father was alive.'

'Yes,' said she, 'that is true. But your papa kept his opinions to himself, except when they concerned matters of great theological importance. Mr Fowle is never short of an opinion on every matter under the sun, nor is he slow to express it.'

'Forgive me for pointing out that neither are you, Mama, nor have you ever been,' said he.

'How could you say such a thing to your poor mother?' said she.

'Because it is the truth,' Captain Harding replied, gently.

'What am I to do?' said she.

'When you are obliged to speak, begin by finding something charitable to say to Mr Fowle. Without irony or malice. If an opportunity presents itself, I will speak to Mr Fowle in my own way and when a suitable time presents.'

Mrs Fowle looked doubtfully at her son and sighed. 'If only I had resisted the temptation to marry for a second time. It would all have been a great deal better,' said she. 'Mrs Beresford is quite delighted with the Colonel's cousin. See how he walks beside her attending to her every word and making himself agreeable. Shall you go to Whitcombe at Michaelmas? I suppose you will do as you please, but I should like you to visit Brinshore.'

'I have no plans to speak of at present. There is business I must attend to. But I shall visit Brinshore before the year is out.'

Lord and Lady Allersham were the last to enter the labyrinth. No sound was to be heard as they approached the centre, and when the place came into view, there was but one person present: Mr Fowle. Mrs Fowle had instructed her husband to wait until the rest of the party appeared so that he may convey a message — that they were to proceed towards the castle ruin.

'I shall not do so myself,' said Mr Fowle, 'for I have walked quite enough for one day. Please inform Mrs Fowle, should she have the inclination to enquire, that she will find me in the Tavern. There I shall stay until it suits her to leave. Excuse me.'

With an abrupt bow, Mr Fowle walked briskly away retracing his steps along the path towards the entrance to the labyrinth by the miller's wheel.

CHAPTER TWENTY-ONE

The day before the Fowles were due to quit Bath, Mrs Beresford fulfilled her promise to accompany Mrs Fowle to the shop in Bath Street on hearing that she was in search of a bargain, something that had so far eluded her during her stay. The promise of cotton stockings, thread and lace at reasonable prices was too great an opportunity to miss. Mrs Fowle proposed to call on Mrs Beresford in Laura Place before noon and from there they would walk to Bath Street to spend a rewarding hour making as many purchases as pleased them for a fraction of the purchase price elsewhere.

The purchases soon mounted up, and as the separate accounts were calculated, Mrs Beresford came upon a remnant of calico sufficient in width and length to make a serviceable pinny for Miss Fox.

'It will make a very fine pinny. Too fine a pinny,' said Mrs Fowle, unfolding the remnant to its fullest length. 'I expect Miss Fox is in greater need of it than I, for I could not help noticing that the hem of the garment she wore to Laura Place was frayed beyond repair.'

Mrs Beresford arranged for the parcels to be delivered to Sydney Place and Laura Place respectively but saw to it that the piece of cloth intended for Miss Fox was wrapped separately.

'I might as well call at Gay Street while I am nearby,' said Mrs Beresford.

'Then I shall accompany you, for I am curious to make the acquaintance of Mrs Price, having heard so much about her. I hope she is just as ghastly as she is painted, and then I shall not be disappointed.'

Their progress to Gay Street was swift, for the breeze was behind them. On arrival, they were admitted to the parlour, and learned that Mrs Price was from home and Miss Fox was helping in the kitchen to prepare a pot of rabbit stew. On hearing that visitors had been received in the parlour, Miss Fox made herself presentable and went to offer her apologies for Mrs Price's absence. Surprised to find that the unexpected visitors were Mrs Beresford and Mrs Fowle, she explained that Mrs Price was not expected for another hour at least.

'Mrs Price is gone in person to supply Mr Ibbotson with a recipe for a poultice,' said Miss Fox, 'for his foot.'

'Please accept our apologies for calling at an inconvenient moment,' said Mrs Beresford.

'It is never an inconvenience to see you, Mrs Beresford, or you Mrs Fowle,' said Miss Fox.

At that moment, one of the younger boarders entered the parlour complaining of a sore finger, unaware of the visitors present. Miss Fox quickly led the girl away, promising to return at once.

While she was absent, Mrs Fowle was drawn to the painting that hung above the fireplace. She got up and moved towards the picture to inspect the scene more closely.

'Well,' said she, 'I am amazed.'

'What is it?' replied Mrs Beresford.

'Come and see for yourself,' said Mrs Fowle.

Mrs Beresford got up to look at the painting.

'Well?' said Mrs Fowle.

'It is reasonably well executed as far as I can see,' said Mrs Beresford.

'Is that *all* you can see?' Mrs Fowle looked at Mrs Beresford in amazement. 'I should have thought you of all people would have recognised the place of your birth.' She pointed to the hint of an edifice in the distance. 'Osborne Castle.'

'Impossible!' said Mrs Beresford.

'Is it? I have often stood in that very spot and glimpsed Osborne Castle on a clear day. See the hounds in the foreground. It is the exact spot in Stanton Woods where your brother's hounds throw off.'

Mrs Beresford took a closer look.

'And there is the lane that leads to the church, and Stanton Parsonage, the place where *I* was born. I should have known the scene anywhere. I'm only surprised that you did not.'

'One such scene is much the same as any other. And why should there be a painting of Stanton Woods in Mrs Price's parlour?' said Mrs Beresford.

'Is the artist's name present, I wonder?' said Mrs Fowle, inspecting the corner of the piece.'

'No,' replied Mrs Beresford.

'Let me look at the back,' said Mrs Fowle, attempting to lift the picture away from the wall.

Mrs Beresford was shocked by Mrs Fowle's audacity and urged her to be quick before they were caught in the act and obliged to account for their actions.

'Here is something,' said Mrs Fowle. 'But I cannot quite make it out. Would you assist me, Mrs Beresford? Thank you. If you would be good enough to hold the painting thus. Ah! Now I see it.'

'What does it say?' said Mrs Beresford.

'*Detested sport, that owes its pleasures to another's pain,*' she replied. 'Oh dear, what message is this?'

'And there is nothing more?'

'Nothing.'

Mrs Fowle, assisted by Mrs Beresford, put the picture back, making sure that it was just as they had found it.

When Miss Fox entered the room, the calico that Mrs Beresford had purchased for her, had been completely forgotten. The visitors' curiosity concerning the picture and how it came to be in Mrs Price's parlour, was the subject uppermost in their minds. On detailed enquiry, Miss Fox was found to have no knowledge of the painting at all beyond being able to confirm that, for as long as she could remember, it had always hung over the fireplace in the parlour. She had never paused to study it in any detail, but on hearing that its subject matter held such a strong association for both women, and consequently for Lady Allersham, Miss Fox assured them that she would never look at the scene in quite the same light again.

'There, you see, is the lane,' said Mrs Fowle, pointing to the picture. 'Further on, although you do not see it depicted here, the lane forks, leading on the right to Osborne Castle and the left to Delham.'

'That cannot be,' said Mrs Beresford, 'for I am certain that it leads to Osborne Castle on the left and Delham on the right.'

'That depends from whence you approach it,' replied Mrs Fowle. 'I am sure I never once had the good fortune to come within its reach from the direction of Osborne Castle. I know every stone, bend, dip and puddle of this lane. Indeed, my brother —'

'Mr Watson? The Croydon attorney —'

'Yes —'

'I remember your brother well. I once assisted him with that business involving Mrs Turner.'

'The business with the redcoat,' said Mrs Fowle.

'I forget the scoundrel's name.'

'The wretch had several. But that is by the by. My brother was never done with complaining about the potholes in this very lane or threatening to indict the surveyor if ever he came upon him. And there, you see as plain as can be, a pothole. The artist has a keen eye for detail. And yet, I always thought it such a pretty lane. And I need not remind you, Mrs Beresford, that the Watsons did not have extensive grounds in which to walk. We had to make do with the lanes and the churchyard. I know them well. I expect that is why you did not at first recognise the scene.'

'I am sorry to admit it,' said she, 'but there is truth in what you say. As a girl, I hardly walked beyond the walls of Osborne Park. But I know the fork in the lane that you speak of very well indeed, for it was the shortest route to Delham by carriage.'

Mrs Fowle was gratified by Mrs Beresford's reply and smiled with satisfaction. 'By the by, Miss Fox, perhaps you will enquire of Mrs Price how she came by this particular painting and to whom the work is attributed. Mrs Beresford and I should be most interested to discover its origin.'

'Indeed, we would,' Mrs Beresford agreed.

The length of cloth, almost forgotten amid their curiosity, was given to Miss Fox and received with a mixture of diffidence and gratitude.

'It is rather too fine for use as a pinny,' said she.

'That is my view entirely. But Mrs Beresford insisted,' said Mrs Fowle. 'It is serviceable and will wash well. It is, I suppose, just what is needed. When do you begin with Miss Ibbotson?'

'This day week,' said Miss Fox.

'Excellent,' replied Mrs Fowle, 'then you will have time to make it up, and I daresay, you will look eminently more presentable on the day.'

On their return to Laura Place, Mrs Fowle and Mrs Beresford continued their conjecture concerning the scene depicted in the painting.

'I do not dispute the likeness to Stanton Woods, for I have sometimes stood in that very spot myself to watch the hounds throw off,' said Mrs Beresford. 'But it is such a long time ago, and my memory at times does not serve me well. Are there not scenes very similar to Stanton Woods in every corner of England? I cannot count the times I have looked at a landscape and thought how similar it appears to Osborne Park or Whitcombe. Indeed, I have viewed portraits in several of the great houses of Surrey, Kent and Somerset combined, and have seen portraits so similar in likeness to my own family, that I have ceased to be astonished by them.'

Mrs Fowle would not be moved; no element of doubt existed in her mind: the scene depicted in the painting *was* Stanton Woods. 'I will not give way to doubt,' said she. 'Nor should I be surprised to find that Lord Osborne is hinted at on horseback.'

Mrs Beresford replied, 'It is exactly the point I was making. You may see my brother represented there, and I see a figure on horseback very like several gentlemen of my acquaintance.'

The debate continued in the same vein until they reached Laura Place where they found Lady Allersham writing a list of tasks to be undertaken in preparation for their return to Allersham Park.

The painting that had created much curiosity, especially on the part of Mrs Fowle, was just as interesting to Lady Allersham.

'I remember the scene well, for I too thought of Surrey when I first set eyes on it. Papa's hounds always throw off at Stanton Woods,' said Lady Allersham.

'There, you see,' said Mrs Fowle to Mrs Beresford.

'I do not dispute the remarkable likeness to Stanton Woods,' Mrs Beresford replied. 'But as so many scenes of the kind look very much alike, I mean only to caution against certainty. And if your aim is to establish a connexion between Miss Fox and Surrey, remember that Miss Fox knew nothing about the painting but for confirming that it had hung in the same spot above the fireplace for as long as she could remember.'

'And on the reverse of the painting was written — how was it Mrs Fowle?' said Mrs Beresford.

'*Detested sport, that owes its pleasures to another's pain,*' she replied.

'But that is Cowper,' said Lady Allersham. 'I am certain it is. For it is a line that was much in dispute in our household. Papa is with the abolitionists but will not apply the same to those pursuits that *draw the sportsmen over hill and dale.*'

'Cowper? Yes, indeed,' Mrs Beresford replied.

'Perhaps the message pertains to another sport entirely,' said Mrs Fowle.

'Whatever do you mean?' said Lady Allersham.

'Sport in its widest sense. It is of little matter,' Mrs Fowle replied. 'You have not enquired as to our reason for calling at Gay Street.'

On hearing of the length of cloth purchased for Miss Fox, Lady Allersham was in full agreement. 'A new pinny is just the thing, for the old one was threadbare and had received several mendings.'

'Advise Miss Fox to cut her old garment into squares and make dusters of it,' said Mrs Fowle.

'I am sure she needs no advice on such matters,' Mrs Beresford replied.

When the subject of Stanton Woods and Miss Fox had been exhausted, Mrs Beresford was disappointed to find that while she had been away from Laura Place, James Beresford had called.

'I regret having misjudged him as I did,' said Lady Allersham, 'for James Beresford has a number of excellent qualities. He promises to call before we leave for Allersham and has every intention of visiting Whitcombe at Michaelmas. He gave me his word that he would keep an eye on Miss Fox and report on her progress. I was amazed to discover that he has already called upon Mr Ibbotson's sister and has answered all her enquiries regarding Paragon Buildings and its inhabitants, of which, I understand, there were many — enquiries, that is. Not inhabitants.'

'I hope Miss Ibbotson does not take advantage of his obliging nature,' said Mrs Beresford.

'Such women inevitably do,' said Mrs Fowle. 'But I expect he will manage Miss Ibbotson well enough. Were she fifteen or twenty years younger, her attentions might have placed him in some danger. Men are at their most obliging when it pleases them. But it does not last long. I should know.'

'Dear Aunt Fowle,' said Lady Allersham, 'Mama wishes to know when to expect you at Osborne Park. Her letter arrived this past hour. Aunt Musgrave is also expecting you in Delham before too long.'

'Well,' she replied, 'I see I am in demand. If only Delham were twenty miles closer to Brinshore, we might see each other very often indeed.'

CHAPTER TWENTY-TWO

The arrival of a letter in the morning's post was met with a mixture of curiosity and mild pleasure by Lady Dalrymple. Its author was Lady Russell and it contained news of Lady Dalrymple's neighbours in Laura Place. The news was disappointing, though not unexpected: the Allersham party had quitted Bath. The information that was less pleasing to the mother, brought respite to the daughter, who now found it conceivable to contemplate a return to Bath without the fear that had first driven her away.

Miss Carteret sighed with relief at the news but sensed a hint of reproach in the tone of her mother's remarks.

'Had we returned to Bath directly, the opportunity to enjoy the pleasure of our neighbours' company a little longer would have been ours. I do not often say so of any acquaintance begun in Bath, but Laura Place will be the poorer for their absence. And I am quite put out when I consider that I am not now at liberty to fulfil the promise I made to Mrs Beresford to pass a morning together in Milsom Street before her return to Whitcombe. I am obliged to postpone our visit to Molland's indefinitely. And why? What has been gained by extending our stay here? One might visit Bristol any month of the year. Indeed, it would not perturb me one whit were I never to see Bristol again! And I may say that it has not escaped my notice how anxious you were to leave Bath, and in so great a hurry. I am beginning to wonder why it was imperative to attend the wedding of the very person whose acquaintance you showed little inclination for when the Elliots resided in Camden Place,' said she.

Miss Carteret was unable to supply a satisfactory explanation and to avoid further probing of the same, retreated to her bedchamber on the less than sufficient excuse of preparing for their return to Bath.

Once arrangements had been made and outstanding invitations honoured, Lady Dalrymple and Miss Carteret expected, by the end of the month, to be settled once again in Laura Place.

Miss Carteret took comfort in the knowledge that she might recover that peace of mind she had lost, now that she was free of the risk of exposure. Explanation would no longer be required; she would continue as before with nothing to disturb or upset her.

Anne Wentworth had, unexpectedly, proved an understanding confidante, and had given Miss Carteret every assurance that nothing of the matter that had been spoken of would pass her lips.

When the day came to leave Bristol, their return to Bath was accomplished without fanfare or fuss. Lady Dalrymple was not inclined to receive callers the following day, owing to a mild rheumatic disorder brought on by the previous day's journey. Miss Carteret, however, wishing to make the most of the day, made up her mind to call on Mr Ibbotson's sister at her new lodgings in Paragon Buildings. The visit must be made, thought she, and might just as well be made sooner rather than later. Knowing that her mother would rather be spared the obligation, an excuse for Lady Dalrymple's absence might easily be made on the grounds of indisposition owing to the exertions of the previous day's travel. Thereby the prospect of spending a morning debating the virtues and vices of Sir Walter Elliot would thus be avoided.

Mr Ibbotson's sister was at home and appeared pleased to receive Miss Carteret. Lady Dalrymple's apologies were presented and accepted with hardly a note of disappointment. Miss Ibbotson trusted that the wedding had lived up to expectations and congratulated the bride's father on finding a husband for his daughter with three thousand pounds a year. It was no small feat, for Miss Elliot who was long past the first bloom of youth could boast of little more than that she was the daughter of a baronet. The wedding remained the focus of Miss Ibbotson's enquiries for almost an hour. How did the bride look? What connexions had the groom's family to speak of? How was the wedding breakfast? How did Sir Walter appear?

One piece of information that surprised Miss Ibbotson was that the Musgroves had not attended the wedding. She was certain, however, that the fault lay not in the actions of Sir Walter, but his daughter. Miss Elliot was certain to be the culprit. Then there was Mary Musgrove's inattentiveness to her father, a fact she believed, that must also have played some part in it. One could not expect anything more from a daughter whose selfishness and obstinacy had been present in her character from birth.

As time went on, Miss Carteret found her resolve to contradict Miss Ibbotson slip away, but offered one closing remark. 'Sir Walter himself was responsible, and had no scruples in admitting it,' said Miss Carteret.

Miss Ibbotson was at first unwilling to believe it possible, but soon found reasons to vindicate Sir Walter for his foresight and prudence.

'Were the Musgroves to be invited, so must the Hayters, Benwicks and the Crofts. And so it goes on. There is no end to it, for where one invitation is extended there are sure to be five and twenty more required to quell the grievances of those who are all too willing to feel slighted. Sir Walter was quite right not to invite the Musgroves. And surely, he would not desire his own consequence to be diminished by those of inferior rank who were quick to claim a connexion with the name Elliot,' said Miss Ibbotson. 'I expect Sir Walter appeared as handsome as ever, and without a wrinkle upon his brow or a hair out of place.'

Miss Carteret was obliged to stay ten minutes longer, for once Miss Ibbotson had begun, nothing would distract her from the subject of Sir Walter. Release came in the form of Miss Fox, who had been expected, and was due to remain in Paragon Buildings for most of the day. In perfunctory fashion, Miss

Ibbotson directed Miss Fox to a far corner of the room where a chair had been placed for her. Beside the chair was a large pile of darning. No opportunity to speak to Miss Fox presented itself, save for a brief salutation; an escape, therefore, was soon achieved, and shortly afterwards, Miss Carteret left Miss Ibbotson, relieved that the visit had been paid and thankful that it might be some time before the courtesy was returned, owing to the varying demands placed upon Miss Ibbotson at her new abode.

Further along the Paragon, Miss Carteret was pleased to find James Beresford walking in a similar direction. He stopped and greeted her with a look of surprise.

'We did not know when to expect you,' said he. 'Your neighbours were sorry to leave Laura Place without having the opportunity of making their adieus in person.'

'Have you news of Lord and Lady Allersham and Mrs Beresford?' said she.

'They are all quite well. Lady Allersham bid me say to you, if ever we were to meet, that she hopes to renew your acquaintance at some point in the future, God willing.'

Miss Carteret replied, 'Please convey my good wishes to Her Ladyship. I should, of course, be happy to renew our acquaintance in due course.'

He asked whether he might have her company as far as Broad Street. The request was accepted, and they walked on.

'I have just called on Mr Ibbotson's sister,' said she.

'I hope she finds her new arrangements comfortable and to her liking,' he said

'She seems pleased with them,' Miss Carteret replied. 'Miss Fox arrived as I left.'

'I trust Miss Fox continues to fare well,' said he.

'I had little opportunity to enquire, for Miss Ibbotson was quick to claim her attention and set her about her duties.'

James Beresford made no reply and continued in silence until they arrived at the place where they were to part company.

'Is Captain Harding aware of your return to Laura Place?' said he.

'Why should he be?' she replied. 'I expect Captain Harding is gone to Allersham Park, or to visit his mother. The name of the place escapes me. It lies a short distance from Sanditon.'

'He is not gone to Brinshore. I was with Captain Harding two evenings ago. I understand he is to remain in Bath for the present.'

'Oh,' said she.

'This is where we part. I continue towards the Abbey. I find myself drawn to the church these days, and the solace it affords,' said he.

'There is little solace to be found in the world. I wish I had the same conviction that it was to be found within the walls of the Abbey,' she replied.

CHAPTER TWENTY-THREE

The splendour of midsummer at Allersham Park was a sight to behold. In the full light of day, as the Hall came into view, it rose stately amid the verdant countryside, resplendent and inviting. Until that moment, Lady Allersham had not felt a sense of belonging to the place; strangely, unexpectedly, it began to feel like home. The path she had once wished for had been laid just as she had pictured it, adding interest and shape to the landscape, leading the eye towards the grove where bluebells flourished, and onwards to the lake.

How the path came to be there, how and when it had been laid were questions to which Lady Allersham eagerly sought answers. Lord Allersham had not left Laura Place for the sole purpose of supervising the repairs to the roof or the abatement of the flood waters on the land adjacent to the Park. The path had also been his object.

'You kept it a secret all this time?' said Lady Allersham. She was keen to put the path to good use, and proposed that as soon as the weather allowed, they were to walk down to the lake as far as the path extended. There was still work to be done to complete the project, but there was already much to see and admire and wonder at.

Laura Place was almost forgotten, and for several days Bath was hardly spoken of. One morning, however, a letter from Captain Harding brought interesting news: Lady Dalrymple and Miss Carteret had returned to Bath.

'I confess, I am surprised to find that the Dalrymples have returned to Laura Place so soon after we left it,' said Lady Allersham to her husband.

'I feel certain that had the Elliots known of our movements, they would surely have altered the date of the wedding to avoid any inconvenience to ourselves,' said he, with a wry smile.

'Do not tease me,' Lady Allersham replied. 'I still feel a little dissatisfied with the manner of our parting. The last I saw of Miss Carteret was at the ball.

Something had distressed her there and I should like to know what it was.'

Lord Allersham sighed and said, 'And what other news does your letter convey?'

'Cousin Robert dined with James Beresford four evenings ago.'

Lord Allersham expected something more than this for the information to be properly described as *news*.

'It seems James Beresford had met Miss Carteret by chance leaving Paragon Buildings. She had been to visit Mr Ibbotson's sister. They walked together as far as Broad Street where they parted company.'

'This, again, is hardly news, my dear.'

'But here is news indeed! Robert called at Laura Place and was received by Lady Dalrymple and Miss Carteret. The wedding was talked of at great length.'

'Wedding? Has Harding made Miss Carteret an offer?' said Lord Allersham.

'You know perfectly well what I mean,' she said. 'And it appears that Sir Walter Elliot snubbed his own daughter. Mary Musgrove was not invited. I am astonished.'

'Perhaps you shouldn't be, Emma,' said he.

'Snub a member of the family and suffer their indignation for years to come?'

'Miss Carteret may have a similar choice to make on her wedding day if she ever marries. Should she invite Sir Walter or should she not.'

'And if I understand the character of Sir Walter correctly, a snub from such a quarter would matter greatly to a man who places the utmost importance on rank and consequence,' said she. 'I suppose it is a

211

very good argument for not marrying at all. If only weddings and funerals were as delightful as baptisms.'

Lady Allersham returned to her letter and read further down the page. 'Miss Carteret has seen Miss Fox. Poor Miss Fox was given little opportunity to speak and had a large pile of darning to complete. I hope James Beresford is as good as his word and keeps an eye on our Miss Fox. Ah! And here is something interesting.'

'I do hope so,' said he.

'Lady Dalrymple has invited Cousin Robert and James Beresford for dinner at Laura Place,' said Lady Allersham. 'Perhaps I should invite the Dalrymples to Allersham, and if neither gentleman has come to the point by Michaelmas, I may have to take matters into my own hands,' said she.

Lord Allersham gave a forbearing sigh.

'It is a joke,' said she. 'But I shall invite the Dalrymples just the same.'

Lady Allersham expected to be alone for the rest of the day as Lord Allersham was due to spend much of it with his steward on estate business, and Mrs Beresford had been invited to luncheon at the Rectory owing to the vast improvement in Mrs Dauber's condition.

There was much to be done at Allersham, and a day without interruption was the very best sort of day to set about fulfilling the responsibilities incumbent upon the mistress of the house. After removing to the library, where the sun shone brightest in the late morning, and writing down every task on an ever-lengthening list of things to be done, Lady Allersham cast her eye over two full pages of items and, daunted by the extent of it, put it to one side. Were there but sufficient hours in the day to accomplish every obligation, thought she. The task uppermost in her thoughts and which claimed a large part of her attention was inspection of the late Lord Allersham's affairs. If it were to be conducted properly and thoroughly she would require help to establish the whereabouts of documents, diaries and letters pertaining to the deceased. A cursory search of the library led her to conclude that nothing of interest was to be found there. Presently, she would need to seek help to locate the items of interest.

Lady Allersham resolved, therefore, to deal with several minor items first, for they might be attended to and crossed out more speedily than those that required greater time and effort. She reproached herself for an hour spent in idleness and daydreaming and took up the list once again with a mind to tackle the least taxing item upon it. But her eyes drifted towards a bookcase by the window where, inserted between a copy of the Book of Common Prayer and Anecdotes of Painting in England, was placed the volume about which there had been so much speculation: *Paradise Lost*. She opened the cover to see how the signature, 'J Carteret', appeared. The recollection that she had within her possession a note written by Miss Carteret at Laura Place, prompted her to find it to compare the hand of both items.

She went in search of it and found it. And as she had expected, the signature inside the cover of the volume and the signature on Miss Carteret's letter matched perfectly, the formulation of the letter 'C' being distinctive and unique.

As she examined the evidence, Lady Allersham was unexpectedly interrupted by the entrance of her husband's steward, who had been despatched to collect plans for the building of some new stables. The documents were quickly found, and as quickly did the steward apologise for the intrusion.

He was about to take his leave when Lady Allersham called him back.

'Where might I find a list of acquisitions to the library? Do you keep one?' said she.

'Indeed, I do. I note with careful attention to detail every acquisition. Your Ladyship will find a record of each volume in the inventory over there,' said he, pointing to the ledger in question.

Lady Allersham took up the book to examine it. 'Where might I find a record of *Paradise Lost*?'

The steward, knowing the library well, was able to direct Her Ladyship to the volume itself, on a shelf at the opposite corner of the library.

'But I discovered this fine volume here,' said she, pointing to the space where she had found it.

There was a simple reason for the omission, he explained. The shelf in question contained several volumes belonging to Lord Allersham's late brother, and as soon as time allowed their presence in the library would be recorded.

'I see,' said she, intrigued by the information.

'They were returned with certain other items belonging to the deceased,' he replied.

'Returned from where?' she asked.

'Portsmouth, I believe, Your Ladyship,' the steward replied.

'Portsmouth? Let me be clear. Are we talking about Lord Allersham's *naval* brother and not his *elder* brother?' said she.

'Yes, Your Ladyship. Captain Fitzroy,' he replied.

'Are you quite certain?' she enquired.

'I am, Your Ladyship,' said he. 'Might I assist you in some way? I shall be happy to enter the volumes formally into the inventory at the earliest opportunity.'

'Thank you. There is nothing with which I require assistance for the present,' said she, and then adding hastily, 'except the whereabouts of any other items belonging to Captain Fitzroy. I believe you said the volumes were among them.'

'The housekeeper may be able to help you there, Your Ladyship. Apply to the housekeeper.'

'Thank you,' said she.

The steward bowed in haste and withdrew from the library, eager to be on his way.

Captain *Fitzroy* and Miss *Carteret*? Confounded by the steward's information, Lady Allersham searched the shelf for further evidence pertaining to a connexion between them. How did Captain Fitzroy have in his possession a volume belonging to Miss Carteret? thought she. How was the connexion established? And why did Miss Carteret fail to mention they had been acquainted at one time? Where did they have cause to meet? Bath, of course. Bath must have been the place. And why did not Lady Dalrymple speak of it? How very curious!

One by one, every volume on the shelf in question was examined carefully and returned to its place. Lady Allersham was a little disappointed to find that *Paradise Lost* alone bore Miss Carteret's signature. She picked up the volume once again and noticed a single ivy leaf pressed between its pages. Its appearance suggested that the leaf had been there for some time, though it showed no signs of fragility or decay.

As a new bride, Lady Allersham had been shown Captain Fitzroy's room on a tour of the house. The housekeeper had performed the service then, and although Lady Allersham had paid little attention at the time, she remembered the general appearance of the room perfectly well. She would not call for the housekeeper's assistance, for the door was unlikely to be locked. Confident that the room must yield more of Captain Fitzroy's secrets, she felt vindicated in making a search of it for the sake of Miss Carteret, of understanding, and of clarity.

The room had not been meddled with, but for the placement of dust sheets over the main items of furniture. A chest of drawers by the door had no dust cover and seemed to be the best place to start her search. Every drawer was opened and all but one was found to be empty. An array of neckties, laundered and folded, were the sole contents of the drawer. She closed it and looked about her, surveying every corner of the room. Her attention was drawn to an item at the foot of the bed. Supposing it to be a trunk of some description, she removed the dust sheet to reveal a beautiful oriental chest inlaid with mother of pearl. A key, placed conveniently within the lock, could not have been more propitious or inviting. The chest was unlocked with ease, and the lid opened effortlessly.

Lady Allersham was not disappointed, for the chest was not empty; though neither was it full. On first appearance, it looked to contain some old maps, a compass and a telescope, items entirely in keeping with the belongings of a naval captain. The telescope was an irresistible object and a very fine one and might still prove its utility were it not hidden away in a chest. Indeed, thought she, it might be put to good use if the occasion required it. She extended the barrel and held the telescope to her eye, moving it slowly around the room until the window came into focus. Yes, thought she. What a very useful object this is!

Continuing her quest, Lady Allersham removed the remaining objects from the chest, one at a time, and placed them on the floor beside her. The most intriguing item was a small wooden box that lay at the bottom of the chest. She picked it up and wiped away the dust. It was an unremarkable box, without elegance or adornment, a box that had seen better days. Unlike the chest, however, the box was locked and missing its key. She would have expected to find the key inside the chest, somewhere near to where the box had lain, but another explanation held greater appeal. A thorough search of the chest and all the remaining items confirmed what she had suspected and wished to be the case: the key was missing. Of course, the key will not be found among Captain Fitzroy's possessions, thought she! For the key is attached to the gold chain worn by Miss Carteret. There could be no other explanation.

The implications of the connexion began to dawn on Lady Allersham more fully than before. There must have existed at some point in the past a degree of mutual understanding between Captain Fitzroy and Miss Carteret. And it was the degree of acquaintance between them that now seemed of paramount interest, and more so because her own husband appeared to know nothing of the matter. More facts might yet come to light, thought she, if only the box would yield up its secrets. Several attempts to force the lock failed, and hearing a horse's canter outside,

Lady Allersham replaced the contents of the chest, but for the small box, and closed the lid. She left the room, taking the box with her, and congratulated herself on her astonishing discovery.

'Well,' said she, greeting Lord Allersham on his return. 'I trust your day has been as fruitful as mine.'

'Judging from your countenance I fancy not,' said he. 'You have something to impart and are anxious for me to hear it.'

'Do you recognise it?' said she, placing the box in his hands.

'It is a box. Not a particularly fine one. Where did you find it?' he replied.

'I found it in your brother's room. It was inside a chest among several other objects, one being a very fine telescope. And before you chastise me for searching Captain Fitzroy's room, I should like the opportunity to explain why I did so.'

'Emma,' said he, 'why should I chastise you? You are mistress of Allersham. Consequently, you are at liberty to do whatever you wish. Consult me by all means if you have need to. My only hope is that you have left the telescope where you found it.'

'I have,' said she. 'I expect it is of great sentimental value.'

'No,' he replied. 'I was thinking only of you and your fascination for espionage. Have you forgotten? It served no good purpose at Brinshore.'

'Do not remind me! Henry, please be serious,' said she. 'I wish to open this box, but the key is missing. That is to say, not necessarily missing, but nor is it present.'

Puzzled by his wife's remark, he asked her to explain the matter further.

'The key is very probably attached to a gold necklace worn by Miss Carteret.'

Lord Allersham was disinclined at first to give credence to his wife's claim and, having heard all that she had to say on the subject, was still doubtful.

'Did you know that the volume belonging to Miss Carteret was found among your brother's belongings?' Lady Allersham observed her husband's expression. 'Ha! I see you did not.'

'There will be a perfectly reasonable explanation,' said he.

'And that perfectly reasonable explanation is that Captain Fitzroy and Miss Carteret had a mutual understanding that they endeavoured to conceal from their family and friends,' she replied. 'Are you not shocked to hear it?'

Lord Allersham laughed at such a notion.

A thought suddenly occurred to her. 'I wonder if Charles Blake knew? That would be even more shocking,' said she. 'Henry, my love, I believe all our answers are to be found within this box. Will you find a way to open it?'

Lord Allersham paused momentarily to consider his wife's request. 'Supposing you are correct in your assumptions,' said he, 'that there was a degree of acquaintance between my brother and Miss Carteret of which his family and hers were unaware, then I believe the contents of this box were not meant for our eyes. If, in fact, Miss Carteret is in possession of the key, it must have been given to her by my brother for safe keeping. It is not unreasonable to conceive that particulars of a personal nature might be best concealed in such a way, and that the only person with the means to unlock them is the person to whom those secrets belong. It is well within my power to break the lock, and it is the type of lock that would not prove difficult to mend. But suppose the box contained letters belonging to either party. How would you or I explain why, if Miss Carteret holds the key, we forced the lock?'

'But you do agree that my supposition is a reasonable one, that a connexion was formed between Miss Carteret and Captain Fitzroy?' said she.

'It is surprising, but possible, I suppose,' he replied. 'But it is by no means certain. As you know, I was estranged from my family for several years. And my brother was at sea during most of that time. All I can say with any certainty is that Miss Carteret was never mentioned in any conversation or document, or indeed within the pages of my brother's will. If you must pursue the matter, and I neither forbid nor encourage it, write to Miss Carteret yourself and ask her.'

'I should rather speak to her in person,' said she. 'My love, do you see what this means? If Captain Fitzroy had not been fatally wounded, Miss Carteret may well have been mistress of Allersham.'

CHAPTER TWENTY-FOUR

Miss Fox had attended Mr Ibbotson's sister for three weeks with unfailing diligence and punctuality before the question of Miss Dauber's wedding was mentioned between them. The assurances Mrs Price had given to Lady Allersham regarding Miss Fox's attendance were now placed in some doubt due to Miss Ibbotson's strong opposition. Miss Ibbotson, who had raised no objection three weeks ago, now found that she could not spare Miss Fox at all. Consequently, Mrs Price was faced with a predicament she declared was entirely of Miss Fox's making; and wishing to break her promise neither to Lady Allersham nor to Miss Ibbotson, with whom she had been on friendly terms for some years, Mrs Price concluded that her only course of action was to work on Miss Fox. She called her into the parlour and proposed a solution to the problem.

'Had you not insisted on going to Whitcombe, I should not have been faced with so troublesome a dilemma. Therefore, it rightly falls to you to solve it,' said Mrs Price.

Miss Fox endeavoured to hide her disappointment. 'Please tell me what I am to do.'

'You will write to Miss Dauber a day or two before the wedding and explain that you have a cold and are not fit to travel. You will make your apologies in the usual manner and wish her joy,' said she.

'You wish me to tell an untruth?'

'With the very best of motives. I think only of Miss Dauber. You would not wish to disappoint your friend on her wedding day. Any other explanation but ill health would seem feeble indeed.'

'Pardon me, Mrs Price,' said Miss Fox. 'Would it not be more honest to say that I cannot be spared? If I should be caught out in a lie, what am I to do then?' said Miss Fox.

'No one will know or care,' said she. 'Now, I suggest that you write your letter and I shall make sure it is received on the appropriate day.'

With an acute feeling of injustice and regret, but without the power to refuse Mrs Price, Miss Fox agreed to the request. She hurried away, anxious to avoid any criticism Miss Ibbotson might level against her for her tardiness were she to reach Paragon Buildings later than the agreed hour.

When at last she arrived at the lodgings of her employer, she was but five minutes late and Miss Ibbotson, distracted by an ambiguous remark present in a note from her brother, appeared not to notice Miss Fox's lack of punctuality. The latter set about her chores directly, discharging them in full, and to Miss Ibbotson's satisfaction within the time set aside. Miss Ibbotson, having received an assurance from Miss Fox that she would not attend the wedding at Whitcombe, was disposed to look kindly on her and, as recompense, allowed her to leave a quarter of an hour before the normal time of her departure.

As Miss Fox left Paragon Buildings, having at her disposal an additional quarter of an hour before she was needed in Gay Street, she decided to walk further on and take a turn in Queen Square. There she might collect her thoughts and enjoy a rare reprieve from the demands of others for a small portion of the day; there she might indulge her feelings of disappointment over the visit she would now no longer make to Whitcombe despite having looked forward to the event for so long. Most of all, she was troubled by the knowledge that she must deceive her friend. She did not blame Mrs Price, for she understood the difficulty that had led her to insist that no other course of action would do. But what would she say to Lady Allersham if she were asked to account for her absence? Once begun, she would have no alternative but to continue in the falsehood. Lost in thought, she proceeded along Queen Square without proper attention to her surroundings and was startled to hear someone call her by name.

'Miss Fox,' said James Beresford. 'It is you, is it not?'

'Yes, sir,' she replied. 'Forgive me, my mind was elsewhere.'

'It is fortunate, indeed, for I had intended to write to Mrs Beresford this very day and I know both she and Lady Allersham are anxious to hear how you go on. He offered his arm which she gratefully accepted.

'You were very much in my mind this last hour,' he continued, 'for I have just left Mr Wood, the physician who attended you in Laura Place. He enquired about you and was eager to have it confirmed that you were now fully recovered. So, you see, Miss Fox, there are many who claim an interest in your welfare.'

'I am sure I do not deserve it,' said she.

'I believe you do,' he replied. 'You would be as surprised as I if you knew the extent to which the inhabitants of Paragon Buildings know each other's business. I have heard it from several sources that Miss Ibbotson cannot do without you. But I trust your employment there suits you well and that you are not overwhelmed by ever increasing and unreasonable demands. Miss Fox, if you ever need assistance of any kind, I am at your service.'

'Thank you,' said she. 'You are very kind.'

'Now tell me, what am I to say in my letter to Mrs Beresford?'

Her eyes sparkled as she suppressed a tear. He searched her face for an answer and seemed troubled by her expression.

'It is nothing,' said she. 'I am perfectly well. Please think nothing of it.'

'I cannot, for I see you are distressed. Something or someone has upset you. I hope it is not I.'

'No!' said she. 'Not at all. It is my own foolishness. Please forgive me.'

'May I be the judge of that? Allow me to say, Miss Fox, that you are the very last person I should describe as foolish.'

She looked away to compose herself and to avoid his searching gaze. After a few moments, she said, 'Mr Beresford, may I ask you something?'

'Of course,' said he.

'Is it ever acceptable to speak falsely, to tell a lie, though kindly meant?'

'That depends,' he replied. 'I have on occasion complimented a host on the soup or some dish or other when in truth I did not care for it so very much. But if I have understood you correctly, Miss Fox, I do not think it is soup that disturbs your mind. You are troubled by the notion of telling a falsehood, and that suggests to me that your instinct is to resist it. I shall assume that your question is a particular and not a general one as we are not engaged in a debate about moral philosophy. Has someone placed you under an obligation to lie on their behalf?'

'I am not at liberty to say,' said she.

'No, of course not,' he replied. 'Forgive me. Perhaps you would feel more at ease speaking to a woman. I understand from Mrs Beresford that you are to visit Whitcombe next week. It is not my place to advise, but might you feel at liberty there to speak to Mrs Beresford or Lady Allersham or one of the Dauber ladies?'

Miss Fox raised her eyes to meet his. She was almost tempted to explain herself, to admit the deception to which she had consented, and lay bare the shame of her weakness and the disappointment that must follow from her actions. The choice was hers: to carry out the obligation placed upon her by Mrs Price and Miss Ibbotson or throw herself on the mercy of Mr Beresford who appeared willing to act on her behalf. She knew that his only object was to satisfy the enquiries of Lady Allersham and Mrs Beresford, but it did nothing to diminish her appreciation for his offer of assistance, if assistance she required. Ultimately, she understood that the wishes of Mrs Price and Miss Ibbotson must hold sway, for to them she was beholden for her existence and livelihood. Moreover, she was prepared to allow that the happiness of Miss Dauber would not be lessened by her absence; and, when viewed from all angles, she could surely endure the disappointment of not visiting Whitcombe.

James Beresford studied his companion for some moments. 'You are silent,' said he. There was sadness and resignation in her look, but when she turned towards him her eyes were full of resolve.

'Mr Beresford, I thank you,' she replied. 'You have helped me more than you can know. I now know how I must act, and though it grieves me to do so, I truly believe it is for the best.'

Miss Fox's decision to maintain her silence and act according to Mrs Price's wishes brought some relief. Her spirit would not be broken, nor would she give way to self-pity. There were others far less fortunate in the world who would consider it the greatest good fortune to be provided with food and shelter and to be of use to others.

As their chance meeting came to an end, James Beresford and Miss Fox parted company at that corner of Queen Square most convenient for their separate destinations. The sensation felt by Miss Fox as she hurried away, quickening her step as she progressed along Gay Street, was one of relief that she had resisted the temptation to explain the cause of her disquiet. James Beresford concerned by the encounter, paused a while and watched Miss Fox disappear from view before continuing towards the Paragon, in contemplation of the conversation that had passed between them.

Two days passed before James Beresford and Miss Fox met again. Having promised to supply Miss Ibbotson with the name of a reliable cabinet maker, he had called on his neighbour shortly before Miss Fox's usual time of arrival. Miss Ibbotson, being without the services of her maid, was less prepared than usual to receive visitors.

'My weakness, Mr Beresford, is that I think more of my servants than I do of myself. You find me in a sorry state this morning, for against my better judgement, I gave way and indulged Frost. I granted her leave to visit her father in his last hours. Frost, said I, you may take one hour and no more, and should your father breathe his last before the hour is fully spent, do not tarry. I shall expect you to return without delay or I shall want to know why.'

James Beresford replied, 'There is no regret greater than that of being denied the opportunity to be present with a loved one, to bid them farewell, in their final moments of life.'

Their conversation was interrupted by the arrival of Miss Fox who was promptly instructed by Miss Ibbotson to prepare a tray of tea for her visitor.

'Good morning, Miss Fox,' said he.

'Good morning, Sir,' she replied.

Turning to Miss Ibbotson, James Beresford said, 'Please do not trouble Miss Fox on my account. I shall not trespass on your time,' said he, rising from his chair.

'Nonsense,' she replied, 'Sit down, if you please. It is no trouble at all. If I may, I should like to speak with you further, Mr Beresford.'

He smiled awkwardly and complied with her request.

'Fox, what are you waiting for? Make sure you bring the best tea chest,' said Miss Ibbotson, calling after her, 'and make haste.'

With a semblance of cheerful diffidence, Miss Fox did as she was directed.

'Fox has proven herself a useful creature and a good deal cheaper than Lady Dalrymple's seamstress. Of course, she requires correction, and appears for the most part to heed it. You would not believe how I have suffered instilling in my servants the importance of heeding directions,' said Miss Ibbotson. 'If you only knew what they put me through. Fox is a little more desirous of learning than some, I suppose. I am to host my brother and my two nieces next week. Fox is to assist in the preparations. In fact, she would not have it any other way. Miss Ibbotson, said she, I would be honoured to help you.'

'Is that before Miss Fox goes to Whitcombe or on her return?' said he.

Miss Ibbotson smiled apprehensively. 'It is not for me to say, Mr Beresford. Fox must answer for herself. But we need not dwell on such matters.' She perused the details of the cabinet maker, provided by her guest. 'May I ask, have you availed of the services of this particular cabinet maker yourself, Mr Beresford? Does the name you have supplied come with your personal recommendation?'

'It does,' said he.

'I hope he does not charge dear,' she replied.

'I am of the view that he charges a fair price for his labour.'

Miss Ibbotson enquired about certain of her neighbours in the Paragon and whether any of them had used the same craftsman.

Miss Fox brought in the tray and set it down gently in front of Miss Ibbotson.

'Thank you, Fox,' said she. 'I am surprised it took you quite so long, but I see that everything is in its place. There are sheets to be folded and deposited in the linen press. I should like them all put away before Frost returns.'

'Of course,' said Miss Fox, without raising her eyes to Miss Ibbotson or Mr Beresford. There was no hint of discontent, no look of reproach, in her manner towards Miss Ibbotson. Mr Beresford wondered at the artless acquiescence of Miss Fox and the apparent contentment she seemed to derive from carrying out her duties, despite the manner in which the directions were given.

Mr Beresford stayed just long enough to consume one dish of tea. Miss Fox did not appear again for the duration of his visit, and with some unease over the scene he had encountered, he took his leave of Miss Ibbotson.

CHAPTER TWENTY-FIVE

When next they met, Mrs Beresford listened in amazement to Lady Allersham's suspicions concerning Miss Carteret and Captain Fitzroy.

'I can hardly believe it,' said she. 'I suppose it explains Miss Carteret's temperament at times. And if it is so, then I am truly very sorry for her. But why did she not make known to you her connexion with Captain Fitzroy when we first made her acquaintance? And Lady Dalrymple? I cannot believe that she would be so furtive. I find it all quite perplexing,' said Mrs Beresford. 'What a time to have quitted Laura Place! At such an interesting moment!'

'It becomes more interesting still,' said Lady Allersham, 'for Robert has dined a second time in Laura Place. He is become quite a favourite there though he hints that he is making slow progress with Miss Carteret. Now we know why that might be. Come, there is something I must show you.' Lady Allersham led Mrs Beresford into the library and placed in front of her the wooden box she had found among Captain Fitzroy's belongings.

'A box?' said Mrs Beresford, with a questioning look.

'Do you remember when first we visited the Dalrymples in Laura Place, Miss Carteret referred to possessing a key without a box?'

'Did she?' Mrs Beresford said, unable to recall the precise conversation. 'I understood her to speak in general terms.'

'But do not you recall my saying to you that Miss Carteret wore a gold chain on which was hung a key. I suspected it immediately. And she confessed to it. It was as though she wished to be found out. Indeed, those were her very words. *You have found me out*, or something to that effect,' Lady Allersham replied. 'Aunt, consider. This may be the box.'

Mrs Beresford picked it up and examined it. 'What reason have you to suppose that this is the box?'

'Miss Carteret's volume was found with Captain Fitzroy's books on *that* shelf,' said she, pointing to the place where she had first discovered the book. The signature "J Carteret" matches exactly the signature on the letter I received from Miss Carteret at Laura Place. The hand is one and the same. Do you see?'

Lady Allersham took the volume from the shelf. 'And there is more,' said she, taking the pressed leaf of ivy from between the pages of the book.

'You know more than I, Aunt, what flowers and fauna signify. Tell me if you will, the meaning an ivy leaf conveys.'

'If my memory serves me correctly, I believe ivy represents fidelity,' she replied.

'There, you see,' said Lady Allersham, 'Miss Carteret and Captain Fitzroy were more than common acquaintances. Neither I nor Henry knew there was any connexion between them at all. And why Miss Carteret never mentioned a word about it is a complete mystery to me.'

'And yet we cannot be certain that the ivy leaf holds any special significance for we do not know the circumstances in which it came to be pressed between the pages of the volume. Should we perhaps take care not to jump to conclusions? I am sure Lady

Dalrymple would have mentioned any prior connexion with Allersham. Remember, it was Lady Russell who made the introductions when we first arrived in Bath and no mention was made then of the Dalrymples having visited Allersham or of their acquaintance with the family.'

'Yes,' replied Lady Allersham, 'all that is true.' She looked at the volume once again as though expecting to gain insight from it. 'Which means that Miss Carteret and Captain Fitzroy must have had a secret understanding. There can be no other view.'

'Unless,' said Mrs Beresford, 'these objects were being held by Captain Fitzroy in safe keeping for another — a fellow officer, perhaps.'

'I see what you mean. But who? Surely not Charles Blake! Charles was Captain Fitzroy's closest friend and confidante. But I confess, such a thought did not occur to me,' said Lady Allersham. 'Surely, it cannot be possible.'

'Whatever the case may be, I believe you must speak to Miss Carteret, for only she has it in her power to explain the matter in full. All else is mere speculation.'

'I have made up my mind to go to Bath. I am to send the carriage for Miss Fox anyway, so there is no reason why I should not make use of it myself,' said Lady Allersham.

'Miss Fox, of course!' Mrs Beresford replied. The mention of Miss Fox gave her the perfect opening for news of her own. 'My dear, I too have news. James Beresford has written to me concerning Miss Fox, and I am sorry to say that it is not good news.'

'What is it? What has happened?' said Lady Allersham.

'He has been as good as his word,' Mrs Beresford replied. 'He met Miss Fox by chance in Queen Square on Tuesday, I believe, and again the day after or thereabouts when he called on Miss Ibbotson in Paragon Buildings. Reading between the lines, I suspect Miss Ibbotson is never done with seeking his advice on one thing or another. She sees that his nature is too yielding, and she takes advantage of it. That is my belief.'

'What does he say of Miss Fox?' enquired Lady Allersham. 'Nothing too disturbing, I hope.'

'Only that from his observation Miss Ibbotson appears exacting in her demands. He fears she may not release Miss Fox in time for the wedding but gives no reason for his suspicion. If it proves to be so, Miss Fox will be vastly disappointed.' said Mrs Beresford.

'No, Aunt,' said Lady Allersham. 'Miss Ibbotson will be vastly disappointed. Mrs Price gave me her word. If I am obliged to go to Bath myself and bring Miss Fox to Whitcombe, that is what I shall do.'

'Oh dear,' said Mrs Beresford. 'If only —'

'I know you are not at liberty to accompany me,' said Lady Allersham.

'I have invited the Daubers to dine —'

'And you cannot let them down,' said Lady Allersham. 'Do not be anxious. I shall manage very well on my own. And I am certain that Henry will not object.'

'Then Miss Fox must stay at Whitcombe,' said Mrs Beresford. 'I should be happy to have some company and at Whitcombe she may visit the Daubers whenever she wishes.'

232

Lady Allersham was delighted by the suggestion and thought it entirely appropriate that Miss Fox should stay close to the Rectory. 'And were Whitcombe to bring forth in Miss Fox a recollection from the past we might yet make progress in our quest.'

Mrs Beresford made no reply. She had a reason of her own for inviting Miss Fox to stay, quite apart from any pursuit concerning the circumstances of her birth. James Beresford's letter, whether intentional or not, seemed to convey an uncommon interest in Miss Fox. There was even a note of fondness in his expression. To determine whether her instinct was correct, and to establish if there existed any trace of affection on Miss Fox's part, Mrs Beresford was curious to observe the young woman at closer proximity. She had no doubt that James Beresford would find Miss Fox, in appearance, character and disposition, appealing; but she was inclined to suppose that a diffident Miss Fox would be less likely to think of James Beresford in quite the same way, there being so great a disparity in their consequence and situation.

When the subject of Bath was broached later that evening at Allersham Park, His Lordship made no objection to his wife's proposed expedition.

'Have you made arrangements for your stay?' said he.

'I shall not stay in Laura Place, if that is your meaning. There is no point in doing so on so short a visit.'

'My love, is the White Hart quite suitable?'

'I have no intention of staying at the White Hart.'

'Then where will you go?' said he.

'Sydney Place, if my cousin will have me,' said she.

'Does Harding know of your plans?'

'He will shortly. I have sent an express.'

'And how long shall you stay?'

'Two nights will achieve my aim,' said she.

'And your maid goes with you?'

'She does,' said Lady Allersham.

'Do the Dalrymples know of your plans?' said he.

'I wish to surprise them, though I may need my cousin's help to keep Lady Dalrymple entertained while I speak to Miss Carteret.'

Lord Allersham smiled, 'I doubt that will present a problem. Why does Harding remain in Bath? What business has he there?'

'More than you might imagine. Do not ask me. It may surprise you to find that I am just as proficient as Mr Dauber in keeping my silence. Mr Dauber is not the sole keeper of secrets.'

'What has Dauber got to do with anything?' said Lord Allersham.

'Mr Dauber is happy to keep you and I in the dark while hinting that Miss Fox is in some way connected to Allersham, and at the same time he is quite content to see the person he placed into Mrs Price's care live a life of drudgery and obscurity without the means of improvement or escape. Is that the action of a good Christian? It is because Miss Fox is a woman that she has no means of making her own way in the world. Her only hope is to marry, but there are few men who will take her without a penny to her name.'

'And what do you say of rich women, of whom there are plenty, who marry poor men?'

'I say they are foolish indeed. For what woman, endowed with riches and independence, willingly surrenders her rights and fortune to another human being? She had better stay single. A woman less fortunate, on the other hand, can aspire only to the protection and shelter that a man of good fortune can provide. No other power but wealth allows a woman to direct her own destiny.'

'Then why did you consent to becoming my wife?' said he.

Lady Allersham was thoughtful in her reply. 'I should not have found a way to live in this world without you. And yet, love alone, without liberality of mind and deed, would not have sufficed. As a woman, I can exercise no power over you. You travel where and when it pleases you. You may consult me, of course, but ultimately the decision to do as you please resides entirely with you. And as my husband, it is within your power to forbid me to act on my conscience if it diverges from yours. But you do not choose to exercise that power. That is what I mean by liberality of mind and deed.'

'You see the world as it ought to be and not as it is. I believe your powers of persuasion are superior to mine,' said he. 'But if you truly hold to such views, surely you should seek to dissuade Miss Carteret from matrimony for she is just the type of rich young woman for whom matrimony is an evil rather than a blessing.'

'If what I suspect is true, Miss Carteret may have no thought of matrimony, at least not for the present. I shall return Miss Carteret's volume. But I shall leave the box where it is.'

Lord Allersham looked up in surprise.

'A little more clarity is needed first, is it not? If Miss Carteret confirms my suspicions, then we shall see.'

'I could not agree more,' said Lord Allersham. 'Such matters are best managed by degrees.'

Lady Allersham's proposed trip to Bath was confirmed by return of post. Captain Harding would be pleased to receive his cousin in Sydney Place.

'He says, after dinner, his housekeeper will see to all my requirements. He is to move to the White Hart to ensure that propriety is maintained. Dear Robert,' said she. 'Have I caused him a great deal of trouble?'

'No more than his own mother, I should imagine,' said Lord Allersham.

'I have never known him quite so fastidious. I am a married woman after all.'

'Nevertheless,' Lord Allersham replied, 'appearances matter, or so I am told by you, my dear.'

'It is too late to undo what is done. We shall make it up to him. Robert must come to Allersham. You, my love, may take him fishing. I only hope that I am able to accomplish *my* purpose.'

CHAPTER TWENTY-SIX

After the Dalrymples' return to Bath, Captain Harding had become a regular visitor to Laura Place. His willingness to place his carriage at Her Ladyship's disposal whenever she had need of it, and his diverting conversation, soon made him indispensable. Miss Carteret, who had viewed Captain Harding in a less than favourable light at their first meeting, now received him with equanimity, and the days that he

236

was not seen in Laura Place, she began to find strangely dull and empty. The change in Miss Carteret had been slow, but as she endeavoured to understand Captain Harding better, she saw that he had certain fine qualities to recommend him. Her gratitude was the greater, due to his uncommon discretion concerning the incident at the ball. He had persuaded her former friend, Mrs Baldwin, to keep her silence. Respect for the deceased naval hero had been his plea, and his appeal to Mrs Baldwin, as the daughter of a distinguished naval officer herself, had won the day. Miss Carteret's secret was safe.

At first, Captain Harding, who had done little more than entertain the challenge of making himself agreeable to Miss Carteret, found that what had begun as a pleasant pursuit, had advanced to something more noble. His attachment to her had grown almost as slowly as her indifference towards him had diminished. He was not without understanding and saw that the probability of a declaration being accepted might still be some way off. Until Miss Carteret was reconciled to the loss of Captain Fitzroy, the only course of action in his power was patience. He would wait for the right moment to make an offer and hope that good judgement in the timing of it prevailed.

The arrival of Lady Allersham in Sydney Place was anticipated with increasing curiosity. Her stay would be short but filled with engagements that left little time for discourse or pleasure.

'How was the journey?' said he.

'Accomplished without incident,' she replied. 'I shall have Miss Fox with me on my return until Whitcombe. She is to stay with Aunt Beresford.'

'And so, Miss Fox will go to Miss Dauber's wedding after all,' said he.

'There is no doubt about it,' she replied. 'I have come to fetch her.'

'That was not my understanding six hours ago when I called at Laura Place. Mr Ibbotson was of a different view. He called while I was there. Miss Carteret made a point of asking about Miss Fox.'

'Well then, Mr Ibbotson must have been misinformed,' said Lady Allersham. 'How do Lady Dalrymple and Miss Carteret go on?'

'The loss of your society is lamented. As you requested, I have said nothing to our friends in Laura Place of your arrival in Bath,' said he.

'Thank you,' she replied. After a short pause, she said, 'I have a commission for you, Cousin.'

'Oh?' said he.

'I should like to contrive a private conversation with Miss Carteret.'

'And you require my assistance? Let me guess. You wish me to distract Lady Dalrymple while you speak to Miss Carteret alone?'

'Precisely. I thought we might find them at the Pump Room,' said she.

'You do not know what you ask,' said Captain Harding, with a good-humoured sigh. 'Lady Dalrymple expects a letter from Lady Russell any day with the latest development in the continuing tale of woe which is the Elliot family. Sir Walter has found himself a rich widow in want of a title. And as she failed to obtain a lord, she is minded to settle for a baronet instead. So that Sir Walter may continue to make progress, he has extended his stay with the Wentworths. Lady Russell is ill disposed to stand by and watch the spectacle, so she is gone to Uppercross to patch things up with Sir Walter's daughter, whose name escapes me. And so it goes on. Has there ever been such a carry on as this? And now I shall be obliged to hear it all again tomorrow.'

Lady Allersham attempted, without success, to stifle a smile.

'I see what you are thinking,' said he, 'and of course you are right. Have I not family enough of my own to equal or surpass the exploits of Sir Walter?'

'Have you heard from my Aunt Fowle since she returned to Brinshore?' she replied.

'You will be pleased to know that my mother and Mr Fowle have lately reached a truce. How long it will last is uncertain.'

Not wishing to acknowledge his own part in bringing it about, Captain Harding replied, 'They have resolved to live separate lives under one roof, and speak without blame, malice or scorn, and only when necessity dictates. For the first time, Trafalgar Terrace is purported to be a haven of peace and tranquillity.'

'But not for the first time, Cousin,' said she. 'Remember, I spent one summer with Aunt Fowle in Brinshore. And what an eventful summer it was! Trafalgar Terrace was a haven then, at least for some of the time.'

'Was it?' said he.

'Did Charles Blake's attachment to our cousin surprise you?'

'I thought of you,' he replied. 'I knew Blake had always been a favourite of yours.'

'It broke my heart,' said she. 'And yet, it mended more easily that I thought possible. Bathing in the sea, walking by the shore, taking the air — there was consolation to be found by the sea. Perhaps Brinshore would be just the place for you.'

'Thank you, Emma,' said he, 'I shall remain here. Bath suits me. I may not stay forever, but at present it affords me the opportunity to pursue certain interests.'

'I wonder Lady Dalrymple does not return to Ireland,' said she.

'I thought you knew, Emma. The estate went to the nephew who made them, for want of a better word, unwelcome. She and Miss Carteret, who meant only to visit Bath for three months in the first instance, have remained in Bath ever since.'

'How strange. I never heard her speak of it,' said she.

'Nor I,' he replied. 'It was Miss Carteret who proffered the information.'

The next day afforded Lady Allersham the opportunity she had sought of a private conversation with Miss Carteret at the Pump Room. Captain Harding kept Lady Dalrymple occupied as instructed; the greater share of the conversation, however, fell to Her Ladyship, as Captain Harding spoke only to seek clarification of a point from time to time and, in the appropriate places, provide an occasional nod of understanding, or an expression of surprise when necessity required.

Lady Allersham led her friend to a quiet corner to avoid interruption or distraction. Miss Carteret was pleased, if a little apprehensive, to see Her Ladyship once again. Happily, the fear of discovery she had once harboured had diminished through the efforts of Captain Harding.

As they exchanged information of mutual interest, news of Miss Fox was uppermost in Miss Carteret's mind.

'Miss Fox is become quite indispensable to Mr Ibbotson's sister. Miss Ibbotson boasts that her furnishings are now fully made and restored, and everything is comfort and practicality. And much of it has been the work of Miss Fox. The Ibbotsons are expected to dine there next week,' said Miss Carteret. 'Mama and I are not invited, which is a great relief. I have never known Miss Ibbotson go to such trouble over her brother and nieces. She hinted that Mr Ibbotson has a matter of import to convey.'

'Oh?' said Lady Allersham.

'She is hopeful of an expectation of some kind but would not be drawn further on the matter. It seems a rich and elderly relative is not expected to last a full week.'

'It is unfortunate then that Miss Fox will not be in attendance to hear Miss Ibbotson's good news,' Lady Allersham replied.

'Will she not?'

'I shall take Miss Fox with me when I return to Allersham. She is to stay with Mrs Beresford at Whitcombe for three days, for I cannot arrange use of the carriage for her return to Bath any sooner than that,' said Lady Allersham.

'Mr Ibbotson's sister will be disappointed,' said Miss Carteret.

'Undoubtedly. But there we are,' she replied. Turning to another subject on which she had wished to enquire, Lady Allersham said, 'And how was Miss Elliot's wedding? I understand Sir Walter snubbed the Uppercross family.'

'And it has caused a great deal of trouble ever since. No doubt Captain Harding has mentioned that Lady Russell is gone to Uppercross to smooth the way. Mama says of Lady Russell that she is not one to shrink from awkward conversations. And another such conversation looms.'

'Sir Walter and the rich widow?'

'I see Captain Harding has given you an account already,' said Miss Carteret.

'My cousin is just as fascinated by intrigue and speculation as the next person, and likes to make the most of it,' said Lady Allersham.

Alarmed by Lady Allersham's remark concerning Captain Harding, Miss Carteret replied, 'I hope Captain Harding does not partake in such idle pastimes at the expense of others. I trust he values discretion above all things.'

Lady Allersham was puzzled by the sudden change in Miss Carteret's tone, the more so because she sought to bring the conversation to an abrupt end and seemed anxious to leave.

'Please allow me a few more minutes of your time,' said Lady Allersham. 'There is something I wish to return to you. I believe it is yours,' said she, in haste. She placed a small parcel into Miss Carteret's hands.

'For me?'

'Yes,' said Lady Allersham. 'Please feel at liberty to open it.'

Miss Carteret carefully untied the string and removed the item from the brown paper. Her fingers began to tremble. She recognised the volume immediately, and for several seconds was unable to speak. Lady Allersham made no effort to fill the silence but observed with interest the look of astonishment and alarm on the face of her companion. Lady Allersham received the confirmation she had sought.

With hesitation, Miss Carteret said, 'May I ask where you came upon it?'

'I found it quite by accident in the library at Allersham,' she replied.

'I see,' said Miss Carteret. 'I…I wonder how it came to be there.'

Lady Allersham spoke gently. 'I thought perhaps you might be able to explain its presence there better than I.'

'Yes, of course,' said she, fixing her eyes on Captain Harding who was standing at some distance, deep in conversation with her mother. 'I see how it is. How could I expect the matter to be concealed? Has my mother has been informed?'

'Are we speaking of Captain Fitzroy?'

'Foolishly, I believed my secret to be safe. I am a greater fool than I imagined.'

'May I ask how you became acquainted with Captain Fitzroy?' she replied.

An awkward pause preceded a deep intake of air before Miss Carteret spoke again.

'In the early autumn of fifteen, after the Waterloo Campaign, I was invited to spend some time with a family by the name of Buller near Cork on the south coast of Ireland. Miss Buller and I were friends but after leaving Ireland our letters and the intimacy that we had once enjoyed ceased. As you might expect in such a place, there was great excitement, dinners, concerts, balls, and among society there were many officers of the Navy. I was eighteen when I first met Captain Fitzroy. We were introduced at a ball. He was accompanied by another captain of the Navy who claimed an acquaintance through the wife of a retired admiral of the blue. His father had served with the admiral in years gone by. The admiral's widow introduced us. The rest is easy to imagine.'

'Do you recall the name of the captain who accompanied Captain Fitzroy?'

'Black, I believe.'

'Blake?'

'Yes, Blake was his name. Captain Blake,' said Miss Carteret.

Lady Allersham smiled but denied herself the opportunity to explain her own connexion with Captain Blake. 'Forgive me if I have caused you pain,' said she. 'May I ask, was there an understanding between you?'

'About a week before his ship was due to sail, Captain Fitzroy asked if he may go to my mother.'

'To seek permission?'

'Yes,' said Miss Carteret. 'Papa died some years ago. There being no son to inherit, the estate went to my uncle, a kind and generous man who would not hear of our removal from the home that had been beloved and precious, but to which we had no further claim.'

'No better uncle to have then,' said Lady Allersham.

'No, indeed.'

'Did Lady Dalrymple grant permission? Was your uncle of the same mind?'

'The following morning a letter arrived informing me that my uncle was gravely ill. I left Cork immediately. But it was too late. The suddenness of my uncle's death and the subsequent removal from our family home made an alliance at such a moment impossible. We decided — I decided, and Captain Fitzroy agreed — to delay matters until a more conducive time. We corresponded for some months. I did not speak of it to Mama. I could not. My uncle's death changed things for the worse, you see. Mama was most deeply affected by it when we had to quit our home. Then, after several months, suddenly, Captain Fitzroy's letters ceased. I assumed it signalled the end our understanding and was persuaded that I had been mistaken in Captain Fitzroy. England being so far away, there was little I could do. Believing Captain Fitzroy to be inconstant, I could not speak of it to Mama, nor did I suppose there to be another explanation for his silence. I fell ill. Mama believed the cause to be the sudden removal from the home of my birth. I allowed her to continue in that belief. My cousin, you see, had not his father's temperament or liberality of mind and heart. To see the place Mama loved fall into the hands of such a man, who sought only to profit from his own good fortune, was unendurable. It was made perfectly clear that our continued presence there was borne under sufferance. We came to Bath. I was at once fearful and excited by the prospect, for I knew that Bath was but a short distance from Allersham. I longed to see Captain Fitzroy again and dreaded it in equal measure. Most of all, I wanted to discover the reason for his silence. I suspected — feared — he had entered into a more suitable alliance. In Bath, our cousins, the Elliots, were anxious to seek a renewal of the good relations we had once enjoyed. I shall not oppress you with the reasons for the estrangement between our two families. Among their acquaintance was Lady Russell, a longstanding friend of the Elliot family from whom an introduction was sought and granted. I knew nothing of Lady Russell's connexion with Allersham.'

'Then you must have been astonished to make such a discovery,' said Lady Allersham.

'I was,' said Miss Carteret. 'One day, not long after the wedding of Captain and Mrs Wentworth, Mama and I were walking in Sydney Gardens when we came upon Lady Russell. I remember her words so clearly. *Lady Dalrymple*, said she. *You find me out of sorts today. I am grieved indeed. I must leave Bath tomorrow. Lord Allersham's health deteriorates at such a pace*. It was the elder brother of whom she spoke. Next came the worst shock of all. She said, *Is Allersham to endure another loss?* And then, you see, only then, did I comprehend the reason for Captain Fitzroy's silence. Several weeks later, I received a small parcel. It had been redirected from Ireland and had taken more than ten months to find me. The parcel contained a key. There was a note from Captain Fitzroy's man of business, which said only, *To the Honourable Miss Carteret, according to the late Captain Fitzroy's instructions.*'

'My dear Miss Carteret,' said Lady Allersham, 'I am truly sorry for all the sorrow you have endured and have borne alone in silence for so long. Forgive me for reviving those memories that must be so painful to you.'

Unable to speak further, Miss Carteret examined the volume in her hands until the page fell open and revealed the pressed leaf of ivy. She picked it up and placed it in the palm of her hand.

'You cannot know what it means to see this once again, to hold it,' said she.

'I pray you never again have cause to know such a feeling as this. But why, may I ask, did you not speak of it sooner?' Lady Allersham enquired gently.

'How could I? I had neither the words nor the courage,' said she. 'My object was to banish all thought of him from my mind. But I could not. And what was there to say about an attachment begun in secret and ended in secret?'

'You said you first heard the news of Captain Fitzroy in Sydney Gardens. Were you standing by the cascade?'

'Yes,' said Miss Carteret. 'How did you know?'

'When we first walked there, I saw how your countenance changed. I knew something had distressed you.'

'Of course. And I should not have ventured that way had it not been my aim to avoid the Misses Ibbotson.'

Lady Allersham smiled. 'And the key?'

'Your suspicions were correct. Several months ago, I lost the key when the chain to which it was attached broke. I thought I should never find it again.'

'And how did you discover it?'

'A maid found it on the stairs and was about to give it to the housekeeper. I saw it and recognised it immediately. But I have still no notion why Captain Fitzroy meant me to have it.'

'And do you still wear the key around your neck?'

'I do,' said she.

'May I look at it?'

Miss Carteret lifted the chain from inside her collar and pulled out the key. Lady Allersham studied it carefully.

'To what does the key belong?' said she.

'I should truly like to know,' replied Miss Carteret.

CHAPTER TWENTY-SEVEN

The key in Miss Carteret's possession was larger than expected, too large for the small wooden box found among Captain Fitzroy's effects; hence, Lady Allersham saw no reason to raise her friend's hopes that the item she had been searching for had been found.

Miss Carteret's story had surprised her. Since first hearing the name, Captain Fitzroy, during the summer spent with her aunt in Brinshore, no mention had ever been made of his connexion with any young woman. Despite lately suspecting an attachment between Captain Fitzroy and Miss Carteret, never had she heard their names spoken together in the same sentence, neither by his closest friend and confidante, Captain Blake, or her own husband. It seems curious, thought she, that he should keep a matter of such substance entirely to himself. What of the key that was taken from Captain Fitzroy's effects and posted to Miss Carteret by his man of business? Who else knew of its existence? What and where was the object to which the key belonged?

Lady Allersham had achieved one objective but had been obliged to leave Miss Carteret with a less than satisfactory promise. She resolved to make every effort to discover the key's purpose even though she could give no assurances that her endeavours would bear fruit.

'Did your interview with Miss Carteret meet with your satisfaction?' said Captain Harding, as they left the Pump Room.

'I believe I accomplished some of what I set out to do. Beyond that, I am not at liberty to say.'

'A matter of some importance then,' said he.

Lady Allersham smiled at her cousin but gave no reply.

Minutes later they were in sight of Gay Street where they parted company, Captain Harding having declined his cousin's invitation to accompany her on her visit to Mrs Price.

'Forgive me, Emma,' said he, 'if I forgo the enjoyment of sitting in Mrs Price's parlour for ten minutes of the day. I shall leave that pleasure entirely to you and you may tell me all about it later.'

'Why do all the disagreeable tasks fall to me?' she replied.

'Because you are more determined than the rest of us, hence you are bound to succeed where others fail.'

'You need not use your flattery on me,' said she.

'It is not flattery, Cousin. It is a fact,' he replied. 'It is poor Mrs Price I feel sorry for.'

'Poor Mrs Price indeed,' said Lady Allersham. 'Though, perhaps you are right.'

Mrs Price was surprised to receive Lady Allersham's card and to learn that Her Ladyship was waiting on her in the parlour; it was not a pleasant surprise, for the purpose of Her Ladyship's visit was easy to imagine. While Lady Allersham awaited Mrs Price, she made use of the time by examining the painting that Mrs Fowle had declared was, without question, a scene from Stanton Woods. The likeness was striking indeed, and on closer inspection she was bound to conclude that the scene bore a remarkable resemblance to the place.

Her reflections on the subject were interrupted abruptly when Mrs Price entered the room, flustered and dishevelled. 'Forgive me, Your Ladyship. Had I known that Your Ladyship might grace us with your presence today I should have made better accommodation — as you see, we are once again in uproar. It is daily to be expected.'

'My apologies, Mrs Price,' said she. 'I shall not trespass on your time.'

The door opened, and a young boarder entered. 'Please, Ma'am,' said she, 'we caught another one.'

Mrs Price signalled for the girl to leave the room immediately.

'Mice?' enquired Lady Allersham.

Mrs Price smiled awkwardly. 'Might I enquire as to the purpose of Your Ladyship's visit?'

'I am come quite simply to take Miss Fox to Whitcombe in accordance with our agreement. I have business in Bath and I am pleased to accommodate Miss Fox in the carriage on my return. Expect my carriage tomorrow morning at nine o'clock. Please see to it that Miss Fox is prepared and punctual.'

'That will not be possible, Your Ladyship,' said Mrs Price. 'Miss Fox has been rather unwell lately. I have been most solicitous of her health. I fear she may likely suffer a relapse of her earlier complaint.'

'Miss Fox is at home then?' said Lady Allersham. 'Would you show me to her room?'

'Forgive me. It is not advisable at present.'

'Miss Fox *is* at home, I take it?'

'No, Your Ladyship,' said she. 'She is presently with Miss Ibbotson. There was nothing I could say to prevent her from her duties, though I fear greatly for her constitution. She would insist on attending Miss Ibbotson. As you know, Miss Fox will not be told. She can be quite determined when she wants to be.'

'Mrs Price,' replied Lady Allersham, 'if Miss Fox is fit to travel and wishes to do so, I shall not countenance anyone who seeks to stand in her way. Is that understood?'

'Miss Ibbotson, you see,' said Mrs Price, 'has great need of Miss Fox — very great need, very great need indeed. A matter of great importance. I cannot stress enough —'

'Mrs Price, might I remind you that you gave me your word. I shall leave you now and return at nine o'clock in the morning. Make sure Miss Fox is ready to travel.'

Lady Allersham left Gay Street for Paragon Buildings, resolved to discover for herself the state of Miss Fox's health and her treatment at the hands of Miss Ibbotson. On being admitted to the drawing room she found both Miss Ibbotson and Miss Fox, the latter seeking further instructions over a chore that had been carried out with less care and attention than had suited her mistress.

'Miss Ibbotson, I thank you for receiving me. I understood from Mrs Price that I would find Miss Fox here. I beg your indulgence for it is Miss Fox I am here to see,' said Lady Allersham. Leaving no opportunity for Miss Ibbotson to reply, she turned to address Miss Fox directly. 'Miss Fox, I am come to take you to Whitcombe. I leave Bath in the morning and I should like you to accompany me. Miss Dauber

251

sends her good wishes and expects to see you at the wedding. Mrs Beresford has asked if you would stay with her at Whitcombe as she resides close to the Rectory. You will find it a great deal more convenient than Allersham.'

'I beg your pardon, Lady Allersham,' said Miss Ibbotson, 'but Miss Fox is required here, and I do not think she is quite well, and certainly not fit to travel so great a distance.'

'Whitcombe is no great distance, Miss Ibbotson. If Miss Fox is well enough to attend you, she is well enough to travel to Whitcombe. And I am certain that Mrs Beresford will ensure that she obtains all the rest that is necessary when she arrives at her destination.'

'Miss Fox,' said Miss Ibbotson, 'would you please explain to Lady Allersham that you are not well enough to travel?'

'I — I do not know what I might be in the morning, Your Ladyship,' said Miss Fox.

'Miss Ibbotson,' said Lady Allersham, 'I should like to speak with Miss Fox in private. A minute or two will suffice.'

Miss Fox glanced timidly at her mistress and received a look of hostile intent in return. Lady Allersham observed the silent exchange between them before fixing her eyes on Miss Ibbotson until she left the room. When the door was firmly shut behind her, Lady Allersham beckoned Miss Fox to sit down. 'Now, tell me truthfully,' said she, 'have you been prevailed upon to abandon your visit to Whitcombe?'

'I really cannot say, Your Ladyship,' said she.

'If fear prevents you from speaking plainly,' she replied, 'have courage. I am here to take you to

252

Whitcombe. Miss Fox, do you wish to attend the wedding of your friend?'

Miss Fox was aware of the consequences of defying Mrs Price and Miss Ibbotson, and the censure that would follow should her resolve to place her own desires above all else triumph. She did not wish to seem selfish or neglectful of their needs. And yet had she not given her word to Miss Dauber? How could she disappoint her friend?

'Courage, Miss Fox,' said Lady Allersham.

Her answer came with a cautious, but affirmative nod of the head.

Lady Allersham replied, 'Miss Dauber will be very happy. I shall attend to any objections put forward by Mrs Price and Miss Ibbotson. You have nothing to fear. Be prepared to leave at nine o'clock in the morning.'

The protestations that followed from Miss Ibbotson were soon crushed when Lady Allersham hinted that Lady Dalrymple had expressed an interest in employing Miss Fox herself.

'Oh yes,' said Lady Allersham. 'It seems Lady Dalrymple's present seamstress has been obliged to find alternative work due to her failing eyesight. She is, therefore, most interested in securing the services of Miss Fox.'

Such a prospect was not to be borne: Miss Fox would not easily be replaced on the very reasonable terms that existed between herself and Mrs Price. But to surrender the services of Miss Fox to Lady *Dalrymple* of all people was insupportable. Without further discussion, Miss Ibbotson relented. 'I am vastly disappointed in you, Miss Fox,' said she. 'I shall expect better than this on your return. Is that understood?'

CHAPTER TWENTY-EIGHT

The journey to Whitcombe the following day was accomplished without obstacle or delay. Lady Allersham was pleased to release Miss Fox into Mrs Beresford's care, and though Miss Fox seemed at first daunted by the grandeur of Whitcombe Park, she was filled with wonder at the enchanting vista that unfolded before her. The house was full of charm, and so completely unlike the image of austere stateliness she had imagined it to be, that she soon felt almost at ease. Mrs Beresford took personal charge by explaining the layout of the house and showing Miss Fox the room which was to be her bedchamber.

When the dust of the day had been washed off and Miss Fox had made herself presentable, she came down to the drawing room where Mrs Beresford had arranged some refreshment. After enquiries were made regarding the journey, Miss Fox's duties in Paragon Buildings, and the health of Mrs Price, Mrs Beresford was pleased to inform her guest that they were to call at the Rectory the following morning.

'Miss Dauber and Mr Sparke will be delighted to hear that Mrs Price was able to spare you,' said she. 'For I understand that your attendance at the wedding was in some doubt. It was Mr Beresford who first suspected something amiss and when the matter came to the attention of Lady Allersham she would not rest until it was settled to her satisfaction. My niece can be very determined at times but never in a malevolent way.'

'Lady Allersham has been very good to me. I do not know why Her Ladyship should show me such kindness. I am sure I have done nothing to deserve it. I have no special talent, no connexions, nothing beyond the ability to sew and mend. And even then, there are many young women in the world whose handiwork is infinitely superior to mine.'

'You do yourself a disservice, Miss Fox. Mr Beresford believes you do, and I am inclined to agree with him.'

'I have never heard Mr Beresford say a harsh word about anyone or anything.'

'Nor I,' said Mrs Beresford. 'On that point we are in complete agreement. I knew little of Mr James Beresford prior to Colonel Beresford's death, for he was brought up at a great distance and spent several years in the East Indies. In many ways, Miss Fox, James Beresford reminds me of my late husband with whom I never had a cross word in my entire life.'

'How comforting to be reminded so agreeably of the Colonel,' said she. 'Does Mr Beresford bear a family likeness to him?'

'Come, Miss Fox,' said Mrs Beresford. 'Allow me to show you a likeness of the Colonel. It is a very good one.'

Mrs Beresford led Miss Fox into the Colonel's study which had been preserved exactly as it was at the hour of his death. There, by the window, displayed in a glass case was a collection of miniatures. Mrs Beresford opened the case and took out a fine portrait of her husband captured several years earlier and encased in silver.

Miss Fox examined it with care and sensitivity, admiring the brilliance of the brushwork.

'He was very handsome,' said Miss Fox.

'And here is another portrait captured in his younger days. A gift from the Colonel on our wedding day.'

Miss Fox studied his features closely, to Mrs Beresford's delight. After some moments, she returned it and said, 'And the portrait that lies next to it bears your image, does it not?'

'Yes. It was my gift to my husband. We had the portraits commissioned in case we should ever be parted. You see, Miss Fox, we lived in uncertain times then. I suppose we still do.'

Mrs Beresford carefully replaced the objects in the cabinet and was about to close the lid, when Miss Fox asked if she might look once again at the younger portrait of the Colonel. It was an unusual request, but one with which Mrs Beresford was happy to comply. Miss Fox studied his likeness for several moments before depositing the item once again under the glass.

'Was Colonel Beresford a tall gentleman?' said Miss Fox.

'He was,' she replied. 'And he looked very smart indeed in his regimentals. There is a larger portrait of him in the dining room in full military dress. Should you like to see it?'

'Very much,' said Miss Fox.

As they entered the dining room, Miss Fox's eyes were immediately drawn to the portrait of the Colonel that hung over the fireplace. She faltered slightly, though her hesitation went unnoticed by Mrs Beresford, whose eyes were fixed adoringly on the painting.

Mrs Beresford turned to her guest and said, 'The artist captured my dear Colonel completely. Does he not look striking in his regimentals?'

'Oh yes. Yes, indeed,' said she. 'I have not seen a finer portrait in my life.'

'It is very good of you to say so, Miss Fox. And, as you know, I am in full agreement. It is my greatest comfort, for when my spirits are low, and I have need of his counsel, here is where I find it.'

Mrs Beresford had observed nothing of Miss Fox's confusion, which began in the Colonel's study. The miniatures first caught her attention, most particularly the likeness captured several years earlier. There was something familiar in his look that confused her. Most puzzling of all, however, was the sensation she felt the moment she saw the portrait of the Colonel in his regimentals. Almost as soon as Miss Fox entered the dining room, an unnerving realisation dawned upon her: she believed she had seen the gentleman in the portrait, met the gentleman in the portrait, once before. The details were uncertain; when, where, how, were questions beyond her ability to answer. But there was little doubt in her mind: Colonel Beresford had played some part in her past.

The astonishing discovery caused Miss Fox to appear somewhat agitated and inattentive during dinner. Mrs Beresford was not unduly anxious about her guest and assumed that the feeling was entirely natural. Unaccustomed to her new surroundings, and having undergone a tiring journey from Bath, Miss Fox's agitation was easily explained.

When dinner was over, and they had removed to the drawing room, Mrs Beresford proposed that they spend no more than an hour by the fire before retiring. 'A good night's sleep in a comfortable bed is the best remedy. You must be very tired after such an eventful day.'

'I am, Mrs Beresford,' said Miss Fox.

'I have become fond of poetry of late. Do you like to read, Miss Fox?'

'I feel ashamed to say that I have little time for reading of my own. I am requested to read to others from time to time. Miss Ibbotson likes me to read when I have nothing else to do.'

'And what is Miss Ibbotson's taste? Poetry? Prose, perhaps?'

'Prose,' said she. '*The Vicar of Wakefield* is a great favourite, for she is much drawn to the character of Squire Thornhill.'

Mrs Beresford suppressed a smile. 'Is she? How interesting. And is Mr Goldsmith a favourite with you?'

'I do not mind Mr Goldsmith,' she replied, 'but I find Mr Crabbe more to my taste.'

'Then let us read from the *Tales*,' Mrs Beresford replied.

'May I?' said Miss Fox.

'Of course. I should like that very much,' she replied. 'There is a copy in the study, and I know just where to put my hands on it.'

Miss Fox was pleased to have a few minutes to herself. The portrait of the Colonel had caused her further discomposure during dinner. Several times she had glanced at the painting that towered over them as they dined. In vain, she tried to recall every possible occurrence that might shed light upon her past encounter with the Colonel. Had the event occurred during her time in Gay Street, she would have been able to recall the details with greater clarity. There was nothing to connect Colonel Beresford with Gay Street, of that she was almost certain. Her recollections of life before her removal there, however, were imperfect, partial at best. There were but two people to whom she could apply for information: Mr Dauber and Mrs Price.

What troubled Miss Fox most of all was the knowledge that Mrs Beresford was utterly unsuspecting. She could imagine nothing worse than that Mrs Beresford should discover a secret concerning her beloved husband, the weight of which would cast a shadow over his most cherished memory. Mrs Beresford must never know or have cause to doubt him, thought she. I must put all thought of the Colonel aside for the sake of those who have shown me great kindness.

Mrs Beresford returned with a volume of Crabbe. 'I knew exactly where to look,' said she. 'I haven't opened the volume for some time. Should you like to read, or shall I?'

'I shall be guided by you,' said Miss Fox.

'Then perhaps you might begin reading, if you will,' she replied.

'With pleasure, Mrs Beresford.'

CHAPTER TWENTY-NINE

A night of restlessness and disturbing thoughts left Miss Fox without sleep, and less refreshed the following morning than Mrs Beresford had anticipated. A wholesome breakfast was prescribed to provide strength for the day ahead. They were to walk to the Rectory to call on the Daubers, as Miss Dauber had a request of Miss Fox prior to the wedding.

'We shall not stay beyond half an hour unless Mrs Dauber insists, for there will be much to do,' said Mrs Beresford.

'I should be happy to be of service to Mrs Dauber in any way I can,' Miss Fox replied.

'That will not be possible, I'm afraid,' said Mrs Beresford. 'We are expected at Allersham Park for luncheon. Lord Allersham is from home today. If the weather is kind to us, we shall walk down to the lake.'

'I should like to see Allersham very much indeed,' said Miss Fox. 'Her Ladyship has been so kind to me. Might I be of service to Lady Allersham? If it is not in my power to assist Mrs Dauber, perhaps I can be of use elsewhere. It is a strange sensation, Mrs Beresford, to be so completely without purpose or employment. Please do not misunderstand or suppose me ungrateful. That I should never be. I am so very grateful to you for your kindness, and I shall never forget it. When I looked out of the window this morning, I thought I was in a dream.'

The visit to the Rectory was a brief but pleasant one. Mr Dauber was not present, for at the last minute he was called away to the bedside of an elderly parishioner. Mrs Dauber, surrounded by her five children, spoke of her satisfaction in contemplating the marriage of her eldest daughter, and her great joy that she should soon be settled less than three miles from the Rectory. Her aim was to see her remaining two daughters also married within a year, and were her wish to be fulfilled, she would die content. Of her sons, she was proudest of all, for one was destined for the Church and the other the Law.

Miss Dauber and Miss Fox sat together in the parlour for five minutes exchanging news and hopes that the fine weather would continue for the all-important day. As soon as her mother began an account of the state of her health, Miss Dauber insisted on showing Miss Fox her wedding clothes.

'I should like to seek your opinion on how I should dress my hair,' said Miss Dauber. And then in a whisper, she continued, 'I am not of Mama's view, for the style she prefers does not become me. And Dent is quite hopeless with hair. It would please me greatly were she to manage my sisters' hair and leave mine alone. And if you were disposed to agree, Maria, I should like you to dress my hair for no one understands hair better than you. Please say that you will.'

'Of course,' said Miss Fox. 'I should be honoured to dress your hair on your special day.'

'I knew you would. And if you would come early in the morning, I should like you to be my particular maid. There is no one I should trust more than you, Maria, to make me look my best. No one in this household at least.'

Miss Dauber was satisfied that her wish had been granted, and when Dent entered with a message for Miss Fox, that Mrs Beresford was ready to leave, she was only too pleased to part with her friend until the morning.

Outside the Rectory, the arrival of the Allersham carriage that had been ordered to collect Mrs Beresford and Miss Fox drew the attention of neighbours and passers-by. As the Rectory family assembled to bid 'good day' to their visitors, the hope that the following day would be a fine one was expressed repeatedly before they departed.

As the carriage moved off, Mrs Beresford said, 'Mrs Dauber appears in better health today, but I do not think she thrives. It would not surprise me to hear, when the wedding is over, that she has taken to her bed, for her constitution is not what it once was,' said Mrs Beresford. 'I am pleased that you had time to speak with Miss Dauber. Had she something particular to say to you? It was my understanding that she had.'

'Yes,' said Miss Fox. 'And nothing could give me more pleasure. Miss Dauber has asked me to dress her hair tomorrow and help with those duties that usually fall to her maid. What an honour it is to be asked to dress the hair of the bride!'

Mrs Beresford had expected Miss Dauber to ask Miss Fox to be her bridesmaid. 'Forgive me,' said she. 'Has there been some misunderstanding? I had not thought your friend would ask this of you.' She wanted to say more, to decry Miss Dauber's request, but saw at that moment that it served the best interests of all to hold her tongue. She had supposed that the reason for Miss Fox's invitation had been borne solely of friendship, not of convenience and usefulness to herself.

'Is there something wrong?' said Miss Fox, observing a change in Mrs Beresford's look.

'No, not at all,' she replied. 'I am vexed with myself, that is all.'

'The young Dauber girls are to be bridesmaids,' Miss Fox replied, brightly. 'And I think it quite wonderful. They are so very excited at the prospect.'

Half an hour later, Mrs Beresford and Miss Fox arrived at the entrance to Allersham Park. The former, still inwardly vexed by Miss Dauber's request, kept her composure by drawing Miss Fox's attention to various points of interest along the way as they passed through the grounds. Miss Fox looked in amazement at the beauty and extent of the Park and longed for the house to come into view.

'Shall we truly walk in the Park?' said Miss Fox.

'Certainly, we shall.'

When the house finally appeared, Miss Fox gazed at the edifice in wonder and disbelief. 'It is so very grand. I shall be afraid to pass through its entrance.'

'The first time, perhaps. But have no fear,' replied Mrs Beresford, 'you are among friends.'

The warmth of her reception made Miss Fox's introduction to Allersham less daunting than she had anticipated. Lady Allersham was eager to hear all her news — how she found Whitcombe — what was her opinion of the Rectory and its inhabitants — what was Miss Dauber's state of mind? Nervous? Calm? Sparkling? When all her enquiries had been answered, Lady Allersham said, 'I have arranged for you to take a tour of the house. My housekeeper is to be your guide and she will be pleased to assist you with any questions you may have. Then you are to join Mrs Beresford and I for luncheon. Mrs Rawlings will show the way.'

Overawed by the kindness shown to her by those so far above her station in life, and more so because she had received so little kindness in the course of it from those far closer to her in circumstance and situation, Miss Fox could think of nothing more to say to Her Ladyship than *thank you*.

'My dear Aunt,' said Lady Allersham, after Miss Fox had been led away by the housekeeper, 'I am almost back to where I started over the matter concerning Miss Carteret. I have been longing to tell you what transpired ever since my return from Bath. While I was there, Henry found the key to Captain Fitzroy's box and presented it to me on my return. And what do you think? It is not the same size or shape of key as the one in Miss Carteret's possession. And so, I had no scruples in opening the box. I cannot tell you how disappointing it was to find a bundle of bills for items of clothing and the like. I have since made a thorough search of Captain Fitzroy's belongings and have found nothing to which the key might rightfully belong. I am mystified. At least I was not wrong about Miss Carteret and Captain Fitzroy. There *was* an understanding between them, and things might have turned out very differently had Captain Fitzroy lived.'

'Poor Miss Carteret,' said Mrs Beresford. 'How did she seem when you left her?'

'A little shaken,' she replied. 'I gave her my word that I would do what I could to help her in her quest. But all I have succeeded in doing is provide false hope. If only the key had belonged to the box.'

'What says Lady Dalrymple?' Mrs Beresford replied.

'It appears she has no knowledge of the matter either.'

A little before Mrs Rawlings ushered Miss Fox into the dining room, Mrs Beresford returned to the subject of the wedding.

'I confess, I was disappointed in Miss Dauber,' said she. 'Did we not conclude that the *very particular request* Miss Dauber desired to make of Miss Fox was to be her bridesmaid?'

'Indeed,' Lady Allersham replied. 'I thought it was settled. Miss Fox *is* to be Miss Dauber's bridesmaid, is she not?'

'Miss Dauber has asked Miss Fox to act as her *maid* on the day.'

Lady Allersham was shocked to hear it. 'And this is how Miss Dauber treats her friend?'

'But, I might add, Miss Fox does not look on the request in the same light. She is delighted to be of service to her friend. I sensed no reluctance on her part to comply with Miss Dauber's request. Indeed, I do not think the idea of being a bridesmaid had ever crossed her mind.'

'I have noticed that Miss Dauber is a little begrudging of the notice her friend receives. Perhaps I should have invited Miss Dauber for luncheon. Well,' said she, 'I see I shall be obliged to attend the wedding, if only to ease Miss Dauber's resentment.'

'You may be right,' said Mrs Beresford. 'Mrs Dauber was shocked to discover that Miss Fox was to stay at Whitcombe. She asked what the Colonel would have said about it and seemed to imply that he would have opposed it completely. But I am quite certain he would never have done such a thing.'

CHAPTER THIRTY

The attendance of Lady Allersham at the wedding of Mr Dauber's eldest daughter instantly elevated the new bride in the eyes of the neighbourhood from an unexceptional young lady who had, against all odds, succeeded in finding a husband as unremarkable as herself, to that of a young bride to whom notice could not be denied.

Invitations from some of the leading families of the neighbourhood to the bride and groom had been thin and slow to arrive, but the presence of Lady Allersham's carriage was enough to occasion several more, to the complacency and satisfaction most particularly of the bride. The new Mrs Sparke could look forward to many occasions of the kind and savour the opportunity it afforded on each one of them to speak of the presence of her good friend, Lady Allersham, at the wedding.

Miss Fox was wholly satisfied with her part in the proceedings, and although no personal recognition of her efforts had been forthcoming, a few complimentary remarks were made in passing, praising the bride for the excellent way in which her hair had been dressed. Mrs Beresford was sorry to see that Miss Fox's handiwork received no acknowledgement; more concerning, however, was the fact that Miss Fox seemed almost invisible to her friend, conduct that, under any other circumstances, would seem tantamount to thoughtlessness and neglect. Perhaps on such an occasion some might deem it permissible, thought she, for a new bride, overwhelmed by attention and scrutiny, to forget what was due to her friend; but, in the eyes of Mrs Beresford, such behaviour must always be reprehensible.

Mrs Beresford and Miss Fox joined the Daubers and the Sparkes for the wedding breakfast; to the dissatisfaction of the bride, Lady Allersham left immediately after the service due to the expected arrival of a visitor at Allersham Park. The surprise express from Captain Harding, announcing his intention to call on his way to Brinshore, puzzled Lady Allersham greatly. She had seen him but three days ago, and he had mentioned nothing of his plans to quit Bath.

On her return to Allersham she found that her cousin had already arrived and was with Lord Allersham in the library.

'Robert?' said she, as she entered the room in haste. 'What takes you to Brinshore? Is Aunt Fowle unwell? Henry? What is it?'

Lord Allersham glanced at Captain Harding and said, 'Emma, I think your cousin requests a private interview. I shall leave you.'

When they were quite alone, Captain Harding said, 'Shall we walk? I find it easier to speak that way.'

'Of course,' she replied. 'We shall walk down to the lake if you wish.'

They walked in the direction of the lake so that she might show her cousin the newly laid path.

Captain Harding made no attempt to exchange pleasantries and came straight to the matter that had brought him to Allersham. 'Emma,' said he, 'there are few people in the world to whom I am able to speak with complete candour. You, my dear Cousin, are one of the very few.'

'I am glad. Truly, I am,' said she.

'Have you any notion of my purpose in coming here?' he replied.

'No,' said she. 'None at all.'

Captain Harding paused to collect his thoughts. 'I doubt it will surprise you, Emma, to learn of my feelings for Miss Carteret.'

She looked at him and smiled. 'I confess, I suspected something of the kind. In return, it may surprise you to know that my suspicions were raised almost from the outset and, I am ashamed to say, I was not at first convinced that such a match would gain universal approval.'

'And I bear you no ill will for believing as you did. I was just as convinced as you of my unsuitability in *her* eyes.'

'But had you not concealed the extent of your inheritance, I should have had no doubt at all that she would have accepted you eventually,' said she.

'I am a romantic at heart, Emma,' said he. 'I hoped, indeed I still hope, to marry for love.'

'And you had reason to believe that you might secure Miss Carteret's affections?'

'Foolishly, yes,' said he. 'But my belief was based on a false premise. Had I known at the outset that her heart belonged to another, I should have proceeded with caution, perhaps entertained a larger measure of doubt, and exercised a greater degree of prudence.'

'But Miss Carteret is not pledged to another.'

'No, she is not, though she might well be,' he replied. 'How does one compete with the revered memory of the deceased? The one who can do no wrong. The one to whom perfection can be applied and allowed to stand unchallenged for eternity.'

'Have you spoken to Miss Carteret?'

'I have,' said he. 'I was refused.'

'I am so very sorry, Cousin,' said she, astounded by his disclosure. 'May I ask, do you suspect that your rejection was due to an enduring affection Miss Carteret has for a person now deceased? Did Miss Carteret speak of her fidelity to the memory of someone with whom she once had hopes of an alliance?'

'I already had an understanding of the matter.'

'What?' said she, all astonishment.

'I happened to be present when an unguarded and untimely remark, made by a former acquaintance of Miss Carteret, was uttered,' said he. 'The night she fled from the Upper Rooms. The night of the ball.'

Lady Allersham replied, 'And you have known all this time?'

'I made a solemn promise to conceal the matter,' Captain Harding replied.

'Do you know the name of the deceased?'

He nodded, glancing briefly at his cousin.

'Then I do not see why we should conceal his name any longer,' she continued.

'But how did you —'

'Discover Miss Carteret's secret?' said she.

'I found an item belonging to Miss Carteret among Captain Fitzroy's possessions. I went to Bath to return it to her. Cousin, there is one thing I do not understand. If you knew Miss Carteret's secret, what convinced you of the notion that she might accept your offer?'

'Until a week ago, I sensed there was some cause to hope. Even Lady Dalrymple hinted at the idea, and Miss Carteret made no attempt to admonish her mother. Emma, when you asked me to distract Lady Dalrymple so that you might have a private conversation with Miss Carteret at the Pump Room —'

'Yes?' she replied.

'— it was then that I asked Lady Dalrymple's permission to apply to her daughter.'

'Dear Robert!' Lady Allersham replied. 'Why did you not say?'

'I wanted to be certain of a favourable outcome. I called at Laura Place the following day, the morning you left for Allersham.'

'What was Miss Carteret's reason for declining your offer?'

'Trust, or rather, the absence of it.'

Lady Allersham hesitated. 'Trust? I cannot believe it. Did she say why?'

Captain Harding shook his head. 'I gave her my word and kept my word completely.'

'And she suspects otherwise,' surmised Lady Allersham.

'Yes,' said he. 'She refused to explain why.'

'I hope nothing I said gave her cause to doubt you.'

'How could it?' said he.

Lady Allersham glanced hesitantly at her cousin. 'I discovered the connexion between Captain Fitzroy and Miss Carteret in the library at Allersham. A book belonging to Miss Carteret was among Captain Fitzroy's possessions. She also has in her possession a key belonging to him. The key was sent to Miss Carteret by his attorney following Captain Fitzroy's death. No note of explanation accompanied the item. I had at first assumed that the key belonged to a box I found in Captain Fitzroy's room. But I was mistaken.'

They walked on in silence until they reached the lake. There they sat down.

At length, he broke the silence, 'Tell me about the key.'

'There is not much to tell. It is a key. Quite an ordinary key,' she replied.

'You don't suppose it might pertain to some object employed at sea?' said Captain Harding.

'You, of all people, would know if such a possibility exists.'

'I cannot say without examining the key myself,' said he. 'Can you describe it?'

'Not easily,' she replied. 'But I believe I can make a drawing of it.'

'Very well,' said he. 'I cannot promise to solve your puzzle.'

'It is not my puzzle, Cousin. I should imagine any service you perform for Miss Carteret to bring her round would be enticement enough to make it your quest.'

'I shall not renew my addresses to Miss Carteret, Emma.'

'Nonsense! Time and patience are all that is required,' said she.

'Miss Carteret could not have been clearer. Any renewal of the sentiments that led me to make her an offer in the first place would be met with the same response. She has made up her mind.'

'She is not ready. That is all,' said Lady Allersham, gently. 'And what says Lady Dalrymple?'

'I left Laura Place immediately. I did not wait to find out,' he replied. 'I shall break my journey at Portsmouth for I have business there. I expect to arrive in Brinshore at the end of the week.'

'Will you not stay here for a day or two?'

'Thank you. I must be on my way. I have spent too long in idleness and foolish hopes.'

The following day brought news from Whitcombe that Miss Fox had tripped and fallen while taking a walk in the grounds. Mrs Beresford decided that the return of Miss Fox to Bath should be postponed until the bruising to her face and arm had subsided.

'Whatever would Mrs Price say if we were to return Miss Fox in such a state? There is a new physician in Whitcombe, a Mr Lane, who came the minute he received my request. He says two weeks and no less is required to make the disfiguring bruises disappear. I must confess, I am in part responsible for Miss Fox's accident. In my absent-mindedness, I forgot to warn our friend of the small step at the entrance to the walled garden.'

'The same step that is covered in moss and weeds? The step I almost tripped over myself?'

'The very same, I am sorry to say. I meant to have it cleared.'

'Well,' said Lady Allersham, 'It is a good excuse to keep our friend at Whitcombe a little longer.'

'I am pleased to have the company,' said Mrs Beresford.

'Mrs Price must be informed,' replied Lady Allersham.

'I have already sent word to Gay Street. Miss Fox is resting. Mr Lane has prescribed a poultice of comfrey for the bruising.'

'Excellent,' said she. 'And so, how was the wedding breakfast?'

CHAPTER THIRTY-ONE

One morning, almost a week after Captain Harding's departure, Lady Allersham was about to ride into Whitcombe when a letter arrived to delay her departure. The letter was addressed in an unfamiliar hand. The message contained within it was as surprising as it was abrupt, for the letter came from Mrs Price and contained an announcement. Mrs Price was to give up her establishment altogether, having accepted an offer of marriage from Mr Ibbotson.

'I cannot believe it,' said she. 'Mrs *Price* and Mr *Ibbotson*? I fancy the Misses Ibbotson will not look kindly on the match. And Mr Ibbotson's sister will not wish to see her influence over the family diminish. Can you imagine how it will be, my love? Mr Ibbotson's sister will be obliged to give way to Mrs Price.'

'I imagine it will be everything you say and worse. Otherwise, I have no view on the matter at all,' her husband replied.

'Then you better have, my dear, for the *matter* is of utmost concern to Miss Fox, and consequently to Allersham. Mrs Price is to give her boarders away to other establishments — how thoughtful of her — and has already begun to do so. Oh! And listen to this. Miss Ibbotson has taken the younger of Mrs Price's maids and no longer requires the services of Miss Fox. Despicable woman! Mrs Price has gathered Miss Fox's belongings together and expects them to be collected by the end of the month. How very charitable of her! As she has been paid until the end of the month, I expect she did not wish to reimburse any part of it. I now see why Miss Fox could not be spared and why Mrs Price made such a fuss about it.'

'And how do you propose to break the news to Miss Fox?' said Lord Allersham.

'I shall speak to Aunt Beresford first,' she replied. 'And if it is not convenient for my aunt to keep Miss Fox at Whitcombe, I believe we are honour bound to take her until a proper position can be found for her.'

Lady Allersham arrived at Whitcombe to find that Miss Fox had received a caller, one of the younger Dauber girls. The two were comfortably settled in the small sitting room, exchanging their stories about the wedding; and Mrs Beresford was happy to leave them alone to the news and chatter that young people enjoy.

The visit of Lady Allersham was timely for Mrs Beresford had also received a communication from quite a different source. Mr Beresford had called on Miss Ibbotson on the day of Miss Fox's expected return, to find battle lines being drawn.

'Poor James was obliged to sit for a full hour listening to Miss Ibbotson's complaints. She had suspected nothing at all, and so the announcement made at the famous dinner came as a complete shock. Miss Ibbotson had quite unsuspectingly invited Mrs Price to dine with them. And there before the soup had gone cold, Mr Ibbotson announced his intentions towards Mrs Price. It has set Mr Ibbotson's sister and his daughters quite at odds with him.'

'Now it all makes sense,' she replied. 'Mrs Price did not want Miss Fox to travel to Whitcombe when what mattered most to her and Miss Ibbotson was the dinner, though both had completely different expectations of it.'

'And I should imagine Mrs Price has great need of Miss Fox at present to help sort out the chaos that surely reigns in Gay Street.'

'Of course,' said Lady Allersham. 'Does Miss Fox know? Has she received a communication from Mrs Price?'

'I do not believe so,' replied Mrs Beresford. 'Indeed, I wished to speak with you first. I should like Miss Fox to stay, at least until Michaelmas. I am happy to have her company at Whitcombe. Then, perhaps, we might see how matters develop.'

'Certainly, a position might more easily be found for Miss Fox at Michaelmas, unless you have another plan in mind?'

Mrs Beresford smiled enigmatically. 'Mrs Price is eager to have Miss Fox's belongings removed. I thought I might ask James Beresford to store them for the time being, unless there is anything Miss Fox has particular need of.'

'Would he?'

'I believe he would.'

Miss Fox was shocked to hear that Mr Ibbotson was to wed Mrs Price. And when Lady Allersham explained that Miss Ibbotson no longer had need of her services, her astonishment was almost as great as her relief.

'The fall has made quite a mess of your face,' said Lady Allersham.

Miss Fox replied, 'It appears far worse than it feels. I have hardly any pain at all.' Her mind was elsewhere, pondering the news that the place that had given her shelter for so long was to be her home no longer.

'I must seek employment,' said she.

Mrs Beresford replied, 'I should like you to remain at Whitcombe, at least until Michaelmas, if you would give me the pleasure of your company, and then we shall see what is to be done.'

'But that is three months,' she replied.

'Yes,' said Mrs Beresford. 'Would that be acceptable to you?'

Miss Fox was overcome with joy and relief. 'It is more than acceptable, Mrs Beresford. I thank you. I thank you too Lady Allersham. But please give me employment. I must be of use. I am happy to do whatever is required of me.'

'At present,' replied Lady Allersham, 'you are not fit to be seen. So, I advise you most strongly, to allow the bruising to heal and enjoy Mrs Beresford's fine walled garden. But be careful of the step.'

When Lady Allersham and Mrs Beresford were alone once again, the former observed, 'I believe I shall pay a visit to Mrs Dauber.'

'Mrs Dauber?'

'Soft fruits are plentiful this year and we have more than we need at Allersham.'

'Yes, I see,' said Mrs Beresford, who did not quite see why the Rector's family, blessed with an orchard and an abundance of fruits to hand, should be thought of when there were families in greater need than the Daubers.

'Do you find Mrs Dauber a rather garrulous sort of person at times?' Lady Allersham enquired.

'More so when Mr Dauber is not present,' replied Mrs Beresford.

'And Mrs Dauber is not bound by the secrets of the confessional.'

'Emma?' said Mrs Beresford, comprehending her niece's purpose.

'I am determined to find out what I can about our Miss Fox. Henry has business in the parish next Wednesday, and Mr Dauber is also expected to attend. Hence, Mrs Dauber will be alone. Would you assist me and arrange for the younger Dauber girls to call on Miss Fox the same day? I should like to pay Mrs Dauber a visit in private.'

CHAPTER THIRTY-TWO

The dearth of callers to Laura Place was greatly lamented by Lady Dalrymple and owed less to Mr Ibbotson's impending nuptials than Captain Harding's sudden departure from Bath. Of the former, Lady Dalrymple had nothing good to say. The news that Mr Ibbotson, whom she had regarded as a man of moderate sense and intelligence, had been taken in by a proprietress of an indifferent establishment that might generously be described as a 'school', was as shocking as it was absurd. On one matter, however, she was less scathing. Word had reached Laura Place that Mr Ibbotson's sister was beside herself with the news and opposed the match in every possible way. To see Miss Ibbotson, therefore, obliged to give precedence to Mrs Price was a spectacle not to missed, and if assurances were given that Miss Ibbotson was to be one of the wedding party, nothing would keep Her Ladyship from attending the nuptials herself.

The departure of Captain Harding was sudden but not entirely unexpected, for the cause was undoubtedly her daughter; and though Her Ladyship would neither persuade nor insist on compliance in matrimonial matters, she suspected that the decision to decline Captain Harding's offer was something her daughter might yet live to regret. Despite his more outrageous contentions, Lady Dalrymple liked Captain Harding, for, unlike a number among her acquaintance, the obsequiousness she most despised in *them*, was wholly absent in him. She had found his conversation to be to her liking; sometimes dazzling and often incisive, he was diverting, and never ceased to amuse her.

At last, Miss Carteret broke her silence and approached the subject of Captain Harding; oddly, Lady Dalrymple was none the wiser, for the reason her daughter put forward for declining his offer was more mystifying than it was revealing. The objection to Captain Harding stemmed neither from lack of fortune and consequence (for she had both in good measure and had perceived nothing in his manner to suggest he was a fortune hunter); nor indeed was it the prospect of having the Fowles as in laws.

It mattered little to Miss Carteret that Captain Harding's mother had married a humourless, self-important physician, for he could boast of his aunt, Lady Osborne, a viscountess and the mother of a countess. No. The defect in Captain Harding pertained to an aspect of his character that she could not forgive: his inability to honour his word. It was a flaw so serious that it amounted to nothing less than betrayal.

The nature of that betrayal, however, remained unclear to Lady Dalrymple; she knew only that, as far as her daughter was concerned, the matter had been dealt with and was now closed.

The tension in Laura Place, that proceeded from the refusal of Captain Harding's offer, persisted for several days, until one morning Lady Dalrymple and Miss Carteret received an unexpected visit from Captain and Mrs Wentworth. The Wentworths were on their way to Kellynch, to the bedside of Mrs Croft, Captain Wentworth's sister. News that Mrs Croft's condition was more serious than first thought was met with some alarm, and the decision was made to pay a visit to Kellynch directly rather than wait until their proposed tour in the autumn. The distance involved meant that the journey would not easily be accomplished in a day, and so they had chosen to travel as far as Bath with the intention of arriving at Kellynch by four the following day.

'And young Master Frederick?' said Miss Carteret.

'It is his first excursion. And he has slept throughout. Nothing disturbs him. Nanny is taking care of him at present. Indeed, I can hardly get a look in at times,' said Mrs Wentworth. 'He is so good natured, I believe he owes it entirely to his father. My family dispute it, of course, which amuses me greatly, but it is perfectly plain to see that Freddie is, thankfully, more a Wentworth than an Elliot.'

'I hear we must wish your father joy,' said Lady Dalrymple. 'I understand Sir Walter has found himself a bride. It may surprise you to find, however, that he is not the only one. Do you remember Mr Ibbotson?'

'I remember Mr Ibbotson's sister,' said Anne.

'It seems her brother is also to marry, though I suspect the case is somewhat reversed. The widow in question has no fortune to speak of, and Mr Ibbotson is wanting in nothing but good sense. Matrimony will likely remedy that defect but, of course, by then, it will be too late to apply it.'

Captain Wentworth smiled. 'I know nothing of Mr Ibbotson, but I cannot think of a better plan for Sir Walter than to marry.'

'That is because you desire a tranquil life, as do I,' his wife replied. 'If my father's alliance succeeds in that respect, I shall ask for nothing more, though I cannot speak for my sisters.'

After tea was brought in, Anne Wentworth took Miss Carteret aside, and with a discreet touch of the arm, drew the latter's attention to the placement of a small package beneath a silk cushion. 'Open it when you are alone,' said she. 'When we were in Bristol, you took me into your confidence. I hesitate to say so, but I understood more of the facts than those you disclosed to me. Forgive me. You must know that the death of a brave naval officer does not go unremarked by the families of other naval officers. My husband acquired the contents through the Admiralty and required no explanation from me save my desire to assist a friend. It is not in his nature to question or pry. My wish for you, Miss Carteret, is that one day you should find such a man. And if I may say so, it is my belief that the loved one whose memory you honour would have wished it too.'

An hour passed before the Wentworths were let go from Laura Place. Lady Dalrymple would not hear of their departure until all her enquiries had been satisfied, and when she could keep her visitors no longer, Her Ladyship released them on the promise that they would repeat their visit to Laura Place on their return from Kellynch if circumstances allowed. The good wishes of the ladies of Laura Place and their hopes for Mrs Croft's full recovery were expressed repeatedly. The Wentworths departed, a half hour later than they had intended, promising that their messages would be conveyed to the Admiral's ailing wife as soon as they reached Kellynch.

After their departure, Miss Carteret was able to retrieve the package when her mother, who was anxious to continue her letter to Mrs Beresford, left the room. The additional news of the Wentworths' visit was more than enough to fill the remainder of the page and would answer completely Mrs Beresford's enquiry of the same.

Miss Carteret felt underneath the cushion for the package deposited by Mrs Wentworth. On retrieving the item, she untied the string, and removed the item from its wrapping. The image of Captain Fitzroy, that had begun to fade from her memory, was now hers to behold. It was as she remembered him. The artist had captured his countenance completely: compassion in his eyes and conviction in his expression. He was a man who cared more for the principles that governed his existence than for any sense of his own position in the world. It is how she remembered him, and always would.

Strangely, as she beheld his likeness, she felt a sense of calm and even raised a smile. She had rarely allowed herself to hope that one day she might again look upon his image. The affection she had for him was no less deeply felt; but it was the possession of his likeness that made the difference. That she would no longer have need to depend on the power of memory allowed her to entertain the possibility that she might in time bear his loss with greater acceptance, and conceive of a future different to the one she presently envisaged.

The letter from Lady Dalrymple provided Mrs Beresford with sufficient reason to call on her niece at Allersham Park. Miss Fox was happy to remain at Whitcombe, having been granted the opportunity to practise upon the pianoforte in a small but pleasant music room which offered an impressive view of the grounds.

When Mrs Beresford arrived, however, she found that Lord and Lady Allersham had set out to walk towards the lake. As the weather was warm, she was pleased to go in search of them. On approaching the lake, she caught sight of her niece picking wild flowers and Lord Allersham seated on a log watching his wife's efforts. As soon as Mrs Beresford caught their attention, they waved and beckoned her towards them.

'You find Emma determined to prove a point, Mrs Beresford,' said Lord Allersham.

'Do not listen to him, Aunt,' Lady Allersham replied. 'He is afraid to admit he is wrong.'

'Wrong?' said Mrs Beresford. 'About what, my dear?'

'Hot house flowers,' she replied. 'Henry says they are superior to wild flowers, and I do not agree. Are these not just as pretty? I shall insist upon Henry's help to arrange them.'

'Pity then that they will wilt before either of us sets foot in the house. One or two have already withered, I see,' said he.

'Well, my dears,' said Mrs Beresford, 'if flowers be your only point of dispute, you will do very well.'

'We shall,' said Lady Allersham, 'as long as the hot house is given over to the growing of fruit for the table.'

Lord Allersham sighed and got up, picked a wild flower and placed it in his wife's hair. 'I have already seen to it that your wishes are carried out.'

'What shall I do, Aunt? My husband delights in teasing me,' said Lady Allersham. 'Are we to have exotic fruits after all?'

'Do not expect them instantly, but, yes, we are,' said he. 'I see, however, that Mrs Beresford has some purpose to her visit, so I will leave you to your tête-à-tête in case there are secrets not meant for my ears.'

'I have received a letter this morning from Lady Dalrymple,' said she, 'but it is no secret.'

'Confirming what we already know from Harding?' said Lord Allersham.

'Indeed,' said Mrs Beresford. 'Lady Dalrymple is completely mystified by her daughter's refusal. And I detect no understanding at all from her letter that she is aware of her daughter's past connexion with Allersham.'

'How can that be?' said Lady Allersham.

'She understands that her daughter's refusal has something to do with some indiscretion on Captain Harding's part, the failure to keep a promise of some kind.'

'I am sorry that Miss Carteret supposes that Robert failed to keep his word,' she replied.

'That seems to be the crux of it,' said Mrs Beresford.

Lady Allersham looked at her husband. 'Did Robert confide in you? He was with you in the library when I found him.'

'Harding said very little to me. It was you he sought, and you he confided in,' said Lord Allersham. 'Might there have been a failure of communication, a misunderstanding of some sort?'

'I believe so,' said Lady Allersham, as a thought occurred to her. 'In fact, I believe I may have been the cause. I said something to Miss Carteret in an unguarded moment that may have given the wrong impression of my cousin. If I am correct in my assumption, I must endeavour to do something to rectify the situation.'

Lord Allersham and Mrs Beresford exchanged amused glances.

'And before you say that I meddle too much, allow me to point out that my meddling yields results,' said Lady Allersham. 'And if it is within my power to promote the happiness of my cousin and Miss Carteret, I shall do so.'

'I thought Harding made it clear that he would not renew his addresses to Miss Carteret. He was given to understand that a renewal of the same would be utterly futile,' Lord Allersham replied.

'Henry,' said Lady Allersham, 'had I been determined to refuse you, I hope you would not have given up quite so easily.'

'You think it the easiest thing in the world for a man once rejected to renew his addresses, Emma,' said he. 'But it is not.' Lord Allersham kissed his wife's cheek. 'I shall leave you to plot and plan. I am sure Harding will be vastly appreciative of all your efforts. In the fullness of time.'

When Lord Allersham was out of earshot of his wife, she said, 'Henry is just as concerned for Robert as you and I, for I know that he has written to him.'

'What more can be done? If Miss Carteret will not have him, that must be the end of it,' said Mrs Beresford.

'Then I am sorry indeed.' Lady Allersham took Mrs Beresford's arm as they walked on.

'Well, perhaps I can do more good by turning my attention to Miss Fox. I *shall* call on Mrs Dauber tomorrow morning for her husband is certain to be out of the way. Henry says they are to meet at the Crown at eleven o'clock.'

'And he approves your plan?'

'I shouldn't suppose so,' said Lady Allersham. 'That is why I haven't mentioned it.'

'Emma,' she replied, 'are you sure that is wise?'

'Quite sure,' said she. 'A pardon is easier come by than permission.'

'I do hope so,' said Mrs Beresford. 'You will be pleased then to know that Miss Fox is to visit Mrs Sparke tomorrow morning. The younger Dauber girls will call at Whitcombe Park on their way. They are all invited to spend the day at Sparke Farm.'

'Excellent. It is just as I hoped,' said Lady Allersham. 'Shall you accompany me to the Rectory, Aunt?'

'That won't be possible,' replied Mrs Beresford. 'I have hopes that I shall see James Beresford at Whitcombe Park tomorrow. I received a letter from him informing me that he is now in receipt of Miss

Fox's belongings and is to send them to Whitcombe in case she should have need of them.'

'That is kindness indeed,' said Lady Allersham.

'I did not discourage him from his plan. I rather encouraged him to send them, but at the same time to take the opportunity of visiting Whitcombe himself.'

'And do you think he will accept your invitation?'

'It is my hope,' said she.

'Then Miss Fox might stay at Allersham for the duration, if you prefer it.'

'Oh no, my dear,' said she. 'I am perfectly happy for Miss Fox to remain at Whitcombe.'

'Then you must all come to dine at Allersham. I insist on it,' replied Lady Allersham. 'Let us hope that James Beresford does not do as Cousin Robert and spend but a night. Impress upon him that no less than a fortnight will do.'

CHAPTER THIRTY-THREE

Mrs Dauber was all amazement at the sight of Lady Allersham's carriage by the Rectory gates for the third time in a month. She began to wonder how she had become the recipient of such marked and preferential attention. Laden with a basket of soft fruits for the Rectory table, the true purpose of Lady Allersham's visit was soon made clear: Her Ladyship had reason to believe that Mrs Dauber might be in possession of knowledge pertaining to Miss Fox's past connexion to Whitcombe.

'I, Your Ladyship?' said she. 'I assure you, I am the last person with whom my husband would share any intelligence concerning his parish. It is his job to know everything and to conceal everything, most especially from his wife.'

'Of course,' said Lady Allersham. 'And I commend him for his discretion in all things.' She sighed. 'Are not men of the cloth the cleverest keepers of secrets in the world? They see everything and say nothing.'

'There I beg to disagree, Your Ladyship,' replied Mrs Dauber.

'Oh?'

'My husband's powers of observation have, at times, been found wanting.'

'How interesting, Mrs Dauber. Indeed, it is my belief that women possess superior powers of observation,' said Lady Allersham. 'You seem to me a watchful, vigilant woman of the highest order.'

'You flatter me, Your Ladyship. You do. Modesty prevents me from blowing my own trumpet.'

'Your modesty is misplaced,' she replied. 'We women never receive the credit due to us.'

'Indeed we do not,' said Mrs Dauber, animated by the suggestion. 'I find that I am party to certain interesting rumours from time to time. My husband says he is above all that and will not discuss anything of import with me. I may say, Your Ladyship, that I am amused to find that the secrets of the confessional are often widely known in the neighbourhood long before those at the centre of them admit their transgressions to my husband. It is almost too diverting for words to hear that Mr So and So or Mrs So and So seeks the favour of a private word with the Rector. And after all is confessed and forgiven, to see Mr Dauber strutting around, thinking himself so very important for being possessed of certain secrets that he alone is privileged to hear, when I, his obscure and docile wife, heard it all and more six months ago! It is all the amusement I am afforded, you see, and so I make the most of it when I can.'

'My Aunt Fowle used to say that a secret was a very well-kept secret if only half the neighbourhood knew of it,' said Lady Allersham.

Mrs Dauber broke into fits of laughter and any stiffness present between them disappeared in an instant. 'Yes, indeed!' said she. 'Your Aunt Fowle has it precisely. The parish is a great supplier and distributor of gossip.'

'And I am sure that someone like you, Mrs Dauber, a very intelligent and perceptive woman, allows nothing to slip by you unobserved.'

'That is true. That is very true, Your Ladyship. You have understood me completely.'

'I have a feeling, you see, that this is not Miss Fox's first time at Whitcombe.'

'Am I to understand that Your Ladyship shares my misgivings about Miss Fox's continued presence at Whitcombe Park?'

Lady Allersham was puzzled by the comment. 'Do you mean Whitcombe *village* rather than Whitcombe *Park*, the residence of Mrs Beresford?'

Mrs Dauber hesitated for a moment. 'Surely the nature of your enquiry relates to Whitcombe Park, Your Ladyship. Forgive me, if I am mistaken.'

'I spoke in general terms,' Lady Allersham replied, cautiously. 'It was not my intention to *exclude* the residence of Mrs Beresford.'

'And the late Colonel,' whispered Mrs Dauber, with a knowing look. 'I see what you mean, Your Ladyship. General terms. We understand each other perfectly. The *neighbourhood* of Whitcombe. Yes, of course.'

Lady Allersham, who was at a loss to comprehend Mrs Dauber's meaning, nodded in agreement.

'I had no objection to Miss Fox's assisting my daughter on her wedding day. None at all. My daughter wished to make use of Miss Fox and my husband made no objection. But when I heard that she was to stay at Whitcombe Park I was shocked. Quite shocked,' said she, as she lowered her voice once again to a whisper. 'You know, with the business concerning the Colonel.'

Lady Allersham was greatly perplexed by Mrs Dauber's remark and, having no understanding of the business to which she was referring, but not wishing to declare her ignorance of it, said, 'I wondered about that myself.'

'It was kept very quiet, of course,' said Mrs Dauber.

'Very quiet indeed,' said Lady Allersham. 'To be perfectly clear, however, and so that we understand each other completely, what aspect of the business in *your* estimation, Mrs Dauber, was the most alarming?' said Lady Allersham.

'Why, Miss Fox and the Colonel! I suppose it was never established that she was his ward, but what other explanation might there be?'

Lady Allersham reached for her tea and sipped it slowly to disguise her bewilderment. Impossible, thought she. That Colonel Beresford should have kept such a secret from his wife, and have taken it to his grave, was inconceivable. How would such a matter as this have been hidden for so long? And yet, if it were the case, what perverse twist of fortune to have come upon and invited unawares into their circle a person so intimately connected with the Colonel and, consequently, Whitcombe Park!

'I witnessed everything, you see,' continued Mrs Dauber. 'Colonel Beresford brought the child — as she was then — under cover of darkness and placed her in the care of my husband.'

'And what did Mr Dauber do?'

'He took her to Bath, I presume, for he had the carriage waiting and said nothing to me save that he had urgent business there. To this day he is completely unaware that I saw it *all*.'

'Who else is party to this information, apart from Mr Dauber, of course?' said Lady Allersham.

'No one but Your Ladyship,' said Mrs Dauber. 'I keep a great many secrets from my husband. That is but one of them.'

'And shall you maintain your silence?' Lady Allersham replied.

'I would not wish the Colonel's secret to become common knowledge, nor for Mrs Beresford to be wounded by it. She has been very good to me.'

Mrs Dauber's revelation could not be doubted, nor any other explanation suffice. And yet, it was inconceivable that the Colonel should have concealed the matter from his wife! And how curious that no part of it had revealed itself after his death.

Lady Allersham now saw the warning issued by Mr Dauber in a new light. The connexion between Miss Fox and Allersham was not as she had supposed. She had long suspected Lord Allersham's brother to be the villain of the piece, but that the Colonel was implicated was troubling indeed. Should she reveal the details to her husband? Surely she must. But in so doing, the extent of Mrs Dauber's knowledge would, unavoidably, be made known; and as Mrs Dauber vowed to keep her silence to save wounding Mrs Beresford, Lady Allersham promised to maintain hers, at least for the present.

The knowledge that her aunt had been deceived, even betrayed, by the man whose death had caused her immense grief was astonishing. There was one question to which she could find no satisfactory answer. If Miss Fox was the Colonel's ward, how could he have left her to her fate so cruelly? That Colonel Beresford should not have made provision in his will for Miss Fox seemed impossible to imagine. Lamentably, the truth was plain to see: the payment of Miss Fox's allowance to Mrs Price must have ceased on Colonel Beresford's death. Everything pointed to the accuracy of Mrs Dauber's account.

As the carriage approached Whitcombe Park, Lady Allersham found that she could not pass its gates without calling on Mrs Beresford, and ordered the coachman to take her to the house. On approaching the sweep, she looked out of the window and observed the arrival of another carriage. As the carriage moved on at a slow pace to the coach house, its occupant was nowhere to be seen.

'James Beresford is come,' said Mrs Beresford, as Lady Allersham was shown into the drawing room. 'It is just as I had hoped. He is to stay a full week. You will see him presently, my dear, for he has just arrived and is giving instructions to the stable hands. One of the horses needs shoeing. I have assured him we have an excellent smithy at hand. But you will not see Miss Fox today. Even I do not know when I shall see Miss Fox, for the Misses Dauber were in such high spirits when they called here this morning and were determined to keep her at Sparke Farm all day. She promised to dress their hair according to the fashion in Bath.'

Lady Allersham heard hardly a word of her aunt's speech for her mind was reeling from Mrs Dauber's revelation.

'And how was your visit to the Rectory, my dear?' said Mrs Beresford. 'Was Mrs Dauber in better health? Did you achieve your aim?'

Before Lady Allersham had time to reply, the door opened to admit James Beresford.

'Ah! I fear my presence is an intrusion,' said he, observing that Mrs Beresford was occupied with a visitor.

Lady Allersham turned towards him and said, 'An intrusion? I think not.'

'Lady Allersham!' said he.

'Bonnets are the best disguise in the world. You are forgiven, Mr Beresford,' said Lady Allersham, 'for I know you did not expect to see me until tomorrow.'

'I am always very pleased to see you, my dear,' said Mrs Beresford. 'And if I can persuade James to stay a fortnight, my happiness will be complete.'

'That, I'm afraid, is beyond my control, for I have business in Bath before then. A week is all I can spare on this occasion,' said he.

'But you will return at Michaelmas. You must give your word,' said Mrs Beresford.

'You have my word. I shall indeed return to Whitcombe at Michaelmas,' he replied.

'Excellent,' said Lady Allersham. 'If only we could be certain of my cousin Robert also. Have you called at Laura Place since the business with Miss Carteret?'

James Beresford was puzzled by her question. 'The business?'

'Perhaps you have not heard,' said Mrs Beresford. 'Captain Harding made Miss Carteret an offer.'

'And she refused him,' Lady Allersham added.

'I had not heard,' said he. 'I know only that Captain Harding is gone to Brinshore and will be absent for several weeks. I am sorry indeed to hear of his disappointment. I must confess, I have been remiss in my visits to Laura Place since you left it. Lady Dalrymple and Miss Carteret attended the Pump Room two days ago. I spoke with them but briefly. The news was of Mr Ibbotson. I expect you have heard it already.'

'Certainly, we have,' said Lady Allersham. 'But what of Mr Ibbotson's sister? Have you seen Miss Ibbotson since the announcement?'

'I happened to call there yesterday and stayed but five minutes. One of her nieces was present.'

'Plotting, no doubt,' said Lady Allersham.

'There was little I could proffer in defence of Mr Ibbotson that either lady wished to hear.'

'I suppose Mrs Price is no longer welcome in Paragon Buildings,' said Lady Allersham.

'Mr Ibbotson's sister and Mrs Price have not spoken since the announcement,' he replied.

'Is it true that Miss Ibbotson is not against her brother marrying again but believes Mrs Price beneath him?' said Lady Allersham.

'That would appear to be the case,' said he.

'And yet I understood that Miss Ibbotson and Mrs Price were the best of friends,' said Lady Allersham.

The conversation halted momentarily when a note was brought in for Mrs Beresford. She opened it and quickly perused the contents.

'Mrs Sparke,' said she, 'wishes Miss Fox's presence until the morning. How very inconvenient.' Turning to James Beresford, she explained, 'Mrs Sparke is Miss Dauber that was.'

'Mrs Sparke likes to make use of her friend,' said Lady Allersham. 'It was our belief that Miss Fox was to be Miss Dauber's *bridesmaid*, but in the end all she wanted was a *maid*.'

James Beresford nodded in agreement. 'It is Miss Fox's misfortune to occupy an indeterminate position in the world, one which exposes her to seemingly inconsequential degradations and ill-treatment of a kind that is rendered liberally and with impunity. And yet, Miss Fox bears it without complaint or reproach.'

Mrs Beresford cast a knowing glance in Lady Allersham's direction. The latter, however, for whom the news of Miss Fox's history remained uppermost in her thoughts, could not return it. If her aunt's purpose was to promote a match between Miss Fox and Mr Beresford, the outcome would surely be disastrous for both parties. She felt keenly the part she had played by intervening in Miss Fox's affairs, and now saw, to her dismay, the consequences of her misplaced interference. Had she left Miss Fox alone, had she not taken up her cause, that which had the potential to inflict untold suffering on more than one person might then have been prevented.

Lady Allersham got up to leave. 'Take advantage of the fine weather, Mr Beresford. Whitcombe Park is glorious in the summer. But remember, we must have our share of you too. I shall expect you all to join Lord Allersham and I tomorrow evening.'

'Of course, my dear,' said Mrs Beresford. 'And if Mrs Sparke does not release Miss Fox in the morning, I shall go to Sparke Farm and fetch her back myself.'

CHAPTER THIRTY-FOUR

Lord Allersham was distracted from his newspaper by his wife's constant pacing back and forth, and on reading the same sentence five times without discerning the writer's intent, he conceded defeat and put the paper aside. He watched his wife, each gesture and expression, each movement of her body, until he could remain silent no longer.

'Are you vexed, my dear, or is exercise alone your object?' said he.

'Vexed?' she replied. 'Whatever put such an idea into your head?'

'Have I said or done something amiss?'

'I haven't given you a thought, my dear. Not a single thought,' said she.

'How comforting it is to know that your husband occupies no place in your reflections,' he replied.

'I didn't mean — you understand me, I know you do.'

'Not at this moment, however,' said he.

Lady Allersham sighed. 'I wish I had not called on Mrs Dauber. She is different to every Rector's wife I have ever known.'

Striving to maintain a serious look, he replied, 'Might I enquire what distinguishes Mrs Dauber from all the rest?'

'You think me ridiculous, I see,' she replied.

'Not ridiculous. A little theatrical, perhaps.'

'Theatrical? How can you say such a thing?'

'It has been my lot to observe you this past half hour. Some matter, possibly connected with your visit to Whitcombe Rectory, disturbs your mind. It may be of little consequence to any other creature in this world, but it is clearly a matter of concern to you.'

'Of little consequence to any other? It is a matter of grave concern. Mr Dauber may think himself uniquely privy to the thoughts and actions of his parishioners, but clearly he is not.'

'Do I understand you correctly, my dear? Does Mr Dauber make his wife his confidante? It seems unlikely.'

'You know Mr Dauber better than I. How certain is he of his wife's ignorance of matters that he assumes to be his sole province?'

Lord Allersham sat up and gave her his full attention. 'Emma, are we speaking of Miss Fox?'

'I really cannot say,' said she.

'That was the purpose of your visit to the Rectory today, was it not?' he replied.

Lady Allersham did not reply. Instead, she took up the publication that her husband had discarded and began to peruse the front page.

The room descended into silence. After some time, Emma peered at her husband over the top of the newspaper. 'I gave my solemn promise that I would say nothing to a soul, including you, my dear.'

'That is perfectly understood, my love. I admire your resolve,' said he. 'And Mrs Dauber would be likewise full of admiration for your tenacity. And should she be possessed of the same determination, I have no doubt that Mr Dauber would also —'

'I see what you are doing, but it will not work on me,' she replied.

'Very well, Emma. Let us say nothing more about it.'

A further few minutes of silence ensued before Lady Allersham spoke again.

'It will not do. I must speak,' said she, defeated by her inability to bear the burden of knowledge alone. 'No one must know. You must give me your word.'

'You have my word, Emma.'

'I have something shocking to tell you. Prepare yourself,' said she.

Lord Allersham gave her his full attention.

'It concerns Miss Fox and Colonel Beresford. Miss Fox was likely his ward. That is her connexion with Allersham. A rather circuitous one, I grant you. Mr Dauber, however, is unaware that his wife is in possession of the facts.'

'Is she quite sure?' he replied. 'How could the matter have been concealed for so long from the wife for whom the Colonel had the highest esteem? Mrs Dauber either labours under a grave misconception or seeks to make mischief.'

'She saw everything,' said Lady Allersham. 'Perhaps it was the Colonel's deep affection for my aunt that prevented him from making such a disclosure. Remember, my dear, you did not know the Colonel as I did. There was nothing he would not do to avoid injury to my aunt.'

'Would not the injury have been the greater were Mrs Beresford to have found out following the Colonel's demise when he was unable to speak for himself?'

'Aunt Beresford will never hear of it from me.'

Lady Allersham supplied the salient points of her conversation with Mrs Dauber as he sat in silence to comprehend the matter. At the end of her speech, Lord Allersham expressed his doubts.

'Did Mrs Dauber hear it from the Colonel's own lips? Did the Colonel confirm that Miss Fox was his ward?' said he. 'Appearances can be deceptive, Emma.'

'There was no mistaking the Colonel's carriage. Mrs Dauber recognised the occupant immediately.'

'If it indeed proves to be the case,' said he, 'what do you propose to do with Miss Fox? Has not Mrs Beresford a right to know whom she entertains under her own roof?'

'I shall say nothing to Miss Fox or my aunt. We shall go on as before. We must,' said Lady Allersham. 'There is nothing else to be done.'

'I wonder,' said he.

'By the by, James Beresford is come to Whitcombe. They are all to dine here tomorrow evening.'

'There is a sweet irony, I suppose, in the notion that Miss Fox is embraced by the family to which she might rightfully belong, except for the fact that she does not know it and neither do they,' said he.

'Are you relieved to find there exists no association closer than Colonel Beresford to connect Miss Fox to Allersham?' said she.

'For your aunt's sake, a connexion with Allersham rather than Whitcombe would have been the lesser evil. There may come a time, however, when Mrs Beresford and Miss Fox may need to be informed. There may be legal implications. Was an attorney appointed? If so, he must be found,' said he. 'One must also consider the possibility that the Colonel was acting on behalf of a third party.'

'Mr Dauber was the third party,' said she.

'There is but one person who may be in a position to provide answers.'

'Mr Dauber is sworn to silence,' she replied.

'Mr Dauber may be sworn to silence, but James Beresford is not a clergyman,' said he.

'James Beresford? Of course!' said she. 'Why did I not think of it? You must speak to him at once. But if he is in possession of the facts, why does he not speak? Why does he remain silent?'

'Perhaps he wishes to determine the extent of Mrs Beresford's understanding first.'

'Yes. You must be right. And therein lies the explanation for his coming to Bath in the first place. Will you speak to him?'

'If you wish,' said he.

'I do.'

When the party from Whitcombe arrived for dinner, Lady Allersham was curious to observe the easy affability that existed between them. James Beresford's attentiveness to Mrs Beresford displayed a genuine fondness for her aunt; and his behaviour towards Miss Fox was cordial, courteous and respectful. Pleasant company, the fine summer weather, and the excellent meal, all contributed to an agreeable evening enjoyed by all. Even Miss Fox, who at first had been overawed by the occasion, found that towards the close of the evening she was at ease enough to smile and even contribute an observation or two.

James Beresford expressed a desire to view the sunset from the terrace, a scene warmly commended by Lady Allersham, and asked whether Mrs Beresford and Miss Fox should like to join him. Miss Fox, who had never had the good fortune to see the sunset from such a vantage point, eagerly assented to the idea. Mrs Beresford, however, declined with the excuse, 'I have seen the sunset many times. Go and enjoy the scene without me.'

'Henry will show the way,' said Lady Allersham, with a determined look in her eye. 'Won't you, my dear?'

Lord Allersham, though reluctant to do so, acceded to his wife's request.

When Lady Allersham and Mrs Beresford were quite alone, the latter was eager to impart a piece of news to her niece. 'Have you noticed it too?' said she.

'Noticed what, Aunt?'

'James Beresford's behaviour towards Miss Fox. He is considerate, protective of her welfare, even, I might say, affectionate. This afternoon, after Mrs Sparke consented to release Miss Fox and return her to Whitcombe in Mr Sparke's old cart, I proposed that Miss Fox show James the Park. She has taken a tour of the Park on two previous occasions and now knows it well. Both parties were exceedingly happy to comply with my suggestion. Do you not see, my dear Emma? I believe James Beresford is on his way to becoming attached to Miss Fox. And what better place for the pair of them to be than at Whitcombe.'

'I never thought of you as a matchmaker, Aunt,' said Lady Allersham.

'Nor I. But I played some small part in the alliance between your mother and father many years ago. And

300

when one sees how these things progress, sometimes all that is required is a little push in the right direction.'

Lady Allersham received Mrs Beresford's news with less enthusiasm than her aunt had anticipated.

'Perhaps,' said Lady Allersham, 'James Beresford seeks only to protect Miss Fox, to show concern for her welfare.'

'Perhaps,' she replied. 'But I perceive something more. He is not the type of man swayed by rank or fortune. He is quite dismissive of those calculating and callous actions of fortune hunters, several of whom are known to him personally. I have heard him express his contempt for such persons. It is my belief, Emma, that Miss Fox has yet to comprehend the nature of James Beresford's fondness for her, or indeed her own feelings for him. She speaks daily of securing a position as soon as one presents itself. I must admit, I promised to help her in her quest but have done little to advance it. I foresee a better future for Miss Fox, you see, in the form of James Beresford.'

'My dear Aunt,' said Lady Allersham, 'you have often advised me against making matches, and now I offer you the same advice. The way forward for Miss Fox may be fraught with complications of a kind that are not to be easily overcome. I like Miss Fox as much as you, but sometimes I wonder whether I have done her any favours at all, that perhaps I should not have interfered in the way I did.'

'And where would she be now? The servant of Mr Ibbotson's sister, whom, I might add, treated Miss Fox abominably. I had it from James Beresford who witnessed it with his own eyes.'

301

'I can well believe it,' she replied, 'and I do not think Mrs Sparke has distinguished herself in that regard either.'

'Indeed, she has not,' said Mrs Beresford. 'I understand that Miss Fox spent most of her time at Sparke Farm darning stockings and altering undergarments when she was not dressing hair and hemming sleeves. And yet, Miss Fox returned delighted to have been of service to her friends.'

As the evening advanced to almost midnight, and the carriage had been despatched from the coach house to return their guests to Whitcombe, Lady Allersham made known to her husband her concerns about Mrs Beresford's endeavour to promote a match between James Beresford and Miss Fox.

'And if Aunt Beresford succeeds and the evidence we most fear then comes to light, what are we to do? Consider, my dear, if James Beresford were to make Miss Fox an offer, and Aunt Beresford urges her to accept him, to whom would she turn to publish the banns? Mr Dauber, of course. And I am convinced that if such an event were to take place, Mrs Dauber would not then keep her silence. Miss Fox's prolonged stay at Whitcombe has already gained disapproval at the Rectory,' said she. 'Henry, you must speak to James Beresford without delay.'

'It may please you to know that I have already spoken to him. We spoke briefly after dinner,' he replied.

'Oh?' said she. 'And what said he about the business?'

'Beresford knew nothing of the Colonel's personal affairs.'

'I suppose you mentioned the possible existence of a ward under the care of Colonel Beresford.'

'Not explicitly. My enquiry concerning the Beresford family was of a general nature.'

'That is truly disappointing. James Beresford may have been guarded in his replies for that very reason.'

'That was not my impression. I believe he would have supplied such information had he been in possession of it.'

'How can you be so certain?' said she.

'I suspect he has very good reasons of his own to do so, but my view is based on supposition and not fact, and therefore carries no weight.'

'Then how shall we ever discover the facts?' said Lady Allersham.

CHAPTER THIRTY-FIVE

The morning's post brought news from Lady Dalrymple of an unexpected nature relating to Captain Harding. She had received the news in a letter from Lady Russell, who had heard it from Mary Musgrove, who in turn had had it from Admiral Croft. The news concerned Fulton Park, a large estate adjoining Kellynch. The name of the new owner had only recently come to light following the demise of a Mr Brooks, the former owner of the estate. Handsome, by all accounts, the estate had, until a month ago, been occupied by a tenant whose lease had come to an end. And although a renewal of the lease had been offered on the same terms as before, the said tenant had decided to move to Deal for the sake of his health and because his wife had a sister there. It happened, therefore, that the estate was in need of an occupant. According to Lady Russell, Fulton Manor was said to be comparable in size and character to Kellynch Hall, but having the advantage of grounds twice as extensive, and an expanse of river of which the best stretch for fishing was to be found in the whole of the county. The news was the more surprising for in making his addresses to her daughter, Lady Dalrymple declared that Captain Harding had never once mentioned having inherited Fulton Park.

'Oh, dear! I feared this would happen. So now that Cousin Robert's secret is out, I wonder if Miss Carteret will suffer misgivings for having turned him down?' said Lady Allersham.

'I really couldn't say,' said Lord Allersham, intent on reading his own correspondence.

'I am quite certain you have heard not one word I have said,' she replied.

'Your cousin has unwittingly presented Sir Walter Elliot with a solution,' said he. 'Were Sir Walter to persuade Admiral Croft to take Fulton Park, he might return to Kellynch forthwith. You see, Emma, I hear you perfectly well and attend to everything you say.'

'That was nothing more than a stroke of luck,' she replied. 'You heard the words *Fulton* and *Park* and *Kellynch* and *tenant* and happened to make a lucky guess.'

'I happened to hear of it yesterday. Harding wrote to me himself.'

'And you did not think to tell me?' said she.

'Your mind was engaged on other matters. And when the moment for speaking of it had passed, it quite slipped my mind, that is, until you mentioned it just now.'

Lady Allersham sighed. 'I wonder whether Lady Dalrymple has written to inform Aunt Beresford.'

'Can there be any doubt about it?' Lord Allersham replied.

'I shall ride to Whitcombe, for Aunt Beresford is not likely to visit Allersham today.'

'Are you sure?'

'She will not wish to compromise the reputation of either of her guests, or of Whitcombe Park, by being absent while they are present even for a morning.'

'Beresford is to join me this morning. To fish in the lake, my dear. Have no fear. The reputation of Whitcombe Park is safe,' said Lord Allersham.

By the time James Beresford arrived, Lady Allersham was half way to Whitcombe. Her aunt, having caught a glimpse of her from the morning room where she was at her desk composing a reply to Lady Dalrymple, got up and went down to greet her.

Of James Beresford, Lady Allersham commented, 'I wonder I did not meet him on the way. I suppose he kept to the lanes. He is not perhaps familiar with the fields round about.'

'He rarely rides, which surprises me,' said Mrs Beresford. 'He took the carriage this morning. I must tell you, my dear, I received a letter not more than an hour ago from Laura Place. Lady Dalrymple has some very interesting news about Captain Harding. But you do not look surprised.'

'Concerning Fulton Park?' said Lady Allersham.

'I see you have heard it.'

'Henry heard of it from Cousin Robert yesterday.'

'Lady Dalrymple is shocked. She wonders why Captain Harding said nothing about it. Does Miss Carteret regret her decision, I wonder?'

'It is altogether regrettable, for my cousin still vows he will not renew his addresses to Miss Carteret,' said Lady Allersham.

Mrs Beresford replied, 'Lady Dalrymple knew nothing at all about the business with Captain Fitzroy, you know. How did Miss Carteret keep it from her own mother for so long?'

'Very easily,' said Lady Allersham. 'Lady Dalrymple does not take the trouble to understand her daughter. I should imagine she understands her a little better now.'

'Perhaps you are right, my dear,' said Mrs Beresford. 'Lady Dalrymple was most anxious to seek your view of the business, and how much of it is known to Lord Allersham. She understands that you spoke of it to Miss Carteret when you were last in Bath and she is anxious that it should not sour relations between our two families.'

'Why should it?' said Lady Allersham. 'If anything, it should bring about closer ties than before. Though I wish she would think of her daughter before anyone else.'

'Quite right,' said Mrs Beresford. 'In fact, I was about to write to Lady Dalrymple when you arrived. What may I say to Her Ladyship?'

'Tell Lady Dalrymple that we expect to see them at Michaelmas and that I am hopeful of a positive response.'

'What a large party we shall be!' Mrs Beresford replied.

'We shall indeed,' said Lady Allersham. 'I am disappointed, however, that my little brother is not to be one of the party. Frank is eager to see the sea again and is not in the least concerned about coming to Allersham. Aunt and Uncle Musgrave are to go to Sanditon at Michaelmas to visit Captain and Mrs Blake and have offered to take Frank with them. Frank, it seems, is beside himself with joy, Mama less so. To keep the peace, Papa thought Frank should go to Sanditon. Captain Blake's mother has been most accommodating, for she has offered to stay with Grandmamma and Great Aunt Turner at the Dower House to make way for Frank. He is to have a room of his own, the room Mrs Blake usually occupies, and so, you see, he will not be obliged to share the nursery with the Blakes' infant.'

'Mrs Blake is very good. But it is a great shame,' said Mrs Beresford, 'for I was looking forward so very much to seeing my young nephew again.'

'Shall you spend Christmas at Osborne Castle?' asked Lady Allersham.

'That depends on whether I secure a situation for Miss Fox if my other plan for her does not come to fruition. Until then, I cannot make up my mind.'

'Will she not be invited to Sparke Farm?'

'She is gone there today, always willing to do Mrs Sparke's bidding. If only James would come to the point. What prevents him from speaking to her, I wonder?'

Lady Allersham looked anxiously at her aunt. 'Perhaps their union might not be for the best.'

'I am sure he could go higher but he thinks as I do. He is not poor, so little is to be gained through marrying for material advantage alone. Had I not married the Colonel, I should not have known happiness. The more I observe James Beresford with Miss Fox, the more I am convinced of their affection for one another. If only there were a way to bring him to the point. Forgive me, my dear. I begin to think of James Beresford as the son I never had. I do not say that he is perfect in every detail, for he is a little grave at times. But I can easily forgive him that, because in other respects he resembles my dear husband so nearly that I can almost see the Colonel in his eyes.'

Mrs Beresford saw that her niece was not in complete accord with her, a circumstance she had not anticipated. 'My dear, I see you are apprehensive. What causes you to doubt? Your concern is admirable, Emma, but you have no need to be anxious on my account.'

Lady Allersham could not, would not, explain the cause of her misgivings. Her aunt's remark had caused her to contemplate the very worst possibility of all: that James Beresford and Miss Fox might be more closely related than she had at first imagined. They might even be brother and sister. What cruel twist of fate might then be visited on her unsuspecting aunt?

'What could possibly occur to spoil the pleasure of seeing Whitcombe Park come to life again. I am certain it is what my dear husband would have wanted,' said Mrs Beresford.

'Of course, he would,' said Lady Allersham. 'Dear Aunt, I wish, in this instance only, to urge caution.'

'Come, Emma,' replied Mrs Beresford, 'look at it this way. Such a match would be providential for Miss Fox, as any duty towards her arising from the connexion with Allersham, of which we have yet no firm knowledge, would be more than fulfilled by so practical an alliance.'

Their conversation was interrupted by the announcement of another visitor.

'We shall speak again, Emma,' said Mrs Beresford, as Mr Dauber was shown into the drawing room.

Expecting to find Mrs Beresford alone, Mr Dauber expressed his apologies for arriving at an inconvenient moment.

'Mr Dauber, you are welcome,' said Mrs Beresford. 'May I enquire after your wife? Is she well? I heard her spirits were a little depressed.'

'I suppose you heard a report of it likely emanating from Sparke Farm. Perhaps Miss Fox should exercise a little more discretion. I do not approve of young ladies telling tales,' said he.

'I did not hear it from Miss Fox,' Mrs Beresford replied. 'I had it from Mrs Dauber herself in a note I received from the Rectory this morning. She was kind enough to send me the recipe I had requested. Please thank your wife. I have given the recipe to Mrs Wilby as I promised I would.'

'I see,' he replied. He paused momentarily to collect his thoughts as though preparing to deliver a sermon. 'Allow me to speak plainly, Mrs Beresford. I believe Miss Fox is an unsettling influence on my younger daughters.'

'Why so?' said Mrs Beresford. 'I cannot imagine any person less likely to unsettle anyone.'

'Mr Dauber,' said Lady Allersham, 'your description of Miss Fox is at odds with my knowledge of her character and behaviour. Why on earth would you describe her as unsettling?'

'Miss Fox may be better served resuming some of those duties to which she was accustomed while a boarder with Mrs Price. She is an impressionable young woman as all young women are and, consequently, susceptible to forming ideas above her station. Since she has had the good fortune to enjoy your hospitality, Mrs Beresford, Mrs Sparke informs me that she has begun to give herself ladylike airs.'

'I have never had cause to think Miss Fox *unladylike*,' said Mrs Beresford. 'She has always behaved with modesty, courtesy and consideration for others at all times.'

'Nevertheless, I have given the matter some consideration,' said Mr Dauber, 'and I believe I have found a solution, a mutually beneficial one. Sparke Farm is in need of a general helper and Miss Fox would be a very suitable candidate. In return for some general duties, Miss Fox would profit by receiving food and a roof over her head. And if you are willing, the matter can be concluded without delay. My daughter thinks only of Miss Fox's welfare.'

'Please thank Mrs Sparke for her kind offer,' said Mrs Beresford. 'However, Miss Fox is not at present without food or shelter, and as nothing in the manner of general duties is required of her here, it is reasonable to suppose that she is better provided for under Whitcombe's roof than under the roof of Sparke Farm.'

'But that is precisely my point,' said Mr Dauber, glancing at Lady Allersham to seek her assistance. 'Your Ladyship, are you not of the same mind? Am I not in the right?'

'I cannot agree, Mr Dauber,' said she. 'Mrs Beresford and I have Miss Fox's interests at heart and will find a solution in time.'

Observing the tension on Mr Dauber's brow, Lady Allersham began to wonder whether Mrs Dauber had confessed to knowing Colonel Beresford's secret.

Vexed by Mr Dauber's accusation, Mrs Beresford delayed the bell for tea.

'I understand from Mrs Dauber that your parish duties are all consuming at present. It is unfortunate that I cannot introduce you to the Colonel's cousin, Mr James Beresford,' said she.

'Lord Allersham has taken him fishing,' added Lady Allersham.

'He will be gone in a day or two. Such a thoughtful and well-read young man. I wonder he does not think of the church as a profession,' said Mrs Beresford.

'Mr Beresford has been several years in the East Indies,' explained Lady Allersham.

'Then I shall be pleased to make his acquaintance at church on Sunday,' he replied.

Mr Dauber would not be moved and stayed on for half an hour more without being granted the opportunity to return to the subject of Miss Fox. Seeing that his mission was unlikely to be accomplished in one visit, he decided to take his leave.

'Mr Dauber,' said Lady Allersham. 'Might I walk with you to the gates? I wish to seek your advice on a particular matter. It is my understanding that you might be able to assist me.'

He responded with a more gracious bow of the head than she had expected in light of their earlier difference of opinion.

'I shall expect you for luncheon tomorrow,' said Lady Allersham to Mrs Beresford. 'You, Mr Beresford *and* Miss Fox. It is the last we will see Mr Beresford until Michaelmas.'

Lady Allersham gave the stable boy instructions to take the horse as far as the gates of Whitcombe Park and wait for her there, for Mr Dauber had arrived on foot.

'It is disappointing to find that we are at variance over Miss Fox,' said he. 'She is unlikely to receive a better position than the one at Sparke Farm. Allow me to take this opportunity to reiterate my concern. I should not like to see Mrs Beresford taken in or imposed upon by that young lady.'

'Mr Dauber,' said Lady Allersham. 'What can you tell me about Miss Fox? If you wish me to help you persuade my aunt, you must tell me what you know. Convince me, and I shall speak to her.'

'Is not my word enough, Your Ladyship?' said he.

'Your word?' replied Lady Allersham. 'Among your flock, your word may suffice.'

'Your Ladyship doubts the word of a clergyman?'

'Supply the name of Miss Fox's guardian and I shall be satisfied,' said Lady Allersham.

'It is not in my power to do so,' said he.

'Mr Dauber,' she replied, 'you placed Miss Fox with Mrs Price. This much I know. If you cannot tell me on whose behalf the service was performed perhaps you would explain to me why you chose to place her with that woman.'

Mr Dauber slowed his pace and looked into the distance and then at Lady Allersham. 'Mrs Price,' said he, 'is the daughter of my father's first wife. My stepsister. After the death of Mr Price, I sought to help his widow secure an income.'

'Mrs Price? The same Mrs Price who dealt harshly with Miss Fox and is now to wed Mr Ibbotson?'

'I beg to disagree, Your Ladyship. Mrs Price provided shelter for Miss Fox where others less charitable would have abandoned her.'

'Mrs Price concealed her connexion with you.'

'My stepsister is estranged from the rest of the family. I maintain the connexion in secret,' said he. 'Mrs Dauber, of course, knows of it. I sent our daughter to Gay Street for she was at one time becoming a little unruly.'

'You sent your daughter to Mrs Price as punishment?'

Mr Dauber made no reply.

'I cannot believe it,' said Lady Allersham.

When Mr Dauber spoke again, it was of Mrs Price. 'May I rely on your discretion in this matter?'

'You may, but in return, I should like to know the name of Miss Fox's guardian and the reason her allowance ceased,' said Lady Allersham.

'The name I cannot supply,' said he. 'Miss Fox's allowance may have ceased for any number of reasons. I can offer no further assistance in this matter. I bid you good day.'

Lady Allersham obtained little from her interview with Mr Dauber except for his curious connexion with Mrs Price. She could not, however, accept Mr Dauber's claim, that his stepsister had dealt charitably with Miss Fox. In their eyes, Miss Fox's worth lay only in her docility and readiness for hard work, for her compliant nature was easy to exploit to their own advantage.

The arrival of the Whitcombe party the following day once again provided Lady Allersham with an opportunity to observe with unease the growing bonds of family and friendship between them.

'We are soon to lose James Beresford,' said Lady Allersham to her aunt. 'And so, he leaves for Bath tomorrow.'

'He does, and we shall be all the poorer for his absence,' said Mrs Beresford. 'I have been given a firm assurance, however, that he will stay a full month when he returns at Michaelmas. What a happy time we shall have!'

Lady Allersham looked at her aunt with compassion, and smiled. There was nothing to spoil the anticipation of his return except the revelation of Colonel Beresford's secret. The truth must never come to light, thought she. And yet, were James Beresford to make Miss Fox an offer, and were she to accept him, withholding such knowledge from them would be impossible.

'What is it, Emma?' said Mrs Beresford. 'You seem very quiet today. What troubles you?'

'Nothing, Aunt,' she replied, attempting a smile.

'Maria, for we call Miss Fox Maria at Whitcombe Park, emptied her trunk of its contents today. You will never guess what object was found among them.'

'No, indeed,' said Lady Allersham.

'The painting that caught our eye in Mrs Price's parlour. The one Mrs Fowle was so certain portrayed Stanton Woods. Miss Fox has chosen to place it in the music room. It is displayed to great advantage there.'

'But do you not see what this means?' said Lady Allersham. 'The painting must have originally belonged to Miss Fox's benefactor. I have observed how Mrs Price adorns her parlour with boarders' ornaments and possessions.'

'The thought had passed my mind. But Mrs Price may have placed it among her belongings by mistake. She may even have tired of the painting and wished to pass it on. If only my dear Colonel were here. He was the best solver of mysteries I know. He knew Stanton Woods well and when he did not pass through them with the regiment he liked to ride with the hounds there,' said Mrs Beresford. She sighed and drew Lady Allersham's attention towards Mr Beresford and Miss Fox. 'Do not James and Maria make a fine couple? My dear, you do not disapprove of the match, do you?'

'Disapprove? Oh no, Aunt,' said she, unconvincingly.

'I can see that you are not in complete agreement. Your countenance tells me so. Should you be very surprised if James were to make an offer before he leaves for Bath? I should not.'

'So soon? Would that be wise?'

'He expressed an uncommon interest in Fulton Park when I mentioned it the other day. And he wrote to Captain Harding yesterday on his return from Allersham.'

'Has he spoken to you about Miss Fox directly?'

'He is not obliged to apply to me,' said Mrs Beresford.

'I would think it a courtesy while she resides under your roof.'

'Emma,' Mrs Beresford replied, 'I feel certain that he will speak when the time is right.'

'He is quite the fisherman,' said Lady Allersham.

'Oh yes, he enjoyed His Lordship's company yesterday.'

'And Henry enjoyed his, despite having to concede to Mr Beresford's proficiency for landing a rather fine carp,' said Lady Allersham. 'Are you sure about Fulton Park?'

'Yes,' replied Mrs Beresford, 'if Admiral Croft does not secure it first, I should not be surprised if James Beresford takes it instead.'

CHAPTER THIRTY-SIX

The absence of James Beresford was felt keenly at Whitcombe Park as the ladies began to count the days until his return at the end of September. In a letter to Mrs Beresford that reached Whitcombe almost a week after his departure, she was pleased to find that he had arrived in Bath twenty minutes earlier than anticipated, having made good progress on the road. He had called on Lady Dalrymple and Miss Carteret in Laura Place and could report that both ladies were in reasonable health and wished to extend their good wishes to their friends at Allersham. He had met Mr Ibbotson's sister and the Misses Ibbotson at the Pump Room. Both nieces were to stay with their aunt in Paragon Buildings after their father's wedding to Mrs Price.

'The Misses Ibbotson are not on speaking terms with their father and have nothing good to say about Mrs Price. I do not foresee any reconciliation before the wedding,' said Mrs Beresford, whose perusal of the letter occasioned an accompanying commentary. 'Oh! And here is something surprising. Mr Dauber is gone to Bath to intercede on Mrs Price's behalf. How strange that he should be drawn into the fray. He will need to work miracles.'

'Mr Dauber will do his best. I do not doubt it,' said Miss Fox. 'I hope that peace will break out.'

'James asks about you,' said Mrs Beresford. 'He has purchased a new volume of Cowper and wishes you to have it for he believes it will be to your liking just as it is to his. That is very kind of him, do not you agree?'

'Very kind indeed,' said she. 'Mr Beresford is always very kind.'

'And handsome,' said Mrs Beresford.

'In looks and deeds,' said she.

'I should not be surprised if he has a notion to marry,' Mrs Beresford replied.

'Oh,' said Miss Fox, without guile or affectation. 'Is Mr Beresford to marry? What a happy thought!'

'It is a happy thought,' said Mrs Beresford, perplexed by her answer.

'Mr Beresford deserves a partner in life who is his equal in every respect. I wish him every happiness,' Miss Fox replied.

'Any young woman who loved such a man should not hesitate to accept an offer were he to make one,' said Mrs Beresford. 'She should not refuse him on the grounds of birth, rank or situation if he should make her an offer.'

Mrs Beresford's remarks were puzzling; Miss Fox was unable to respond to them in any meaningful way and, consequently, fell silent.

'Now, my dear,' said she, 'I shall call on Mrs Dauber this morning for Mrs Wilby has written down a rather fine recipe for plum bread and wishes her to have it. You took a slice with your tea and said that you had never tasted better.'

'Yes, indeed,' said Miss Fox.

'Shall you walk to Allersham today? Lady Allersham is expecting you.'

'I shall,' she replied.

'Perhaps go by the lane. I do not advise crossing the fields for the mud is thick in parts. It will spoil the hem of your gown, and your boots will not fare well,' said Mrs Beresford.

The Rectory parlour was quiet owing to the absence of the Dauber girls who, having spent the night at Sparke Farm, were not expected until the afternoon. Mrs Dauber was pleased to receive her visitor, and though her pleasure in receiving Mrs Wilby's recipe for plum bread was less fulsome, she asked Mrs Beresford to convey her thanks to Whitcombe Park's famous cook. Mrs Dauber had always supposed her own recipes to be superior to any others in the neighbourhood and congratulated herself on having improved the standards of cookery enjoyed in the parish through distribution of the same to anyone in need of assistance, more so those in charge of the kitchens in the great houses.

'I see Mrs Wilby leaves out the peel and is a little heavy-handed with the nutmeg,' said Mrs Dauber, perusing the chit. 'A slight alteration to the ingredients will, I suppose, yield a tolerable loaf.'

Mrs Beresford smiled. 'I find Mrs Wilby's plum bread exceedingly good. You will also be pleased to find that I have spoken in glowing terms of your curd tart. And should you be good enough to provide the recipe, I would be happy to recommend it to Mrs Wilby.'

'It would be a pleasure,' she replied. 'Allow me to say, however, that a lightness of hand in pastry making ensures the best results. An understanding of the ingredients alone will not suffice. I am sure Mrs Wilby's skill in the kitchen would be vastly enhanced were she to attend to this point. My dear Mrs Beresford, I fear for you at Whitcombe, not least for your palate.' Mrs Dauber was all compassion. 'And I am sorry to hear that Miss Fox continues to impose upon you and your good nature.'

'Impose upon me?' said Mrs Beresford. 'You have it quite wrong. Miss Fox's company is no imposition. She remains at Whitcombe at my request. It is my express wish.'

'And yet Miss Fox would be put to greater use at Sparke Farm. Mrs Sparke speaks of nothing else,' said Mrs Dauber. 'And I understand, though my husband knows not from whence my knowledge proceeds, that Mrs Price, soon to be Mrs Ibbotson, may send for Miss Fox herself after the wedding. Mrs Price is at odds with Mr Ibbotson's sister and is disinclined to seek a reconciliation. If Miss Fox were to return to Mrs Price, the sister may consider it a provocation, for she is not quite as satisfied with her new domestic arrangements as she at first appeared to be.'

'Were Miss Fox to return to Bath neither Mrs Price nor Miss Ibbotson would succeed in their aims,' said Mrs Beresford.

Mrs Dauber replied cautiously. 'There are rumours, I am told, of an astonishing nature concerning Miss Fox. Perhaps you have not heard.'

'No, I have not,' said Mrs Beresford.

'My dear Mrs Beresford,' she replied. 'I should not wish any harm to come to you because of false reports or gossip of any kind. You must know, I think only of your good name.'

Mrs Beresford made no reply; consequently, Mrs Dauber was encouraged to proceed.

'I am reliably informed that Miss Fox is determined to set her cap at the Colonel's cousin. The rumours are certain to reach Bath by one means or another if they are not dismissed in the strongest of terms.'

'Nothing could be further from the truth, Mrs Dauber,' said Mrs Beresford. 'Indeed, I wish it were so. Were Miss Fox to set her cap at James Beresford and succeed, I should be the first to wish them joy.'

'Oh, my dear Mrs Beresford, that cannot be. I see you are unaware of the delicacy of the situation,' said Mrs Dauber, moving to occupy a chair beside her guest.

Footsteps in the hall advanced towards the door which opened to admit Mr Dauber at the very moment Mrs Dauber declared to Mrs Beresford, 'There is something you must know.'

'Mrs Beresford,' said the Rector in his Sunday voice, 'it is a pleasure indeed to see you again. I fear our last meeting came to a less than satisfactory conclusion. Might I seek your forgiveness for speaking with such candour.' Turning to his wife, he said, 'I see that I have interrupted an important disclosure. Mrs Dauber, please continue, if you will. What is it that Mrs Beresford must know, my dear?'

'Nothing in particular. We speak of recipes. It is of no consequence at all,' said Mrs Dauber. 'Indeed, it is quite forgotten.'

Mr Dauber was unconvinced by his wife's protestations. 'Why have you not provided tea for our guest?' said he.

'I had a mind to do so, of course. We were waiting for you, my dear. Mrs Beresford has hardly had time to catch her breath.'

'Then I shall be pleased to join you, for I should never refuse a dish of tea,' he replied. 'I hope I find you well, Mrs Beresford.'

'You do indeed, Mr Dauber,' said she.

'And did Mr Beresford approve of Whitcombe? I hope he did not cast his eye over the estate as those with expectations have sometimes the impertinence to do.'

'The matter never crossed my mind, nor, should I imagine, his,' said she.

'It should, Mrs Beresford, it should. Let me advise you to be on your guard,' he replied. 'May I enquire, have you thought further of the matter we spoke of recently?'

'Miss Fox?' she replied. 'No, I confess I have not, Mr Dauber. I believe your wife was about to speak to me concerning Miss Fox when you arrived.'

Mr Dauber directed his gaze toward Mrs Dauber in search of an explanation.

'It was nothing,' said she. 'Nothing at all. Indeed, I have quite forgotten my train of thought.'

Mrs Beresford was perplexed by the awkwardness that followed as the exchange between Mr Dauber and his wife was less than cordial; and, not wishing to witness the spectacle in its entirety, she made her excuses and rose to leave.

'Forgive me,' said she. 'There are matters I need to attend to. I only meant to stay long enough to enquire after your health, Mrs Dauber, and to place Mrs Wilby's recipe into your hands as she desired me to do. Would you now excuse me?'

The following day Mrs Beresford received word from Allersham Park that Mr Dauber had requested a private conversation with Lord Allersham and was insistent that she should also be present. The note made no reference to Lady Allersham but appeared to be a matter of some urgency. Lord Allersham expressed the hope that Mrs Beresford would be at liberty to meet with Mr Dauber at such short notice and would send a carriage from Allersham Park to collect her. There was no indication as to the subject, but as the clergyman had sought Lord Allersham's ear, and being somewhat intrigued by the urgency of the matter, she consented to the request and arrived at Allersham after the heat of the afternoon had subsided.

'Dear Aunt,' said Lady Allersham, 'I cannot understand why Henry asked you to come here in all this state. Does Miss Fox accompany you?'

'My presence alone has been requested. That is all I know.'

'Henry would not have asked you on a whim,' said Lady Allersham.

'Certainly I should not,' said Lord Allersham, as he approached to welcome Mrs Beresford and apologise for the disruption to her day.

'Why are you so furtive, my dear? Will you not explain why Mr Dauber issues his demand that we all must obey? And why am I to be kept in the dark?' said Lady Allersham.

'Enquire of Mr Dauber, if you will. I know only that it is a matter of some seriousness and that Mrs Beresford's presence is requested,' said he.

'And what of my presence? Am I not to be party to the gathering?' she replied.

'Indeed, you should,' said Mrs Beresford. 'We can have no secrets between us. I shall insist on your presence, my dear.'

'Secrets? No, indeed,' Lady Allersham replied. She dare not raise her eyes to her aunt, for being in possession of a secret concerning the Colonel, any indignation she might otherwise have felt now seemed hollow. 'Whatever could Whitcombe's esteemed cleric have to say, I wonder?'

'We must wait and see, Emma. Will you mind very much if your aunt and I comply with Mr Dauber's request in the first instance?' said Lord Allersham.

'Is he come?' she replied.

'Mr Dauber awaits us in the library,' said he.

'Then I shall await you in the drawing room,' said Lady Allersham.

'My dear Emma,' Mrs Beresford replied, 'for my part I should insist on having you with me, but I will give way until more is known. Mr Dauber must have his reasons.'

'Yes,' said Lady Allersham, 'I am sure he does.'

Five minutes later brought Lord Allersham and Mrs Beresford together with Mr Dauber in the library. Lady Allersham resisted the impulse to follow and listen at the door. Instead, she took to the long gallery and, pacing back and forth, vented her vexation with Mr Dauber for his interference and pompous self-regard. What nature of man is he? whispered she under her breath. That he should have the temerity to issue a command and expect it to be followed. Poor Mrs Dauber! Were I married to such a man I should leave immediately, and I should not care for anyone's poor opinion of me!

The thought occurred to her that the purpose of his visit might be to further the interests of Sparke Farm, to persuade her husband and aunt to agree to Mrs Sparke's request. And yet Sparke Farm was clearly not a matter of urgency to anyone but Mrs Sparke. Moreover, she dismissed the possibility that Mr Dauber would reveal Colonel Beresford's connexion with Miss Fox, for he had been adamant in his refusal to reveal anything pertaining to the affair.

Presently, Lord Allersham entered the gallery alone. 'I expected to find you in the drawing room.'

'Where is Aunt Beresford?' said she.

'She is with Mr Dauber,' he replied.

'How long must he insist we all stand on ceremony? He should save his sermons for the pulpit. Why are you here?'

'My presence was no longer required.'

'And might I know the something of the matter or are there to be secrets between us?'

'Emma,' said he, 'I have your aunt's leave to explain everything. Shall we sit for a while?'

'I hope it is nothing very disagreeable,' said she.

'Mrs Beresford called on Mrs Dauber this morning. Mr Dauber came upon them as his wife was about to impart something important. The moment was lost, and your aunt left the Rectory and thought no more of it. After your aunt's departure, Mr Dauber insisted that Mrs Dauber reveal all to him, more particularly the information imparted to you.'

'I see,' said Lady Allersham. 'And so Mrs Dauber confessed to having discovered some secret concerning the Colonel.'

'Yes.'

'And no doubt Mr Dauber asked whether she had revealed the secret to anyone else, and she admitted that she had spoken of it to me. And assuming that I, being a woman, was not to be trusted to keep a secret, he decided to speak. He saw that he, and not Mrs Dauber, must inflict the pain on my aunt himself. Despicable man! But what must she think of me now? How she must despise me! How am I to face her? I suppose now that Mr Dauber has done his worst, it will make the way easier for Mrs Sparke,' said she.

'Mrs Sparke?'

'Do you not see? His object is to send Miss Fox to live at Sparke Farm and keep her there as little more than a maidservant.'

'Emma,' Lord Allersham replied, 'Sparke Farm was not mentioned.'

'I expect Mr Dauber is prevailing upon my aunt even as we speak. Is she very distressed?'

'I shall leave you to hear out Mrs Beresford. It is better that she speaks with you directly.'

'What if she will not see me?'

'Come,' said he.

Lady Allersham waited anxiously for the appearance of Mrs Beresford in the drawing room, preparing what she might say to ease her aunt's pain.

It was not long before her aunt came in. Emma went to her at once.

'Dear Aunt,' said she, 'can you forgive me for causing you pain?'

'Causing me pain?' Mrs Beresford replied. 'You have never caused me pain, Emma. What an extraordinary thing to say!'

'You were obliged to hear something disagreeable from Mr Dauber in this sensational and severe way! Can you forgive me?'

'My dear, I am delighted! Quite delighted to find that my dear Colonel was able to be of service to Miss Fox of all people!' said Mrs Beresford.

'I don't understand,' Lady Allersham replied.

'It is a mystery solved,' said she. 'Several years ago, the Colonel came to me after receiving an intriguing letter from a former member of his regiment, quite out of the blue, seeking help with the delivery of a valuable item to a recipient in the neighbourhood of Whitcombe. It had quite gone from my mind until Mr Dauber spoke of it this afternoon, for I supposed the delivery to be an inanimate object — a vase, or something of the kind. My dear husband always exercised the utmost discretion in such matters. The item was to be deposited at the gates of Whitcombe Park. I recall that the Colonel had taken it upon himself to deliver it personally to a house in the neighbourhood. I now know that house to be the Rectory, and the person to whom the item was delivered, Mr Dauber. And of course, the item was not a vase but a child, hence the need for secrecy. Mr Dauber explained that my dear husband had sought his assistance in finding a suitable situation for the child. The application was timely, for Mrs Price had not long opened an establishment in Bath, eminently suitable for girls and young women in similar circumstances. And so, my dear Emma, I am sure you have guessed it by now. The child was our own Miss Fox, and Mrs Price, Mr Dauber's stepsister! Is it not beyond comprehension?'

'It is certainly beyond mine! But Aunt, has not your opinion of the Colonel altered in light of the discovery that he took the secret of Miss Fox to his grave?'

'It has,' said she. 'In fact, it has improved my opinion of him, if such a thing were possible. I know that his assistance was sought precisely because his complete discretion was assured. And now I understand why he acted as he did. Miss Fox, it seems, is the product of a past indiscretion. The welfare of all parties concerned was contingent upon secrecy being maintained. There is but one piece in the tale that is less satisfactory than the rest, and that is the reliance on Mr Dauber's recommendation of Mrs Price. Of course, my dear husband was not to know, I suppose, the callous nature of the woman, and yet Mr Dauber sent his own daughter to Gay Street. So I must allow that, whatever reservations I may have in that regard, Mr Dauber acted in good faith towards Miss Fox.'

'And so Miss Fox is the natural daughter of one of Colonel Beresford's regiment? I am relieved to hear it!'

'Why so, Emma? Why relieved?' said Mrs Beresford.

'Because I had imagined Miss Fox to be the Colonel's ward. Forgive me. How could I have allowed myself to entertain such thoughts.'

'I see what you mean, my dear,' Mrs Beresford replied. 'But I believe you were purposefully led in that direction by another.'

'I was. Nevertheless, I should have dismissed the idea immediately. I did not.'

'Mrs Dauber must not be blamed,' said Mrs Beresford. 'It was perfectly understandable, seeing the Colonel that night, to suppose that he was acting on his own behalf.'

'Why did Mr Dauber choose to disclose this information when he has resisted doing so for so long?' said Lady Allersham.

'Oh, Emma,' said Mrs Beresford. 'It was my doing. During my visit to the Rectory, Mrs Dauber indicated that she was about to tell me something important when Mr Dauber entered the room and asked her to explain herself. His suspicions were raised and he insisted on knowing everything. Poor Mrs Dauber. I should not like to be on the receiving end of his wrath. It was only when Mr Dauber came to realise that his wife had misunderstood the nature of the Colonel's involvement in the matter, that he decided to act. He wished, above all things, to ensure that *the late Colonel's memory was not sullied by false speculation and innuendo of a cruel kind.* Those were his words exactly. So, you see, we now have our answer. And is it not the greatest coincidence that Maria should come to be under my care?'

'What would the Colonel have thought of it all?'

'He would have been delighted to know that his actions had brought about the happiest of endings.'

'Did Mr Dauber approach the subject of Sparke Farm? He must believe that it now strengthens his case,' said Lady Allersham.

'He did,' replied Mrs Beresford, 'but I would have none of it. He will not attempt the subject again. Until we are certain of Maria's parentage, which may never be established, I shall act as her guardian.'

'Then her origins remain a mystery?'

'Apparently my husband never told Mr Dauber the name of Maria's father,' said Mrs Beresford. 'Her allowance was forwarded by an attorney until, of course, the payments to Mrs Price ceased and the gentleman in question became *unreachable*.'

'Poor Miss Fox must have felt utterly abandoned.'

'She is enduringly sanguine and thinks only of the good that has come her way. It is quite extraordinary,' Mrs Beresford replied. 'But now I shall leave you. I intend to search the Colonel's correspondence to see what might come to light.'

'What shall you say to Miss Fox?' said Lady Allersham.

'Nothing at present,' she replied, cautiously. 'Let us see if we can reach a better understanding of the matter through further investigation.'

Lady Allersham replied, 'I suppose Henry has a full understanding of the affair?'

'He has,' said she.

Lady Allersham stood at the window and looked out onto the lake. It appeared perfectly still, illumined by a stream of light that caused its surface to sparkle.

'There you are,' said Lord Allersham, on entering the drawing room.

'How splendid the lake appears before sunset,' she replied.

He came and stood by her. 'My thoughts entirely,' said he.

'Will you walk with me to the lakeside?'

Lord Allersham offered his arm.

'What a day of revelations!' said she. 'I can now say with equanimity that I have no regrets for having taken Miss Fox under my wing. Nor has my aunt.'

'Shall you continue your quest?'

'My quest?'

'I know you, Emma. Does Mr Dauber's intelligence suffice?'

'Not entirely. However, I may, in part, have misjudged Mr Dauber. When he realised the nature of the falsehood perpetrated by his wife, he acted quickly to put right the blemish to Colonel Beresford's reputation. Alas, I believe I should have drawn the same conclusion as Mrs Dauber. And yet, I do not see why I was excluded from the business this afternoon. I suppose he offered no explanation for that.'

Lord Allersham replied, 'He fears you, Emma. Mr Dauber fears any woman who dares to question his authority. Where you perceive righteous indignation, he sees invective against the Church, against all he stands for.'

'Did he say so?'

'Not explicitly,' he replied. 'It is an observation.'

'But who has right on their side?'

'Your question surprises me. Is not the answer as clear as day?' His ironic smile was met by a look of puzzlement.

They walked on towards the lake and, on reaching their favourite spot, they sat down to admire the scene in all its beauty.

'Since Mr Dauber's revelation this afternoon, it occurs to me that you should perhaps focus your efforts nearer home,' said he.

'Osborne Castle?' she replied, astonished by the suggestion.

'Stanton, perhaps?'

'What could possibly come to light there?'

'I was thinking of the painting. If Stanton Woods is indeed its subject — was not the Colonel acquainted with the neighbourhood of Stanton, Delham and Osborne Castle?'

'Aunt Beresford is certain to know the extent of his past acquaintance there.'

'And you might consult your mama and Mrs Fowle. Consider Emma, if your Aunt Fowle is determined to grace us with her presence at Michaelmas, to forsake Brinshore and leave her husband behind, it proffers endless possibilities for speculation and intrigue.'

CHAPTER THIRTY-SEVEN

An extensive search of Colonel Beresford's effects yielded nothing — no name, no hint of a name or place, nor any allusion whatsoever to the service rendered by the Colonel. After every box, drawer and cupboard had undergone meticulous examination, Mrs Beresford was obliged to cease her endeavour and admit failure. As the summer drew to a close, and Michaelmas was but a fortnight away, her mind turned to other concerns. Chief among them was the return of James Beresford. Since his last visit to Whitcombe, he had corresponded with pleasing regularity, providing a constant source of news and commentary on their acquaintance in Bath. His latest missive, however, had brought disappointing news: Captain Harding, who was also expected at

Whitcombe was now prevented from honouring his commitment.

'He knows that Miss Carteret is to come, and he wishes to avoid causing pain and embarrassment,' said Lady Allersham.

'It is a great pity,' said Mrs Beresford, 'for, were they to be thrown together, they might yet reach an understanding. Is Captain Harding's mind quite made up?'

'The point is, Aunt, Robert is convinced that Miss Carteret's mind is made up,' said Lady Allersham. She hesitated momentarily before proceeding with a request of her aunt. 'There is something I must ask of you. Lady Dalrymple has expressed a wish to stay with *you* at Whitcombe, for she looks upon you as a friend.'

'Yes, indeed,' said Mrs Beresford. 'Of course she must stay at Whitcombe. I should like that very much.'

'And I should like Miss Carteret to stay at Allersham so that she might understand better something of Captain Fitzroy's home,' said Lady Allersham.

'An excellent arrangement. Perhaps the experience may afford Miss Carteret some release from her sorrow,' said Mrs Beresford.

'Perhaps,' said Lady Allersham. 'My hope is that it does not add to it. And if you desire it, Aunt, Miss Fox might also stay here. Or have you other reasons for keeping her at Whitcombe? Are you still hopeful that James Beresford will come to the point?'

'He always enquires after Miss Fox. His letters are proof of his fondness, but I believe his propriety and restraint create uncertainty which puts everything in doubt. All that is needed is his return, for it is impossible to begin a courtship at such a distance,' said Mrs Beresford.

'Might the question of Miss Fox's birth stand in the way?' said Lady Allersham.

'Knowing him as I do, it would seem unlikely. If only my dear husband's effects had yielded results,' said Mrs Beresford.

'Mama is as intrigued as Grandmamma by the story of Miss Fox,' Lady Allersham replied.

'When do your parents arrive?' said Mrs Beresford.

'Friday,' replied she. That is, if the weather is favourable and the road out of Delham is mended. Shall you dine with us?'

'Friday?' said Mrs Beresford. 'No, my dear. I know your father after a long journey. He has little to say and if he utters two words together it will be a wonder. It was ever the case.'

'Very true. Saturday, then,' said Lady Allersham. 'Mama is anxious to see you and to meet Miss Fox.'

The arrival of Lord and Lady Osborne at Allersham was awaited by their daughter with eagerness, and their son-in-law with pleasant anticipation, and took place in mid-September under blue skies and a soft breeze. Lady Allersham had looked out every half hour since midday until the clock struck five and the Osborne carriage entered the gates of Allersham Park.

'What a journey!' said Lady Osborne, removing her bonnet and gloves. 'Your papa will tell you all about it. I was never so relieved as when we passed that little coaching inn outside Whitcombe and knew that we were but five miles from Allersham. We had intended to call at Whitcombe Park on the way, just for a minute or two, but neither your papa nor I were in a fit state. My dear Emma, how well you look! All summer I have counted the hours to this moment. Your grandmamma begged to come, and Aunt Turner too, but the journey is quite beyond them. To secure my release, I had to promise to write every day and account for every hour spent at Allersham and miss nothing out. They are most interested in the progress of Miss Carteret and Miss Fox. Your grandmamma wagers both young women will be wed by Christmas, but Aunt Turner is of the opinion that your cousin Robert will not succeed with Miss Carteret and is sure she will receive a better offer.'

'They are just as they ever were then,' said Lady Allersham, 'I am so very happy to see you! If only Osborne Park were as close to Allersham as Whitcombe, I should be the happiest being in the world.'

'Emma,' said Lord Osborne, 'have you a word of welcome for your papa?'

'Papa!' she replied. 'I hope you have not entered into any wagers with Grandmamma. And if you have, you must tell me later when we are not in earshot of Mama!'

'Very wise, my love,' said Lady Osborne to her daughter. 'Presently, they are much occupied by a dispute concerning the garden.'

'Your grandmamma favours a fountain, Aunt Turner a figure,' said Lord Osborne.

'Of Eros,' Lady Osborne interjected.

'Can they not combine the two?' said Lady Allersham.

'That would involve compromise, Emma. And that would never do,' said Lord Osborne.

The appearance of Lord Allersham, welcomed by all, was accompanied by an apology for his tardiness.

'I was not aware of your arrival until a footman came to find me,' said he. 'How was the journey? You suffered no delay, I see.'

'None at all,' said Lord Osborne.

'Henry,' said Lady Osborne, 'how good it is to see you again. Lord Osborne and I are amazed by the changes to Allersham Park. You have done wonders to the landscape. How beautiful it looks at this time of year.'

'It does, indeed,' agreed Lord Osborne.

'Much of it is Emma's doing. I merely carry out your daughter's wishes,' said he, with a smile. 'What news from Brinshore?'

'Charles Blake sends greetings,' replied Lord Osborne.

Lady Osborne whispered to her daughter, 'Your papa took Frank to Sanditon and stayed the night there. Your brother was wild with excitement. He gazed at the sea all the way from Brighton to Waterloo Crescent and did not once turn his head to look at his papa, even when spoken to.'

'I thought Frank was to travel with Aunt and Uncle Musgrave,' said Lady Allersham.

'He was,' said her mother, 'but I asked your father to take him. It was an excuse to bring Mrs Blake back with him. I did not want her to travel post. The Dower House could not wait to receive her.'

'No doubt Grandmamma and Aunt Turner with expect to be entertained with all the goings on between Brinshore and Sanditon,' said Lady

Allersham. 'Has Mrs Blake given up Osborne Cottage completely?'

'Not entirely, no. But Mrs Blake's visits to Sanditon have become more frequent of late.'

'You must miss her society, Mama.'

'I do,' said Lady Osborne. 'But I cannot complain. Osborne Castle is rarely without visitors. I see your Aunt Musgrave almost daily.'

'And Aunt Fowle?'

'Almost one week in every four. Though lately it seems matters have improved a little in Brinshore.'

'And will the Croydon families spend Christmas there?'

'They talk of nothing else,' said Lord Osborne, catching the thread of conversation.

'Your papa happened upon your cousin Robert when he dined with the Blakes.'

'Cousin Robert dined with the Blakes?' said Lady Allersham.

'He had some business there,' said Lord Osborne.

'Perhaps he threatens to buy a house in Sanditon. It would vex the Fowles greatly. How does he fare?' she replied.

'Your papa said he appeared a little subdued, did you not, my dear?'

'Harding seemed surprisingly dull company,' said Lord Osborne.

'Miss Carteret is the likely cause,' said Lady Allersham. 'Did you call on Aunt and Uncle Fowle, Papa?'

Lord Osborne smiled. 'No. I was obliged to forgo that delight.'

CHAPTER THIRTY-EIGHT

Lady Osborne was anxious to call on Mrs Beresford the following morning and resisted all attempts by her husband to persuade her to take a tour of Allersham Park instead.

'My sister will not expect it for she is to dine with us this evening,' said Lord Osborne.

'Nevertheless,' said Lady Osborne, 'I should like to visit Whitcombe. I said we might call there on our way to Allersham, and we did not.'

The matter was settled without further ado, and Lord and Lady Osborne set out after breakfast to visit Whitcombe. They found Mrs Beresford within and were received with the warmest of welcomes.

'You have just missed Miss Fox,' said Mrs Beresford. 'The Dauber girls called earlier and persuaded her to join their expedition to Whitcombe Hill. I do not think she was inclined to go, but they made such a fuss about her being of their party and would not leave without her, that she was forced to yield to their entreaties.'

An hour passed as news and expressions of good wishes were exchanged, and enquiries satisfied. There was still much to hear and say, and the coming days promised to provide many happy opportunities of a similar kind.

During the hour, the Osbornes brought news of the new incumbent at Stanton, his musical wife, and their six children. It was not long thereafter before the mention of Stanton brought to mind the painting that Mrs Fowle had mentioned in a letter to her sister. Lady Osborne expressed a particular interest in viewing it.

'The painting?' said Mrs Beresford. 'Oh, yes. There has been much speculation about it. Mrs Fowle believes Stanton Woods is its subject.'

Lady Osborne replied, 'Penelope was in no doubt that the scene was Stanton Woods. If it proves to be so, it would be a remarkable coincidence, would it not?'

'Should you like to see it?' said Mrs Beresford.

'I should indeed,' Lady Osborne replied. 'And you, my dear,' said she, turning to her husband, 'will decide the matter if our views are at variance, for you know Stanton Woods better than anyone. I remember when you first invited me to watch the hounds throw off there.'

'I do not know what my brother was thinking of when he wooed you with the prospect of a meet,' said Mrs Beresford.

'No one was more surprised than I when the incomparable Miss Watson appeared in Stanton Woods that day. I could not believe my luck,' said Lord Osborne.

'Your presence on that day gave my brother hope,' said Mrs Beresford to her sister-in-law. 'For I remember he was never done speaking of it.'

'I don't believe I ever said a word about it,' said Lord Osborne.

Disbelieving of His Lordship's protests, Mrs Beresford and Lady Osborne exchanged a smile of mutual understanding.

'Come this way,' said she, leading them to the painting. 'It hangs in the music room. It has a most curious inscription on the back. *Detested sport, that owes its pleasures to another's pain.* A line from Cowper, I believe.'

Lord Osborne made a close examination of the artist's endeavour. 'I can say with absolute certainty that no one past or present connected with the family of Osborne would have ever mounted such a sorry apology for a horse. Have you ever seen such a creature?'

'My dear brother, the horse is not the point in question, as you well know,' replied Mrs Beresford.

'Then it undoubtedly ought to be,' said he.

Lady Osborne was silent, her countenance curiously difficult to read. 'I know this painting,' said she, with a calm affirmation that left Lord Osborne and Mrs Beresford confounded by her claim.

'I know this painting,' she repeated. 'Mrs Beresford, would you be so kind as to remind me of the inscription on the reverse of the canvas?'

'*Detested sport, that owes its pleasures to another's pain,*' said she, slowly and deliberately, enunciating every syllable.

'What if, in this instance, the remark refers not to the sport of *hunting*, but to another kind of *hunter*?' said Lady Osborne.

'You are speaking in riddles, my love,' Lord Osborne replied.

'Would you indulge me for the present?' said she. 'I should regret raising hopes only to dash them, and my instinct may well prove to be flawed. My dear,' said she to her husband, 'I shall require your assistance.' Then, turning to Mrs Beresford, she said, 'Emma wrote to me of a silver vinaigrette in Miss Fox's possession.'

'Yes,' replied Mrs Beresford. 'A fine piece and much treasured.'

'I have a rather irregular request. Would you ask Miss Fox if she might give up the item for a day or two?'

'What reason should I give?' she replied.

'Say that the prospect exists of having the item examined in the hope that more light might be shed on its origins. Make no promise. I should, of course, take great care of the trinket,' said Lady Osborne.

'Of course,' said Mrs Beresford. 'I should be delighted if —'

'But should I fail —'

'Then we will not speak of it again,' she replied.

On leaving Whitcombe Park, Lady Osborne said, 'I should like to know whether a journey to the village of Kilston, known to be in these parts, might be accomplished in a day,' she replied. 'If not, we will need to secure a room for the night.'

'Kilston?' Lord Osborne replied.

'Yes,' said she. 'I daresay you will find the expedition thoroughly disagreeable, but I am of the view that it should be undertaken. And I shall require your help.'

'I am ready to offer it.'

'Do you recognise the name?' said she.

'Kilston? Should I?'

'Certainly you should. Your mama announced some sad news concerning one of its inhabitants not so very long ago.'

'Not —'

'Yes, my dear.'

Lady Osborne was obliged to wait until dinner to satisfy her curiosity regarding Miss Fox. Her thoughts had, from time to time, returned to the scene depicted in the painting that was so remarkably familiar to her. The possibility that it might have been copied could not be discounted or that her recollection of the past was defective and incomplete. She lacked only the opinion of her elder sister, Elizabeth, to give her the assurance she needed to establish with certainty the painting's origin.

Without having the benefit of Elizabeth's eye, Lady Osborne was eager to study Miss Fox for signs, looks and gestures that might confirm her suspicions. Her eventual appearance, however, did little to strengthen the reliability of the suppositions that had taken shape in Lady Osborne's mind. Miss Fox was, in character and countenance, quite different to the notions Lady Osborne had formed of her. Mild and modest, courteous and unaffected, Miss Fox had surprising qualities that caused Her Ladyship to question her own judgement and almost retreat entirely from her reasonable supposition.

Miss Fox said little while at table, and even less after the ladies moved to the drawing room. Mrs Beresford quickly seized the arm of Lady Osborne and led her to a quiet corner of the room for a private conversation. At one and the same time, Lady Allersham guided Miss Fox to the pianoforte and prevailed upon her to play the country dance she had learned.

'Mrs Beresford said that you play it very prettily. The piece is a favourite at Osborne Castle,' said Lady Allersham. 'Do not be anxious. You are among friends.'

'May I play it quietly? If I should make a mistake —'

'Do not worry about mistakes. I make mistakes all the time and no one cares one whit.'

While Miss Fox played, Lady Osborne and Mrs Beresford returned to the subject they had spoken of earlier in the day. Mrs Beresford, swiftly and stealthily, placed Miss Fox's vinaigrette into Lady Osborne's hand.

'Miss Fox surrendered the object without question. I mentioned only that I wished to make enquiries concerning a particular silversmith and that it might throw light on the piece,' said Mrs Beresford. 'Shall you require it for long?'

'I shall return it within a day. Your brother and I are to call on an old acquaintance. We shall leave early,' said she. 'I am assured that the journey will be accomplished in a day.'

Lady Allersham caught a little of the conversation as she approached the pair. 'What journey will be accomplished in a day?' said she.

'Emma,' said her mother, 'Your papa and I promised your grandmamma that we would call on an old acquaintance and offer our condolences.'

'Who had died?' said Lady Allersham.

'An acquaintance of your grandmamma. And as she is not able to pay a visit in person, she insisted that we make it for her.'

'Just like Grandmamma! She must have her way. Shall I accompany you? Do I know the person?'

'No, my dear. It is of little matter and I know that you would find it wearisome. You had better stay where you are. Your papa and I will manage very well on our own.'

'And what about Aunt Beresford? Are you to be of the party, Aunt?' said she.

'Not I. I should also find it wearisome, my dear. I am happy to remain at Whitcombe.'

'Oh,' said Lady Allersham. 'I see. In that case, I shall ride over to Whitcombe myself. Miss Fox's adventure climbing Whitcombe Hill has put me in mind of doing the same. I shall take Henry with me. He proposed to me on Whitcombe Hill, you know. I should like to see it again.'

CHAPTER THIRTY-NINE

A carriage bearing the Osborne coat of arms neared the church in the inconsequential village of Kilston. Lady Osborne drew her husband's attention away from the journal he had been perusing for a large part of the journey and reminded him of the part he was to play.

'It is important that you keep him occupied while I speak to Mrs Howard in private,' said she. Her eyes were drawn to a distant figure in the churchyard. 'Look! Over there! Is that not Mr Howard making his way to the church?'

'Unmistakably so, I should say,' said Lord Osborne. 'You wish me to go after him?'

'Yes. No,' she replied. 'Wait here, or tarry in the churchyard until he returns, for if he sees you directly, he will likely return to the parsonage. Do what you can to delay him. Ask him to direct you to Mr Edwards' grave. There you might trespass on his time further and oblige him to render lengthy prayers for the deceased, and in turn offer condolences on behalf of your mother, Aunt Turner, and the entire neighbourhood of Delham if you so wish. Then you might ask to see his pigs. Say that you are considering purchasing a dozen yourself and —'

'My love, Mr Howard is an intelligent man. I have not seen or corresponded with him for many years. Do you not suppose that a conversation over the purchase of pigs would seem somewhat irregular under the circumstances?'

'I am sure you will think of something. Ask if he has news of Charles.'

'Charles Blake? I have more news than he. I saw Charles but a fortnight ago as you well know.'

'Then convey Charles' good wishes. Talk to him of Sanditon and Mrs Blake and Frank and —'

'You had better go before the opportunity to speak to Mrs Howard eludes you altogether!' said he.

Lady Osborne was received by a maidservant unused to opening the door to a viscountess.

'Please ma'am,' said she, 'let me send for my master.'

'There is no need to disturb him. Lord Osborne has gone to seek him out and desires a private conversation. Is Mrs Howard within?' said she.

'Yes, Ma'am, but my mistress does not receive callers.'

'Nevertheless, I should like you to take me to her. Where might she be at this hour?'

'In the garden, Ma'am. But —'

'Thank you. I shall find my own way.'

Seated on a wooden bench beside an ancient yew, Mrs Howard, head slumped to one side, had drifted into a deep slumber. Lady Osborne sat down beside her and shook her gently.

'Mary. Mary. Wake up,' said she.

Mrs Howard opened her eyes wearily and whispered, 'So tired,' and closed her eyes once again.

'Wake up, Mary. I need to speak with you,' Lady Osborne replied.

Slowly, Mrs Howard opened her eyes once again. 'Emma? Emma Watson? Is it really you? I must be dreaming.'

'It is I,' said Lady Osborne. 'You must wake up properly, Mary. I must speak with you before Mr Howard returns. It is important. I do not know what time we have at our disposal.'

Mary yawned into the palm of her hand and sat up. 'Why are you here?'

'Mary, listen to me. There is something I must ask you.' She took out the silver vinaigrette belonging to Miss Fox and placed it into Mrs Howard's hands. 'Do you recognise this box?'

Mrs Howard examined it and was silent.

'Mary?'

'How did you come by it?' said she. The sight of the item startled her and rendered her fully awake.

'I borrowed it,' said Lady Osborne.

'That is not possible,' Mrs Howard replied.

'Why is it not possible?'

'Why did you come here?'

'Because I want to help you, if I can,' said Lady Osborne. But first of all, I need your help. Can you tell me how a young woman might have come by this small trinket, an object I recognise, and which bears your initials?'

'Not mine. M. F., as you see,' said Mrs Howard.

'The engraving is worn, Mary. The initials are yours. M. E. Mary Edwards. Do not deny it. We have little time.'

'How did you —'

'Tell me what you know, but quickly, and I promise to do likewise. Do not hide any particular from me. Captain Hunter is implicated in some way, is he not?'

Mrs Howard nodded. 'What do you require of me when you are already in possession the facts?'

'It was a lucky guess.'

Mrs Howard sat up and straightened her apron. 'You recall the circumstances of my marriage to Mr Howard,' said she.

'Your father discovered your plan to elope with Captain Hunter and sent you to London. There, I believe, you were thrown together with Mr Howard and when he made you an offer, you accepted him.'

'How you must have despised me when he was such a favourite with you.'

'I did not, nor do I, despise you. My feelings were injured at first, but I understand why you acted as you did,' said Lady Osborne.

'Mr Howard never cared for me. He desired only my money and connexions. I was desperately unhappy from the start and sought happiness from another source. When Captain Hunter followed me to London, we met in secret. His marriage to Miss Styles did not put an end to our encounters, you see. After his removal to Somerset, something Mrs Hunter insisted upon, our encounters naturally became less frequent.'

'Mrs Hunter persuaded him to leave London?'

'She has family here. I believe she suspected her husband. The renewal of an old acquaintance near Bath provided me with the means of resuming the affair. I would, from time to time, visit Somerset under the pretence of caring for a sick friend. Mrs Hunter found out and wrote to Mr Howard, and to the friend I had made use of. I had nowhere to go. I could not return to Mr Howard. Mrs Blake was very kind, but she did not know the extent of my troubles. I did not know it then, but I was with child. When I realised my predicament, I wrote to Captain Hunter. He arranged lodgings for me until the time of my confinement. I went under the name of Fox and dressed as a widow. In the fullness of time, my daughter came into the world and the same day was taken away from me. I never held her in my arms. I was told she was placed in the care of a wet nurse and remained there for some time. I know not where.'

'By whom was she taken?'

'Captain and Mrs Hunter, of course,' said Mary. 'I was obliged to comply or face the consequences. Whatever *he* might have done, *her* word meant nothing, for after my daughter had been taken away, Mrs Hunter saw fit to inform Mr Howard. You see, she discovered that I had written to Captain Hunter asking him for information concerning the whereabouts of my daughter. I just needed to know that she was safe. I lived daily without a moment's peace of mind. Captain Hunter proffered just enough information to assure me that she was alive, and agreed to my request to place with her some items in my possession, this little vinaigrette being one of them. My hope was that she might look for me in time and seek to understand the circumstances of her birth. My only desire was for forgiveness. One glimpse of her would have sufficed. Mr Howard's incontrollable rage, on receiving Mrs Hunter's letter, led ultimately to his removal from London. He wrote to my father, who took his side completely. My father immediately informed my uncle without giving thought to the consequences, and my uncle, being high and mighty in church circles, and believing me to be beyond redemption, advised Mr Howard to find a new situation. Ironically, my husband was obliged to accept the only offer he received: a living in Somerset. Again, I was cut adrift. In time, Charles Blake found lodgings for me, a short distance from Kilston. The mother of a young midshipman who had lost his arm at sea wished to let a room, which Charles paid for. I had no money of my own. An arrangement was reached after some months that my father should move to Kilston on the understanding that he would leave his estate in its entirety to Mr Howard on his death. In return, I should be reconciled with my husband and admitted once again to our marital home to tend to the needs of my ailing father. In recognition of my husband's leniency, I was obliged to agree to any conditions he chose to impose upon me. This is how you find me. Mr Howard and I live under the same roof. Friendships are banned, letters intercepted, replies dictated by Mr Howard. I have food and shelter, and despite the perpetual reprimands, I have come to accept my situation. All that has transpired has been of my own doing. In a moment of naïve optimism several years ago, I had contemplated the possibility that Mr Howard, who had shown mercy to me, might show mercy to an innocent child and accept her as his own. The suggestion caused outrage. Mr Howard wrote to Captain Hunter, demanding that he took full responsibility for the child and that nothing more was to be spoken of or known about the matter at Kilston. Mr Howard, you see, was quite as determined as Mrs Hunter, and threatened to expose her husband as a philanderer and profligate. Captain Hunter feared such a threat above all things because, curiously, in the meantime he had fallen in love — with Mrs Hunter.'

Mrs Howard looked down at the vinaigrette in her hand. 'I had nothing to give my daughter but this silver box, and a painting that hung in my father's house in Delham. A reminder of happier times.'

'And did you inscribe a line from Cowper on the back of it?' said Lady Osborne. '*Detested sport, that owes it pleasures to another's pain.*'

'The detested sport of seduction. I thought only of my daughter's pain. The pain of separation, obscurity and disgrace: all the evils of the world to which she would be subjected without the protection of family, without the knowledge of having been loved. I have learned to care for nothing and no one else in this world but the child I was forced to give up. Have you come to tell me something dreadful? I expect it. Daily I expect it. Has my little one been taken from this world?' said Mrs Howard, wearily.

'I have promised to return the trinket to its owner who is very much alive,' replied Lady Osborne.

Suddenly, the gate squeaked open and voices were heard approaching.

'You have told me what I need to know, Mary. And I thank you.'

'But you have told me nothing,' she replied.

'I have told you that the person to whom you gave this trinket is alive. I can tell you that she is safe and cared for. Take comfort from that and have patience,' said Lady Osborne in haste. Any further opportunity to speak was lost. 'Ah, Mr Howard, I see you have found my husband.'

'Lady Osborne,' replied Mr Howard, 'it is an honour to receive you. Had I been forewarned, I should, of course, have received you properly.'

'We don't stand on ceremony, do we, my dear,' said she, turning to Lord Osborne with a searching look.

'Mr Howard kindly directed me to Mr Edwards' grave. Mrs Howard, I wish to join my wife in expressing my condolences to you on the loss of your father. My mother and Mrs Turner were most insistent that we pay our respects while in Somerset, for they are unable to do so in person.'

'Thank you, Sir. You are most kind,' said Mrs Howard.

'Mrs Howard and I were recalling the times when my sisters and I were invited to the house of Mr and Mrs Edwards to dress and dine on the evenings of the local assembly in Delham. You may remember my father,' said she.

'Mr Watson,' said Mr Howard. 'He had the living at Stanton.'

'He and Mr Edwards were the best of friends and keen card players,' Lady Osborne replied.

'I remember Mr Watson. Your father was full of praise for a sermon I once delivered during a visitation. I have pleasant memories of those days,' said he, fixing his gaze on Lady Osborne, 'and some profound regrets. I have never forgotten the time you honoured Wickstead with a visit to my sister when you first entered Surrey.'

'Profound regrets? I confess, I have none,' said Lord Osborne, with a casual smile.

Lady Osborne smiled in admiration at her husband's remark.

'Come and take tea inside,' said Mr Howard. 'You must excuse my wife today. Mrs Howard is indisposed.' Turning to his wife, he continued, 'Your room is prepared. Twigg will assist you. A tray will be sent up to your room presently. You may say your goodbyes now.'

Addressing Mrs Howard directly, Lady Osborne said, 'We had hoped to enjoy your company a little longer.'

Mrs Howard looked at her husband and replied, 'If you will excuse me, I must lie down. Forgive me.'

'Mary,' said Lady Osborne, 'before you leave us, there is something I wish to ask of you. And you, Mr Howard. Mary and I were rather caught up in reminiscences of Mr Edwards and it quite slipped my mind, you see. Mrs Beresford has a cousin. He is in fact the late Colonel's cousin. A Mr James Beresford. He is not long returned from the East Indies and proposes to buy an estate in Somerset and is eager to secure Mrs Beresford's opinion. I understand that the route from Whitcombe would take my sister-in-law through Kilston.'

'I should be honoured to receive Mrs Beresford at any time she chooses,' said Mr Howard. 'I receive few callers in Kilston.'

'I shall convey your kind invitation to my aunt. She may be accompanied by Mr James Beresford, a gentleman of fine character.' Lady Osborne turned to

Mrs Howard and directed her gaze to the small vinaigrette concealed in her hand. Relaxing her fingers so that the object was visible to Mrs Howard alone, Lady Osborne said, 'And we have hopes that we may soon wish Mr James Beresford joy.'

Mrs Howard's eyes expressed the gratitude that she could not convey in words. Satisfied that the mother of Miss Fox had understood her meaning, Lady Osborne released Mrs Howard into the care of Twigg so that she might enjoy the prospect of a day unlike any that had preceded it. The knowledge that had been denied Mrs Howard for so long, was now in her possession: her daughter was alive and safe.

Lord and Lady Osborne did not sit long with Mr Howard and, after Her Ladyship had paid her due respects at the graveside of Mr Edwards, they were soon on their way.

'Are we indeed to wish Mr Beresford joy?' said Lord Osborne, as their carriage left Kilston and turned on to the road towards Allersham.

'My love,' said she, 'I needed to convey a message to Mary by the only means available to me. Did I speak out of turn? Your sister is quite certain that James Beresford will come to the point. Eventually. And had you allowed us but five minutes more before making your appearance, I am sure I should have satisfied Mary's enquiries in full. You granted me time only to hear Mary's part in the affair.'

'A long-winded tale then,' said he.

'And not a pleasant one. I had little sympathy for Mrs Howard all those years ago and now as I look back, I feel ashamed that I ceased all notice of her. She atoned for her mistakes long ago and in full, but forgiveness has never been afforded her. She has been dealt a most cruel hand by Captain Hunter *and* Mr Howard, and, I believe, her own father.'

'And so your suspicions were confirmed,' replied Lord Osborne.

'They were,' said she. 'I shall consult your sister, of course, for I suspect that Miss Fox alone may not be the only party affected.'

'You mean the Blakes,' said he.

'Charles Blake and his mother were both active in effecting a reconciliation between Mr and Mrs Howard. Neither Charles nor Mrs Blake knew about the child. Mr Howard prevailed upon Captain Hunter to make the problem, that is Miss Fox, disappear, and threatened to expose him if he failed to comply. So there you have it.'

'And Mrs Howard knew nothing of the child's progress?' said Lord Osborne.

'Nothing at all,' said she. 'She has no knowledge of the fact that Miss Fox was delivered to Bath with assistance from the Colonel, nor does she know the whereabouts of her daughter. Had you not appeared with Mr Howard at that moment —'

'The less Mrs Howard knows for the time being, the better. She now has the most important facts in her possession,' said Lord Osborne.

'Perhaps so,' Lady Osborne replied.

'Where is Captain Hunter?' said he.

'Mrs Howard did not say. She may not know. Was Captain Hunter part of Colonel Beresford's regiment? He was certainly known to him. They both attended the Delham Assembly. I remember being introduced to Captain Hunter at my first assembly. Mary danced with him to the dismay of her parents. And you, my love, danced with no one at all and, if memory serves me correctly, sent Tom Musgrave to engage me on your behalf.'

'But you only had eyes for Mr Howard.'

'Do not remind me. Poor Mary! I had a very lucky escape and largely at her expense. If only Mr Edwards had relented and given his permission. Mary might have married Captain Hunter and their daughter would have had a mother and a father. Mr Edwards would not have been obliged to settle his entire estate on Mr Howard and each in his or her own way would have been a great deal happier.'

'What shall you say to Emma of the matter?' said Lord Osborne.

'I must first speak to your sister.'

CHAPTER FORTY

The arrival of Lady Dalrymple and Miss Carteret was anticipated with interest at Allersham and took precedence over the return of Lord and Lady Osborne from Kilston. The knowledge that her parents' journey to Kilston had been accomplished without incident, and that they were once again safely returned was enough, and necessitated no further enquiries beyond establishing where they changed horses, whether they had found adequate refreshment on the way, if the stone had already been laid on the deceased's grave, and whether they had been well received by the mourners. Lady Allersham's interest was raised further, however, when her father inadvertently referred to the grave of the deceased as belonging to Mr Edwards.

'Mr Edwards?' said Lady Allersham. 'Had he any connexion with the Mr Edwards we knew in Delham, Papa? You remember Mr Edwards, Mama. Grandmamma thought him quite ridiculous in his pursuit of Aunt Turner, he being a gentleman of great age.'

Mrs Beresford looked to her brother for an explanation. 'Mr Edwards? Had he a brother in the Church?'

Lord Osborne glanced helplessly at his wife.

Lady Osborne turned to Mrs Beresford and said, 'Would you be so kind as to walk with me? I should like to take a turn in the gallery. We might mount a lookout for Lady Dalrymple's carriage, for I understand there is a very good view of the road from there.'

'I had the very same thought,' she replied.

'Will you excuse me, Emma?' said Lady Osborne, in a whisper. 'There is something I should like to discuss with your aunt.'

'Of course, Mama. And I have some news to convey to Miss Fox. Cousin Robert has written. He had a letter from James Beresford concerning Fulton Park, but with a most interesting postscript. The elder daughter of Mr Ibbotson is engaged.'

'Not to James Beresford, I hope?' replied Lady Osborne.

'I am not quite certain. I forget how he worded it.'

'Perhaps you had better read it again before you say anything to Miss Fox.'

Lady Osborne and Mrs Beresford entered the long gallery, the latter anxious for news of Kilston.

'When Osborne mentioned Mr Edwards, I could no longer remain silent on the matter,' said Lady Osborne. 'Have you guessed?'

'Mr Howard. Is it he who has the living at Kilston? It is so long since the Colonel and I had dealings with him. I knew, of course, that Mr Edwards had given up the house in Delham and had gone to live with the Howards,' said Mrs Beresford. 'Why did he do such a thing, I wonder?'

'Mr Edwards was frail and needed the care of his family, but he was obliged to enter into an arrangement with Mr Howard for the privilege of doing so. Do you remember Mrs Howard?' said Lady Osborne.

'Mr Edwards' daughter?' Mrs Beresford replied.

'Prior to and during her marriage, Mary Edwards as she was then, had a liaison with a redcoat. Captain Hunter.'

'Captain Hunter wrote to my husband at one time. Something to do with the local militia.'

'Colonel Beresford and Captain Hunter were acquainted in Delham, were they not?' said Lady Osborne.

'They were in the same regiment,' said Mrs Beresford. 'I remember the trouble Captain Hunter caused my poor dear husband.'

'Captain Hunter, I believe, used his connexion with the Colonel to his advantage. You see, Captain Hunter is the father of Miss Fox.'

'And so I take it, Mrs Howard is her mother,' said Mrs Beresford, taking possession of the nearest seat as she absorbed the news. 'Are you quite certain?'

'I am. The first notion I had of it was the painting and the inscription written on the reverse. The *detested sport* led me to think of Captain Hunter almost from the outset. I recall very clearly the first time Mary Edwards, Mrs Howard that is, introduced us. And when I saw Miss Fox, the likeness to her father was unmistakable. I had expected to find a likeness to her mother. I never liked Captain Hunter; but Mr Howard is no less culpable than he. Perhaps he is more so, for Mr Howard thought only of fortune and connexions. Captain Hunter would have married Mary Edwards for love.'

'I see,' said Mrs Beresford. 'Does Mr Howard know about Miss Fox?'

'He instructed Captain Hunter to rid himself of the problem. Mrs Howard has not seen her daughter since the day of the infant's birth.'

'And yet Mrs Howard remains under Mr Howard's roof,' said Mrs Beresford.

'A prisoner in all but name. She is weak, without spirit or vitality. I hardly recognised her. Mrs Howard may have a roof over her head, but it is at a very great cost. In return, Mr Edwards made Mr Howard his sole beneficiary.'

'Did you speak with Mrs Howard in private?' Mrs Beresford asked.

'I did. But before I had the opportunity to give an account of Miss Fox, Mr Howard appeared.'

'And the silver vinaigrette? Did she recognise it?'

'Even I recognised it,' said Lady Osborne. 'Indeed, the silver trinket and the painting were all Mrs Howard had in her possession to give to her daughter. Mrs Howard recognised the vinaigrette immediately, of course.'

Mrs Beresford sought a full account of Lady Osborne's conversation with Mrs Howard and persisted in her enquiries until each question was answered to her satisfaction.

'I confess, all that you have told me has come as a complete surprise. Why did you not say before your visit to Kilston that you suspected Mrs Howard?'

'There was a chance that I may have been wrong. A small one, I grant you.'

'You know what this means,' said Mrs Beresford.

'Miss Fox is not as poorly connected as we thought,' replied Lady Osborne.

'It means that Miss Fox is connected by marriage to the Blakes. Charles is, therefore, her half-cousin.'

'And Charles' wife, Anne, is my niece,' said Lady Osborne.

'Surely the Blakes must be aware of Miss Fox's existence or at least that Mrs Howard bore a child,' said Mrs Beresford.

'When Mr Howard discovered the truth, he insisted on secrecy. Not for Mary's sake, but for the sake of his own reputation. He thought only of himself. Mr Howard dictates and prescribes every particular of Mrs Howard's existence. She sees little society, no letter is private, no reply authorised without Mr Howard's consent or authorship,' said Lady Osborne. 'I fear I have been exceedingly neglectful in my dealings with Mrs Howard, and I do not yet know how to right that wrong. She may be guilty of many things, but to be deprived of her daughter so cruelly and compelled to live as a virtual prisoner, deprived of society and friendship, is contemptible, whatever her past transgressions might have been.'

'How is Mrs Howard to be reunited with her daughter? If what you say of Mr Howard is true, how is he to be circumvented?'

'There is one aspect of my conversation with Mrs Howard that I do not look on with pride. I was denied the opportunity of explaining the whereabouts of her daughter, for our conversation was brought to an end by Mr Howard's appearance. In a foolish attempt to convey some modicum of hope, I mentioned James Beresford. I said that you were likely to visit him when he was settled in his new residence and that the road to Fulton Park passed through Kilston. Of course, I do not know that it does, nor am I certain of anything pertaining to Mr Beresford's movements or plans. The part I regret most is that I intimated that he was shortly to marry. It was not meant to be mischievous. I wished only to convey that which mattered most to Mrs Howard at such an awkward moment: that her daughter lives and flourishes.'

Mrs Beresford smiled. 'And did she understand your meaning?'

'Yes, I believe she did.'

'It is my greatest wish that they should marry. Miss Fox's stay at Whitcombe has allowed me to observe her disposition more closely. Her desire to be of use, her quiet strength to withstand the condescension of others, without bitterness or indignation, has confirmed my opinion of her. The goodness I see in Miss Fox, I also see in James Beresford. And I should certainly be happy were they to wed.'

Suddenly, they were distracted by the sight of Lady Dalrymple's carriage, and stood to watch its progress towards the Hall from the upper window.

'They are here at last,' said Mrs Beresford. 'Are you acquainted with Lady Dalrymple or her daughter?'

'I have not had that pleasure,' said Lady Osborne.

'Therein lies another story.'

'Does it involve my nephew, Captain Harding?'

'You have guessed it.'

'Emma has furnished me with some of the details,' Lady Osborne replied, 'that I might avoid the awkwardness of a careless word or blunder should an innocent remark slip out unawares.'

Lady Osborne and Mrs Beresford smiled at each other.

'I believe my daughter mistakes me for my sister Penelope,' said Lady Osborne.

'It is perhaps fortunate then that Emma is spared the task of performing the same service for your sister. Mrs Fowle is apt to speak her mind rather more often than one would wish,' Mrs Beresford replied.

'Indeed. Discretion is not one of my sister's most obvious virtues,' said Lady Osborne. 'Nor does she find any merit in it. Desirable as it might be, my sister is happy to remain a stranger to prudence.'

The whole party assembled in the drawing room to receive the Dalrymples and to hear news of their journey and the latest gossip from Bath. Miss Carteret smiled when a smile was required of her, and spoke when spoken to, but said little else as she endeavoured to acquaint herself with the home of Captain Fitzroy, the place of his birth.

Amid the clamour, for there was much to say and hear, Lady Allersham took Miss Carteret aside and said, 'It is my hope that you may derive some comfort from your stay at Allersham Park, Miss Carteret. Would you walk with me in the morning? I should like to show you the church where lies Captain Fitzroy's remains.'

'Thank you,' said she. 'I should like that.'

'I may not be able to answer all your questions, but please apply to Lord Allersham if you so desire. He can speak of his brother with greater authority than anyone.'

Across the room, Lady Dalrymple had news to convey on a subject of great interest and speculation. 'I was pleased to receive a rather lengthy missive in the second post from Lady Russell. Was it yesterday, Jane, or Thursday?'

'Yesterday, Mama,' said Miss Carteret.

'Yes, of course,' she replied. 'And yet, I should not be surprised if you have heard the news already, for it concerns your family more than mine. James Beresford has purchased Fulton Park. Lady Russell confirmed it. She had it straight from Sir Walter. There had been some speculation about Admiral Croft vacating Kellynch and moving to Fulton. But it is not to be, for Mrs Croft is not to be moved at present, and when the inevitable occurs, the Admiral is certain to quit Kellynch for good. It will be too large for his needs, you see. Lady Russell believes he will go to Portsmouth, though the Wentworths may insist he takes a house nearby. And so it is that Sir Walter is likely to return to Kellynch once he is wed. I forget the name of the widow who is to provide for him the means.'

'Poor Mrs Croft,' said Mrs Beresford. 'I am sorry to hear that the Admiral faces so bleak a prospect. It is a comfort to know, however, that the purchase of

Fulton Park has been accomplished. I understood that it was imminent, for James wrote to me, explaining that he would be obliged to delay his arrival until the papers had been signed. I expect we shall see him very soon.'

CHAPTER FORTY-ONE

Lady Allersham and Miss Carteret set off for their walk to the church. Miss Carteret stepped out of the door and looked about her; there was no one to be seen but for a distant labourer laden with fallen apples for the kitchen. Lady Allersham had expected their progress towards the church to be accompanied by silent reflection in view of the gravity of their purpose. She was surprised, therefore, when Miss Carteret spoke as soon as they left the Hall.

'You must think me a wretched and ungrateful creature,' said she, 'but until now the opportunity to thank you for the object you sent to Laura Place was not within my power. It is more precious than you can imagine. Its arrival, the day before Mama and I set out for Allersham, was sensitively and thoughtfully executed. For this I thank you with all my heart. I was afforded the liberty of examining its contents in the quiet and seclusion of my room.'

Puzzled by Miss Carteret's gratitude for an act of kindness about which she had received warm attribution in error, Lady Allersham said, 'You are mistaken, Miss Carteret, for I am most certainly not the person to whom gratitude is due.'

'I had assumed — for it arrived —'

'What, pray, arrived?' said Lady Allersham.

'Captain Fitzroy's writing slope. A perfect match for the key he had entrusted to me. I cannot tell you the joy and the agony that was contained within it.'

'A writing slope?' said Lady Allersham.

'Was it not sent from Allersham?' replied Miss Carteret.

'Not to my knowledge.'

'Then the matter is easily explained,' Miss Carteret continued. 'Captain Fitzroy's attorney must have discovered that the item was still in his possession, realised his error, and sent it forthwith.'

'Without a note of explanation or an apology?' said Lady Allersham.

'If you recall, the key arrived in quite the same manner.'

'You must be right,' said Lady Allersham, in wonderment at the timing of its discovery. 'The important thing is that you have it.'

'Yes, indeed,' said Miss Carteret. 'I must tell you that among the contents locked away were letters I had written to Captain Fitzroy. I am, of course, pleased to be reunited with them, for I should not have wished to imagine them in another's possession.'

'A thoughtful act on the part of Captain Fitzroy in his dying days,' said Lady Allersham

'And just like him,' replied Miss Carteret. 'To my surprise and joy, I found among the contents an unfinished letter in Captain Fitzroy's hand. It must have been written near to the end for the writing was unsteady. He knew, Lady Allersham, the imminence of his demise.'

They stood momentarily to survey the view and collect their thoughts.

At length, Lady Allersham broke the silence. 'Were you comforted by the letter?'

'I was,' replied Miss Carteret. 'Much comforted by it.'

'I am pleased to hear it, for while the mystery remained unsolved you were denied peace of mind.'

They soon reached the gates of the church and stood for a moment to admire the beauty of the building.

'Captain Fitzroy's remains are buried in the churchyard. I shall leave you to your own thoughts,' said Lady Allersham.

'Thank you,' said she.

'Shall I call for you in an hour?'

'That will not be necessary, Lady Allersham. You have been so kind. I shall be pleased to make my own way back.'

As the morning was a fine one, Lady Allersham chose to take advantage of the weather and return to Allersham by the lane to Whitcombe rather than through the Park.

The recovery of Captain Fitzroy's writing slope and its delivery to Laura Place was uppermost in her thoughts. She turned into the lane that led from Whitcombe to Allersham to discover Miss Fox, a short distance ahead. The quickness of her step meant that Lady Allersham was unable to narrow the distance between them until a cart passed by on the road and Miss Fox stopped to wave and say 'good day' to the farmhand. Catching a glimpse of a person approaching, Miss Fox saw that it was Lady Allersham. Surprised to find her there, she walked towards her, carrying a basket full of blackberries.

'Your Ladyship,' said Miss Fox, 'I did not expect —'

'I have come directly from the church. It is a fine day for walking and so I decided to return to Allersham by the Whitcombe lane. Where are you bound, Miss Fox?'

'For Allersham. I hope you like blackberries. They are in such abundance and as they must be eaten soon, I should be sorry to see them go to waste. I have given some to Mrs Wilby. She promises to bake a pie for Mr Beresford when he arrives. I left some for Mrs Dauber at the Rectory and some I took to Sparke Farm.'

'You have been busy,' she replied. 'I have not picked blackberries since I was girl.'

'Oh,' said Miss Fox, attempting to hide the scratches on her wrist and her stained fingertips.

'Come,' said Lady Allersham. 'We shall go to the kitchen together and find cook. She will know the best way of removing blackberry stains.'

As they walked through the Park, Lady Allersham enquired whether blackberry pie was a favourite with Mr Beresford.

'Mr Beresford? Oh, yes,' she replied. 'He said so himself when he visited Whitcombe some weeks ago. The blackberries were not ready to be picked then, of course. Mr Beresford said that care must be taken when picking the fruit because of the sharp thorns.'

'And I see that you bear the marks.'

'It is nothing compared to the pleasure of gathering them.'

Lady Allersham smiled at her companion. 'You find pleasure in the most curious of pursuits. Tell me,

Miss Fox, what is your opinion of Mr Beresford. Do you think him a good man?'

'I do not believe I have met a kinder one. The world would be a poorer place without him. Mr Beresford is expected today at Whitcombe.'

'Then we must do something about those stains and scratches or I do not know what he will think, for when he last visited Whitcombe you had cuts and bruises on your face.'

'Due entirely to my own clumsiness, Your Ladyship.'

'My mother and I used to collect blackberries. They were always found in abundance in Stanton Woods.'

'Is Stanton Woods far from here?' said Miss Fox.

'Stanton Woods is where I grew up in Surrey.'

'How lovely to have picked blackberries with your mama,' said she.

Lady Allersham had given no thought to something so seemingly insignificant that would mean so much to one who had never known what it was to have a mother. 'Were your mother to be found, what should you feel?' said she.

'As any daughter who has lived in this world without her mother. It is my greatest wish.'

'Of course,' said Lady Allersham. 'A foolish question.'

'Oh, no, Your Ladyship. Not foolish. A question impossible to answer, for words alone cannot express such a feeling.'

When Lady Allersham appeared again, it was at luncheon where an additional place had been set.

'Where have you been, my dear?' said Lady Osborne. 'Miss Carteret and I have been out of our minds with worry.'

'I was about to send out a search party,' said Lord Allersham.

'Really, Henry —'

'And I was about to lead it,' said Lord Osborne.

'Papa, what could possibly have become of me walking to and from the church?'

'I fear I am to blame, for it was I who raised the alarm when I returned to Allersham and you were nowhere to be found,' said Miss Carteret.

'I took the Whitcombe lane and came across Miss Fox collecting blackberries. Well, not quite collecting them. She had set out from Whitcombe to bring the fruits of her labour to Allersham for a pie, though cook insists on topping them with apple dumplings instead of pastry. A minor point of contention.'

'And they must be eaten without delay if one is to avoid bad luck,' said Mrs Fowle, appearing at the door.

'Aunt Fowle?' said Lady Allersham. 'I was not told of your arrival.'

'Nor anyone here present, it seems. Did you not receive my letter?' said she. 'I received no welcome. Even my own sister appears startled to see me.'

'Come now, Penelope,' said Lady Osborne, 'I am surprised, but that does not mean your arrival is unwelcome. I am always pleased to see you.'

'We are all pleased to see you, Aunt,' said Lady Allersham.

'Your pleasure will increase tenfold when I tell you I have left Mr Fowle behind in Brinshore.'

'But we had such a jolly time when we last entertained Mr Fowle at Osborne Castle,' said Lord Osborne wryly.

'Yes, I see what you mean,' said Mrs Fowle. 'I was quite put out. Tom Musgrave was the joker of the piece, as I recall. And he received a good telling off from Elizabeth afterwards, I can tell you.'

'What happened, Aunt?' said Lady Allersham.

Mrs Fowle turned and looked at her sister.

Lady Osborne returned her glance and said, 'Your uncle *and* your papa were equally blameworthy. They feigned an array of indescribable infirmities and sought Mr Fowle's expertise on a cure for them. Your uncle, Emma, was not alone in receiving a reprimand.'

'It was some time ago,' said Mrs Fowle, 'and I have since come to consider it exceedingly diverting. By the by, James Beresford sends his apologies. He would not be persuaded to break his journey. He seemed anxious to continue onwards to Whitcombe without delay.'

'Mr Beresford?' said Lady Allersham.

'Yes. He offered me a seat in his carriage and I accepted it. What a gentleman he is,' said Mrs Fowle. 'Did you not know? I have been in Bath this past week. Sydney Gardens is a delightful place, is it not?'

Lady Allersham glanced apprehensively at Miss Carteret. 'Where is Cousin Robert? Is he come too?'

'No, indeed,' said Mrs Fowle. 'He sends his apologies. He brought me as far as Bath. We left Brinshore a week ago. My son had business with Mr Beresford, you see.'

'The sale of Fulton Park?' said Lady Allersham.

'Quite so,' said Mrs Fowle. 'James Beresford got it for a very good price in my view. And I do not see why my son should have sold it at all. I should have been happy to visit Fulton Park myself, for I have heard it is a fine estate. Nothing on the scale of Allersham, of course.'

'Cousin Robert promised to spend Michaelmas with us,' said Lady Allersham.

'Mr Beresford tried his best to change his mind, but Robert would not be moved. My son can be very stubborn at times. Just like his father,' said Mrs Fowle. 'My journey from Bath to Allersham was all comfort and convenience, unlike the agony I suffered every inch of the way from Brinshore to Bath.'

'Captain Harding's carriage is one of the most comfortable carriages I know. And very well sprung,' said Mrs Beresford.

'Indeed, it is,' said Lady Allersham.

'On short excursions, perhaps,' said Mrs Fowle. 'But you have not travelled between Brinshore and Bath in that contraption, and I do not recommend it. As soon as I stepped into the carriage and sat down, what do you think he did?'

Mrs Fowle's question was met with a sea of blank looks.

'He loaded the coach with boxes of this and that, until I felt like a smuggling privateer caught in the bowels of a ship, buried beneath its cargo. It was just like travelling with Mr Fowle. I had a hat box at my feet, and a parcel of books tied with string beside it, two blankets folded and stacked on the seat beside me. One will do, said I. I am not an invalid. But no. Two it had to be. And that was not the end of it. The coachman handed him a large parcel which he set down on the seat beside him. What is *that*? said I. It is a parcel, said he. I know it is parcel, but what in heaven's name is inside it? It is of little matter, said he. Then tell your coachman to remove it at once. I cannot, said he. And so it continued. I got it out of him in the end.'

'I hope it was something purposeless and outlandish,' said Lord Osborne, in a whisper to his wife.

Possessed of a keen ear, Mrs Fowle caught His Lordship's remark but gave no regard to it. Determined to continue her tale of woe whether anyone wished to hear it or not, she went on. 'Where did I get to? Ah, yes. A slope? said I. You *have* a slope. What need have you of another one? Had you consulted me first, you might have had your father's old slope for it is of no use to me. And there you have it. I tried my best. I always do. And what did he do? Continued in unyielding silence all the way to Brighton. But for refusing a sugared almond I offered him as we passed through Sanditon, for I knew something would be needed to sweeten the crossing of that town, he uttered not another word until we reached the Steine. I am glad I am not a man. One can never determine what occupies their thoughts or sometimes whether they think at all.'

Miss Carteret excused herself from the table and left the room almost unobserved but for Lady Allersham's notice.

'Mama,' said she, 'will you see to matters here? I must go in search of Miss Carteret in case she needs me. I shall explain it all presently,' said Lady Allersham.

CHAPTER FORTY-TWO

The arrival of James Beresford at Whitcombe Park was awaited with impatience by one of its residents. At the first sight and sound of his carriage, Mrs Beresford went out to greet him.

'You find me quite alone this afternoon,' said Mrs Beresford. 'Lady Dalrymple is gone to her room to lie down and rest her eyes. Miss Fox is gone on foot to Allersham to take a basket of blackberries.'

'Allersham?' said he. 'Then I am surprised I did not meet her on the road, for I left Allersham this last half hour.'

'Oh?' said Mrs Beresford. 'Miss Fox may have taken the path across the field by Sparke Farm. Come, your room is prepared. The fire is lit, and I shall have hot water sent up to you. Come and find me when you are ready, and I shall send for tea. Then you can tell me all the news from Bath.'

An hour passed before James Beresford reappeared. Still, there was no sign of Miss Fox, and Mrs Beresford was anxious for her return.

'I wonder what has happened to her? If she does not return before the sun sets, I fear she will not be able to find her way. She carries no lantern. I have sent the stable boy to look for her for he knows the fields well.'

'Had I known Miss Fox was at Allersham, I should have brought her back with me,' said James Beresford.

An anxious wait was somewhat eased by the appearance of tea and curd tart.

'I must congratulate you on a fine purchase. I hear Fulton Park is a pretty estate,' said she. 'Now all you need is a wife to manage the house.'

James Beresford nodded and kept a thoughtful silence.

'Have I spoken out of turn?' said Mrs Beresford. 'Forgive me.'

'Not at all,' he replied.

'You seem a little subdued,' said she. 'Are you not pleased with your purchase?'

'May I speak in confidence? I must speak to someone and I should like it to be you.'

'Of course,' said she, hopeful that it concerned Miss Fox.

'Yesterday I was presented with something of a dilemma, entirely of my own making. Had I declared my intention to buy Fulton Park, had I sought the recommendation of the person most qualified to give it, I might have acted differently.'

'Have you second thoughts about the purchase?'

'I have,' said he, 'but not for the reasons you might suspect. I had cause to visit Mr Wood.'

'Mr Wood the physician? Mr Wood of Queen Square?'

'Yes,' said he. 'Mrs Beresford, perhaps from the beginning I should have made plain my purpose in coming to Bath. I did not. Now, I fear I must. Forgive me, if you can, for my lack of openness. It was my hope that —' He paused momentarily. 'I came to Bath to avail of the services of Mr Wood on the recommendation of a ship's surgeon I came across in Ceylon. He advised me to place myself into Mr Wood's care. He is, as you yourself can attest, an excellent physician.'

'Yes, indeed,' she replied.

'But all the curatives, all the treatment in the world cannot mend a weak heart.'

'You mean a *broken* heart?' said Mrs Beresford.

'A broken heart is more easily mended. Excellent as Mr Wood is, he cannot turn a weak heart into a strong one.'

Mrs Beresford could do nothing more than listen in astonishment and dismay to all he had to say.

'My life has been full, and I have latterly found true friendship and goodness here at Whitcombe, at Allersham, and in Bath.'

'I did not expect this,' said Mrs Beresford, moved by his account and horrified by the implications of it. 'Surely, it cannot be. Surely, something can be done.'

'There is nothing to be done. Forgive me, Mrs Beresford. Forgive me. I see that I have ruined this day for you,' said he.

Their conversation was interrupted by a footman who had come with a message. Miss Fox had been found and was now safely back at Whitcombe. Almost before the footman had completed his report, Miss Fox appeared at the door.

'I am so very sorry to have caused you anxiety. Please forgive me,' said she, her hair a tangle, and her frock hemmed with mud. 'Oh, Mr Beresford, forgive me, please. I did not see you there. I trust you had a pleasant journey. Would you excuse me?'

'We shall dine in an hour,' said Mrs Beresford. 'A little earlier than our usual hour. Lady Dalrymple is to dine at Allersham this evening. Would you be good enough to call the carriage when she is ready to depart and see her to the door?'

'I shall, of course,' said Miss Fox, closing the door quietly behind her.

'My dear James,' said Mrs Beresford, when they were once again alone, 'words fail me. What is to be done?'

'I am advised that the disease, unpredictable as it is —' He broke off. 'I find there is solace to be had in not knowing too much. Ignorance can often be a blessing.'

The quietness of Mrs Beresford at dinner led Miss Fox to suppose that the cause must have been her tardy return to Whitcombe.

'Mrs Beresford,' said she, 'I fear I have disappointed you. If —'

To prevent even a hint of the true state of affairs, James Beresford enquired, 'Had you a busy day, Miss Fox?'

'I came upon Lady Allersham in the lane. Her Ladyship insisted on taking me to her cook because of my stained fingers.'

'Stained fingers?' said he.

'From picking blackberries,' she replied.

'Have you been at Allersham all this time?' said he.

'I left Allersham and called at Sparke Farm, for Mrs Sparke wished to see me. I sat in her parlour for half an hour. And as I left, Mrs Sparke asked me to deliver some apples to one of the labourer's cottages. A Mrs Todd. I found the way without difficulty. Well, not perfectly, for I had to ask the way. Mrs Todd would have me stay and sip some broth and was most insistent. But when I left the cottage, I lost my way. One of the stable boys found me or I do not know what I should have done.'

The conversation did not flow as it had when James Beresford had last visited Whitcombe, and sensing that something was amiss, Miss Fox made her excuses after dinner and went up to her bedchamber early.

When they were alone once again, Mrs Beresford, anxious to know his plans for Fulton Park in light of this most terrible news, enquired as to its fate. Would it remain empty? Should a tenant be found? Or would he leave Bath and make the estate his home?

'I have no fixed plans for the present,' he said.

'There *is* another possibility,' said she. 'Whitcombe. You must consider Whitcombe your home for as long as you require it.'

'A most gracious offer indeed, but I would not burden you,' said he. 'In all likelihood a tenant shall be found for Fulton Park, and I shall remain in Bath.'

'What you say grieves me greatly,' said Mrs Beresford.

'Believe me when I say that I am reconciled to my fate. I am at peace,' said he. 'There is, however, something I should like you to know concerning my estate after I am gone. I have given the matter much thought and my mind is made up.'

'Must we talk of such things?'

'We must,' said he. 'I should like you to know my intentions, the more so because I seek your approval.'

'Very well,' said she, endeavouring to keep her composure.

'Forgive me for speaking plainly. The Colonel made adequate provision for you after his death,' said he.

'I am very comfortably situation,' Mrs Beresford replied, 'and want for nothing.'

'As you know, I have no heir. It is my belief that if I cannot make a difference in this life, perhaps I might do so in the next. I should like Miss Fox to inherit. I can think of no act more fitting.'

Astounded by his admission, Mrs Beresford replied, 'Are you quite sure?'

'I am.'

'Dear James,' said Mrs Beresford, 'this is a bittersweet irony.'

Curious to understand the meaning of her remark, he looked to her for an explanation.

'Now it is my turn to speak candidly,' said she.

'Please do,' said he. 'I should, of course, welcome any view you might put forward.'

'Since you were last at Whitcombe, I have entertained the notion that — Yes. I will declare the hopes I had for you,' said she. 'I thought I observed a growing attachment between you and Miss Fox. Please do not imagine that I sought to prevent it. No. Indeed, the opposite was true. It was my dearest wish. I confess, I believed such a union would prove to be a most prudent match for Miss Fox. She would be afforded a surname of distinction and a proper place in society. You and Miss Fox share the same temperament. You see, I have grown fond of you both. But more than this, when I observed you together in the Park, I was reminded of the first time I met Colonel Beresford and of the happy years we spent together. That is why I feel such great sorrow now, for you are to be denied the years of happiness I enjoyed. Let Miss Fox inherit if it pleases you, but let me speak plainly. If there exists between you any affection, any love, offer her your hand also. Offer your *heart* for as long as it is yours to give.'

James Beresford replied, 'In turn, I shall tell you that it was my desire to make Miss Fox an offer. I endeavoured to complete the purchase of Fulton Park for that reason. I had, of course, no firm expectations of a favourable reply, but I allowed myself to hope. Nothing more than that. Mrs Beresford, it is now impossible entertain any prospect of the kind for, were she to accept an offer from me, I should be in danger of making her a young widow. As an heiress, she might have whom she chooses — a man with strength and vitality, not an invalid lain upon a sick bed.'

'Then you do not know the character of Miss Fox or any woman who truly loves. Do you think that Miss Fox would reject the man she loved in order to accept the attentions of a man she did not love? There are women who have done so and women who will yet do so, but Miss Fox is not one of them. I believe you do yourself and Miss Fox a disservice,' said Mrs Beresford. 'And I do not see before me an invalid lain upon a sick bed. I see a young man who is possessed of life. Do not allow uncertainty to restrain you or curb your capacity to love and live your life. My dear James, you have not sought my advice, but I shall give it all the same. Make Miss Fox an offer and if you succeed, take Fulton Park. Make it your home for as long as you have life. We, none of us, know whether we shall live to see another day. Life holds no certainty for any one of us except the certainty that one day it will end. Do not dwell on that day to the exclusion of every other day. Let there be a wedding breakfast at Whitcombe long before there is the whisper of a wake.'

CHAPTER FORTY-THREE

Lady Allersham found Miss Carteret seated in the long gallery, staring out of the window. The information conveyed by Mrs Fowle, who lacked any understanding of the significance of her disclosure, settled the matter on which the two women had spoken earlier that day. The writing slope had been delivered to Laura Place by Captain Harding.

'How could that be?' said Miss Carteret.

Lady Allersham replied, 'He came to me. We spoke of Captain Fitzroy.'

'Captain Harding gave me his word that he would say nothing about the incident he witnessed the night of the ball,' said Miss Carteret. 'I am most grateful that the item has been recovered, and by his efforts. But I was utterly convinced that he would keep his promise to me. He did not.'

'His promise to conceal your secret?' said Lady Allersham.

'Yes,' she replied. 'Or how could I ever believe his word again? How could I accept a man whose word meant so little? And so I refused him.'

'My dear Miss Carteret,' said she, 'Captain Harding kept his word to you. He revealed nothing of your secret to me. I first discovered the extent of his knowledge when he visited Allersham, and that was *after* you refused him. And only when he had fully established my understanding of the matter. I am sorry to say, Miss Carteret, that you have misjudged him. I can vouch for my cousin. Whatever else he may be, I have never had cause to doubt his word once given in earnest. It is I who am culpable. I have ruined everything. I recall with shame how I spoke of my cousin's love of intrigue. Such a remark must have prejudiced your view of him.'

'Oh, no. I see now that I was at fault, and I alone,' said Miss Carteret.

They sat for some minutes in silent contemplation of their own thoughts. Miss Carteret was first to break the silence. 'May I ask, where and how came he to discover the slope?'

'I do not know,' said Lady Allersham.

Miss Carteret made her excuses and went to her room; Lady Allersham, satisfied that she had succeeded in plea to vindicate Captain Harding, returned to the dining room. Finding the room empty, she entered the drawing room, and found not a soul there either. The library proffered the next best possibility of company, for her husband was most likely to be found there.

'My love,' said she, on entering the room, 'the house is deserted. Where have they all gone?'

'Your parents have gone for a walk. Mrs Fowle is gone to her room to lie down. I have no idea where Miss Carteret is gone.'

'I wonder where Cousin Robert found Captain Fitzroy's slope?' said Lady Allersham.

'Has Harding delivered it already?' replied Lord Allersham.

'What do you know of the business?' said she, as she sat down beside him and looked enquiringly into his eyes.

'I wrote to Charles Blake and asked him to search the attic at Waterloo Crescent. Some of my brother's belongings were stored there. It was remiss of me, I know. But I had not the means of removing them to Allersham at the time. When Charles bought the house, he had no objection to storing them in the attic. There was but one item among them that required a key. I had forgotten all about it. My brother's writing slope. I asked Charles to let Harding have it.'

'And you didn't think to tell me?' said she.

'I wanted to establish its whereabouts first of all,' said he.

'Your instinct was correct. There is but one thing I should like to know. What did Charles Blake know of the business? He was present when your brother first met Miss Carteret in Cork,' said Lady Allersham.

'We are not party to all the secrets of a friend. If Charles Blake had any notion of the understanding that existed between my brother and Miss Carteret, it would not be in his character, or the character of any man, to disclose it. I trust Miss Carteret is now content.'

Lady Allersham resisted the temptation to furnish her husband with every particular of Miss Carteret's current state of mind. 'I believe Miss Carteret might now find comfort in the notion that Captain Fitzroy thought of her in his final hours,' she replied. 'Do you miss your brother?'

'Yes. Of course I miss my brother,' he replied, and returned to the study of some agricultural plans he had been perusing.

CHAPTER FORTY-FOUR

Michaelmas Day saw a vibrant array of daisies blossom amid the fading summer verdure of Allersham Park. Ten sat down to goose and onion gravy and gave thanks for a good harvest. Mrs Fowle expressed the hope that the goose, reared especially for the fine table at Allersham, might secure the promise of a good income and a prosperous year. Lady Allersham glanced at her husband and observed that without having once given thought to arithmetic, the table comprised an even number.

'We are missing only Mr Fowle and my son, and I am sure I do not mind the absence of the former, and as I am vexed with the latter, you will not hear any complaint from me,' said Mrs Fowle.

'You are fortunate indeed, Mrs Fowle, to have so very fine a son. And had I a son such as Captain Harding, I should count my blessings. I lament his absence among us. How he entertained us all in Laura Place!' said Lady Dalrymple.

'What a merry lot we are,' said Lord Osborne. The solemn expression on the face of his sister puzzled him. He whispered to her, 'You don't seem quite yourself today.'

Mrs Beresford replied, 'No brother, I am not. But I beg you, do not draw me out.'

'Michaelmas daisies are a beautiful sight, are they not? They bring so much pleasure at this time of year when the summer colours begin to fade and die,' said Lady Osborne.

'I expect they are just as beautiful at Osborne Park, Mama,' said Lady Allersham. 'Grandmamma will insist on having a supply cut and brought into the

Dower House. How do you like the daisies, Mr Beresford? I remember it was you who said you hadn't seen them in years. I don't suppose they grow in Ceylon.'

'I don't see why they should not, but it is true, I cannot remember when I last had the pleasure of seeing them,' said he.

'Aunt Beresford knows the meaning of flowers,' said Lady Allersham. 'What is the meaning of Michaelmas daisies, Aunt?'

'I believe it is *farewell*,' said she.

'A rather dispiriting thought,' said Mrs Fowle. 'Though seen in a different light,' she continued, thinking of Mr Fowle, 'one might consider it curiously uplifting.'

'I like to think of *farewell* as two words, not one. *Fare* and *well*. What better hope than this: to wish a friend fares well as they go,' said Miss Fox.

James Beresford replied, 'A fine sentiment.'

'There are many who say one thing and desire the reverse. People do not wish others to *fare well*. Another's misfortune is often a cause of great rejoicing,' said Mrs Fowle. 'Mr Fowle is a case in point. He would no more wish Mr Granby to fare well than Liverpool.'

'*Liverpool?*' enquired Lady Dalrymple. 'My late husband once visited Liverpool, but I have not had that pleasure.'

Lady Allersham whispered to her father. 'I am a little confused, Papa. Do Lady Dalrymple and Aunt Fowle speak of the *place* or the *person*?'

'I am as mystified as you, my dear,' said he.

'Might I propose, when we are done here, a reading for Michaelmas Day?' said Lady Allersham.

The proposal was well received, and general agreement prevailed until shortly afterwards when it was replaced by equally general disagreement.

'I propose *The Lady of the Lake*,' said Mrs Fowle. 'Sword rattling will likely suit the gentlemen among us, and I am not wholly opposed to it.'

'I do not think Scott is at all appropriate for St Michael's Day,' said Lady Dalrymple. 'Let us have something from Mrs Radcliffe.'

'Mrs Radcliffe? A singular recommendation,' said Lord Osborne. 'Milton is the obvious choice.'

Mrs Fowle sighed with exasperation. 'Not *Milton*!'

'What better day than this to hear *Paradise Lost*?' he replied.

'What? *All* of it?' said Mrs Fowle. 'My late husband, Lady Dalrymple, was in holy orders, and one was never more aware of those *orders* than on certain days in the Church's calendar one could not escape. I have slept through hours of Milton. And every Michaelmas the same! Thankfully, before the Archangel had chance to wield his sword, I slipped into a deep slumber and did not awake until Dr Harding went *hand in hand* with his book, on his *solitary way*.'

'Then Milton it must be,' said Lord Osborne to his daughter in a whisper. 'And I shall make sure a copy is to hand when your Aunt next proposes a visit to Osborne Castle.'

'*Nor love thy life, nor hate*,' said James Beresford. 'I forget the rest.'

'*But what thou livest live well*,' continued Miss Fox, glancing in his direction. In a lower tone, she said, '*How long, or short, permit to Heaven*.'

They exchanged brief looks: his, a searching smile; hers, reassuring and resolute.

'I see you are familiar with Milton, Miss Fox,' said Lord Allersham.

'I had the good fortune to read at the bedside of more than one admirer of Milton's works,' she replied.

Lady Allersham glanced enquiringly at Miss Carteret. 'I hope this talk of Milton does not distress you,' said she, in a whisper.

'I am not distressed by it, Your Ladyship,' she replied. 'I should find it a great pleasure to undertake the reading of a passage, if that would please you.'

'It would,' said Lady Allersham. 'Have you your volume to hand or shall I ask Lord Allersham to seek out his own copy?'

'I should be happy to fetch mine,' Miss Carteret replied.

'I can think of no more fitting tribute to Captain Fitzroy,' Lady Allersham replied.

On the last day of September, Lady Allersham proposed a tour of the Park. A chill in the air and the lack of a warm shawl deterred Lady Dalrymple from the excursion. Mrs Beresford similarly declined the offer, citing Lady Dalrymple as the cause. 'I, too, shall forgo the exercise and settle, instead, for a comfortable chair beside the fire and the pleasure of Lady Dalrymple's company,' said she.

Lord and Lady Osborne were of the same mind, resolved to stay indoors and take a walk in the long gallery. Mrs Fowle likewise declined the invitation, for she had no wish to be obliged to keep pace with the rest of the party. 'Let the young people walk if they will. I should only delay them and then, you see, I would never hear the last of it. They will make better progress without me.'

The party, which was once ten, was now five. Lord and Lady Allersham, Miss Carteret, James Beresford and Miss Fox set out amid a cool easterly breeze to make a tour of the Park. Lord Allersham and James Beresford walked on ahead, the former curious to hear about the purchase of Fulton Park and the neighbourhood thereabouts. The women gathered posies made up of Michaelmas daisies entwined with ivy. As they passed the path to the church, Miss Carteret asked to be excused, leaving Lady Allersham and Miss Fox to walk on without her.

On entering through the churchyard gate, Miss Carteret found the place deserted. She closed the gate and took the path that led to her destination. There she knelt to uproot a weed and clear the grave of fallen leaves. She ran her fingers along the letters carved into the headstone.

'Farewell, my love,' said she, placing a posy of daisies on Captain Fitzroy's resting place. Quietly, she stood at the foot of the grave and watched as the fallen leaves, scattered by the breeze, came to settle at her feet. A sudden gust of wind encircled her as though impelling her to move on. She shuddered momentarily, and submitted herself to its bidding, retracing her steps until she came to the door of the church. The latch was heavy; she lifted it, pushed open the door and went inside. Slowly, reverently, she walked the length of the aisle alone, and sat down.

Almost half an hour elapsed in quiet contemplation before she heard footsteps in the porch. She turned to find James Beresford standing there, hesitant to proceed further.

'Mr Beresford,' said she.

'Forgive me,' he replied, 'I disturb your devotions.'

'Not at all. Please,' said she, beckoning him to enter. 'You once told me that the Abbey was your refuge.'

'I take pleasure in the silence of a church, most especially when I am oppressed by indecision or my spirit fails me.'

'And do you find the remedy you seek?' she replied.

'It affords me an occasion to alter my thinking. To see the world, and my insignificant place in it, differently.'

He moved quietly towards a pew on the opposite side of the aisle. Miss Carteret watched his movements as he knelt, head bowed, before taking his seat some moments later.

On determining that he was not at prayer, Miss Carteret remarked, 'I came here to say farewell.'

He turned to look at her, his expression full of compassion.

'How does one say farewell? It sounds so final,' she continued. 'Do you ever have cause to regret certain past actions, Mr Beresford?'

'Are we not all regretful of the past in some way?' said he.

'I hesitated, you see. Had I not requested a delay — Had I not — The person lost to me forever, Mr Beresford, lies here in this very churchyard.'

'Had you chosen a different course, might he yet have lived?' said he.

'No,' said she, 'for I could not prevent the ocean or the fire of a cannon from doing its worst.'

'Then you have no reason to reproach yourself. Seen in a different light, have you not been saved the life of a widow?'

'*Saved*? No, Mr Beresford. I have not been *saved*. I have been *denied* that which matters to anyone who has ever loved. The life of a widow, as you describe it, would have afforded me the prospect of a tolerable existence: to own my grief. The liberty to mourn, to acknowledge my sincere feelings to the world, would then have been a true blessing.'

'A *young* widow? To be so briefly united —' said he.

'What I would have given for a day, an hour, even a moment!' she replied. 'You seem surprised, Sir.'

'I confess, I am,' said he. 'And what of the present?'

'Those memories will remain with me for the rest of my life; my love shall never cease. It will not. It cannot.' Miss Carteret stood up to leave. 'How strange. Inexplicably, I find I am at peace, though perhaps I have disturbed yours. I shall leave you to your prayers.'

'That will not be necessary,' said he. 'Shall we go?'

'If you wish,' she replied. 'But I have afforded you few moments for your own thoughts.'

'I believe my petition has been heard,' said he. 'Curiously, I have received that which I came for. I have what I need.'

They left the church and followed the path through the churchyard to the gate. As they proceeded towards the Hall, the breeze began to strengthen. James Beresford offered his arm to Miss

Carteret as they walked slowly against the wind. Gusts came and went, making constant conversation impossible.

Having set out on the shorter route to Allersham Hall, they emerged from the path by the lake and made their way upwards through the grove. In the distance, moving towards them was the figure of a man, at first indistinguishable from any other. He walked at a fast pace, taking the same path as theirs and was soon upon them.

'Captain Harding!' said James Beresford. 'How good it is to see you! This is a most pleasant surprise. Is it not, Miss Carteret? Miss Carteret and I have just come from the church.'

Captain Harding greeted them in haste. 'I trust you find Allersham to your satisfaction. The Park is exceptional, is it not?' said he, in haste. Addressing Miss Carteret, he enquired after Lady Dalrymple.

'My mother is in good health. I thank you,' she replied in some confusion.

'I seek Lord Allersham. I understood he was one of your party.'

'I saw His Lordship and Lady Allersham almost an hour ago walking in the direction of the walled garden,' said James Beresford. 'Miss Fox was obliged to return to the Hall directly to receive a visitor. A Mrs Sparke, I believe.'

'Yes,' said Captain Harding. 'I looked in on them briefly. Please excuse me.'

The sudden and unexpected appearance of Captain Harding deprived Miss Carteret of any means of preparation. Their meeting was brief; it began and ended before she was afforded an opportunity to express her gratitude for the service he had rendered.

Had she walked alone, he would not have encountered her on the arm of James Beresford. The chance to speak with him, to proffer her thanks, to make plain her error, and her subsequent regret, would not then have been denied her.

Perturbed by the brevity of their encounter, her mind was filled with the lack of expression in his eyes, his words, and, most of all, the absence of feeling in his tone of voice. His manner towards her had not been resentful, but she sensed in his demeanour something of polite indifference. He seemed anxious to be on his way, to escape her presence at the first opportunity. Regretful of the terms on which they had parted, she now concluded that his purpose in coming to Allersham had nothing to do with *her*. *She* had not brought him there. His was a more urgent mission; and she bore no part in it.

On entering the Hall, James Beresford proceeded to look for Miss Fox. The small sitting room where she had received her friend was empty; he concluded that Mrs Sparke had left Allersham and Miss Fox had likely set out to accompany her friend as far as the gates.

Miss Carteret took to her bedchamber to sit at the window and watch for the return of Captain Harding. As she contemplated with dissatisfaction the errors in her dealings with him, the list of her failings grew. She would wait for the right moment to speak with him; and if no opportunity offered, she would contrive it if it were in her power to do so.

After some time, Captain Harding's carriage was brought to the entrance of the Hall and there it stood for several minutes until Mrs Fowle emerged, dressed in travelling attire. Lady Osborne appeared and seemed concerned for her sister, anxious to placate her. It was then that she caught sight of Captain Harding advancing in haste from the direction of the coach house with Lord Allersham.

Lady Allersham joined her mother and seemed similarly concerned. Mrs Fowle was wished a safe journey by all who attended her. Captain Harding then assisted his mother into the carriage and climbed in after her.

Miss Carteret watched the scene unfold before her, powerless to act. The opportunity to secure a private conversation with Captain Harding was now lost forever, and she watched as the carriage pulled away and disappeared beyond the gates of Allersham. 'Farewell, Captain Harding,' she whispered. 'Farewell.'

CHAPTER FORTY-FIVE

The visit of Mrs Sparke to Allersham was met with curiosity by more than Miss Fox. Mrs Sparke, who had a great desire to be received there, found the perfect excuse in Miss Fox. Unfortunately for Mrs Sparke, Captain Harding had arrived shortly before her, and had important news for his mother. Having been directed to the drawing room, he had found Lord and Lady Osborne, Mrs Beresford, Mrs Fowle and Lady Dalrymple engaged in lively debate about the fortunes and exploits of Lady Forbes. The journey several summers ago of the Dowager Lady Osborne and Mrs Turner to Lady Forbes' residence in Brighton was the subject that most enthralled the party. When Captain Harding burst into the room and requested a private conversation with his mother, Lord Osborne was in mid flow.

'Surely it can wait,' said Mrs Fowle.

'Captain Harding!' said Lady Dalrymple. 'This is a most welcome surprise! We are delighted to have you among us once again.'

'Forgive my intrusion,' said he, 'I do not wish to disturb your gathering, but I must speak with my mother on a matter of some urgency.'

'Then speak,' said Mrs Fowle. 'I have no secrets here.'

'It concerns Mr Fowle,' Captain Harding replied.

'Is he dead?' she replied, hopefully.

'No, he is not,' said he.

'I thought not,' Mrs Fowle sighed. 'I suppose he has sent you to beg me to return to Brinshore. You may speak plainly. I have nothing to hide. Anyone may know my opinion of Mr Fowle.'

'I received an express this morning from Charles Blake. He had cause to visit Brinshore three days ago. Indeed, he called on Mr Fowle in Trafalgar Terrace and was alarmed to find preparations were underway for his removal to Fowle Lodge.'

'Fowle Lodge?' said Mrs Fowle. 'That old dank and draughty apology for a dwelling. Impossible!' Mrs Fowle explained that after they were married Mr Fowle had given up Fowle Lodge and had moved to Trafalgar Terrace. 'It was my one stipulation. I should never have entertained the notion of residing at Fowle Lodge. Not for a moment. Mr Fowle has a tenant there now who is not too particular in that regard.'

'And that tenant has quit Fowle Lodge in favour of a smart townhouse in Sanditon.'

'Well, Mr Fowle may do as he pleases. But I shall not be moved,' said Mrs Fowle.

'I expect you will when you know what he intends. He has let Trafalgar Terrace and has begun to remove certain items of furniture.'

'What?' said Mrs Fowle. 'He cannot do such a thing! Trafalgar Terrace is mine. He has no right to it!'

'I understood that your brother, the Croydon attorney, settled the matter of your legal entitlements some time ago,' said Mrs Beresford.

'He did,' Mrs Fowle replied.

'And was Trafalgar Terrace included in those arrangements?' said Lord Osborne.

Mrs Fowle fell silent, unable to confirm that it was.

'Oh, my dear Penelope,' said Lady Osborne. 'What is to be done?'

'I must go,' said Mrs Fowle. Alarmed by what her son had told her, she looked to him for direction.

Captain Harding replied, 'I have come to take you to Brinshore. Make haste.'

When the sudden appearance and disappearance of Captain Harding had been explained to Miss Carteret, she understood better the reason for his visit and applauded his swift action in returning his mother to Brinshore.

'Mrs Fowle is fortunate to have such a son,' said Lady Dalrymple, as they all sat down to dine.

'What an abominable thing to do!' said Lady Allersham. 'I now wish I had not promoted the match at all.'

'You promoted the match?' said Miss Carteret.

'Sadly, yes,' Lady Allersham replied. 'Mr Fowle was all smiles and compliments then. He seemed violently in love. Do you remember the first time he danced with Aunt Fowle at the Brinshore Ball, Mama? You were there. You saw him. You saw it all.'

'I did,' said Lady Osborne. 'But one never knows how matrimony will turn out.'

'I am glad you married Papa,' said Lady Allersham, 'and not —'

'Emma!' said Lady Osborne, to prevent her daughter from going further.

'Forgive me.' Lady Allersham observed the looks that passed between her mother and father and Mrs Beresford. Each, in turn, appeared to glance briefly at Miss Fox.

When the ladies rose from the table, Lady Allersham took her mother's arm to seek a private word.

'Mama, is there some reason why Mr Howard's name must not be mentioned among us?' said Lady Allersham.

Lady Osborne replied, 'For the present, please avoid mention of his name. I cannot explain why, but you will understand in time. It is not in my power to determine when that time might be.'

'You speak in riddles, Mama. What is so secret that you cannot tell your own daughter?' said Lady Allersham.

'I shall leave you to answer that question yourself when you have a daughter of your own,' Lady Osborne replied, with a smile.

Lady Allersham's dissatisfaction with her mother's reply caused her to consult Mrs Beresford. On receiving a similar response to the one provided by her mother, she then applied to her father.

'Emma, my dear,' said Lord Osborne, 'it will all come out very soon, I am sure. It is a delicate matter and one that must be left to your mama.'

'Does it involve Miss Fox?' said Lady Allersham.

'Why should it involve Miss Fox? Whatever gave you that idea?' replied Lord Osborne.

'You, Mama and Aunt Beresford all glanced in Miss Fox's direction when Mama prevented me from mentioning Mr Howard's name,' she said.

'I do not recall — Was not Lady Dalrymple seated next to Miss Fox? I expect it was nothing more than a misunderstanding.'

'But then, Papa, why should you, all three, glance at Lady Dalrymple?' said Lady Allersham.

'Do you not find that Her Ladyship eats her soup in a most peculiar fashion?' said her father.

'I cannot say I have noticed anything unusual,' said Lady Allersham.

'Perhaps you should look a little more closely next time,' he replied.

'Lady Dalrymple was eating a pear. Perhaps, Papa, you might invent something a little more plausible next time,' said she.

Lord Osborne smiled. 'You have my solemn promise, Emma, that you will be the first to know —'

Lady Osborne appeared, and before His Lordship had chance to end his sentence, she said, 'Emma, my love, will you play for us? Lady Dalrymple has requested a selection of Scottish airs.'

CHAPTER FORTY-SIX

The morning brought Lady Osborne to Whitcombe. The call was not unexpected, as both women not only enjoyed each other's company, but had much to discuss, the topic of the moment being Miss Fox and her mother. Lord Osborne and Lord Allersham had planned a morning's fishing at the lake, and Lady Allersham, whose mind was set on writing to Captain and Mrs Blake to seek further information concerning Mr Fowle's present course of action, provided Lady Osborne with the perfect opportunity to spend a morning at Whitcombe Park in the company of her sister-in-law.

James Beresford had declined the invitation to fish, having another aim in mind. It was not long after setting out for a walk in the grounds of Whitcombe Park that he had the good fortune to meet Miss Fox also intent on a morning's walk.

'Might I join you?' said he.

'Of course, Mr Beresford,' Miss Fox replied.

They walked on, commenting on the weather, the beauty of the landscape and the previous day's events at Allersham. At length, a break in the conversation provided James Beresford with the moment he had been seeking.

'I had hoped to speak with you today Miss Fox, for I return to Bath in the morning.'

'Yes,' said she. 'I know.'

'I find the words more difficult than I imagined,' he replied, 'and I beg your forgiveness in advance. I may find it impossible to express myself as clearly as I should like.'

'I have never found your speech unclear,' said she.

'Miss Fox, I wish to ask you a question. It is a question that brings with it certain complications. Those complications I must lay before you in advance. Do you understand me?'

'I believe I do,' said she.

'Miss Fox, I wish to ask if you would do me the honour of becoming my wife.'

Miss Fox listened in silence, her eyes fixed on the ground.

'I am in poor health,' he continued.

She glanced at him and said simply, 'I know.'

'You know? Has Mrs Beresford —'

'Mrs Beresford has said nothing,' she replied.

They walked on, quietly attending to their own thoughts. At length, Miss Fox broke the silence. 'May I say something, Mr Beresford?'

'Of course,' said he.

'Before we were introduced I suspected it to be the case,' she replied. 'I often had occasion to pass through Queen Square to purchase items from the haberdasher in Bath Street for Mrs Price. I saw you enter Mr Wood's residence on several occasions and, knowing Mr Wood to be a physician, I assumed it was not likely to be a social visit. Then when we were introduced, forgive me for saying so, I was able to study you more closely. I have seen ill health, you see. And when I began to work for Miss Ibbotson in Paragon Buildings I also noticed that, on occasion, Mr Wood visited you. We have walked together in Whitcombe Park several times, have we not? And when we reach a particular incline, you find it hard to catch your breath. Forgive me if I speak out of turn, but I do not see that anything is to be gained by pretence or disguise.'

'Nor do I, Miss Fox.'

'Do I surprise you, Mr Beresford? Are you displeased?'

'I confess, I am surprised. But I am not displeased. Not at all. I did not expect — Allow me, Miss Fox, to complete the picture you have described so faithfully. I have a weak heart. It is not altogether certain how long I might continue in my present state.' He paused to compose himself. 'How long my heart will serve me. You must understand that it may not be long. And given this knowledge, know that were you to refuse me, I should understand completely, and I hope we might remain friends.'

'We shall always be friends, Mr Beresford.'

They walked on towards the entrance to the walled garden and entered through the gate. Once inside, and away from prying eyes, she turned to him and said, 'Mr Beresford, I cannot accept your offer.'

'I see. Of course, I do. I should not have spoken. You do not wish to watch a man hasten towards his end,' said he. 'But I thank you, most sincerely, for your honesty, Miss Fox.'

'Mr Beresford, I cannot accept your offer because I am not sure that you love me,' said she. 'In my life, I never expected to receive an offer of marriage, but I always supposed that, in the unlikely event that it should happen, it would be for the sake of love alone.'

'What an utter fool I am. Love. I spoke of death when I should have spoken of love. Of course,' said he. 'I have made no declaration. I thought only of the disadvantage to you. But be assured of my love. Miss Fox, you have my love. I have watched you. I have seen how graciously you have borne the ill temper and impossible expectations of others. You have done so without complaint or malice. I know of no one who would have suffered the whims and temper of others as patiently as you. I love who you are, what you are. There is no one worthier of love than you and no one less worthy a recipient than I.'

Miss Fox placed his hand in hers. 'I began to love you more each time I saw you in Queen Square, or at least I thought myself in love. A foolish infatuation would better describe it. I said to myself, if I should ever meet such a man, I should be the happiest being in the world. And then, with an extraordinary twist of fate, we became acquainted through the strangest of circumstances. Nothing altered my opinion of you, except that my attachment grew all the stronger,' said she.

'I had no idea —'

'Mr Beresford, all my life I have been obliged to conceal my feelings. But I have also learned neither to disown them nor to indulge them. In so doing, I find contentment,' she replied. 'Without family or fortune, what right had I to hope. I had reconciled myself to the notion that one day you would marry if your health prevailed. I was quite prepared to see you marry *and* to wish you joy.'

'And now?'

'My answer is yes, Mr Beresford. Yes. With all my heart.'

'You shall want for nothing when I am gone,' said he.

'But I shall want for you,' she replied. 'When that time comes, we shall face it together, but let us not be governed by that fateful day. I wish to think only of the present, to love and be loved. To take pleasure in this day and every day to come.'

Mrs Beresford and Lady Osborne received the news with delight.

'It is just as I had hoped. I am so very happy for you both,' said Mrs Beresford. 'You must be married from Whitcombe. I insist. And let it be very soon.'

Amid the congratulations and plans for the couple's forthcoming nuptials, the business of revealing the name and whereabouts of Miss Fox's mother was abandoned until James Beresford mentioned the matter in private to Mrs Beresford one day.

'To whom should I apply?' said he. 'Mrs Price?'

Mrs Beresford furnished him with a full account of Miss Fox's parentage and situation: the Osbornes' visit to Kilston, Mr Dauber's involvement in the matter, and her own husband's intervention. Mr Beresford listened carefully to each and every detail.

'I have been at a loss to find the right moment to explain the matter,' Mrs Beresford replied.

'Of course,' said he, thoughtfully. 'Then I believe the duty should henceforth fall to me. Do you not agree, Mrs Beresford?'

'I do. Thank you. Yes,' said she.

When news of the engagement was known, the Daubers expressed their astonishment. Mrs Sparke's joy at the prospect was somewhat constrained by the fact that Miss Fox had done better in her choice of partner than she had done for herself in marrying Mr Sparke. Nevertheless, the advantages of such a connexion were not in doubt, and, seeing the possible benefit to herself, Mrs Sparke was determined to continue her friendship with Miss Fox after her marriage.

And so it was, that on the eleventh day of November, Miss Maria Fox married Mr James Beresford in the presence of their closest friends and relations. The wedding took place without fuss or fanfare. The bride wore a pale muslin dress, unadorned but for a single gold chain, given to her by the groom. Five in all partook of the wedding breakfast; at the invitation of Lord and Lady Allersham, the bride and groom, and Mrs Beresford dined together at Allersham Park. The day was spent with laughter and light hearts, and no one gave heed to the future.

CHAPTER FORTY-SEVEN

Confirmation came from Whitcombe that the wedding of Mr Beresford and Miss Fox had taken place. The news was received with joy in Laura Place. Miss Carteret was curious to hear the every particular and attended closely as Lady Dalrymple read the account aloud and responded to her daughter's enquiries.

'And do Mr and Mrs Beresford intend to remain at Whitcombe for the present?' said Miss Carteret to her mother.

'They are to move to Fulton Park at the end of the month. In time for Christmas, I suppose,' Lady Dalrymple replied.

'Miss Ibbotson observed the removal of Mr Beresford's belongings, or some of them, from his residence,' added Miss Carteret.

'That woman never misses a trick,' said Lady Dalrymple. 'She likely drove him away. If you ask me,

Mr Beresford couldn't wait to leave Paragon Buildings.'

'What else does Mrs Beresford say?' Miss Carteret enquired.

'Never mind that. How very inconvenient to be obliged to address Miss Fox as Mrs Beresford as well as our good friend. One will never be sure of whom one is speaking. I suppose we might refer to Mrs Beresford of Whitcombe to distinguish her from the new one.'

'We might refer to Miss Fox as the young Mrs Beresford,' said her daughter.

'Certainly not,' Lady Dalrymple replied. 'That would imply that Mrs Beresford of Whitcombe is old. And as I am two years her senior, such a description is wholly inaccurate.'

'What does Mrs Beresford of Whitcombe say in her letter?' said Miss Carteret.

'She is to travel to Fulton Park with the happy couple. She makes a point of saying that they are to break their journey in the village of Kilston. I have never heard of it. With such a name, it is bound to be an unremarkable place. Ah! Now it is explained. They are to visit the parish church there, or rather, the parson's wife of whom Mrs Beresford claims an acquaintance. And then, I suppose, they will continue on their way. I daresay the Beresfords — all three — will come across Admiral and Mrs Croft now that his wife is over the worst. No one expected her to rally, least of all the Admiral. The Wentworths' visit must have done the trick. The Crofts are certain to remain at Kellynch now. Sir Walter will have to make do with his bride's exceedingly comfortable arrangements elsewhere. Now here is news indeed! Mr Fowle has upped and gone to Eastbourne. And he is not expected to return. There was such an outcry in Brinshore, apparently, over his treatment of Mrs Fowle that every one of his patients have gone over to Mr Granby.'

'What? All of them?' asked Miss Carteret.

'All of them,' her mother replied. 'And Mr Granby is to assume responsibility for Brinshore's spa. Mrs Fowle will continue to reside at Trafalgar Terrace. I wonder how Captain Harding brought that about?'

'Why should Captain Harding have had anything to do with it?' said she.

'Because Mrs Beresford writes that it was all his doing. He managed everything, and to everyone's satisfaction. Perhaps Mrs Fowle will prove to be tolerable company now that she does not have Mr Fowle to complain about.'

'And does Mrs Beresford say whether Captain Harding is expected to remain in Brinshore for long?' said Miss Carteret.

'There is nothing left for him in Bath now that all his friends are gone,' replied Lady Dalrymple.

About a week later, on one of Lady Dalrymple's usual morning visits to the Pump Room, she had cause to observe an intriguing encounter: all the Ibbotsons, including the new Mrs Ibbotson, by accident rather than design, met face to face.

'Jane!' said Lady Dalrymple, 'Look over there! Have you ever seen anyone as cross as that woman?'

'Mr Ibbotson's sister?' Miss Carteret enquired.

'How very vexing it must be to be obliged to acknowledge one's foe in a public place.'

'Mrs Price seems just as cross. I mean Mrs *Ibbotson*, of course.'

'And Mr Ibbotson's daughters are not much better,' said Lady Dalrymple. 'And now, do you see, Mr and Mrs Ibbotson are leaving. I expect they can't get away quick enough from that woman.'

Miss Carteret turned away, refusing to make the scene into a spectacle. Lady Dalrymple, eyes fixed on the couple, followed the retreat of Mr and Mrs Ibbotson until they disappeared through the door. At that moment, she observed another familiar face emerge through the same doorway and glance apprehensively in their direction. Miss Carteret, whose back was turned, knew nothing of the gentleman's approach and Lady Dalrymple had no time to proffer a warning.

'Lady Dalrymple,' said Captain Harding. 'I did not expect to find you here. Is it one of your usual days?'

'It is,' she replied. 'What a pleasant surprise! Is it not a pleasant surprise to see Captain Harding, Jane?'

Miss Carteret, with a look of surprise, raised an awkward smile.

'I hope I find you well,' said he, addressing Lady Dalrymple.

'I was not particularly well, but now I feel much improved, dear Captain Harding.'

Captain Harding acknowledged Lady Dalrymple's daughter with a similar enquiry. 'Miss Carteret. I trust I find *you* well.'

She replied with a slight nod of the head and a brief glance towards him.

'How good it is to see you again, Captain,' said Lady Dalrymple. 'You have been missed. Bath is the poorer for your absence. Do you stay long?'

'Not long,' said he.

'There will always be a welcome for you in Laura Place. I hope you will honour us with your presence before you leave.'

Captain Harding forced a smile.

'Dear me!' said Lady Dalrymple, 'I have just spied Miss Ibbotson and her nieces. Would you excuse me, Captain? I must have a word with them or they will think me neglectful. Such dear friends! I beg you will excuse me.' Turning to her daughter, she said, 'Jane, I seek a private word with Miss Ibbotson. Excuse me if you will. You may stay where you are. Do not let Captain Harding slip away before I return.'

Before her daughter had chance to reply, Lady Dalrymple sallied forth, leaving Miss Carteret to the company of Captain Harding. Unsure of his reception, he was about to move on when she requested a few moments of his time. He assented to her request with a courteous bow and led her to a place where they were unlikely to be disturbed.

'Captain Harding,' said she, 'I have long wished to thank you for the service you rendered. When I took delivery of Captain Fitzroy's writing slope, I had no idea that it was due to *your* kindness. I learned of it through your mother. Mrs Fowle inadvertently supplied the information when she first arrived at Allersham.'

'It was nothing,' said he. 'Indeed, I had little to do with its discovery. It was Lord Allersham who suggested a search of the Blakes' attic.'

'I did not expect, after what had passed between us —'

'You think me incapable of any small benign act?'

'Not at all. Forgive me. I meant — I know that you defended your mother from Mr Fowle's unkindness,' said she. 'What it must have cost you! If only — I misjudged you. My behaviour was unforgiveable. Can you forgive me? Must you leave Bath so soon?'

'I have another commission to fulfil. A delivery of a different order,' said he.

'A naval commission?' Miss Carteret enquired apprehensively.

'Nothing of that nature,' he replied. 'The newly married Mr and Mrs Beresford have entrusted me with the task of conveying Mr Beresford's mother-in-law, Mrs Howard, to Fulton Park from her present abode in a small village that goes by the name of Kilston.'

'Mr Beresford's *mother-in-law*? Miss Fox's *mother*? How was the discovery made?' said she, in astonishment.

'It was my aunt, Lady Osborne, who solved the mystery. She was acquainted with Mrs Howard many years ago. Indeed, another connexion exists that may interest you,' said he. 'Mrs Howard is Captain Blake's aunt by marriage.'

'I once met Captain Blake. How strange,' said she.

'I have no doubt that your friends at Allersham and Whitcombe will furnish you with the particulars of the case in time,' said he. His eyes surveyed the room, as though eager to be gone. 'Lady Dalrymple appears to have much to say to Miss Ibbotson.'

'Yes,' she replied. 'I do not think Mama has ever had so much to say to her in the whole of her life, though she has often had much to say about her.'

'I do not wish to trespass further on you time, Miss Carteret,' said he.

'Oh, no!' she replied. 'Please stay. Please stay, Captain Harding. There is something I must say to you.' She continued in haste, as though time was fast slipping away from her. 'After speaking with Lady Allersham, I realised my mistake and have regretted it ever since. When Her Ladyship discovered the nature of my acquaintance with Captain Fitzroy, I assumed that her information had initially come from you.'

'You assumed I had broken my word to you,' Captain Harding replied.

'Yes,' said she.

'And that is the reason you refused me?'

'Yes.'

'Without a word of explanation? Without affording me the right of reply, the right to defend myself?' said he.

'Yes.'

'I went to great lengths to ensure Mrs Baldwin's discretion. Why should I have broken my word at such a moment? Miss Carteret, I sometimes have occasion to break a promise,' said he, 'but not usually a promise of that nature. I may promise to write a letter on a certain day and subsequently find that I have neither the time nor the inclination to honour it. I suppose with you a promise is a promise no matter how serious or trivial the matter.'

'My judgement was harsh, and my understanding flawed. Not a day has gone by since — I have, and still do, regret how I acted then.'

'I see Lady Dalrymple has concluded her interview with Miss Ibbotson, or perhaps it is Miss Ibbotson who has brought an end to it. Either way, your mother approaches.'

'Then I thank you, Captain Harding, for granting me these few minutes of your time. Allow me, finally, to wish you well.'

'Likewise, Miss Carteret,' said he. 'Good day.'

She watched as he moved on, taking leave of Lady Dalrymple, before acknowledging a party of fashionable people with a smile of recognition. Further on, he stopped abruptly, his path impeded by the sudden appearance of one of the young Ibbotson women. She could not tell whether his expression was of pleasure or indifference, for his face was hidden from view. She observed only the great delight on the young woman's countenance. Why should he not transfer his affections to another? Had she not rejected him completely? He would not renew his addresses, of that she was certain, for his behaviour towards her, though polite, was remote and cold.

If only we possessed the power, thought she, to return to the past and correct each of our mistakes and misapprehensions. How much happier we should be!

Lady Dalrymple was eager to be on her way. There was no carriage to call, for theirs required the attention of a wheelwright and was awaiting repair. Her Ladyship was obliged, instead, to rely on the hire of a chair to return to Laura Place.

Miss Carteret declined a chair of her own, preferring to walk, to ponder all that had passed between herself and Captain Harding. She waited until Lady Dalrymple was safely on her way, before setting out in the direction of the bridge.

She had not expected to find Captain Harding at the Pump Room, and though she had seemed awkward and unprepared, she had been afforded the opportunity to speak with him, to express her gratitude, and her regret. She could do no more than that; in future, she would endeavour, however hard that might be, to be content in the knowledge that she had done her best to make amends for her failings.

As she turned the corner, she heard the approach of footsteps from behind.

'Are you bound for Laura Place?' said Captain Harding.

She stopped and turned towards him. 'I am,' said she.

'Sydney Place is my destination. I thought perhaps as we are heading in the same direction we might do so together,' he replied.

She was surprised and pleased to be once again in his company.

'I fear I may occasion your displeasure,' said he. 'This time you would be entirely justified in your censure for I am determined to break a promise I made to you when you refused me,' said he.

'I do not recall what it was,' Miss Carteret replied.

'You gave me to understand that a renewal of my addresses would be met with a similar reply. Consequently, I promised faithfully never to renew my offer to you.'

'I was upset.'

'I was astonished,' said he.

'I was in error. Can you forgive me? It is true. I gave you no opportunity to defend yourself. Had I expressed my fears openly —'

'I have given much thought to that day. It occurred to me that the timing of my offer was also at fault. Your heart belonged to another. Miss Carteret, I must warn you, however, that I still love you and I am willing to wait. If you are absolutely decided against me, then say so, and I shall never speak of it again.'

'Yes,' said she.

'Yes?'

'My answer is yes, Captain Harding.'

The walked on in jubilant silence.

At last he turned towards her, smiled and said, 'Shall we be happy together?'

Placing her arm in his, she replied, 'What a strange question at such a moment.'

'I expect we will do considerably better together than some,' he remarked, thinking of his mother and Mr Fowle.

'Are you convinced of my love?' said she.

'Unless it is my chaise and four you covet, I have no reason to doubt it. You refused me once. If you had a mind to do so, you would surely have refused me a second time,' said he.

'I saw you from the window of my room. At Allersham Park. The day you came to take your mother to Brinshore. I watched you depart, and I was certain then what my feelings were — what they are. But I do not know for sure when —' said she.

'When your disapprobation began to subside? At almost our first meeting I formed the notion of making you fall in love with me, not thinking for a moment that the reverse might happen,' he replied. 'I know something of how it feels to be bereft, though in my case death did not part us. It was not an ocean that decided the matter, but a larger fortune than mine. I suppose when you and I first met, I was curious to understand why you seemed at once present in body but not in mind.'

'And your curiosity was satisfied the night of the ball,' said she.

'Everything then made sense,' he replied. 'I have often been the bearer of grave news to the loved ones of good men lost at sea. When all that remains is a box of belongings, the only material evidence a loved one lived, breathed and loved. Each commonplace item that meant so little in life becomes infinitely more precious in death.' He looked at her, and hesitated, as though debating with himself whether to continue.

'What is it?' said she.

'There is something I believe you should know. I recently had cause to visit Captain Blake. He was curious to know whether Captain Fitzroy's writing slope had been delivered to its rightful owner. He said that Fitzroy was a changed man after he left Cork, and though he had given nothing away, even to his best friend, Blake believed love was the cause. Fitzroy astonished the physicians. He fought death with every ounce of strength he had. In the end death defeated him, but Blake believed that had it not been for love, he would have succumbed far sooner. He would have lived if he could. He would have lived for you. Fitzroy was a good man and will not be forgotten. We shall find a way of honouring his memory.'

The time passed more quickly than it should, and Laura Place soon came into view. 'Shall we go in together and break the news to Lady Dalrymple?' said he.

CHAPTER FORTY-EIGHT

The news of Captain Harding and Miss Carteret's engagement was received within the week at Allersham Park. Lady Allersham went directly to find her husband after skimming the contents of Captain Harding's letter.

'There is to be another wedding, my love,' said she. 'Can you guess the names of the happy couple?'

'My imagination fails me,' he replied.

'Nonsense, Henry. You must know. Here is a clue. Laura Place,' said she.

'Has Lady Dalrymple acquired an admirer?'

'She is happiness itself at the prospect of Captain Harding and Miss Carteret's alliance. And I am sure you needed no clue at all. They are to be married in Bath. In January. Cousin Robert has bought a house. You will never guess where.'

'The Crescent?' said he.

'What put you in mind of the Crescent?' said Lady Allersham, with surprise. 'It *is* Royal Crescent. What do you know of the matter?'

'Harding told me he was considering it,' he replied.

'And you did not think to tell me?'

'I should have told you immediately had Harding confirmed the purchase. The house will afford ample room for Lady Dalrymple should she be inclined to give up Laura Place.'

'Give up Laura Place? Impossible! When she has the pleasure from time to time of such amiable neighbours as ourselves? Henry, my love, I *should* like to go to Bath in January. You will be pleased to know that I could not possibly stay there beyond March.

Are you not eager to witness the wedding? After all, it was you who brought it about.'

'It had nothing whatsoever to do with me.'

'It was you who advised a search of the attics at Waterloo Crescent. My cousin's endeavour in retrieving your brother's writing slope and delivering it to Laura Place did much to further his cause. I believe it was my cousin's actions and the discovery of your brother's final letter to Miss Carteret that set in motion certain events that have now reached so delightful and satisfactory a conclusion.'

Lord Allersham humoured his wife with a smile.

'There is another piece of news,' said she. 'Mrs Howard is safely installed at Fulton Park. I will save you Robert's description of his interview with Mr Howard. It seems Mrs Howard is overjoyed to be reunited with her daughter, and Miss Fox, or rather the new Mrs Beresford with her mother. The Beresfords insist on Mrs Howard making Fulton Park her home for as long as it pleases her to remain there. I do not think she will return to Kilston. Mr Howard insisted that his wife leave all her jewellery behind. What need has Mr Howard of necklaces and earrings? Indeed, what need has Mrs Howard for such ornaments when there is kindness and hospitality to be had instead. I regret my initial reservations about James Beresford. Did you know he made enquiries concerning the whereabouts of Captain Hunter and found him languishing in a debtor's prison? That is why the allowance paid to Mrs Price ceased. I am sure, years ago, I heard Grandmamma speak of Captain Hunter. He was in Colonel Beresford's regiment. James Beresford has settled Captain Hunter's debts and now he is a free man, though a weakened one. Mrs Hunter has taken him back. She must love her husband, I suppose, even after all he has done.'

Lady Allersham turned the letter on to its side to read the crossed lines. 'I can just about make out Robert's hand here. He says, James Beresford thanks Lord Allersham for his help in finding Captain Hunter and intends to write to him in a day or two. Henry? For a man who professes indifference over the concerns of others, you have a remarkable talent for involving yourself in their affairs. You are full of surprises, my love.'

'Here is another. Mr and Mrs Ibbotson are to spend Christmas with the Daubers. Perhaps you knew that already. I had it from Mr Dauber.'

'I did not know that,' said Lady Allersham, all astonishment.

'Thankfully, there are no more surprises to come,' her husband replied.

'Except one,' said she. 'I have a surprise for you.'

'Have you found another Miss Fox to rescue?' said he.

'No.'

'Has Mrs Fowle invited herself for Christmas?'

'No.'

'Has Mrs Beresford discovered another relative of the late Colonel?'

'No,' said she. 'But should we have the good fortune in January to enjoy the company of our good neighbours in Laura Place, I shall be obliged to quit it in March, in good time for my confinement.' Lady Allersham observed with amusement the look on her husband's face. 'What did you say, my love?' said she. 'No more surprises to come?'

413

CHAPTER FORTY-NINE

For all the expressions of joy at the union of those who hold a special place in the hearts of many, there must follow sorrow. As surely as light contrasts with shade, and pleasure gives way to pain, so life encompasses both, and every degree between. Without shade there can be no light, without pain we would know no pleasure, without sorrow joy would have no meaning.

James Beresford departed this life on the twelfth day of November in the year twenty-four. As his life drew to a close, Maria Beresford remained at her husband's side, day and night, until his final breath, just before eleven o' clock in the morning as the easterly wind whipped up the fallen leaves.

In that same year the birth of Robert John Harding was welcomed in Royal Crescent; an announcement in the *Chronicle* carried the news that the infant was born into the world on the twenty-ninth day of September to parents whose joy was no less complete than the joy of the infant's grandmothers, Lady Dalrymple and Mrs Fowle. And though neither grandmother would brook the interference of the other, neither succeeded in determining who should take precedence over the other, to the amusement of the child's parents.

The death of another caused great sorrow at Allersham, Whitcombe and Osborne Park. Lady Allersham felt deeply the loss of her grandmother, and in equal measure, Mrs Beresford the loss of her mother. The Dowager Lady Osborne, who had viewed life as a series of delightfully perverse events, all the more enjoyable for having found herself at the centre of them, had the satisfaction of leaving this world the victor of one final wager. 'And should you outlive me,' said Mrs Turner to the Dowager, 'let that insipid fountain, indistinguishable from drizzle, be replaced by a fine statue of Eros.'

The Dowager had triumphed; and though Mrs Turner was quite at liberty to do exactly as she pleased, due to, rather than despite, the Dowager's demise, the fountain remained, for Mrs Turner was as opposed to its removal as she was to any word being uttered against her dear departed friend.

Mr Howard was not reconciled with his wife, nor did she ever return to Kilston. Fulton Park became Mrs Howard's home, a place of respite as well as laughter, where she was free from the judgement of others, to be to her daughter a mother, a pleasure that had long been denied her. Mrs Howard endeavoured to make amends for the mistakes of the past and, with a grateful heart and wisdom attained through pain, she found that her spirits, which had long been depressed, revived; and she was restored to health once again.

When Mrs Beresford (of Whitcombe) was not at home, she divided her days between the houses of Allersham, Fulton and Osborne Park. And during the season, there was always a welcome to be found in Laura Place and Royal Crescent. She did not marry again but enjoyed the fortune and independence that widowhood afforded her, and the contentment obtained through precious memories, and the love and friendship of others.

Allersham Park welcomed two births in as many years. The first to be announced was the birth of Lady Henrietta on the twenty-fourth day of April in the year twenty-one. The arrival of a second child, a sister, Lady Elizabeth, was announced in the year twenty-three on the sixth day of January.

One spring afternoon when Henrietta was in her fifth year and Elizabeth her third, Lady Allersham sat by the lake, her husband at her side, and gazed at their daughters, who chattered all the while as they watched fish swim beneath the surface of the water.

'You seem wistful?' said Lord Allersham.

'I was thinking of our girls and all the joys and sorrows that await them. In their innocence, they know nothing but joy, nothing of what might lie ahead. They know only the pleasure they feel now,' Lady Allersham replied.

He placed her hand in his. 'What hope do you cherish for our girls?'

'That they learn to love life through living it to good purpose.'

LIST OF CHARACTERS

During the course of the trilogy, some characters names change through marriage and situation. Names by which they are also known appear in brackets.

ALLERSHAM

Lord Allersham (Henry Fitzroy), spouse of Lady Allersham (Emma Osborne), brother of Captain Fitzroy.

Lady Allersham (Emma Osborne), daughter of Lord and Lady Osborne, spouse of Lord Allersham (Henry Fitzroy).

BERESFORD

Colonel Beresford, spouse of Mrs Beresford (Miss Osborne), son-in-law of the Dowager Lady Osborne, brother in law of Lord Osborne.

Mrs Beresford (Miss Osborne), spouse of Colonel Beresford, daughter of the Dowager Lady Osborne, sister of Lord Osborne, aunt of Emma Osborne (Lady Allersham), sister in law of Lady Osborne (Emma Watson).

BLAKE

Mrs Blake, mother of Charles Blake (Captain Blake), sister of Mr Howard. Widow.

Charles Blake (Captain Blake), son of Mrs Blake, nephew of Mr Howard, spouse of Anne Musgrave (Mrs Anne Blake).

Mrs Anne Blake (Anne Musgrave), daughter of Tom and Elizabeth Musgrave, spouse of Captain Charles Blake, cousin of Emma Osborne (Lady Allersham).

CARTERET

Miss Carteret, daughter of the Viscountess Lady Dalrymple, character in *Persuasion*.

DALRYMPLE

Viscountess Lady Dalrymple, mother of Miss Carteret, cousin of Sir Walter Elliot of Kellynch Hall, characters in *Persuasion*.

DAUBER

Mr Dauber, clergyman of the Parish of Whitcombe, father of Miss Dauber (Mrs Sparke), spouse of Mrs Dauber, relative of Mrs Price.

Mrs Dauber, spouse of Mr Dauber, mother of Miss Dauber (Mrs Sparke).

Miss Dauber (Mrs Sparke), daughter of Mr and Mrs Dauber, spouse of Mr Sparke of Sparke Farm, friend of Miss Fox.

ELLIOT

Sir Walter Elliot, cousin of the Viscountess Lady Dalrymple, father of Anne Elliot (Mrs Anne Wentworth), father in law of Captain Wentworth, characters in *Persuasion*.

FITZROY

Henry Fitzroy (Lord Allersham), brother of Captain Fitzroy, spouse of Emma Osborne (Lady Allersham).

Captain Fitzroy, brother of Henry Fitzroy (Lord Allersham).

FOX

Miss Fox, friend of Miss Dauber (Mrs Sparke), boarder at Mrs Price's establishment in Bath.

HOWARD

Mr Howard, Rector of Wickstead, tutor to Lord Osborne, spouse of Mary Edwards (Mrs Howard), uncle of Charles Blake, brother of Mrs Blake (widow).

Mrs Howard (Mary Edwards), daughter of Mr and Mrs Edwards, spouse of Mr Howard.

IBBOTSON

Minor characters mentioned in *Persuasion* as 'the Ibbotsons'.

MUSGRAVE

Tom Musgrave, friend of Lord Osborne, spouse of Elizabeth Watson (Mrs Musgrave), father of Anne Musgrave (Mrs Anne Blake, spouse of Captain Charles Blake).

Elizabeth Musgrave (Elizabeth Watson), sister of Emma Watson (Lady Osborne), spouse of Tom Musgrave, mother of Anne Musgrave (Mrs Anne Blake).

OSBORNE

Lord Osborne, son of the Dowager Lady Osborne, brother of Miss Osborne (Mrs Beresford), spouse of Emma Watson (Lady Osborne).

Dowager Lady Osborne, mother of Lord Osborne and Miss Osborne (Mrs Beresford).

Miss Osborne (Mrs Beresford), daughter of the Dowager Lady Osborne, sister of Lord Osborne, spouse of Colonel Beresford, aunt of Miss Emma Osborne.

Lady Osborne (Emma Watson), daughter of Mr Watson, niece of Aunt (Mrs) Turner, spouse of Lord Osborne.

Miss Emma Osborne (Lady Allersham), daughter of Lord and Lady Osborne, spouse of Lord Allersham, niece of Mrs Beresford (Miss Osborne).

RUSSELL

Lady Russell, friend of Mrs Anne Wentworth (Anne Elliot), friend of Sir Walter Elliot, and Lady Dalrymple. Character in *Persuasion*.

TURNER

Mrs Turner (Mrs O'Brien), spouse of Mr Turner of Shropshire, clandestine and false marriage to Captain O'Brien, aunt of Emma Watson, friend of the Dowager Lady Osborne.

Mr Turner, spouse of Mrs Turner.

WATSON

Emma Watson (Lady Osborne), brought up by Mr and Mrs Turner in Shropshire. Daughter of Mr Watson, clergyman of the Parish of Stanton, sister to Elizabeth, Penelope, and Margaret. Spouse of Lord Osborne, mother of Miss Emma Osborne.

Elizabeth Watson (Mrs Musgrave), spouse of Tom Musgrave. (Mrs Musgrave)

Penelope Watson (Mrs Harding/Mrs Fowle), spouse of Dr Harding, mother of Captain Harding. Second spouse, Mr Fowle.

Mr Watson, clergyman of the Parish of Stanton, father of Emma, Elizabeth, Penelope, and Margaret.

Robert Watson, son of Mr Watson, brother of Emma, Elizabeth, Penelope, and Margaret. Croydon attorney.

Margaret Watson (Mrs Hemmings), sister of Emma Watson.

WENTWORTH

Mrs Anne Wentworth (Anne Elliot), spouse of Captain Wentworth, daughter of Sir Walter Elliot, sister of Elizabeth (Elliot) and Mary (Musgrove), character in *Persuasion*.

Captain Wentworth, spouse of Mrs Anne Wentworth (Anne Elliot), character in *Persuasion*.

Books by Ann Mychal
in the Watson Novels series:

Emma and Elizabeth

Brinshore

Laura Place